LITTLE UNIVERSES

LITTLE UNIVERSES

Heather Demetrios

Henry Holt and Company

New York

For Sarah

Henry Holt and Company, *Publishers since 1866*
Henry Holt® is a registered trademark of Macmillan Publishing Group, LLC
120 Broadway, New York, NY 10271 • fiercereads.com

Library of Congress Cataloging-in-Publication Data
Names: Demetrios, Heather, author.
Title: Little universes / Heather Demetrios.
Description: First edition. | New York : Henry Holt and Company, 2020. | Summary: Two sisters
    struggle with the secrets brought to light in the aftermath of their parents' sudden death.
Identifiers: LCCN 2019018790 | ISBN 9781250222794 (hardcover)
Subjects: | CYAC: Sisters—Fiction. | Substance abuse—Fiction. | Adoption—Fiction. | Death—
Fiction. | Tsunamis—Fiction. | Family life—Fiction. | Dating (Social customs)—Fiction.
Classification: LCC PZ7.D3923 Li 2020 | DDC [Fic]—dc23
LC record available at https://lccn.loc.gov/2019018790

Our books may be purchased in bulk for promotional, educational, or business use. Please
contact your local bookseller or the Macmillan Corporate and Premium Sales Department
at (800) 221-7945 ext. 5442 or by email at MacmillanSpecialMarkets@macmillan.com.

First edition, 2020 / Designed by Liz Dresner
Printed in the United States of America
10 9 8 7 6 5 4 3 2 1

I'm ready
To meet what refuses to let us keep anything
For long.

—TRACY K. SMITH, *The Universe as Primal Scream*

Part 1

The Universe as Primal Scream

Mae

THERE ARE PIECES OF STARS IN OUR GUTTERS.

(!!!!!!!!!).

It wasn't a Nobel-winning astrophysicist who made this discovery, but a Norwegian jazz musician named Jon Larsen. A completely random human who's into the cosmos and got to thinking.

His experiments led to the observation that these micrometeorites are EVERYWHERE—gutters, yes, and in our hair, the tops of cars, on the rosebushes in your front lawn. Stick out your tongue long enough, and perhaps you can SWALLOW THE STARS.

In case you didn't know, these micrometeorites are older than the planets themselves, some of the oldest matter in existence. Some of them are older than the sun, even. One hundred metric TONS of stardust crashes into Earth—Every. Single. Day.

And it's just raining down on us, all the time.

Hannah

My mom has this book called *Acorn* by Yoko Ono and, I'm warning you right now, if you read it, you will never be the same again. It should maybe come with a warning label.

Say her name to yourself, softly: *Yooooooh . . . kooooohhhhhh.*

Mom says Yoko's presence in the world is the universe's way of reminding us all that we don't have to spend our lives wearing business casual. Or sensible shoes.

Spend our lives. Minutes as currency. It's like we're paying God, handing Her our time in exchange for more breath: Here's a minute, here's another minute, another. And sometimes I want to be like, *Can I have a refund?* Or maybe an exchange. A new life. A new me. Because I'm only seventeen and I feel broke. Like I spent my life already.

Do you ever feel like your skin is a little too baggy, like a pair of jeans that you should probably get rid of, but can't bring yourself to because maybe you wore them the night you lost your virginity or they're your good-luck charm on test days? But you really want to get a new pair. Or some days your skin is too tight, like all of you got stuck in the dryer too long?

And that's where Yoko comes in. She is the great reminder that It Doesn't Have To Be This Way.

Yoooooh . . . koooooohhhhhh.

Whisper with me. Come on.

Do it.

I'll wait.

The sound of her name is just like these wooden wind chimes my mom keeps on our back porch. The wind comes in off the beach and bumps them around, soft wood clunking out poetry. Sound medicine. An incantation.

Good word. *Incantation.* Almost as good as *Yoko.*

Yoko fronts her own rock band even though she's a senior citizen, and she sees the truth of the world and writes about it and draws about it, too, and one time I got to see her art for real, and it made me cry, it was so good. Most people only know about Yoko because she was married to John Lennon. You know, the Beatle. He's the *imagine all the people* guy. I'm a George girl, 'cause he's the silent, sexy one who's all enlightened and plays the sitar, but even I have to admit that John is the man.

People say Yoko broke up the Beatles, but that's just dumb humans blaming a girl for boy problems. The thing is, people change. You know? You love someone, you make things with them, and then you realize you don't *fit* anymore. And that's what happened for John and Paul. They understood that it wasn't working. No matter how good it was. Before.

In her book *Acorn,* Yoko has all these suggestions that she writes down for people to do. Like in "Connection Piece I":

Whisper your name to a pebble.

Sometimes late at night I sneak out of the house and walk over to the beach. I go past the boardwalk, past those iconic Cali lifeguard huts, and the homeless guys and stoners, right down to where the water kisses the shore. I pick up a pebble and I whisper my name to it. Then I throw it into the ocean.

Maybe it will tell the crabs or jellyfish or dolphins my name when they come by.

Maybe someday the whole ocean will be whispering

Hannah. Hannah. Haaaaaa . . . naaaaaahhhhhhh.

I always have a Sharpie in my pocket, and when no one's looking, I write my own acorns. They're not like Yoko's. They're more like secrets I whisper to the whole world. Or just thoughts I want to share, but have no one to share them with because if I did they would give me that blank look they always do when I say things like what I write down with my Sharpies. I say stuff like that and Dad goes, "Maybe we should make an appointment with Dr. Brown," and then I say I don't really need to sit in her stupid paisley chair and talk about my problems and I walk out before he can start rattling off statistics about adolescent junkies, though he would never use that word. Neither would I. Because I'm not one—a junkie, no matter what they say in group. Mom tries to sweeten the deal with some Reiki from her friend Cynthia after the Dr. Brown appointments, to balance things out.

There isn't enough Reiki in the world to fix me, but I don't tell her that.

I wrote this on a stop sign a few days ago, after my first week of senior year:

i am invisible.

Mae would say this is a *scientifically unsound assertion*, but she doesn't understand that some things are true even if you don't have proof.

I don't know why I do them. The acorns. It's weird, I guess, to leave little pieces of yourself all over Los Angeles and never go back to pick them up.

1

Mae

ISS Location: Low-Earth Orbit
Earth Date: 29 August
Earth Time (PST): 20:10

I find out in waves.

My grandmother picks up her cell phone in Florida and dials my number. She calls me because I'm the commander of our crew while my parents are in Malaysia. And also because, even though she doesn't know what my sister did in March, doesn't know about the stuff Mom found in Hannah's room and the counseling sessions and her failed classes, Gram somehow knows that Nah is not okay right now. It's hard to talk on the phone to someone who only speaks crying, or doesn't speak at all. So Gram calls me.

My phone rings, and I answer in the way I always do, our way, which is to tell her something I've learned today. She says this is good practice for my NASA interview. Never mind I still have to get three degrees and become a test pilot in between now and then. Sometimes, just to see if I'm in fighting shape, she'll throw a devilishly hard calculus problem my way. That's what you get for having a grandmother who's a retired math teacher.

"Gram. Hello! I can't get in touch with Dad—have you tried? It's just after breakfast in Malaysia and he's probably on the beach, but maybe the guesthouse has a number? It's of the *utmost importance* that I call him immediately because I was reading today's *Bad Astronomy* post and it's all about how Dad's quintessence theory about dark energy is getting more support from that Harvard string theorist nemesis of his! This paper came out, and in it, they mentioned Dad by name: *Dr. Winters's theories gain more credence* . . . That's my Scientist Voice, in case you didn't know. I'm aware of the neurological benefits of rest when one is on vacation, but this is a DARK MATTER EMERGENCY, so—"

"Sweetie—"

"These physicists are seeing that Dad's probably right about string theory not being compatible with the rapid expansion of the universe. Finally! Of course, we have to see from the experiments up in space if the rate of acceleration is constant, because if it's not, that's a whole other—"

"Mae."

I stop talking. The way she says my name causes tiny electrical pulses to spread across the tips of my fingers. I'm not like Mom and Nah—I don't believe in vibes, and I certainly don't allow Cynthia to do "energy work" on me (good grief). But I do get tingles. Specifically in my fingers. And that's never good. Never. I know it's only a biological reaction to external stimuli, but Mom insists it's an indication of my female intuition; never mind that *female* is a concept up for debate, anyway.

There's a pause while my grandmother's phone converts her next words into an electrical signal, which is then transmitted into radio waves to the cell tower nearest her. The network of towers carries that wave across the country from a condo in Fort Lauderdale to my cell phone in Venice Beach, California. My phone converts her radio wave to an electrical signal and then back to sound.

And the sound I hear is Gram's crinkly, butterscotch-candy-wrapper voice whisper, "Honey? Something's happened."

i am not enough.

Elevator Door

Hedrick Hall, UCLA

Westwood, Los Angeles

2

Hannah

hate cell phones. They skeeve me out. Priscilla, this circus aerialist who basically lives on the boardwalk and used to sell weed or pills to me sometimes—okay, more than sometimes—she told me that the government can track where you are—and listen in on you—through your cell phone. I'm not a conspiracy theorist or anything, but that's messed up. Mom's yoga friends say that cell phones fuck with your vibes and so they're always setting amethysts on top of their phones to clear the negative energy or whatever. I don't need any more bad energy than I have, so I figure keeping a safe distance from my cell is the smart play.

And then after March, after what happened, it got annoying, my friends texting me *Are you okay?* They finally got the hint and now they don't text me anything anymore and I'm okay with that. I became the Hermit card in Mom's tarot. I got off social media, too—and, you know, it's kind of true that if you're not online you don't really exist to the rest of the world. Besides, what would I post pictures of? Here's an empty Suboxone package—physician-approved nicotine for opiate users! Here's my flat stomach. Here's my stupid/pointless/lame group therapy Circle of Sad. Here's the vegan chocolate cake Mom made on day sixty that says *Clean Machine* in pink frosting, even though I'm not vegan. It was good, though. Here's the Death card I keep getting.

So when Micah picks me up in his ancient Jeep, I leave my phone at home. Mom and Dad are halfway across the world—there'd be no check-in calls, no curfew. Mom said we're almost eighteen now, so she's going to trust us. Or at least trust Mae to make sure I don't fuck up too much. Cynthia has already come by twice, and taken me to the Circle of Sad herself—I'm sure she's sending Mom reports.

"You hungry?" Micah asks.

He has to shout because the top is down and we're on the 405 and there's magic happening somewhere close because there isn't much traffic. Blond hair flying around his face—perfect California boy. I shake my head.

"Mind if I get a burrito?"

"Whatever you want." I smile; he smiles.

When we get to UCLA, we squeeze onto his twin bed with the striped comforter I helped him pick out at Target. The roommate took a three-day weekend to roll in the desert, so we have the place to ourselves.

A poster of Bob Marley hangs on the wall beside us, and Bob looks down, giving us his blessing, one hand holding a joint, raised in benediction.

Normally we would smoke a little, but I can't, haven't since last spring—golf clap for my five months of sobriety—so we have to try and remember how to be together without any help. It's awkward. We've forgotten. Even though we've done this so many times since what happened in March, we still can't remember how it was Before.

Micah should have come that day.

He wasn't there because I told him not to be—I knew he'd rather be anywhere else. He'd looked so relieved when I said it was okay not to come. Smiled. I wanted him to come anyway, to, like, *be* there for me, but the only guy who came through the door was this dad-aged dude wearing a polo shirt, and that made me think about how Dad offered to come, which was actually really sweet, but I was like, *this isn't Take Your Daughter to Abortion Day*, you know? Mom kept trying to feed me Life

Savers, those wintergreen ones, until I told her the name was kind of ironic, wasn't it (*lifesavers*, get it?), and then she stopped.

Micah looks down at me. "Could we have a drink? Or is that against the rules?"

Yes, it's against the rules. And he knows it, or at least he should know it. I start to say *yes, but you go ahead, I'm cool* like I have been since April, but Jesus, I've been so good. And a drink is not a pill, and the pills are the problem, the main problem, right? One drink is not the same as one pill. I'm good now, I am. Before, I never could have gone *five months* without a diamond. I could hardly go five *hours* without one. Before.

And the thought of doing this—spending the night, a *whole night*, with Micah and not being a drag like I know I am: I need help. Just a little something.

I bite my lip. Nod. "A drink would be nice."

"You're sure? I'm not, like, fucking with your serenity or whatever?"

Some tatted-up college guy who came to speak at group used that phrase once, and I dig it.

"I'm sure. Yeah. Totally. It's not, you know, Percs."

Just one little blue pill, one teensy-tiny Percocet, and I'd be fine.

Micah reaches under the bed and grabs a bottle of Popov, which is like drinking Windex, and we drink it straight because the only thing in his fridge is a suspicious-smelling carton of chocolate milk. When we're done, he sets the bottle on the desk behind us. We will need it later, I think.

The relief is almost instant. Not being me anymore.

It is so warm.

And then I realize: I am no longer sober.

"Hey." Micah rests a hand on my arm. "You good?"

He's not in my Circle of Sad, where we try to be honest when people ask questions like that. So I say:

"What? Yeah. Totally. All good."

All those days of denying myself, of doing the right thing, all that torture—down the drain. So I take another drink, then another.

"This is what got us in trouble in the first place," Micah says, running his finger along the edge of my lacy bra. He's just teasing—he's *trying*, you know?—but it isn't funny. *Trouble?* There are no words to describe what happened in March, but some are better than others, and *trouble* isn't one of them. *Gutting*, maybe. That would be a good one.

This is Micah, I remind myself. *He loves you.*

But in the elevator up here, when he was tapping his foot and talking about the waves he'd caught this morning, I realized I didn't give a shit about the waves, and the foot tapping might make me commit a homicide, it really might.

And, look, I know he was right. About what I had to do back in March. The pills, who knew what they would have done to the acorn inside me? Before it happened, the counselor and I talked, and she said that a pregnancy is an acorn—not the tree, not yet—but it contains the possibility of a tree. *Acorn.* Perfect, right? She didn't know about Yoko, but it was like she kind of *did* know, on a psychic level only the sisterhood operates on. And she said it was okay to do whatever I wanted. Did I want to do this? And I told her about the pills and we talked about damage to acorns exposed to high levels of opiates and about risks, but how it's also possible the acorn would be fine. And I told her about all the trees I wanted someday, I really do, and am I a bad person if I do this? And she hugged me and she said no, but that this decision was mine.

I don't know what makes you a woman, but I don't think it's getting your period or losing your virginity or having guys suddenly notice you and the harassment beginning, especially when you have hips like mine. I think it's the moment when you get to decide something for yourself, something that will affect the rest of your life.

And this decision: It grew me up.

I told the counselor that I'd had this idea, like this momentary thought that maybe, maybe if I *had* a baby, then things would be okay. Like, I'd have some value in the world. Someone would need me and maybe that need would be the thing, the thing that would make me good and also would keep me from the pills. And maybe take the sadness away. But the thought, the thought of ending up like Mae's birth mother, with the drugs and child protective services and then this acorn-that-is-now-a-tree having to go into foster care because I'm such a fuckup—Micah was right. The clinic, it was the right thing to do. I'm glad I had the choice. That no one took it away from me.

I just wish I hadn't had to make it in the first place.

The counselor looked at me for a long moment: She had red hair and green eyes and it was like this Celtic priestess had come to hear my confession. And she rested a hand on my knee and she said, "Whatever you decide, Hannah, remember this: You are enough."

When she left the room, I put on the scratchy gown, lay down, and closed my eyes.

What haunts me isn't what happened—I don't think it was wrong. But what is killing me is how something got taken off the table. Taken by the look on Micah's face when I showed him the stick with the two lines. And because I'd made other choices, bad ones. I didn't really get to decide—am I ready to be a mom yet?—because of what was in my blood, all those diamonds I couldn't stop swallowing because they fill me with sparkling, glittery light. Like binge-eating starlight.

But the universe gave me this wake-up call and I didn't ignore it. I didn't. Five months clean.

Until today. Because a drink counts. Which means I'll be back to day one, if I get to day one, and day one fucking sucks.

They say *you're clean*, but then why do I still feel so dirty all the time? There is no *clean*. Not for girls like me.

"Where've you gone, Nah?" Micah murmurs. He runs a finger between my eyes, to the thinking-too-hard wrinkles between them.

"Nowhere," I say.

He smiles. He doesn't understand what *nowhere* means to me.

"I miss you." He rubs the tip of my nose with his. "I miss my girl. I know it's been hard. That you've been sad. I want us to be okay. Me being here, in college—this isn't going to change anything. I promise."

And this is why love is so confusing: because now he's my sweet surfer boy who makes my heart beat a little fast again.

"I love you," I whisper.

"I love you more than the best wave in the ocean."

I reach for the bottle next to his alarm clock and gulp down more fire. I notice the time, written in big red numbers that glow in the dark of the room: 8:06 p.m. I am suspended in this minute, just for a moment—drunk girl's prerogative—and I see them, I see my parents. I conjure them.

It is morning in Malaysia, and the sun is beating down, and Mom's wearing that wide-brimmed hat Mae and I got for her, the one with the red bow that matches her swimsuit.

Wow, Mom says, way out there on her island in Malaysia. *The current's strong today. Look at how the water is pulling back into the ocean.*

Dad lifts up his phone and takes a picture to show to his oceanographer friend. Then he points.

Look at the water breaking, way out there. He takes another picture. It is a wave and it is coming.

Micah whispers, *I remembered a condom this time.*

. • • .

"Holy *shit*. Wake up, Nah. Baby, wake up."

Micah is shaking me and something has died in my mouth and my head is full of shards of glass. Fuck. Why do I do this to myself?

"The universe is telling you something, Nah," Mom is saying when we walk out of the clinic. I ask her what the hell the universe could possibly be telling me other than to practice safe fucking and she doesn't even blink at my use of the word fucking. She just shrugs and says, "She speaks through the gut." But I can't think about my gut because it's empty now and all I

want to do is fill it with pills, real pills, and those bitches inside only gave me Tylenol. And I don't ask Mom what she means by speak. What does that mean when you can't hear the universe—or when it doesn't speak to you at all?

When we get home, Mom grabs a bundle of sage and sits me down in front of her altar. On it is a picture of Amma, this lady famous for hugging who Mom says taught her how to love, and also a picture of Yoko, looking kick-ass in a bowler hat and shades. "Okay," Mom says, lighting the sage, "I'm gonna smudge the shit out of you."

I have promised I will do better. No more almost-failing my classes, no more being stoned and pregnant and generally useless. I told Mom I was doing better. I was. Technically, I *was*. I told her to go on this trip. I wanted her off my back. And how was I to know I was going to drink half a bottle of vodka last night? I didn't mean it, didn't *plan* it.

Fuck. Fuck me and fuck my life and I fucking hate myself so much.

Hungover as a mother. But not a mother. Because who would want me, who would want to be a copy of *this*?

You'd think getting knocked up and almost failing the eleventh grade would be rock bottom enough for any girl. Ha.

"Hannah," Micah says, his hand on my arm.

"Go to class," I mumble, throwing his pillow over my head. "You can take me home after."

It's too late to go back to Venice and get to school on time. Ditching school on a Friday is what any self-respecting senior would do.

His phone rings. "Mae? Sorry—sorry. I just saw your text. Fuck. I'm freaking out. I just woke up. My phone was on silent, so I missed all your—No. She's asleep." Micah's voice veers in my direction. "*Nah.* Seriously, wake up. Please."

I turn over. "Just tell her I'm ditching. Christ, she has to stop micromanaging my life. Only one of us is going to be an astronaut someday, and it isn't me. The world will be *fine* if I cut a few more classes."

I wonder what it must be like for Mae, to know that she matters, that she will maybe change the world. Dad is delighted by her. Mom is in awe of her. It's like the universe had to even out her being adopted. I might have my parents' genes, but she's the best of them.

I'm so fucking basic.

"I'm looking now," he says to Mae. "CNN."

The room fills with the sound of people screaming. I bolt up. Micah's at his desk, staring at his laptop.

"What is that?" I'm getting out of bed. *What?*

He turns toward me. Tries to say words, but all that comes out is a croak. Like when I said, *Hey, I have to tell you something,* and held up that stick with the two lines.

And I know, I think. I don't know *what,* but it's like I *know* everything in my life is turning to utter shit. Again.

"Was there a terrorist attack?" I ask.

He shakes his head. What scares me isn't the fear on his face. It's the confusion. Like the tables have been turned. Like whatever is on CNN is actually personal, like it's going to be more than just some randomness you talk about, not a school shooting across the country or a famine on the other side of the world.

I hold out my hand and he gives me his phone.

"It's me," I say.

I hear words and Mae has the kind of voice doctors on TV use when they come into the hospital waiting room with really bad fucking news. But I don't know what she's saying because I'm looking at Micah's screen. And I see it.

I see the wave.

3

Mae

ISS Location: Low-Earth Orbit
Earth Date: 30 August
Earth Time (PST): 09:52

A tsunami can travel at 500 miles per hour, as fast as a commercial jet.

The tallest tsunami ever recorded was in Alaska. It was 100 feet.

Rossby Waves, which aren't tsunamis, just large-scale ocean waves, take roughly 221 days to cross an ocean. A tsunami? *One* day. Sometimes *less* than one day.

Tsunamis rush the shore at the speed of a major league pitcher's fastball. Faster, even.

They're caused by underwater earthquakes, volcanic eruptions or other explosions under the ocean's surface, movement in glaciers—even meteorites crashing down from space.

Many survivors report that a tsunami sounds like a freight train and that the water is gray-brown because it's churning up the ocean floor.

The water is full of all sorts of things:

- Metal
- Pieces of buildings

- Cars
- Shards of glass
- Toys
- Palm trees
- Beach umbrellas
- Gold watches
- Cell phones
- Bathing suit tops
- My parents

It takes eight to ten minutes to drown in seawater. Fresh water is two to three minutes. You die from cardiac arrest. I didn't know that. I thought it was your lungs filling with water, but it's your heart that gives out. That gives up.

For the past seventeen minutes and thirty-two seconds, I have been on a mental EVA—Extravehicular Activity, more commonly referred to by laypersons as a *space walk*.

It is ten years in the future, and I am on the International Space Station, scrunched into a tiny window seat.

There's a bright blue line on the horizon, mixing with the emerald smoky green of the aurora that swirls over Earth's surface like a potion in a cauldron—another sunrise, one of the sixteen I get to see up here every day on the ISS. Since we orbit Earth every ninety-two minutes, that means sixteen sunrises and sixteen sunsets. How's that for a life?

We race toward it, toward the light, and neon cerulean turns to blinding gold as the sun rises over the east, spilling across the beaches of Malaysia right below us.

Up here, I can just make out the rocky coastline of the islands, edged by white sand, green water giving way to the darkest blue of the ocean. A raft of clouds floats by, covering my view, and then we're speeding past those beaches, heading toward our next sunset.

Mad Matter Magazine Vol. 4, No. 12

Today, we're sitting down with theoretical physicist Dr. Greg Winters to talk dark matter, the nature of the universe, and time travel.

Mad Matter: Dr. Winters, you are one of the world's leading physicists, doing groundbreaking research on the very nature of the universe. NASA calls you when they're stumped. People say there might be a Nobel Prize sitting in your office someday. Yet you've taken a sabbatical. Why?

Dr. Winters: My research on dark matter and dark energy—

Mad Matter: For our readers, I'll just interject here: This is the stuff that makes up ninety-five percent of the universe, but we have no idea what it is.

Dr. Winters: Correct. My work in this field has inadvertently created a, shall we say, event horizon of sorts in my life—not to get all heavy on you with general relativity and spacetime.

Mad Matter: [Laughs] Give us your best explanation of what an event horizon is.

Dr. Winters: An event horizon is the point of no return. It's a terrain in spacetime that's created when the gravitational pull of a massive object is so great that escaping it is impossible. Imagine a huge magnet, pointed at you, and you're covered in metal. There's no avoiding its pull. When that massive object is coming your way, it's creating that point of no return. You can't escape the object. You have to face it.

Event horizons are mostly discussed in relation to black holes, but they're a great metaphor for life, too.

Mad Matter: How so?

Dr. Winters: Well, all of us, at one time or another, are going to have something happen that creates an event horizon—a point of no return. The first thing is to accept that we can't escape it, and so we need to face it head-on. Next, we need to look for the potential this event horizon presents us with.

Mad Matter: What is the potential of an event horizon?

Dr. Winters: Theoretically, if you could actually make it across the event horizon, you could see the entire history of the universe playing out before you. You see Napoleon on his horse and your ancestors in the fields and the suffragettes marching in the streets of New York City, and you see your children sleeping in bed in the other room and you see the cancer diagnosis you will get five years from now. You see every bit of it. All of time is happening at the same moment all around you.

   Now, here on Earth, we can't get ourselves to actual event horizons that let us see the future and thus help us make better choices in the present. We can't time travel. Yet.

Mad Matter: So how does it help us—knowing event horizons are out there, and that there's potential to see all of time playing out at once?

Dr. Winters: For me, it makes life on Earth a little more bearable: There's comfort in knowing that whatever is going to happen *is already happening right now*. In spacetime. It takes the pressure off. The deaths and births and screwups and victories—it's already playing out. There's nothing you can do to stop it.

4

Mae

ISS Location: Low-Earth Orbit
Earth Date: 30 August
Earth Time (PST): 11:30

Anything can happen in space.

It's an environment in which human life is impossible. But if you're an astronaut, you're human. WHICH MEANS YOU'RE DOING THE IMPOSSIBLE. You're floating around in a tin can with a finite amount of oxygen, in a very vulnerable body, hoping that the math is right because it's the only thing that's going to keep you alive.

Actually, that's not entirely accurate. There are things you can control, like how well trained you are, the ability to stay calm under pressure—literal and figurative—and your intelligence. And if you've got a good crew, like the kind that would go into Mordor with you, and *they* are well trained and intelligent, then you exponentially increase your chances of survival.

The fact that we can go to space and survive there is proof positive that we can do impossible things. That's what my dad is always saying—*We can do impossible things.*

When I was six, I alerted my father to the fact that maybe there are certain conditions in society that make it impossible for female members of our species to do impossible things. Such as, women make up less than eleven percent of humans sent into space. I informed my father that the probability of me wearing a NASA space suit wasn't great. His answer was to sit me down to watch an interview with astronaut Peggy Whitson, who would go on to become the commander of the International Space Station and would break records for time spent in space: 665 DAYS, the most of any American woman. "We can do impossible things," he said. Then we went to the Griffith Observatory to look at stars.

And this year? Fifty percent of NASA's astronaut candidates are women. FIFTY PERCENT!

Someday I'm going to be up there. I'm going to be on the International Space Station and I'm going to do space walks and listen to "Starman" while watching my sixteenth sunrise of the day and I'm going to call my dad *from space* and it is going to be SPECTACULAR.

That phone call is going to happen because my father is alive. We are going to find him and he'll come up with a great metaphor about this wave. *Just another opportunity to visit the event horizon,* he'll say. And Mom will announce she's going to make soup and we'll help her and it will be so good, the best soup anyone has ever eaten, and maybe we'll call it Miracle Soup, even though only half our family believes in miracles. I'm not in that demographic, but maybe I could be, if they came home.

I started training to be an astronaut when I was six years old, but I think I actually began preparing when I was born. I had to learn, from day one, to adapt to hostile environments that threatened my existence.

Not being picked up when you cry is a hostile environment.

Having a social worker come into your home and realize your diaper hasn't been changed in an entire day is a hostile environment.

By the time I was three, when my parents adopted me after my biological mother officially chose drugs over me, I'd been in *seven* foster homes.

The thing about being an astronaut is that you have to spend your whole life training. From the second you decide you want to be in that big white suit someday, to the moment you're strapped in, listening to that *ten, nine, eight, seven, six*—you never stop getting ready for the mission.

Your whole life is a sim.

Practicing for disaster. For the worst-case scenario. For *Houston, we have a problem.*

Expecting the unexpected.

The worst happens and you work the problem. Right away. That's what you do. You do not cry or have a panic attack or pray or get angry at the engineers on Earth who did incorrect calculations or blame it on the Russians or have a deep-space existential crisis. No. You work the problem.

Work the problem is NASA protocol when there's bad news or flashing red lights or space debris in your trajectory: Work the problem.

My favorite scene in *Apollo 13* is when the engineers all get in a room and one of them holds up a cylindrical carbon dioxide filter and says, "We need to fit this"—and then he holds up a square one—"into this"—and then he points to a bunch of junk he's thrown on the table—"using this." The *Apollo* crew is up there breathing in CO_2, dying, in a shuttle that might not have enough juice to make it back to Earth. These engineers on the ground have to figure out how to turn what those astronauts have on the shuttle into the ultimate breathing hack. In outer space. *And they do it.* They save the astronauts. *That's* working the problem.

Astronauts spend hours in simulators, dying every single day so that they can stay alive on the day that counts.

A good astronaut knows that anything—rejection, failure, death—can be a sim. Everything in your life is preparation for the mission.

I start working the problem before Hannah gets to the house, which means I have been on hold with the Red Cross or the State Department for the past twelve hours. From the time Gram called last night, I had to alternate between calling my sister's boyfriend and trying to ascertain whether my parents have survived a wave that has destroyed a good portion of the Malaysian coast.

My vitals are good—coffee and math have assisted in this—but

Hannah's are not. This is apparent as soon as I see her step out of Micah's Jeep. I suspect she cried all the way down the freeway.

There is a part of me—irrational, I understand—that is surprised to see her. Somehow, in calling and not hearing from her and in calling Dad's and Mom's cells and not hearing from *them*, I started to think that Hannah had been caught in the wave, too. That, somewhere in Malaysia, my sister was floating facedown.

And so, when her feet hit the driveway, I run. Her mouth opens in an O, an expanding galaxy, because I am not given to displays of emotion and have never run *toward* her, just beside her, but I can't help it when I throw my body against hers, which is much taller and softer than mine.

"You're *alive*."

I don't know why I say this, because of course she is. I attribute this cognitive malfunction to a severe lack of sleep.

Nah cries harder, her whole body sagging against me, as though we are doing a trust exercise for AP Psych. I shift my weight as we start to fall, keeping us upright because she can trust me. I am working the problem. I will find them.

"We got here as fast as we could," Micah says. "Fucking 405. You know."

Nah pulls away, just a little. "Have you heard anything? Like, *anything*?"

I didn't notice at first: the smell. In my rush to catch our fall, with my nose pressed against the clothes she left the house in yesterday, my olfactory system was hoodwinked. But the breath is an excellent carrier of alcoholic substances.

I check her pupils first: normal-sized. No opiates. But that just means no pills in the past few hours. I couldn't check her pupils last night, because she didn't come home. Didn't check in.

I should have known. When she didn't check in. But I trusted Micah—and I shouldn't have.

I am perfectly capable of handling a natural disaster. My sister is another matter entirely. All those nights, holding back her hair. Lying to

Mom and Dad for her when I caught her buying from Priscilla because, she promised, this was the last time. Becoming smaller to help make her feel bigger, talking less at the dinner table, after she made that joke that wasn't a joke about how, since I'm six months older, I'm the heir and she's the spare. "You're the Elizabeth," she said, "and I'm the Margaret." I don't read the magazines my sister does, but because of my extensive research for an AP Euro paper on sibling dynamics in the monarchies of Europe between the fourteenth and twenty-first centuries, I did get her reference about sibling rivalry in the House of Windsor.

I have never been angry at my sister for the drinking, the drugs. I have felt scared and sad and sorry for her, but never furious. Until now.

How can she choose to drink instead of look for our parents? What kind of person *does* that?

I pull away from her. "I have been trying to call you since 8:17 last night."

"That's my fault," Micah says. "My phone wasn't on."

I am just now realizing how often we all make excuses for Hannah. It is Micah's fault because his phone wasn't on, not her fault because she didn't bring one in the first place.

It was Dad's fault—according to him—that Hannah had a drug problem, because he worked such long hours. Or Mom's theory: Pappoús was also tempted by the devil more than once. Like grandfather, like granddaughter. It's in the blood. Their blood, not mine, since mine is different. Hannah's addiction, the counselor said, was also, in part, attributed to me: Having a high-performing sibling can, she noted, trigger a user's lack of self-esteem.

The literature on addiction says it's no one's fault, that you can't blame yourself for a loved one's substance abuse, but I don't buy that theory. Every time a rocket goes down, there is an inquiry. Someone is always to blame.

Hannah's lower lip trembles. "I'm here, okay? I'm sorry. I'll start . . . doing whatever you think I should."

"I'm not sure how much assistance you'll be if you're not sober," I say.

"Dude, Mae. Lay off her—" Micah starts.

"Don't." I give him the look my father gives exceptionally obtuse graduate students, then turn back to Hannah. "Have you seen the videos online? Of the wave?"

She nods.

"And you thought the best way to help our parents survive that was to get *drunk*?"

Hannah steps back, as though I have hit her. And I want to. I have never wanted to slam the back of my hand against her cheek, but right now, that would feel really excellent.

"*Hey.*" I have never heard this edge in Micah's voice. "She is *not* drunk. We had *some* drinks last night. Responsibly. Don't make her feel worse than she already does. It's not helping anyone."

I cover my face with the palms of my hands because I am very, very tired. And perhaps I have made a tactical error. The psychologist would say this response of mine could result in Hannah falling into a shame spiral—and more nights of me looking for her on the boardwalk at three a.m. before Dad and Mom realize she's not in bed.

"I'm sorry, Mae," Nah says. "It was just *one night*. Just *drinks*. I'm here, okay? How can I help?"

Does this mean it all starts again? The using and the lying and the detoxing and the days when there is even less light in my sister's eyes? And will it be the wave's fault—or mine?

"Do you know who's going to be blamed for you drinking when they get home?" I ask her. My vocal cords are masking my fear with the sound of anger, a higher pitch than usual, and I'm grateful for that. "Not you. Never you. It will be *my* fault. And maybe it is. You told me to lay off, and I did, but I shouldn't have. I should have followed Mom's rules, and now—"

"Oh, like you'd actually get in trouble." Maybe she is still drunk and this is why she says: "Besides, I wouldn't worry, because they might not even *come* home."

I stare at her.

"I didn't mean—" Hannah stops herself, looks around in a panic, then lunges toward the wooden fence that forms a lazy barrier to our front yard.

Three knocks.

The thing about working the problem is that you can't work all the problems at once. And I don't have time to work the problem of my sister.

I need to help my parents come home.

there is no point to me.

5

Hannah

On this first night, we sleep in Mom and Dad's room. I lie on Mom's side and Mae lies on Dad's and we hold hands and watch CNN, which is the only light in the room. It's on mute because they keep replaying the cell phone videos where everyone is screaming.

We made up. It took ten hours, but when she offered to braid my hair, I knew we were okay.

It wasn't like the vodka just fell into my mouth. I know I made a choice, the wrong choice. But it's hard to explain to my sister about *why* I did it. Hard to explain to myself. I'm not saying Mae's lucky for what happened to her before she officially became one of us (Mom says she's *always* been one of us, and I agree), but I think it made her strong. Maybe knowing you are safe and loved and that all your needs will be met is the trade-off for my weakness.

If Mom and Dad were here, it would all begin again, right away: the random drug tests at home, more meetings in the Circle of Sad, extra appointments with Dr. Brown. As it is, Mae keeps checking my pupils, and her nostrils flare so much I know she's checking for whiffs of booze on me.

"It was just one time," I say. "A slipup. It won't happen again."

Mae's eyes slide toward me, and you can almost see her brain working behind the bright turquoise of them, like her brain is a really fast, expensive computer: assessing, calculating, sorting.

"I don't think it works that way, Nah. All the websites say—"

"Can you at least let me be the expert on my own shit? You can know best about everything else—space is all yours, okay? The whole universe."

Nobody gets under my skin like my sister.

That thinking crinkle we both get—it's like our bodies know we're sisters, even if our blood doesn't—forms between her two pale eyebrows. When Mae gets it, it means she's confused. Which means you rarely see the crinkle on her face.

"I'm just trying to help," she says.

"You can help by trusting me, for once." In the blue light of the TV, she glows a little, milky-white skin and hair the color of wheat. Light to my dark. How cliché is that? "I'm clean. I didn't take any pills. And I'm not going to. I just fucked up because Micah had the stuff and—"

"He shouldn't have let you."

"He's my boyfriend, not my boss. Micah doesn't *let* me do anything. Drinking isn't my problem, anyway."

She gives me a look.

"Legit addicts are way worse than I ever was," I say. "*I* was the one who told Mom and Dad I was using. I wasn't, like, stealing from them to buy smack on the boardwalk or something."

Everyone keeps telling me I'm an addict. I'm not. I had a problem, and now I don't. I'm only seventeen—you can't be an addict when you're seventeen. What happened to sowing wild oats and experimenting and all that? They've written me off before I'm even legally allowed to vote.

Mae squeezes my hand. "You can talk to me. Just because we're not the same doesn't mean I can't understand."

"You can't. This one thing, Mae—you *can't.*"

People that don't wake up every morning feeling like what's the point will never understand. It's impossible. They say: exercise, meditate, think happy thoughts, snap out of it, wear this crystal, drink this tea, find your goddamn bliss. But I literally—and I am not exaggerating—do not remember a time when I was truly happy. Except for when I was on Percocet. Those fuckers in their fancy labs actually figured out how to bottle happiness. Thing is, when you don't have those diamonds in you, it's all worse. So much worse. The Sad is so big it's like, I don't know, it's like that movie Mae loves where the astronaut can't get back to the ship and he just floats off into the complete, utter, terrifying darkness of space listening to cowboy music. My sister studies the void—but I look into it Every. Single. Day.

The universe is so big and terrifying, and we are so small and weak. What is the point of getting out of bed in the morning when you are so utterly insignificant?

I turn away from her, push my face into the pillow, and the tears come fast and hard because—

"It smells like her," I say into the cotton, into the pretty forget-me-nots Mom picked out.

Mae scoots closer and presses her nose to the pillow. "Roses."

She rubs her palm between my shoulder blades, which always makes me feel better, I don't know why. After a while, after she smooths away my crying, I hear her sit up, and when I look over, Mae is holding Dad's pillow to her face. I know exactly what it smells like: my great-grandpa's cologne, Brut, which Dad started wearing after he died. Sweet and cedary. Dad says it keeps his feet on the ground, since his head is mostly in space.

"It smells like morning hugs," Mae says.

He's a scientist, but I'm pretty sure Dad thinks it's bad luck not to hug people when they leave the house in the morning.

And I realize: "I didn't get to hug him. When he left."

Mae got up early to see them off, but I slept in. Why do I always do the wrong thing?

"I hugged him for both of us," she says.

I wish the bed didn't smell like them, because I know that if they don't come back, there will be a moment when it stops smelling like them, and I don't want to know that moment, not ever.

I curl back into the pillow.

Sometime around eleven, Micah comes back from his shift at the restaurant and squishes onto the bed next to me without a word, him on one side, Mae on my other.

I can't even look at him, I can't, because I hate him. I suddenly just hate him. *Fuck you for fucking me while my parents were dying.*

There is nothing rational about grief. I'm already learning this.

I'm also worried his scent will eat up Mom's.

"Anything new?" Micah asks.

"I don't think so," Mae says. "Let's see." She turns the sound back on.

"It's hard to believe, but this is even worse than the tsunami that hit Indonesia, Thailand, and Sri Lanka back in 2004," a reporter is saying.

The landscape behind her is still bright, since it's not even sunset yet over there. Every few minutes, they cut to footage of the wave. I've memorized all the cuts they have—I'll never forget them. Her voice talks over someone's cell phone video, the camera jumping around as they run, and you keep hearing *oh my God, oh my God* and then crying and screaming. There's one taken by someone who was standing on the roof of a resort while the wave covers the pool below, a perfect, clear shot. There's the one of the wave surging up over a dock, taken by someone too fucking stupid to run. There's the satellite map, the graphs showing the earthquake's radius on the ocean floor. And dozens of other things people caught and sent in.

"Malaysia's never seen this level of devastation, and aid workers are struggling to respond," the reporter says.

The wave is a monster, devouring everything. It covers whole hotels, throwing cars around. It moves like a starving, wild beast. I try to picture my petite mother in that water. I try to picture her swimming, but I can't. You can't swim in that.

"Fuck," I say. I draw my knees up and push my eyes against my knee-caps. Micah rests his hand on my back. *I hate you! I hate you!*

"Hannah." Mae presses closer to me on my other side. She smells like oranges and sugar. "Listen, the chances of dying in a tsunami are one in five hundred thousand. Obviously the fact that they actually experienced a tsunami raises the odds, but even so, people survive these things all the time. I mean, look at all the survivors they've interviewed so far. A lot of people are going to live, so why shouldn't Mom and Dad be two of them?"

This is self-preservation. This is Mae hiding in her books, behind her telescope. Numbers and formulas and theories. She has to say this because nothing else is allowed to be true.

I look at her so I can't see the images in my mind: Mom choking on the ocean she'd been deliriously happy about—*Did you get the pictures, Nah? Look how BLUE it is!* Dad, his body bashing into a wall that surrounds the seaside bed-and-breakfast they were staying at. He'd lose his glasses. Wouldn't know which way was up.

Micah tries to hold my hand, but I pull away and stick my hands in my armpits and stare at the TV. He doesn't get mad. Just keeps calling the embassy in Kuala Lumpur again and again while Mae turns her focus to the Red Cross, since they already have people on the ground. I can hear through their speakers: *Due to high volumes . . .*

"I love you," I say to him, after a bit, because I do, right now I do, and because I feel guilty for hating him, too. He's not perfect and I'm not perfect and maybe I've just been too hard on him all these months.

"Love you back." He kisses my forehead. "They're alive. I know it."

I nod. "Right. Yes. You're right."

"The death toll is astronomically high—at least two hundred thousand people," a doctor is saying when I change the channel.

His scrubs are bloody, and his eyes are so heavy I'm surprised he can still stand up.

The anchor's voice cuts in. "Please be warned that what you're about to see contains graphic imagery that may not be appropriate for children."

Hell.

Behind the doctor, there are bodies covered in white sheets, and people crying and brown skin and white skin and chaos. A little boy is screaming for his mom and he hasn't got any pants on.

"How can people find their loved ones?" the reporter is asking. She shoves a mic in the doctor's face.

"We're working around the clock to update our list of patients. At this point, anyone being brought in is . . . They are beyond our help. Most bodies don't have any identification, of course, so we're taking photographs." He gestures toward a wall filled with Polaroids. Tons of people are gathered in front of it, and every now and then someone sobs as they recognize someone they're looking for.

"They're taking pictures of *dead* people?" I say.

Mae begins typing furiously. "It's probably unethical to put the photos online, but . . ."

"We're not looking at them," I say.

"But—"

"Mae. We are not looking at photos of dead people because our parents are not *dead*. Okay?"

She hesitates for a second, the knowledge-seeker in her warring with the sister in her, then finally nods. "All right."

"The worst damage is in Langkawi Island," the reporter is saying. "We expect—"

"Where are you going again?" I ask Mom.

"Langkawi," she says.

"Ohhhh," I say, sounding snooty. "Lang-cow-eeee."

She hits my arm, playful. I hit her back.

"—been over thirty hours since the tsunami hit," a reporter says. "The American embassy in Kuala Lumpur says they're making every effort to—"

"Why can't anyone fucking *answer* this shit?" Micah growls into his phone.

Due to high volumes . . .

A McDonald's commercial comes on. Fuck Happy Meals and Ronald McDonald, that creepy-ass clown. Probably a pedophile. My eyes fill, and when Micah reaches for me, I let myself collapse.

"I'm sorry," I whisper.

Why can't I be strong like Mae? Why do I always have to be an open wound?

"Nothing to be sorry about," he murmurs, fingers in my hair.

Later, half-asleep, I hear Mae and Micah talking.

Mae tells him how she just read on the National Geographic website that many bodies are never found after a tsunami because they're washed out to sea. Jesus *fuck*. So there's actually something even *worse* than them dying.

I get that Mae has to know how things work so she can form a hypothesis—*If many bodies wash out to sea, then we may never find our parents*—but I don't care how things work, just that they actually freaking *work*. I need unicorns in the sky shitting rainbows, not data.

"Do you think they made it?" Micah asks quietly.

I stop breathing. There's a long pause. Too long. Remember: Mae knows all the things.

"Ask me at ninety-six hours," she says.

Four days. In the modern world, if you can't contact someone within that amount of time, you are incapable of contacting them.

"But what's your gut feeling?" Micah says. His voice is so hopeful, so broken.

I can imagine the look on her face. "I need more data."

my mom is terrible at holding her breath.

Death Tarot Card
4302 Seaview Lane
Venice, CA

6

Hannah

I think I might fall off the wagon again.

Preferably today. Preferably now.

Are wagons really that hard to climb back onto? They don't say *fall off a skyscraper, fall out of a plane*. It's just a wagon.

A single pill.

On a loop, in my head, never ending: *I told her to go. I told her to go.*

We haven't heard a thing.

Anyone would want a pill if they hadn't heard a thing. Not Mae, but a normal person, maybe.

At twenty-four hours, I got a second wind when some lady on CNN found her daughter alive in the hospital. She was in a coma, which is why no one knew her name and couldn't put her on a list of survivors. So I decided both of my parents were in comas. All we had to do was go find them. Or maybe they were being heroes. Rescuing kids in trees. Huddling on top of floating debris. Calling out to rescue workers: *Here! Over here!* They are alive, and when they get back, they will write a memoir of survival and it'll be made into a movie starring Hugh Jackman with a Boston accent, and Rachel Weisz, maybe, or that Greek actress Nia Vardalos.

But then we are told that the coma theory is a long shot. At least for *both* of them. But Dad always says the long shot is the best shot. And then he starts talking science and I don't understand him anymore, but my point is that they might be in a coma, but in a cave or a boat, right, not like in a hospital. And someone is taking care of them or, I don't know, maybe Cynthia is right and there really are angels. She said she dreamed of one last night.

Cyn's curled up on the recliner in the living room, which I'm avoiding because she's texting with all of Mom's friends and students from their yoga studio and if one of them comes to the house and is all *namaste* I will cut a bitch. I really will.

It's night two, the second night after the wave, and when Gram and Papa arrive I feel a momentary sense of relief because they're old and have wisdom and will know what to do. But their panic is so present, so palpable, that I've started avoiding them as much as I can. It's hard watching old people try not to cry. Every now and then Papa will look around, as if he's just realized where he is. "I can't believe it," he'll say, shaking his head. "I just *can't* believe it."

Mae's not any better, but for different reasons. Every time I leave a room and come back in, she studies me, like I'm something in one of her labs. To see if I took anything.

"Do you want me to pee in a cup?" I finally snap, around the forty-eight-hour mark.

My sister is doing calculus homework—to relax, she says. This is why she'll jump in a spaceship someday and go be amazing and never be scared and have all the answers and I will be here, forcing myself to get out of bed in the morning. If I'm still here.

Because fuck here. Really. Fuck it.

Mae cocks her head to the side, in that birdlike way of hers, eyes narrowing. Checking my pupils.

"No," she says.

We don't talk for the rest of the night.

On day three, Mae and I start filling out a missing persons report for the International Red Cross.

And it's here, at seventy-two hours, that I realize something:

The forgetting begins almost immediately.

Nobody tells you that.

The stuff they ask you about is the kind of thing they would ask when your missing person is probably not a person anymore. Otherwise, why would they want to know about scars and jewelry and tattoos—they say it's so much easier to identify the body if the person has tattoos. Dad doesn't have any tattoos. Nobody can remember which ankle Mom's Om is on.

We don't have pictures of Mom's feet. Why don't we have a single picture of her feet? Her feet in the sand or on her yoga mat or propped up on the coffee table when she's reading one of those murder mysteries she likes.

"I think it was on her right ankle," Mae says, scrolling through the yoga photos on Mom's website. In all the pictures she's wearing leggings that cover her ankles. "But it doesn't matter because they'll just be looking for a tattoo and see it and then—"

"But what if someone *else* has an Om tattoo on her ankle?" I say. "I mean, it's a common symbol, yeah? And the shape of her ears—are they serious? I don't even know the shape of my own ears."

Mae rubs her eyes, then slides her hands down her face. "Birthmarks?"

"Dad has that one on his back," I say. "Remember that time Gram told him to have it looked at because she thought it was cancerous, and Dad explained, like, the entire history of skin cancer to her and she still made him go to the doctor?"

"And she said it was shaped like Italy," Mae says. "I remember that. Should I write it down like that? *Shaped like Italy?*"

I nod, then close my eyes and try to remember my mother's ears. I'm such a horrible daughter. What kind of person doesn't remember what her mom's ears look like? I mean, really? Did I ever even see her—like *really* see her?

When we're done, Mae takes the papers to Dad's office to scan and send them to the Red Cross.

It's been over five months since I've slipped a diamond between my lips, and my body wants its Percocet fix. My bones hurt. My actual *bones*. Like growing pains. Like how it was in detox, back in March. My bones remember and they want and they whisper, begging, *Please, Hannah, please.*

But I can't. I told her to go. I *convinced* my mother she had to go on this stupid trip, and so I don't get relief. I don't get oblivion. I don't get to fall off a wagon or a skyscraper or anything else because I don't deserve to feel better.

I killed my mother.

I grab a glass of water and pull myself up the stairs, to where my parents keep the Advil, because maybe that will make my bones shut up for a little while. It's the strongest thing I can give them. Our Venice bungalow is essentially a sober house. Mom and Dad stopped drinking at home in solidarity, and once I got back from detox and started the outpatient Circle of Sad bullshit, I never smelled Mom's weed in the backyard late at night, when she thought we were asleep.

I feel like I'm trespassing when I enter the master bathroom. For some reason, I feel them here more than in other places in the house. They were in a rush the morning they left, and so things are scattered on the counter: a tube of lipstick, a bottle of Brut cologne, Dad's little silver scissors. I run my hand across the dry bar of soap in the shower—who used it last? Probably Dad. Mom likes to take her showers at night. A lump gathers in my throat, and I remember how Cynthia says that, according to Reiki, this means my head and my heart are having problems communicating.

I open the cabinet, grab the bottle of Advil, but I'm crying again, the smell of them all around me, and the bottle slips from my hands and the pills go everywhere.

I get on my knees, start picking them up, when I see it. Wedged under the sink, behind the toilet bowl cleaner.

My mouth waters at the sight of that little orange bottle.

Vicodin from when Dad got his knee surgery a few months ago, hidden so I'd never find it.

My mind—it doesn't think. It has no say as my body, as my hands, reach for that bottle, twist off the child safety cover: thirty pills—a whole month's supply.

This is almost like how it all started.

Gram had left some Vicodin at the house after a visit. A year and a half ago. Weed wasn't doing the trick anymore, making the sad go away, so I grabbed the bottle. Just to see if there was something that could help me feel better. About life. About being me.

Because it feels like the universe keeps telling me to step aside.

Mom's always saying to read the signs, and I'm telling you, they are loud and fucking clear.

People don't want me. They don't see me. Like, literally, I am *invisible*.

When I stand in line, the cashier actually looks *past* me to the person behind me. When teachers pair everyone up, I'm always out in the cold and, later, when we're halfway through the assignment, they're like, *Who's your partner, Hannah*? And I'm like, *You tell me, bitch*.

Back when I had friends, when I cared about that sort of thing, I'd be sitting at a table in the caf and they'd walk right by—not to be mean. There was always a moment when one of them would sit down and kind of look around and then shrug. After, they'd be all, *Where were you at lunch?*

Back when I was online, I'd post things and get, like, two likes. Cool things—found poetry and the beach and Priscilla's circus tats—but no one cared. It's like everyone had cracked some code, some code of being seen, and I just couldn't.

There's no place for a zero-followers person in this world. If you don't exist on the internet, you don't exist at all.

Add that to real life, with Dad's colleagues at every party being all, *Oh, you're the other daughter.* I don't know shit about astro-whatever, but I know this: Mae is this crazy-cool star like what you see on posters in science class, and I'm space debris orbiting her. You don't see the debris. You can't. All that light.

And, okay, boo-hoo or whatever, *privilege, first-world problems,* all the things I'm supposed to say, but here's the point: I'm fucking sad and I feel like a goddamn ghost, okay, and I'm sorry if that's politically incorrect, I'm sorry if my invisibility comes with my own savings account and mat-cha lattes, but it's mine, okay, it's mine and it's real to me, so just let me freaking have it. I know, I *know* that other people, so many other people, are invisible in ways that can get them killed or never have a good job or a seat at any table. I know this. But invisibility is a spectrum, like anything else. And I'm on it. So when some white kid in my Circle of Sad was all, *white fragility, white tears, check your privilege* after my turn, I was like, DUDE. Really? *Really?* So sad is just off the table for me. Like I can't feel it. Or express it. I'm in a freaking *therapy group,* what the fuck? I'm just trying to explain, to explain how the entire cosmos is like flashing these neon signs about how I'm a worthless piece of shit and don't you ever wonder what's the point of you and maybe there's no point at all?

And I hear Micah tell me in March, when things were so bad: *I can't carry you.*

I had to get help, he said. *I can't carry you.* I love you, he said. But. *I can't carry you.* Sometimes, he said, you're too much. *I can't carry you.*

I'm that astronaut, floating away to cowboy music.

I had my first pill with Micah. Summer before junior year. A little over one year ago. We said it would be for special occasions.

But it made me so happy. So we decided: weekends. Only on the weekends. We'd lie on the beach all day after he was done surfing or late at night. Percocet, mostly. Hydrocodone. Vicodin. Whatever he could get from kids at school who had the hookup. But he didn't really like it. Preferred weed. And he didn't like when I was on it. Said I was too out of it. And it made me not want to be with him. In that way.

So we stopped taking the pills. He thought we stopped. But I wanted to go back to the moon. I asked around on the boardwalk—you can get anything there—and Priscilla, she got them for me. Percs, usually. Hydro sometimes. Oxy on a really good day. The money wasn't a problem, since I had a job and whatever I made was for me to do with as I pleased. Plus I had tons of savings from all those big birthday checks from Gram and Papa. If you have two parents with good jobs who love each other and you, then being a junkie is the easiest thing in the world. I knew this. Even before I went to the Circle of Sad and that boy talked about what he had to do to get his pills. And the girl who couldn't stop crying because she stole from her sister, who was a single mom on benefits. Spend enough time on the boardwalk and you see the kind of bartering people do for their diamonds.

I took the pills at night, when I was alone. Not every night, at first. Usually when Micah had to work and we didn't hang out and when I felt like I needed to get away from myself.

I felt sad and the pills made me happy. Simple as that.

But then a couple nights became every other night, then every night. By Valentine's Day, seven months after stealing my grandma's pills, I was on them all the time. It happened so fast. It's not like I planned that. It just . . . happened.

Mom and Dad weren't idiots. They knew something was up. I'd failed most of my classes the first semester of junior year and stopped hanging out with anyone but Micah, stopped going to the bonfires he would have with the other surfers on the beach, and I lost my job at the coffeehouse because it was so hard to concentrate. To care.

Mom thought it was depression, and she found weed and booze in my room around New Year's, so that's the stuff she thought I was into. I don't think they imagined I could be such a loser. To pop pills after all those assemblies at school, all those years of drinking Mom's homemade kombucha. I let her believe it was just booze and weed, just too much partying. I started going to Dr. Brown, who is about as fun as her name sounds. But after what happened at the clinic in March, I told Mom and Dad everything. There was detox, group after school, random drug testing, and Dr. Fucking Brown. I got sober. Got good. Even though I didn't feel *normal* without the pills. Not right. Fuzzy.

I did summer school so I could still start my senior year, graduate on time. Smudged myself with sage and went to Mom's yoga classes. Told her to go to Malaysia because I promise I'm fine, it's all good, and yes I'll go to meetings and yes Cynthia can check on me and we all know Mae will watch me like a hawk even though she pretends not to. So Mom went. To Malaysia.

You should totally go, Mom. I'm fine. I want you to go. You deserve a break.

And now I'm sitting on my maybe-dead parents' bathroom floor, thinking about stealing my maybe-dead dad's Vicodin.

I can see myself in Mom's makeup mirror on the counter, and I tell that waste of space in the glass, "You don't deserve them, you fucking piece of shit."

It is so hard to do what I do next, but I do it because I deserve to hurt. I deserve to have my bones grind and scream against one another.

I told her to go. I deserve whatever's coming to me.

So I put the pills back under the counter, behind the cleaner. Where Mom and Dad will find them, all there, when they come home.

I walk into the bedroom and I scream, loud and long and oh my God, oh my *God*—

"Mom!"

She is on the floor, wearing her favorite pale green yoga outfit, and she is in fish pose. She doesn't move, doesn't speak.

"Mommy—"

I stop halfway through my rush to her.

My mother, my beautiful mother, is lying on the ground, just her back arched so that the crown of her head is resting on the blue rug we bought together two weeks ago, her upside-down eyes staring at the wall behind her. Her chest is still.

I take a deep breath and I smell her, smell the roses. I smell the ocean.

"Hannah?" Mae is pounding up the stairs and she bursts into the room, a meteor. "What happened? What's wrong?"

Mom sinks into the floor. Disappears. A fish, swimming to the bottom of a sapphire sea.

"Nah?"

I shake my head.

"What are you looking at?" Mae is staring at the carpet. But there is nothing there.

"Mom can't hold her breath," I say.

Even though I've already forgotten so much about her—the shape of her ears, maybe everything, I'm remembering this: We had a contest in the pool at the Cape last summer, to see who could hold their breath the longest.

Mom lost.

Fifteen seconds. That's all she could do.

Mae blinks. Her computer brain whirs, sifting through memories, until I see in her eyes she has found the one from the Cape.

"Adrenaline rushes can produce surprising effects." She steps closer. "Most moms can't lift cars, but if their kid is trapped under one—"

"The ocean is bigger than a car."

My mom is not coming home.

I know this like I know my belly is empty.

I turn and start to walk out of the room, but Mae looks around, her head cocked to the side.

"What?"

"Are you—are you wearing Mom's perfume?" she asks.

I stare at the rug, willing her back, but she's swum too far away.

"No."

Please don't take them both. Bring him home, I tell the universe, *and I swear I will never use again.*

I won't even bother making promises about what I'll do if the universe ignores me.

7

Mae

ISS Location: Low-Earth Orbit
Earth Date: 2 September
Earth Time (PST): 02:36

The last time disaster struck, Mom made minestrone. That was when Hannah's pregnancy test had two pink lines instead of one. At the time, I didn't know about the test, I just knew something was wrong, because Mom was making soup.

I didn't find out about any of that until after they got back from the clinic. Mom, Dad, Nah—they were all weird about me knowing. Because my bio-mom had been a teen. One with a problem. Except hers was meth, and Nah's is opiates. Same difference, at the end of the day. They thought it would be "triggering" for me. Mom's word. What was "triggering" was the fact that I'd been left out of the loop. This big thing was happening, and nobody told me. Hannah was trying to get sober, like what happened woke her up, so I decided it was not of use to express my hurt, which seemed much smaller in comparison to her hurt.

Emotions, really, are just fractions. You reduce them as much as you can, get to the essence of them, and sometimes you get lucky and they're whole numbers in the end, or even prime numbers—which means they're one thing now and so much easier to make sense of. Five, for example. Five is a natural number greater than one that cannot be formed by multiplying two smaller natural numbers and is therefore prime. Singular. I'm a five about that situation with the lines on the stick and all that came after. Five is just simply *mad*. I don't want to be defined by my adoptedness—it's just a part of me, not all of me. A fraction. But, for some reason, even the people closest to me have determined that being adopted bothers me. It doesn't. Them *thinking* it bothers me is what bothers me.

I'm still mad about all that. I'm still a five.

Now that I'm in the kitchen, though, the mad turns to something else because I'm remembering better: the last time Mom made soup was a few weeks ago—Italian wedding. I forgot because she ended up giving it all to her friend who was sick. She never would say why she made it. That soup was the only one in our entire lives that she insisted on making alone. She wouldn't let any of us in the kitchen, and she played Joni Mitchell's "A Case of You" on repeat. I'll never know what was hurting her or why she made Dad's favorite soup without giving him a bite.

Dad calls Mom's soup habit *soup meditation*. No matter how stressed Mom is about whatever is making her pull out the soup pot in the first place, by the end she's calm. Relaxed, even. Able to see the problem clearly and know what to do about it. Nah calls it Mom's cauldron, like the soup pot is for divination and spells.

I say she's just found another way to work the problem.

When you're making soup, all you need to think about is chopping and pouring and slicing and stirring. And you can't mess it up, not really. It's not like baking, where you have to consider thermodynamics and its effect on various chemical compounds. Baking is science. Soup—maybe soup is art. To make it, you have to engage the right side of your brain. Your imagination. And you need to use all five senses, not just sight. You give the left side of your brain a break—the logic part of it. Wait. WAIT.

MY MOTHER IS A GENIUS.

I am just now realizing: The reason we make soup when there is a crisis is because soup is a creative act that engages your imagination, allowing you to work through the tangles of a problem and connect new, heretofore unseen dots. MAKING SOUP IS LIKE EINSTEIN PLAYING THE VIOLIN.

He was always carrying around "Lina," as he called all his violins, and Dad wrote a whole paper once on the connection between musical theory and quantum theory and showed that part of why Einstein's mathematical equations are so elegant is because, when he was stumped, he'd play music, which would open up new channels in his brain. New pathways to work the problem. Dad joked that we should give partial credit of $E=mc^2$ to Bach and Mozart.

Maybe because none of us play instruments, Mom found another way to open up all those channels in our brains. And how sneaky of her, as usual, not to tell us she's doing it.

I miss her.

It's the middle of the night on what is now technically day five, and I left Hannah asleep on Mom's side of the bed, her head resting on Micah's chest. His arms are around her like he can shield her from the world, and maybe he can. Maybe love can do that sometimes. Hide you. I wonder if Riley would be here if he hadn't had to move a million miles away. Then again, he returns seventeen percent of my emails, so I suspect he would not, in fact, be here.

The kitchen is chilly, but I open the window anyway to let in the salty smell of the air and Mom's garden scents: basil, rosemary, lemon. I pull the big soup pot out of the cabinet. It's after two in the morning, but that never stopped Mom. I press PLAY on the old stereo Dad installed on top of the wine rack, and suddenly I am back in the only church I ever liked being in. The Tallis Scholars, singing in Latin, a cappella. I remember Dad putting the CD in here just a few days before they left for Malaysia. He'd been making his famous egg bake, a breakfast casserole that Mom says will give all of us heart disease. There's half a tray of it still in the freezer. He'd made extra so we could eat it while they were gone. Knowing that egg bake is here when he's not scoops something out of my insides.

I close my eyes and hug the soup pot against my chest as dozens of voices swoop around me, high then low.

I time travel: back to the Cloisters, back to New York City last fall. Just Dad and me, walking through a medieval museum on a hill after doing a tour of Columbia, even though we both knew my heart was set on Annapolis.

It's like that scene in *Interstellar*: I'm in my wormhole, looking through time and space into the past, into my life, with my dad. I'm pushing books out of my own bookshelf, trying to get my past self's attention. But the me in the Cloisters doesn't see the me in the wormhole, the one who is on the other side of the wave, who knows it's coming, who's begging Past Me to warn them.

I watch as Dad and I walk into the cathedral-like space, drawn by the Latin chorus that had been floating down the hall. The music reminds me of the one time I went to Midnight Mass at Saint Cecilia's with my grandmother, when the choir sang just like this and the hair on my arms stood at attention. But in this chapel, there are no singers or pews. It is an empty stone room with slightly vaulted ceilings. Raised speakers form a huge circle in the center, as though they are participants in an ancient rite. Dad silently points to a small placard, and we read how each speaker represents a different choral member's voice. The voices of the invisible singers reach up into the ceiling, mournful and reverent, and I wish I could put this feeling into numbers, into an algorithm, because words will never explain what these notes do to me on a cellular level.

Dad and I join the visitors who stand in the middle of the circle of speakers, and we all listen together, silent. An old woman is smiling, her eyes closed as she sways along with the voices, one hand gripping her cane. A guy not much older than me is sitting on the ground, hands folded in his lap. Others stand with heads bowed as though the music is a prayer. And it is, I think. It doesn't matter, not really, that there is no one who can answer it.

I think the asking is what matters.

Because of the music, we are no longer strangers. The words weave us all into the same tapestry, cream and brown and black and gold. Somehow, we are in four dimensions in spacetime, past and present and future all together, all at once. We are on the event horizon. I decide to add this music to my Golden Record, my own imaginary collection of things I would launch into space for life-forms forty thousand years away to find so they could learn about humanity, just like Carl Sagan did with *Voyager 1* and *Voyager 2* in the seventies. There is a voice recording on his Golden Record of a child saying, "Hello from the children of planet Earth."

This music, it's a kind of a hello, too. If human souls existed, they might sound like this. Or like David Bowie, maybe.

Dad takes my hand and closes his eyes. When I look over, tears are sliding down his cheeks. I have never loved him more than in this moment, this man who chose me to be his daughter. Who fought the system for me. He could have picked any other unwanted kid, but he chose me.

We let the sound waves sweep us up, up, up, toward the ceiling, gathering speed past the sky, then cresting across the atmosphere, until we're nothing but foam among a beach of scattered stars.

Hand in hand we slide to the shore, into the silence.

Something in me breaks, and the tears finally come, a slow, thick stream. What kind of a daughter takes SEVENTY-EIGHT hours to cry after finding out her parents might be dead?

I stand there sobbing for two full songs and it is only after the second one ends and I see the title displayed that I realize I'd been listening to a requiem. A song for the dead.

I want to go back to the Cloisters and whisper in Dad's ear to not ever go to Malaysia because if he goes I will be alone in the kitchen in the middle of the night listening to the Tallis Scholars sing his life goodbye.

Aunt Nora, Mom's sister, flew from Boston to Malaysia yesterday. She says she's looking for them, but I know she's really just going to look at the pictures. Polaroids of the dead. The internet is down all along the coast and no one in the hospitals can upload them, if they'd even be allowed to. We wanted to go, too, but Nora said no and I was upset because there is finally something to *do* and we're almost eighteen and have every right to go ourselves, but Nah was relieved, I think, so I let it go. I called Nora before I came into the kitchen because it's day there. And she told me what I had already figured out for myself, when one considers the effects of exposure, infection, lack of clean water, and all the other things that might make it impossible to stay alive long enough for a rescue crew to find you:

They are not finding any more people that are alive.

There are no pictures with my parents' faces, and no one who is in a coma matches my parents' descriptions. They are not stuck in a tree or wearing a life vest in the middle of the ocean or waiting in the hills because they're too hurt to walk down.

Aunt Nora began to cry and I knew, I knew.

My parents are dead.

I set down the pot and run the back of my hands across my eyes.

"I'm making soup, Mom," I say.

She can't hear me. I know that. I know what happens when an organism dies. I can't help it, though. I want to talk to my mom. I want her to walk down the stairs in her old man's plaid bathrobe that she stole from Pappoús before he died. I want her to start putting things on the counter.

But there's just me.

I open the fridge and scan the contents. It's still pretty full, since Mom and Dad only left a week ago. There are veggies in the drawer. Broth in the cupboard. Cans of beans and tomatoes.

What is a soup for the dead?

Mom made avgolemono—Greek chicken soup—when Yia-yia died, back in the old country, where she bought a house surrounded by olive trees. Mom cried the whole time, her tears falling into the pot as she stirred. As I juiced lemons, she'd told me how her mother had taught her to make soup when she was a little girl, just like she had taught Nah and me. Our religion: the Gospel of Soup, the salvation of the spoon. It'd be nice to make avgolemono for her, but we don't have chicken. Dad hates lentil and Mom only likes vegetable when she's just come back from the farmers' market. Besides, I should use these serrano chiles. Mom hates when things go to waste.

Chili. Chili nights are always fun. I don't know why—maybe it's the spiciness. The last time we had chili, Dad did his impression of the dean of the physics department and Nah got video of him pretending to fall asleep halfway through a lecture on quantum mechanics. Why didn't we take more pictures? Why didn't we take video of *everything*? Dad drinking his morning coffee, Mom watering the basil plant on the windowsill above the kitchen sink. She always insisted on talking to the plants when she watered them. Said it made them grow better, which is actually true. I pull out my phone and add watering plants to the list of things to do—keeping things alive is a way to work the problem of death. I haven't told Nah about this list because she lives in an alternate reality pretty much all the time. For example, she still doesn't know which clothes aren't supposed to go in the dryer.

She thinks they are coming back to water plants and get oil changes and pay the electricity bill. I don't know how long it's okay to let her keep thinking that.

I take out the green peppers, the cilantro, the onions, and the chiles, which add lots of heat. Mom's mason jar of seasoning is in the pantry, and I grab that, too. I run my fingers along the antique spice jars lined up on a small shelf to the left of the stove. Little white ceramic pots with the name of the seasoning written on them in blue paint. *Coriander. Paprika. Oregano.* They'd been passed down from my grandmother to my mom. The jars were a present from my pappoús to my yia-yia after he got his first paycheck in America.

I have a horrible thought, one I try to get rid of as soon as it comes into my head: If Mom is gone, really gone, Hannah will get the jars. Because she is connected to the line of Karalis women in a way I will never be. Mom would say that's ridiculous, that I am as much a Karalis as Hannah, but I'm not. Put my blood under a microscope and you'll see that we're the same species, and that's where our similarities end. I don't have those telltale Greek purple circles under my eyes and black-as-deep-space hair like Hannah does. I don't have ouzo in my blood.

My hair is haystack blond, and my hips are just two bony protrusions, and when we're on the beach, I burn instantly while they just lie there, turning bronze, like perfect plates of *saganaki*.

"Stop," I say to myself, out loud, because out loud feels four-dimensional.

I scrub the peppers clean, then set them on the cutting board. I turn off the Tallis Scholars, too. I begin to chop, and the sound of the knife against the wood is a lullaby. It's Einstein's bow on the strings.

For so long it didn't matter, not a ton, that I didn't come from my mother's womb. Now it does. I can't shake it, this little voice that keeps whispering *they don't belong to you—they never did*. If I had one wish, it would be to have the same genes as the rest of my family, to share the same blood. To look at old black-and-white photos in the green leather album in the living room and see myself in all the faces. Hannah and I have been treated like twins for as long as I can remember, because my parents got me when we were both three. We have always been *the girls*. *Lila, can you pick the girls up from school today? Greg, the girls need some lunch money—do you have any cash?*

When I was little, I tried to color my hair black with a marker. It didn't work. The good thing about Dad being a direct descendant of a Puritan on the *Mayflower* is that people assume I just take after him. So we never get the confused looks from strangers that Lisa, my friend who's also adopted, gets. Her family is white as cream, and she's got skin the color of the cello she plays. So they get lots of questions. One time she snapped at a lady in a grocery store, "No, I'm not my parents' starving African charity case—I was born in Riverside, but thanks for filling my ignorance quota for the day."

I was very impressed with her for producing such an articulate zinger on the fly.

I only have one memory from before becoming a Winters. It's just a shard: I'm being put in a car—a red car. I think maybe someone was smoking—something about the scent of cigarettes always brings this memory right to the surface of my mind. Was this my birth mother? A foster family? I don't know, and I'm glad for that. I don't want to remember being left.

Hannah is all I've got now.

As though I've summoned her, my sister shuffles in, those dark circles under her eyes the color of the fried eggplant she loves so much, Mom's *melitzanes tiganites*. Her hair is a tangle of waves, and she looks so much like Mom it hurts. She's wearing one of the UCLA shirts Dad bought both of us, the same one, but hers is a size bigger because she's five-eleven. I get a crick in my neck just looking her in the eye. She got Dad's height. Mom thinks I'm so short because I wasn't held enough as a baby, which has been proven to affect growth.

"What are we making?"

"Chili."

She nods, then crosses to the pantry to get out the stewed tomatoes and beans: kidney, pinto, cannellini. She grabs a can of sweet corn, then another. Dad likes it with extra corn.

Hannah opens cans while I keep chopping. It feels good to be in here, to be doing something so familiar. We can control at least this one thing.

I throw the onions into the pot with some olive oil and let them sting my eyes as I stir them. What are the odds, I wonder, of being orphaned twice?

The last time a parent left me, child protective services came and took me away. Could they do it again?

And what happens to Hannah? Based on my extensive research, a traumatic event can trigger a relapse into addictive behavior. No one in the family knows about Nah's addiction—Mom said that was my sister's story to tell, when she was ready. She said it wouldn't be fair to Nah, for her to be seen as this one thing. And that's true, but now I am the only Winters who knows how to check her pupils.

What if the end of my parents' lives is also, in a way, the end of ours?

When the onions are soft, I add the garlic, and the sizzle sounds like hope. We wait until the kitchen fills with its meaty scent, and then we pour all the other stuff into the pot, plus Mom's bell jar mix of cumin, chili powder, garlic salt, pepper, oregano. Hannah reaches up and grabs Mom's secret ingredient—coffee. She sprinkles it over the top. Then she looks over at me, holding the open jar.

"You want a cup?" she asks.

"Okay."

I stir the chili while Nah takes down the French press, Mom's favorite way of drinking it. When the coffee's ready, we pull ourselves onto the counter and watch the chili simmer. There's a draft in the window behind us and cold ocean air slips up my spine.

"They're dead, aren't they?" Hannah says.

I take her hand in mine. Her nails are covered in chipped blue polish.

"Yeah," I say, soft.

I keep my hand in hers as silent sobs roll through the body beside mine, the one my parents made.

i will never see them again.

Windowsill in Bedroom
4302 Seaview Lane
Venice, CA

8

Hannah

The universe didn't uphold its end of the bargain, so I'm not upholding mine.

That's why I've been in my room all day, floating on the hooked rug that Mom found at a garage sale in the Valley.

There's a crack in my ceiling. I never knew that.

Outside my door, there are voices. Mae, Papa, Gram. Doors open and shut. A phone rings. On the street, cars drive by. A skateboard rolls. A dog barks. Somewhere at UCLA, Micah is riding his bike to class. He has texted me ten times, all variations on: *I love you. I'll be there soon.*

That is all in the world. I am not in the world. I am somewhere else. I think I'll stay here for a while.

It's time for another pill. I know this because I can feel my body again. I can feel the knife in my heart and the hollowness in my belly. I know it's time for another pill because I can remember.

Everything.

If I close my eyes, I can hear Mom reading us *The Little Prince*. It was always Mae's favorite because it's about space and planets and stars. It was always my favorite because it's a love story.

It's about this boy, the Little Prince, who lives on an asteroid. He's got itchy feet. He wants to see the world. And there's this rose on his planet and she's kind of high-maintenance, so he ditches her and goes exploring the universe. But it's not all it was cracked up to be. The universe. It's full of all these funky planets that he's not into, with the kind of people you meet on the boardwalk every day—dropouts and weirdos. Then he lands on Earth and meets a downed pilot—which to me feels like stranger danger, but it ends up being all good—and the Little Prince is sad because he realizes he *does* love his thorny rose, even though she's needy as fuck. He wants to go back to his asteroid and be with her, only now he's stuck on Earth.

See, in order to get back to where she is on Asteroid B-612—their planet—he has to get bitten by a poisonous snake. Supposedly he gets back to his asteroid and his rose at the end, but honestly? I'm not really sure the Little Prince is alive—I think he has to let the snake kill him so he can leave Earth. I think the pilot is telling his story to keep his *memory* alive. Don't take my word for that. I got a D in English last semester.

But the reason this story is everything to me is because the Little Prince loves his rose so much that he's willing to die for her. I want to be loved like that. I want a boy like him.

Micah should have come. To the clinic. To be with me. He should have come. If there were a wave like *the* wave and we were on the beach, he'd probably run as fast as he could. Leave me behind when I slow down. He already said he'd do that, didn't he? *I can't carry you.*

The sun spreads over me, and I close my eyes against the light. It hurts. So does the remembering.

I am seven, and Mae and I are lying on either side of Mom on the pull-out bed in the living room at Gram and Papa's house on the Cape. We are squished against each other, and I breathe in Mom's faint rose scent, which reminds me exactly of Gram's garden of wild beach roses. Mae and I each hold a flashlight so Mom can see the words in the book.

"It is such a secret place," Mom murmurs, *"the land of tears."*

I run my fingers over the illustration of the Little Prince's abandoned rose, sticking to the side of his small planet, all by herself, with nothing to protect her but four thorns.

Then Mom reads what has always been my favorite line from the book, which the rose says to the Little Prince when bragging about her thorns, which deep down she knows aren't big enough to protect her, but she's proud and she doesn't want him to pity her and she doesn't want to pity herself, so she says: *"Let the tigers come with their claws!"*

I whisper the words into the silence of my room: "Let the tigers come with their claws."

It sounded better when the thorny rose said it in Mom's voice. I open my eyes and look at the yoga mat I laid on my floor this morning, waiting, but she's not there.

"Come back," I whisper. I guess Mom can't hear me. Where she is.

I pulled a card today from the tarot deck Mom bought me when I turned thirteen—Rider-Waite-Smith, the classic.

I got Death. That skeleton riding on his horse, looking fucking satisfied with himself. Maybe the card is telling me she's not coming back, ever again. Maybe it's telling me that my parents aren't the only thing in my life that has died.

There is a knock on my door. I ignore it.

Poor little rose with all her bravado, all that insecurity coiled up inside her petals. Doesn't she know that trying to be strong never works?

More knocking, louder this time. "Nah?"

"Yeah."

The door creaks and I open my eyes when I can feel the heat of my sister over my face. She leans above me, her short, blond hair sticking up in every direction. Her blue eyes, a tropical blue like Malaysian water, stare into my green ones. She knows. I know she knows. My sister is the smartest girl under eighteen in the world. If she can figure out how to fly to the moon, she can figure out I'm currently on it.

The late-afternoon sun cuts into the room so that her face is half light, half shadow. What goes on in there, in that head? Is it all math, or is she as confused as I am? I haven't seen her cry, not once. But I know she's sad. Yesterday, Mae forgot what the capital of Norway was. She was talking about stars in gutters and said the guy was from . . . and then her face scrunched up. It was the first time I saw my sister not know something. I guess sad hits people in different ways.

"There's food," she says.

"I'm not hungry."

"Are you nauseous?"

Here we go. I expected a lecture. Instead, I get Dr. Mae, who has done so much research on my disease that Harvard will likely give her an honorary degree. Opiate abuse results in nausea and vomiting, loss of appetite, loss of parents.

"Not yet, Dr. Winters."

Mae looks down at me. "What did you take, and how much?"

My sister. So good. It would never occur to her, like it did to me, to steal our dead father's opiates.

I lie, because I'm good at it, and because it never occurs to Mae to lie. She's so smart, but kind of dumb, too.

"Vicodin. I just had one pill left," I say. "I hid it. For an emergency. That's all I took. I promise."

Her eyes search mine the way they search the night sky for falling meteorites. "Okay," she finally says. "But that's it?"

"That's it. I just miss them. You know?"

She nods, then lies next to me on the rug. We are quiet.

That kid in group was right about all of us in the Circle of Sad: I am a piece-of-shit lying junkie.

"There's a crack in your ceiling."

"Yeah."

Right now, my sister radiates calm. Usually she's buzzing, like a third rail, zzzzzzzzz, never stops, but right now she's like putting your hand on a stone that's been sitting out in the sun for hours. A rock. Me? I'm water. A puddle. Sludge at the bottom of a well.

I wait for her to tell me I'm a piece-of-shit junkie. She won't say it like that. She will use big words and be precise and reasonable. But underneath, we'd both know I'm a piece-of-shit junkie.

"The Red Cross called," Mae says. She almost whispers it. "They need DNA."

I turn my head to look at her. Push the cobwebs out of my brain. *Dee-en-nay.*

"What?"

She swallows. "To help them identify the bodies, Nah."

There's not enough Vicodin in the world.

"Fuck no. Fuck that."

I have decided that my parents are just floating. Forever. Whole and forever and they will float on the sea with sunlight and moonlight. Hand in hand.

She ignores this and explains how, in order to prevent disease, the Malaysian government has dug mass graves. Our parents might be in one of those. Mom, with dirt and other people on top of her. She'd hate that. She never liked closed spaces, always had mini panic attacks on elevators. We took the stairs a lot. "Good for our hearts," she said. Then she would grin. "And our asses."

I push up onto my elbow, which is goddamn hard when you're made of sand. "They're not *bodies*, they're our parents, Mae." I have a hard time zeroing in on her face, but I do my best. "Don't get fucking clinical on me."

I fall back down, and Mae's hand reaches across the rug and grasps onto mine.

"I'm sorry," she says. "I was trying to use the most efficient way to explain the process." She takes a breath. "We have to find them, Nah. We can bring them back."

In a cardboard box, probably. Ashes.

I close my eyes. Imagine Mom floating on a calm sea in corpse pose.

Dad floats beside her, and he even managed to keep his glasses on. They could be the illustration for the Two of Cups in one of Mom's tarot decks, love and harmony.

When there's no . . . body, it's hard to know when to stop looking. I don't ever want to stop—but this kind of looking, *only* looking for a dead body. No. I can't. I *can't.*

I keep my eyes closed, shake my head.

"We have to do this, Nah."

I am so tired.

"Fuck the Red Cross. It won't bring them back."

She sighs. "I'll do it myself. I don't want them to be so far away."

I'm such a selfish piece-of-shit junkie. Why couldn't I think of that? Of doing right by them.

"Jesus." I groan. "Just help me up."

We get me vertical, and when Mae's out the door, I slip another pill in my mouth before following her into my parents' room.

"They said hair is good. Toothbrushes. Stuff like that." Mae holds up two ziplock bags, and I take one, then follow her into the master bathroom.

"I'll do Dad's," she says.

For a second we stand there, staring. At the rug I puked on when I drank too much vodka at Julie Cirna's party, back when we were thirteen. The shower curtain with the kitschy Paris theme that Dad hates—hated—and Mom loved. The orderly row of Dad's bottles of cologne and aftershave and shaving cream. I can see him, running the razor down his skin, Mom brushing out her long, witchy hair. Talking about the book club they didn't want to go to or if we should grill out for dinner or just get tacos.

"This is fucked up," I say.

Mae squares her shoulders. "We're gathering data. That's all we're doing. Okay?"

Mae World must be really nice.

I open the drawer between the two sinks and grab some of Mom's hair out of her brush. It's darker than mine. I hold it up to the light and notice strands of gray that twist through the black. That bit of silver is like a switch that turns off any bit of light inside me. It's so dark in here.

"I feel bad about teasing her," I say.

Mae looks over from her search through the cabinet on Dad's side of the counter. "What about?"

"A few months ago, I noticed she had a gray hair and I gave her shit for it. Just kidding, you know, but I could tell she was upset."

"Doesn't seem like her." Mae carefully places one of Dad's used razors in her plastic bag. "She's always said she can't wait to be that old lady with flowing gray hair. *Miss Rumphius.*"

"I know. I thought it was weird. I mean, she's all about *au naturale.*"

It hits me then, with the force of the wave itself.

"She's never going to be an old lady," I whisper.

We stand there, holding our bags. It's like an upside-down version of when we got goldfish that one time, after Dad won them in a carnival game for us. We each took a goldfish home in a Ziploc. Mae reaches out and takes the bag from me.

"I'm gonna mail them. Want to come?"

I shake my head. In about an hour, once this next pill kicks in, I won't be here anymore. I'll be on Asteroid B-612, the Little Prince's planet, with my thorny rose and the prince, too. *Let the tigers come with their claws*—I won't give a flying fuck.

"Micah will be here soon," I say.

"Oh." She shrugs, looks like she might say something, then changes her mind.

I see Mom's perfume, a special rose blend that Cynthia makes, and bring it up to my nose. Mom is pulling me in close for a hug, leaning over me to check my homework, twirling in a spray of scent before she heads out the door. I raise the bottle and spray it just above my head, then turn in a slow, slow circle as a shower of rose petals rains down on me.

Mae hesitates by the doorway. "I'm going by school to pick up home-work and stuff. Later. Do you need me to grab your assignments?"

"Are you serious?" I hold Mom's perfume close. "Our parents are *dead* and you're worried about *homework*?"

I'm a mean junkie. Nice sober. I don't know why.

Her fingers twitch. That stress thing she does. A tell. Dad said she would have been terrible at poker if she ever had her hands above the table. Otherwise, she'd kill it. Freaking sphinx, most of the time.

"Look, it might help, okay?" she says. "You can't just sit in that room, Nah, taking pills and—"

"What is wrong with you?"

For once. For *once* I would like it if she could freak out. Acknowledge that this is really bad and I am not crazy for feeling like we just drove off a cliff.

"With *me*? You're the one who's *high*—"

"Our parents are *dead*, Mae. We are literally collecting fucking DNA samples and you want to go get your *homework*?"

I'm shouting. I don't care.

"What else am I going to do, Nah?" Her hand grips the doorway. "I don't have a Micah to come hold me and kiss me and love me. The only person I have is *you*, and you're not here, not really. Not when you're on that stuff. So what am I supposed to *do*?"

We stare at each other, surrounded by my mother's scent. Let the tigers come with their claws.

"You didn't even cry," I snarl.

As soon as I say it, I wish I hadn't.

Her blue eyes darken a little. Like clouds covering the sun.

I don't care. I really, really don't fucking care. She is the enemy. The one who will try to keep me from floating and I want to fucking float, okay, I want to go away. And I want her to go away, too, I want to be on my planet, alone.

"I'm going to bed," I say.

She zips the bags shut. Won't look at me. "My cell's on. If you need me."

Mae goes, and maybe I should feel bad about snapping at her, but I don't. Not really. I'm starting not to feel bad about anything, which is nice. I see why they call them painkillers. They really do kill the pain. Murder it.

I take Mom's brush to my room and set it beside a candle, like it's a relic. I don't know whether or not I want them to be found. I hate the idea of them being separated. Dying alone. So if they were both in the grave, then maybe it meant they were together until the end.

I've imagined the wave so many times. In one version, Mom and Dad are together at the beach. They hold on to each other as the water covers them. They die in each other's arms. But I know that isn't possible. Mae said the water was too strong. Something about force and acceleration. Nerd stuff. I don't know.

In another version, they're at their bed-and-breakfast, and they make it to the roof, but it's not high enough and the water sweeps them away. Or they cling to palm trees that topple over. Or a piece of metal decapitates them. Or a floating car crushes them.

There are so many ways to die.

I lie back down on the rug in corpse pose and stare at the ceiling. Maybe it's my imagination, but the crack seems bigger.

i ignored the last call I got from my dad because i was watching a movie on TV.

Kitchen Cupboard
4302 Seaview Lane
Venice, CA

9

Hannah

My parents have been dead for one week.

I am running out of Vicodin.

Fuck my fucking life.

It's early evening, and shadows crawl over the carpet. I don't know when that happened—the sun leaving. It was here, just a minute ago. Whatever. I live here now. On this carpet.

There's a soft knock on my bedroom door. Someone is always knocking on the fucking door. No one can take a hint. I make sure the rest of my pills are in the envelope inside the throw pillow, not on the desk. Then I turn on the bedside lamp.

"Come in," I say.

Aunt Nora is barefoot but still wearing her lawyer pantsuit. She looks a lot like Mom—dark hair, olive skin, mysterious smile. Uncle Tony's behind her. He's in his usual uniform of Red Sox shirt and jeans.

"Hey, kiddo," Tony says. "You doing okay?"

"I'm tired, I guess."

I wish Dad had left behind more Vicodin. I wish Priscilla delivered. It's hard to sneak out to the boardwalk. Maybe there's an app for that.

"Got time for a little chat?" Nora asks. I nod, and she perches on the edge of my bed.

Mae comes in. Plops down on the floor, leaning back on her hands. As usual, something has been decided without me. I don't know what.

"Do you want me to lead up to what I have to say, or should I just say it?" Nora asks.

I like how blunt she is. Nora always cuts to the chase.

"Say it," I say.

"Tony and I"—she looks at Tony, who nods—"want you to move in with us."

"But you live in Boston." I look over at Mae, panicked. She's watching me with her thinking face on: brows furrowed, eyes a little glazed, biting her lip.

"They told you already," I say to her.

"You were sleeping."

The heir and the spare. Of course they told her first.

"There's a really good high school by us—Saint Francis," Nora is saying. "Nate's in the dorms at MIT, but he comes home most weekends. We've got plenty of space in the house—you'd have your own rooms."

"I can't . . . I . . . Micah lives here," I say.

Nora nods. "I know, sweetie."

I close my eyes, see him and Dad painting the house sky blue. Days and days of them covered in paint, then trooping in like conquering heroes, Dad's arm slung around his shoulder.

I see Micah climb through my window at night and act out all the waves he caught that day, me trying not to laugh too hard so Mom and Dad would hear.

I see the look of pure bliss on his face when he overhears Mom refer to him as "my son, Micah." He turned to me and whispered, "We can still get married, right?"

Now I don't have time to make things right between us. To bury what happened in March and stop blaming him for what that day did to me. I need time. More time. But it's run out.

This is a nightmare. I'm living in a nightmare. Jesus, somebody wake me up.

"Why can't we just stay here?" I say. "I mean, can't Gram and Papa live here until . . . like, graduation or something?"

"It's not good for Papa's health," Nora says. "It gets too cold at night. His rheumatism acts up. And I think it'll be too much for them. They're getting on, you know. They don't really know how to live with teenagers."

Mae clears her throat. The faintest blush spreads across her pale-as-milk cheeks.

"Is there . . ." She frowns, like she's translating words in her head. "With my adoption. Is there any way that social services could—"

Aunt Nora stares at her. "No. Oh, Mae, honey, no. Have you been worrying about that?"

Mae looks at her hands, nods.

I feel like an asshole for not knowing she was stressing about that stuff. For not asking. Has she been worried this whole time that she was going to be taken away?

"I'd never let that happen," I say. "Ever."

"I was just . . . curious," she says.

"You're a Winters," Aunt Nora says in her firm lawyer's voice. "And my niece. And your uncle and I love you so much. It's going to be okay, Mae. I know it doesn't feel like that, but it will be. I promise."

Her voice trips, stumbling in that way all of us do now.

Uncle Tony reaches out and squeezes Mae's shoulder. "When we get to Boston—"

"No." I grab the throw pillow Mom helped me make for a YMCA quilting class my counselor made me do when I first got sober. I hold it like a shield. "I'm sorry, but we can't leave. I mean, this is crazy. We've been here our whole lives. It's our senior year—"

"We have nowhere else to go, Nah," Mae says. Her voice is so soft.

All my sympathy for her suddenly evaporates. I am so fucking sick of her these days, I really am. I used to have a sister. Now I have a narc jail warden.

"Can you just stop being logical for two-point-five seconds and have my back?"

Nora frowns. "Hannah—"

"I'm thinking about what makes the most sense for us," Mae says. "We can't stay here alone—"

"You're not Mom, so stop trying to be." Her face scrunches up and, for a second, I think I'm about to make my sister cry, which is impossible, but then she nods.

"Okay."

The room is very quiet. Why do rooms get so *quiet* after I say things?

"I'm just trying to, like, articulate that I get a say in this. It's not, like, Mae's decision just because she's smarter."

Nora puts a hand on my arm. "Sweetie, it's not a decision for either of you to make. Your parents would never want you to feel that kind of pressure. Their will is very clear: If anything happened to them, they wanted you to be with us. We agreed to it years ago, back when you were both really little."

"So, like, *legally* we have to go with you?" I ask.

I need a pill. An escape pod. What would happen if I just got up and walked out of the room—if I just decided this wasn't happening? Is there any universe in which my opinion on the subject would count?

"Yes," Tony says. "Legally, you come with us. But we don't want you to look at it that way, kiddo. We love you girls. That's why we agreed to this. And Boston is a great city—you always have a good time when you come to visit. It'll give you a bit of distance from all this. It can be really good to breathe new air, you know?"

I've heard the word *hopeless* so many times in the Circle of Sad. I used it myself. Then, I didn't know what the word really means, what it feels like to live inside these eight letters, how they circle around you, a whirlpool.

I'm literally losing everything in my life.

There are no tears, like usual. It's so bad that I can't cry. I stare at them all as my entire chest caves in on itself, as I become hollow. It burns. How can you burn when you're empty?

Mae stands and sits beside me, and I let her pull me against her and rub circles on my back with her palm.

"What about the house?" I ask.

We've lived here our whole lives. I learned to walk in the living room. Got my first period in the bathroom. Made soup with Mom and egg bakes with Dad and—

Nora puts a hand on my knee. "We're gonna have to sell it, honey."

Mae's hand stops. "What?"

For a moment, she and I look at each other and I can almost see that event horizon thing Dad tried to explain to me once—can see Mae and I building mud pies in the backyard after an unexpected spring storm, can see her across the dining room table, helping me with my math, or on the roof, pointing out stars—Cassiopeia, Ursa Minor . . .

Mae turns to them, and, for once, she fails at words. "But . . . but . . . we grew up here. We can't just . . . This is our . . . This is where—"

"That's what your parents wanted," Tony says, his voice gentle. "In their will. They said they wanted the house and yoga studio sold and the money saved for you two in a small trust. College tuition, whatever you need. Fifty-fifty."

I wonder if they had protections in place for me, before Mae. Or if they only thought about it after. Sometimes it's hard, knowing that they picked her. That they *chose* Mae to be their daughter. I was the *oops* baby, the mistake. I wasn't wanted at first. Probably a worst-nightmare scenario. The way Mom tells it, they saw Mae and Dad said, "That's her. That's our daughter." I once overheard Mom telling Aunt Nora that getting Mae was one of the best decisions she'd ever made, that it would have been lonely if it were "just Hannah."

That's me: *Just Hannah*.

I shake my head a little because everything in me is getting bad, really dark, and I can't go there, not unless I can pop this pill in my mouth without anyone noticing.

An acorn comes to me, the sort of one Yoko would write, not like my one-liners:

> Get a cardboard box
> Open it
> Stare at it until your heart stops

I curl into a fetal position, my eyes on the wall. Mae starts rubbing my back again. Nora and Tony keep talking: ". . . Thanksgiving at the Cape, ice-skating on Boston Common, Red Sox games . . ."

And I think: *I want a wave to swallow me up, too.*

Mae

Nobody likes a sad astronaut.

Most people didn't know that when Neil Armstrong went up to the moon, he was still grieving the death of his little kid. It didn't fit the hopeful narrative, so they cut it out.

Before today, the day of my parents' funeral, I would have said for certain that death is the end of a human's existence, at least as this life-form. I know that this wanting there to be an afterlife is a cultural response to grief: It's anthropology—not physics. And yet.

I can feel them.

Almost as if they were standing right behind me.

How would I be able to feel them if they were really gone?

Maybe it's what Stephen Hawking was talking about in his last paper, on memory and black holes. About the possibility that the "hairs" of light surrounding black holes can actually encode information before things pass into the black hole. Before, we always assumed that whatever falls into a black hole would be swallowed up, all data erased so that it's nothing more than pure energy. But if it's true that these beams of light are actually encoding the information of the matter that passes through, saving the data for all time, the same thing might happen when we die.

Death is the ultimate black hole.

Which means it's possible that Hawking discovered a theory for immortality before his own all-systems fail in his last days on Earth. Not, of course, a Philosopher's Stone kind of immortality, but it might be possible that whatever is left of my parents is somehow being saved for all time in what amounts to a giant cosmological database. Dad's theory on quintessence, Mom's memories of the day she and Dad picked me up from social services, all the things they ever wanted to say to us and didn't. Perhaps all of it's still out there, somehow. Maybe that light at the end of the tunnel people like to talk about is just those hairs encoding everything we are before we're nothing at all.

Most likely, this thought process is a stage of grief, demonstrating that I am just as susceptible as every human who has ever grieved to magical thinking. Dad would be so disappointed.

We're holding the memorial under the rotunda at the beautiful library in downtown Los Angeles that Mom had once said was her church, and that Nah and I practically grew up in. It's an art deco masterpiece, full of beautiful chandeliers and murals and wood paneling and marble.

A podium beneath the exquisitely painted ceiling has been placed before rows of already-full chairs, and behind it sits a projector screen on a stand. Gram, Papa, Aunt Nora, Uncle Tony, and our cousin Nate are gathered near the podium, going over last-minute details. Various relatives from both sides have flown in from Boston—Mom's Greek side and Dad's *Mayflower* crew.

Cynthia glides over in one of her gauzy sundresses straight from 1969. This one is dark purple. She's laden down with amethysts that hang from her neck, and her burgundy hair is in a Frida-inspired braid—she and Mom did an online tutorial to figure it out last year. The ribbons woven into her hair are sage green, Mom's favorite color.

"*Mis hijas*," she says, wrapping her arms around us both.

I breathe in her lavender scent, and I suppose there is some truth to the calming effects of certain essential oils.

"She's here," Cynthia says, leaning back. "I can feel her. Can you?"

"I can't tell what's her and what's me," Nah says.

Maybe Nah is undergoing the same grief psychosis as me.

"That's because she's a part of you," Cyn says.

But she's not a part of me. Not technically. We don't share blood, DNA. I didn't grow inside her.

"It might feel like we feel them," I say. "But I think it's a game our minds are playing. Some sort of defense mechanism against grief—"

"Mae." Hannah shakes her head. "You can't prove everything."

"You can try. You *should* try."

Cyn gets that smile, the one that makes her look like the goddess cards on Mom's altar. "Spirit doesn't fit in a beaker or a test tube, *hija*."

I wish Dad were here. You can't reason with a coven.

Later, when Nah and I are alone again, I watch Cyn do all the things Mom would do: check to make sure the coffee's hot, rearrange the food. Discreetly throw out the daisies Mom hates from the flower arrangements people brought.

"I need a drink," Nah says.

She keeps scratching at her arms, pulling on her hair, like she wants to peel herself off her bones.

I can't believe we're here again, so soon.

I look up at her. Wait until she meets my eyes. They flit away, almost immediately. This is a very bad sign. Avoiding eye contact almost always means she's using.

"Please don't make me do this on my own, Nah."

Her skin goes blotchy, a sure sign of an increase in epinephrine. "What the hell does that mean? I'm here, wearing this shitty black dress—"

But Aunt Nora is motioning us over, and I start walking toward the podium. Then I stop. Turn.

My sister stands behind me, motionless. There are enough reasons to cry today. I don't need to add to them.

I walk back to where she's frozen still. "I'm sorry."

It's possible I am being too hard on her. I need to find a way to speak her language.

"What's a tarot card for us?" I ask.

Hannah smiles a little. Just a little, but it's something. She cocks her head to the side. "The Two of Cups. It's about relationships. Leaning on each other."

"Okay. Then let's . . . Two of Cups the shit out of today."

She laughs a little. "I can't believe you just cursed in church."

"The library understands. It's a special occasion." I hold out my hand and she takes it.

"I'm sorry about the playlist," she says.

"It's okay. I understand."

I'd asked Nah to make one of her famous playlists for the slideshow I put together of Mom and Dad. That was going to be her contribution to the funeral. When she's not on pills, Hannah is the family DJ. She would make Mae Is Stressed About AP Tests playlists that had funny things like the Cookie Monster song on it. Or a Dad Has Physicist Enemies playlist, where it was just all the villain songs from movies. Mom got a playlist called Music Smudgefest after some famous lady came to her studio and was totally awful. Micah got Surfer Boy playlists with songs about the ocean.

But Hannah's on pills, which means no playlists, not even for today. Opiates aren't good for creativity. They aren't good for anything but relieving physical pain and ruining lives.

We walk toward our family.

I've always liked Nora. She's got Mom's brown eyes, like good soil in the garden. When the Karalis women cry, their skin gets all blotchy. Aunt Nora and Hannah look like checkered picnic blankets right now. It's Hannah who really looks like my mother. Except for the eyes—she has Dad's eyes. So green. Sometimes, if I look quickly, I could swear she's Mom, back from the bottom of the ocean.

Uncle Tony is Boston Italian, the odd one out, with his thick North End accent and insistence on lasagna at Thanksgiving. He's stocky and usually jovial, but he doesn't muster up a fake smile now, and I really love that about him. Nate is a sophomore at MIT. Nah gets annoyed with us sometimes, when we're together. Says no one can get a word in unless they understand quantum mechanics. That is probably true.

"Hey, Buzz," he says, sliding an arm around my shoulders. "Fucking sucks."

Nate's been calling me Buzz—after Buzz Lightyear, of course—since we were kids. My parents picked up the habit, too. I hope Nate calls me this forever, for all the times they can't.

"Yes," I say. "It does."

He's wearing skinny jeans and a blouse trimmed with lace and pearl buttons, and his dark brown eyes stand out even more with his mascara.

"I hope your mascara's waterproof," Hannah says.

"Of course." He picks up her hand and studies her nails. I never paint mine, but she always has a different color. "I'm giving you a mani when we get home."

"Don't you know chipped polish is all the rage here in LA?"

"Ah." He nods sagely. "Of course. Us Bostonians are so provincial, you know."

I appreciate Nate for not being saccharine or using a grief voice. It is an actual tone of voice I am becoming familiar with. Hushed, underscored by a pitying whine.

Hannah starts to cry. I don't know why, maybe because Nate isn't being grief-strange. My cousin drops his arm from around my shoulders and places his palms on her cheeks.

"You are going to be okay. Not for a long time, but someday," he murmurs, the way you speak to a spooked horse, an agitated dog.

Nate's sister died when we were little, so he knows. I remember how awful it was, watching Annie waste away at Boston Children's, her little head shaved, the cancer eating through her day by day.

Nah swallows. "Promise?"

He holds up a pinkie and hooks hers with it. "Promise."

"This family has such shitty fucking luck, I can't even," Nah says.

Micah comes up behind my sister and wraps his arms around her waist. He doesn't say anything, just buries his nose in her neck. That anger in her dissolves, like he's a chemical solution pouring into her. It's always been this way. Hannah's got that Karalis fire and Micah's all water.

She reaches back with her hand and rests it on his tanned neck. "My Temperance card," she murmurs.

"Which one is that again?" I ask.

She smiles just a little. "Balance of energies." Fire and water.

When we told Micah they were dead, he tried so hard not to cry, not to turn into water. Because they were his parents, too. His family.

We sit. The slideshow starts playing, with "Starman" in the background. A picture of Dad and me comes up, early on. I love this one. We're at the Kennedy Space Center and I'm sitting on his shoulders, looking up at the *Atlantis* shuttle. I'm pointing my little finger at it, my mouth in this huge O. Nate squeezes my knee, and I give him a wobbly smile.

Hannah bolts up and leaves about halfway through the slideshow, when it shows our favorite picture of Mom: Nah had caught her dancing in a rare thunderstorm, her mouth eating the sky. I think maybe I should follow my sister, but then Micah gets up, so I stay.

I want a Micah. Someone who will come find me when I run away. I might have had that once with Riley, but he's on the other side of the world. Literally. His family moved to China. It's hard to have a boyfriend or girlfriend who lives in a different day than you.

Maybe I'll be like Dr. Stone in *Gravity* when she says that she has no one to pray for her and that she can't even pray for herself because no one taught her to pray and now I'm realizing that no one has taught *me* to pray except Gram that one time but I wasn't paying attention and so what if I'm in space in a Soyuz with no thrust and I can't get back to Earth?

They will ask me about this, about the wave, at my astronaut interview. At the psych eval. They'll be worried I'll be like Dr. Stone and have to reconcile with the death of a loved one while in imminent danger in space. And then they'll reject me. And I will never see the Ganges from four hundred kilometers above Earth.

I want to cry so bad, but tears won't come. I am wrong—there's something wrong with me. Who doesn't cry at their parents' funeral? This might be something that comes up in the psych eval, too.

After the service, I hurry to the bathroom. When I get into a stall, away from all the staring eyes, the grief voices, I pinch my skin, hard, and the pain zings up my arm, but my eyes stay dry.

"Those poor girls," someone says as the bathroom door opens.

I go still, trapped in the stall.

"Hannah's the spitting image of Lila. I almost thought it was her!"

"Isn't she? It's uncanny how much they look alike," another woman says. "Except for the eyes, of course. All Greg there. And Mae . . . Can you imagine being orphaned *twice*? Jesus."

"Oh God, the whole thing is so horrible."

There's the sound of running water and the whine of the paper towel dispenser. How can they talk about us like this while they redo their makeup, like we're small talk, the weather?

"But do you think this is a little easier for Mae, though—dealing, I mean? That sounds bad! But you know what I mean? They weren't *really* her parents. But Hannah . . ."

They weren't really her parents. Is that why Uncle Tony made sure to say that the inheritance would be split fifty-fifty? Would he have felt the need to say that if I weren't adopted? Does everyone in my extended family see me like these women do?

"Well, they got her when she was two or something. They always saw her as their child."

Three. Not that it's any of their business.

"Of course. But you know what I mean. There's that bond. When I had Jack, it was this whole chemical thing, right? I can't imagine my actual body responding in the same way with an adopted baby."

I close my eyes, try to imagine it: Mom holding me as a baby. Is that why she and Nah are closer? It wouldn't be Mom's fault—she can't fight her biology. I was never good at twisting my body into weird shapes on the yoga mat, like Nah. And I'm better at math, but she has Dad's genes, so I don't know what happened there. I used to think those were our only differences. Genetics. But maybe it was always something more. Deeper. Primal. What about me didn't turn on that primalness in the woman whose body I grew in?

I don't like this train of thought.

Water, splashing. Paper towels being scrunched up. "Still, they loved both those girls something fierce."

I know what they said was ignorant, about bonding, of course I do. There has never been any distinction between Hannah and I. Sometimes I think about the lost years—those three years when she had them and I didn't. I wonder who I'd be if I really had Mom's and Dad's genes. If I had Dad's genes, would I be even better at science? Brilliant. Not just good. Because maybe there were drugs when my mom was pregnant, not just after. Maybe brain cells were taken from me, right in the beginning.

I remember feeling jealous when I realized that Mom and Hannah have the same feet and that she curls her toes when she's talking, just like Dad does. I wanted Mom and Nah's Greek-ness, to have come from a line of women who make fantastic avgolemono. Mom says I come from that line, but I don't, not in the way that I want to. I want to know who my ancestors are. The blood ones. Maybe they came on the *Mayflower*, too, like Dad's. Or were Irish indentured servants. Or Russian princesses on the run. Or maybe Vikings. My blond hair and blue eyes—very Viking.

Even though I don't fit in the way Hannah does, I never once doubted my parents' love for me. The love they gave was equal and constant, deep and wide. One Valentine's Day, Dad wrote on a Post-it, *I love you girls from here* . . . and then we had to go find the other Post-it, which was all the way on the backyard fence and it said, *to here.* There was a box of chocolates for each of us and little teddy bears holding hearts at that end.

That love—from him and for him—is what makes me throw open the stall door and walk slowly to the sink. I take a long time washing my hands. Long enough for the women to see me and know that I heard. Long enough for them to feel mortified.

I don't say a word. I just grab some towels, dry my hands, and leave.

There are people everywhere and I avoid eye contact so they won't talk to me and I push out the doors, looking for Nah. I find her and Micah on a bench near the reflection pools in front of the library. Her legs are over his lap, her body turned into him, head lying against his chest. He's running his fingers through her hair, and he holds her like he'll never let her go.

I want to fall apart like her, but I can't. I'm not built that way, and even if I were, I'd have no one to catch me when I fall. Maybe that's why that woman thinks I'm not hurting as much—Nah is so obviously shattered.

But, I want to say to them all, is there anything lonelier than an astronaut in space whose parents are dead?

In Japan, they select astronauts by putting them in an enclosed space with other candidates for ten days. There are cameras everywhere, documenting every move they make, all their interactions. The testers make them fold a thousand paper cranes to see who works best under pressure. Traditionally, in Japan, the cranes are given to sick people. They're meant to bring long life and health. The trick is that, if you want to be an astronaut in Japan, your thousandth crane needs to look as perfect as your first one. Otherwise, *sayonara.*

Calm under pressure. That's maybe the number one trait of being an astronaut, other than not having motion sickness or a fear of heights.

People might think I don't miss my parents because I'm not sobbing every other second. But I do miss them. Terribly.

I'm just practicing.

can a person return to sender?

11

Hannah

We divide up all the jobs: packing, sorting, throwing away, organizing. I keep getting too blubbery as we go through things, so Mae tells me to do the paperwork. Dad's laptop is still on his desk, so I turn it on and start with his email. My sister will probably be recruited by both NASA and the CIA, since, apparently, she can also hack into people's emails. She figured out Dad's password is *Starman715*, which is his favorite song and birthday, so I guess maybe it wasn't *that* hard. I'm really going to miss calling Dad a nerd—of course an astrophysicist would love "Starman." This is our bit:

> **Dad:** (says something about math or science that .000003 percent
>   of the world could understand)
> **Me:** Nerd alert!
> **Him:** Takes one to know one.
> **Me:** You're confusing me with your other daughter.

One of the jobs Mae gave me was to create a vacation responder that lets people know that Dad's gone, and that if they need to get in touch regarding his research or anything else, to email our family lawyer. I guess we have one of those.

There are dozens of unopened emails, and I have no intention of reading any of them until my eye lands on a name I recognize: Rebecca Chen. Dad's research assistant. He'd never brought her to the house to come help grade papers and eat chili, like the others, but we met her at the funeral. She kind of looked like Constance Wu, with glossy black hair and big brown eyes. They were red and puffy when we met her, but so were many of the eyes in the room that day. She was older than us, maybe late twenties. I was pretty high by the time we started chatting, but I remember Mae looking horrified because they were talking about quasars, and I said that sounded like a venereal disease.

There are a lot of emails from Rebecca, the last one two days after the tsunami. I click on it, in case it's important—about his research or the book. I could tell Mae and she'd know what to do.

Call Me 8:12 AM (August 31)
Rebecca Chen <rchen@mail.com>
To Greg <gwinters@mail.com>

I am freaking out. Please, I know it's got to be insane over there, but please call me. Please. I'm so scared. Are you okay? How can I help? Do you want me to check on the girls?

I love you and I'm sorry about pressuring you, I am. Please be okay. I love you so much it hurts.

B.

I stare at the screen.
"What. The. Fuck?"
I push away from the desk and stand up so fast the chair topples over. I can hear Mae in the kitchen, talking about our parents' wedding

china with Aunt Nora and Cynthia. They bought special stuff to pack it in. Uncle Tony's in the garage, doing man stuff while Nate pretends to do man stuff with him. Gram and Papa are on a walk. It's just me and this computer and the heat racing through my body, so fast I can hardly breathe.

I lean on the desk and read the email three more times before I grab the laptop and tiptoe upstairs. I lock my bedroom door and sit on my bed. My hands are shaking so hard I can hardly scroll through the emails, but there is no fucking way I'm not reading them. I start with the ones just before Dad left for Malaysia.

Soon 10:15 PM (August 12)
Greg Winters <gwinters@mail.com>
To Rebecca <rchen@mail.com>

Sweetheart, I know it's hard to wait. I *know*. But I need more time. The girls are still in school and I don't want to pull the rug out from under them. And you know everything Hannah's dealing with. I can't risk her sobriety.

I have to do right by Lila, too. None of this is her fault. We will be together. I promise. You have my heart. You've had it since the first moment I saw you.

I love you with everything in me.

—G

"Fuck, fuck, *FUCK*."
I grab my pillow and scream into it.
Then I keep reading.

Don't Go 9:17 PM (August 17)
Rebecca Chen <rchen@mail.com>
To Greg <gwinters@mail.com>

Please don't get on that plane tomorrow. Please.

Re: Don't Go 11:34 PM (August 17)
Greg Winters <gwinters@mail.com>
To Rebecca <rchen@mail.com>

I don't like this any more than you do, sweetheart. Every time I touch her I feel like I'm cheating on you. I tried to get out of this trip, but every excuse I had wasn't working, and I couldn't afford for her to get suspicious. I can't miss out on this last year with the girls at home. I know I'm asking a lot, but, please, this is what we need to do. I want Hannah and Mae to love you as much as I do, and they won't if they think you've broken up our family. They're too young to understand. And I don't want to live apart from them, not yet. Please trust me. What's a year more when we'll have the rest of our lives together? I promise that by the time I get home, Lila will know that forever is off the table. That's reserved for you. I'll be home before you know it.

–G

Re: Don't Go 2:00 AM (August 18)
Rebecca Chen <rchen@mail.com>
To Greg <gwinters@mail.com>

Baby, there will never be a good time to do this. I don't want to be your secret anymore. I've been doing it for almost a year, lying to everyone I know.

If you don't tell Lila by the time you get home, then I'm done.

B.

I'm sorry 6:23 AM (August 19)
Rebecca Chen <rchen@mail.com>
To Greg <gwinters@mail.com>

That wasn't fair, what I said. I'm sorry. I'm just tired of pretending. And there's a reason we can't wait—maybe we can talk about it, if you can get away. I love you. I want everything with you. It's killing me that she gets to wake up next to you every morning.

Tell me we're okay.

B.

Re: I'm sorry 7:30 AM (August 19)
Greg Winters <gwinters@mail.com>
To Rebecca <rchen@mail.com>

We're okay. I'll be home before you know it. Gotta run—the airport shuttle's here. I'll call from Malaysia, okay? I love you.

—G

I scroll back, past this summer, reading every email. It goes on like this for almost a year. All of her emails hidden in a file marked GRADING. He's been fucking her since I was sixteen.

I pick up my phone to call Micah, ready to lose my ever-loving mind, when I realize: Dad's the only father Micah's ever really had. If I tell him this, he'll lose that. And Mae: I can't tell her. She and Dad were crazy close, and this would do nothing but fuck her up as much as I am right now.

I hold Dad's laptop and go to my door, listening. It sounds like they're still downstairs, so I creep to Mom and Dad's room and get Mom's laptop. Back in my room, I search through her emails, but there's nothing, no sign that she knew. Ignorance is bliss, right? Maybe Mom had no idea, and she died with the man she loved, end of story.

Because if she knew, if that wave was coming and she knew . . .

"I can't do this," I say out loud.

There's a long, low breath behind me. The scent of roses.

I turn. My mother is doing a headstand.

I slump to the ground.

"Are you really here?"

I'm not high—yet.

Her hair is matted down with sweat. Or seawater. Her forearms rest on either side of her head, keeping her in balance.

I crawl to her. "Mommy?"

Her eyes stay focused on the mat, her long body in perfect alignment. That breath—*ujjayi* breath—which sounds like the sea. Like waves sliding to the shore.

I want to touch her, but I don't want her to fall. She exhales a wave of breath, and I try to catch it with my mouth. How can the person who made you be gone?

I follow the line of her leg, up to her ankle, and I burst into tears: her right. The Om is on her right ankle.

"Did you know?" I whisper. "Mom. Did you know?"

Mom moves her left leg so that it bends at the knee, makes a four. A sort of upside-down tree pose, but with her foot sliding just behind her knee, so that her left shin rests against the back of her right thigh.

"Tell me what to do. I can't do this, Mom. Please."

Her muscles begin to strain just a little, and I remember her holding my feet as I wobbled on my hands: *I can't do this!*

And almost like she can see that memory playing through me, Mom looks at me, smiles, and lands back on her feet like a cat.

And then she's gone.

I lunge toward the mat, too late. There is one strand of long black hair—but it could be mine. I don't know. I don't know.

I collapse into child's pose, and I cry for my mom like a little girl. I dig my forehead into the rubber, and I see the emails, hear them almost, and I see Mom hold a spoon of soup up to Dad's lips for him to taste and I see Rebecca Chen at the funeral, see her puffy red eyes, and I see the wave, cresting over the beach—

"I don't know what to do," I tell her, even though she's gone.

Do I tell Mae? Do I keep the secret forever? Can I hold this knowledge in me for the rest of my life?

It's almost like a dream, the way I shove the laptop under my bed and reach for the pills and swallow one of the few I've got left with the warm can of Diet Coke on my bedside table. I lie down and wait for the floating and the forgetting and the not-me-ness of the Vicodin. I wait for the wave to wash over me.

In a few minutes, it won't matter that my dad was a lying, cheating bastard.

In a few minutes, nothing will matter.

. • . •

I like mail with no surprises, and it seems romantic, in these last few days here, to check our little postbox one last time.

It's pale green, with orange California poppies painted on it. Mom did that. It sits right at the end of our walkway, peeking over the fence onto the sidewalk like some nosy old broad. Our house is your typical Venice cottage, with a rickety wooden fence and a wild garden and wind chimes and gnomes, so the postbox fits right in. Kind of magical.

As I put my hand on it, I have a sudden urge to just rip the thing out of the ground and take our little friend with me. Carry it on the plane or check it as oversized luggage. This metal box that has always been filled with *Yoga Journal* and *Scientific American* and birthday cards from Gram and Papa with embarrassingly big checks inside.

I half expect it to be empty, but it's not. There's one thing sitting in the dark. I slip my hand in and pull it out.

I hear a wave.

The postcard is a bit banged up. The picture on the front slightly faded, like it'd been sitting out in the sun too long.

My knees buckle and then my ass is on the cold curb and now the wave is a roar.

Can you hear it? Can you hear the cars and people and houses it sweeps up with it?

My hands shake so hard that I have to put the card on my lap just to look at it properly. I stare at the beautiful cove tucked against low green hills, white sand on the beach. Crystal-clear water.

LANGKAWI: ISLAND OF LEGENDS.

Hills. There were so many hills around the beach. Why couldn't they get to the hills?

The back has a printed GREETINGS FROM MALAYSIA centered on the card, and there's a stamp and all the mail things. They sent it two days before the wave. Just enough time for the card to get safely out.

Dad's handwriting—that sure hand. Cursive, of course. Always cursive. Very professorial. And a little note from Mom at the bottom in her swooping print. Blue ink, where his is black.

Hi, ladies!
Don't mind us, we're just over here in Paradise doing absolutely <u>nothing</u> and loving it. Wish you were here to soak up the sun with us—
    N: you and Micah would love it.
    M: Remind me to tell you a physics joke an Australian guy here told me.
    Love you both from here to the farthest exoplanets—

                                         Dad

Hi, beautiful girls! Guess what? I overcame my fear of the deep and snorkeled! I also cut off ALL MY HAIR. A German lady at our guesthouse did it. Can't wait to show you! Be good and don't do anything I wouldn't. ;) xo Mom

The door opens behind me.

"Nah?"

I don't think. I just stuff the postcard down my shirt and stand, unsteady. It's not because I don't want to share this with her. It's because I know that it will kill Mae, never hearing that joke Dad wanted to tell her.

I turn to face my sister.

"Yeah?"

"We have to finish packing."

I stand. Walk. Ignore the searching look Mae gives me. Enter the almost-empty house. It echoes now, when we talk. It will be filled again, soon, with different things and people. It sold almost right away. To a nice family from Thousand Oaks. I hate them.

The things we decided to keep are in storage or in boxes going to Boston.

There has been *a lot* of stuff to deal with. Part of me doesn't want to let go of a thing. Part of me wants to burn all of it.

I am so angry.

At Dad.

At Rebecca Fucking Chen.

At the wave.

At Micah for not being a little more noble.

There is one item we can't do without: Mae and I both insist on bringing Mom's soup pot with us. It's my carry-on for the plane. I pack two books—*The Little Prince* and Mom's copy of *Acorn*. Mae takes some of Dad's physics books.

When we've packed the last box, it looks like the Grinch has been in here, stealing Christmas. Empty but for hooks and nails in the wall, bits of trash on the floors. It would break Mom's heart, I bet, to see how quickly our family can disappear.

The day we leave, exactly one month after the wave—September 29—Cynthia comes to say goodbye. She takes me aside and presses a tarot deck into my hands. It's a Rider-Waite-Smith deck, like the one I have but a different version.

"I read your mom's cards with this the day before she left," Cyn says. "This was the deck she bought me, years ago."

I stare at the box, which has The Magician on the front, holding a wand up high, an infinity symbol traced over his head. As above, so below.

"Did she get Death?"

Cyn shakes her head. "She got The Fool."

"The Fool?"

Starting a journey. I guess that makes sense.

"I've been thinking about it a lot," she says. "You know what I've decided?"

"Huh?"

"Death is just the beginning." She wraps her arms around me. "You have so much of her in you, honey. Don't forget that. She was magic. So are you."

I almost tell her what I know, about Dad, but then Micah's there looking shattered. I let go of Cyn and follow Micah to the little wall that runs along the bike path on the beach. He sits down and pulls me onto his lap and I bury my face in his neck. I hear him sniffling, and when I look up, there are tears rolling down his cheeks and I hate the world. I hate it so much.

"I can't believe this is happening," he says.

He looks as lost as I feel.

"I love you," I whisper. "I'm so sorry."

Is this the end—the real end? I don't want to be alone. And I can't imagine losing him, too.

"There's nothing to be sorry for," he murmurs.

His arms tighten around me, and I can't help but think about the stories of people whose kids or wives or parents were pulled out of their arms by the wave. It doesn't matter how tightly you hold on to someone. Eventually you have to let go.

But I don't know how.

We stay like that until Mae softly calls my name.

"The airport shuttle's here," I say.

He presses his lips to my forehead. "Call me from the airport." My cheek. "Call me when you get in." The tip of my nose. "Call me in the middle of the night, and every second of every day." My lips. "Call me."

I can taste his tears and mine. "I will."

"I'll be there for Christmas. And we'll make lots of hot Los Angeles love."

I laugh a little. "It's a deal."

"It'll be perfect. Just a couple months away," he says, his fingers trailing along my jaw. "And then you'll come back and we'll get our own place and . . . It's just nine months, right?"

That number. Why does it have to be that exact number?

"Yeah."

Except that the last time someone I loved got on a plane, I never saw them again. Everything feels like it's made of glass: me and Micah, the future, my body.

I start to walk away, but he pulls me back. "You're not just my girlfriend—you're my family. We'll get through this."

Later, on the plane, I catch myself staring out the window as we fly over fields and cities and rivers and highways. Looking hard at the clouds, at the rips between the white and gray. I think I'm looking for them. I don't know where they are, *what* they are. I don't know if they were taken on purpose or not. Can they see me?

I catch myself looking for Micah, too.

It feels like he's a ghost already.

Mae leans her head against my shoulder. "They have *Toy Story*. Want to watch together?" She tries to smile. "'To infinity and beyond.'"

Our thing.

I look away. "Disney lied. Infinity doesn't exist."

"Well, actually, if you consider—" I give her a look, and she stops.

I don't want to be conscious anymore. Then I have to think about new schools and a house that smells different from mine and a whole life of waking up and remembering they're gone.

I push an eye mask over my eyes. Mae rests her head on my shoulder, and we sleep our way across the country.

i want to go home, but i don't have one.

Baggage Claim Carousel
Logan Airport
Boston

12

Hannah

There's a place between waking and sleeping, and I try to stay there.

It's warm, like bathwater. It tastes like forgetting.

I just want to never leave, huddled under the blankets, curled in on myself. Floating.

I have three Vicodin left of Dad's month supply. Mae kept me from going to the boardwalk to get more from Priscilla. I need to conserve them until I find a dealer here. I had a quit attempt yesterday, but by noon I gave up. I'll get good again—I just need to get through the next . . . I just need to get through.

I hear the door open—it creaks, this strange, new door in my strange new room.

"Nah?"

I don't say anything, just scoot closer to the wall. Mae lies down and throws an arm over me.

"I feel like I'm in a black hole," I say. This is speaking Mae's language.

"Did you know that a black hole is actually a collapsed star?" she says. I shake my head. "To escape it, you'd have to travel FASTER than the speed of light. Which is really fast."

"How fast?"

"Six hundred seventy million miles per hour."

"Fuck."

"Right?" she says. "That's why a black hole is black—not even the light can escape it."

Mae sits up, pulling her knees against her chest. She's wearing her favorite striped vintage pajamas, with embroidered roses stitched along the collar. "I keep thinking about Dad's book. How he's not going to write it."

I'm scared to touch on Dad. I think I kind of hate him now.

"Maybe you can write it yourself someday."

She bites her lip. "I'm not going into theoretical studies, though. I mean, maybe on the side, but when you're in the space program, you give up a research career." She brightens a little. "Maybe I could talk to Becca—you know, his research assistant. We could cowrite it, maybe. I bet she has all his notes. She's super into axions."

I close my eyes. I could tell her. I *should* tell her. I think Mae was pissed about not being asked to go to the clinic with me. About being left out of something so important. I don't want her to feel like I'm hiding something from her. But when I look at my sister in the dim light of my room, I see a spark in her eyes that hasn't been there for a month.

"What about Tim? He worked with Dad longer," I say. "Or one of the MacDougal genius guys."

"MacArthur. It's a *MacArthur* Fellowship."

"Okay, whatever—you know what I mean. Get the most qualified person. Not some assistant."

She nods. Then, because she's Mae: "Hey, you want to know what I just read?"

"Huh."

"Apparently, one of the prettiest things in space is when the astronauts dump their urine and it flash freezes. So when the sun hits the drops of urine, they're like these diamonds floating in the sky."

"That's disgusting."

"But kind of awesome."

We're silent for a while, each lost in our own thoughts.

"I haven't been able to cry," Mae whispers.

The hurt in her voice carves out my insides.

"I know," I say. "It's okay. People, like, deal in different ways. You know?"

Like with prescription drugs you stole from your dead father. I want to tell her about Mom doing a headstand in my room, but I don't want her to tell me I imagined it. That it's not possible.

She nods. "I feel like . . . I think it's a distinct possibility there's something wrong with me. Just a hypothesis. I need to conduct some experiments."

I sit up on my elbow. Mae is talking about feelings. This is . . . unprecedented.

"There's nothing wrong with you." I sit up all the way, cross my legs. "You came out fucking great. *I'm* the one with struggles. You know that."

She shakes her head. "My parents died and I only cried once, when I was making the soup. I'm fucked-up."

She *never* curses. This is serious.

I rest a hand on her knee. "Are you sad?"

"Of course."

"Then you're reacting in a totally normal way. Not everyone is a shit-show crier like me. If you're sad, we can rule out total psychosis." She laughs a little—my work here is done. Almost. I grab the bottle of Mom's lotion off my bedside table. "Hold out your hand."

She smiles. Runs a finger over the bottle. How many times did we see Mom hit the pump of this Jergens bottle after cooking in the kitchen, or gardening?

I squeeze a dollop onto her palm, then rub it into her skin, which is so translucent you can see bright blue veins running beneath it, like rivers on a map. My skin is darker, olive. Light, but with a dash of Mediterranean.

"Magic potion," I say. "Remember how she used to stand by the kitchen window and rub it onto her hands for the longest time?"

"And she'd be playing Joni Mitchell or Enya."

"Yeah."

My sister's hands are small, but her fingers are long and thin. Elegant and scholarly. Not stubby like mine. Her nails aren't bitten and covered in chipped black paint like mine, either. They are neatly filed, bare with little half-moons peeking over the cuticles.

"Remember how Mom and Dad were always trying to get you to take piano lessons, because of your fingers?" I say.

She snorts. "And they didn't give up until I proved that proficiency in math does not guarantee musical aptitude."

Finished, I reach over and press the bottle once more, creamy white Jergens spreading onto my palm.

"Why Jergens?" Mae asks. "Always this cheap drugstore stuff."

Original scent. Cherry almond essence. She never switched it up.

"It's what Yia-yia used," I say. "Her whole life, after she came to America. When she died, I remember Mom going into her bathroom at the nursing home and taking out the bottle. She was kind of hugging it to her chest. She told me how, when she was little, Yia-yia used to give Mom manicures, and she'd always rub this lotion on her hands first."

"I never knew that," Mae says. She runs her fingers over her palms. "Mom painted my nails the night Riley left for China. Do you remember? Each nail a different color."

I nod. "Breakup nails." I look down at my hands, at the chipped polish, the nails I've bitten so much they bleed. "What's gonna happen to us?"

"It's already happening," she says softly.

"God, I miss Micah so much. And I saw him just, like, twenty-four hours ago."

I don't remember what it's like to be mad at him. Absence maybe does make the heart grow fonder. I don't know.

"You guys have been together for three years—you have nothing to worry about." Mae's lips turn up a little. "He worships you."

I give her a sly glance. "Maybe you'll find a nice Boston boy. Or girl."

She shakes her head. "No. I have to stay focused. There's no point. I'm joining the military in July."

I never thought about it that way, but she's right. If Mae gets into Annapolis, which she will, she'll be in the navy for the next nine years. Then she'll be in Houston or wherever astronauts live these days. Russia, maybe. God, that's far.

It hits me then. I haven't just lost my parents and Micah. I've lost Mae, too. Somehow in all of this, I'd forgotten that there are more goodbyes.

I slide my hand under my pillow, touch the tiny envelope of pills. Later. I will be able to float later.

"Sometimes I . . . It feels like they're . . . here. Sort of. Can you . . ." I take a breath. "I know you don't believe in this stuff, but—can you feel them?"

She looks up at me. "Yes."

I blink. "Really?"

I thought my sister would give me that look. The science one.

She nods. "But I still think that's just our imaginations playing tricks on us."

"Where do you think they are now?" I ask.

Mom believed in Something Else. I do, too—I just don't quite know what it is. It's the feeling I get when I go to Saint Cecelia's and light candles with Gram or when we're doing Kirtan chanting at the yoga studio. Places Something Else lives full-time.

"I think they're somewhere in Malaysia. Decomposing." She looks stricken. "Sorry. I just mean—"

I shake my head. "I know what you mean. But you're wrong. They're out there—their essence, spirit, *something* is out there. A knowing thing. A remembering thing." I rest my palm against the place in the middle of my chest where I feel Something Else. "I think we all have a part of that—in us. Our soul, maybe, or just. I don't know. Carl Jung called it a *collective unconscious*. I read that in one of Mom's books. Like all of humanity has this giant spirit hive mind we can tap into."

She raises her eyebrows. "I didn't know you read Jung."

There's a lot people don't know about me. Don't see. I just shrug. "He's cool."

"Stephen Hawking thinks it's possible we . . . encrypt ourselves on the universe when we go. I mean, this is a really simplified explanation. He wasn't able to prove that, though, and now he's gone. So it's possible you and Carl Jung are a little correct."

I roll my eyes. "But only if you can prove it."

"Well, if you can't prove it, it's just a theory. It might be *workable*, but it's still not conclusive."

Sometimes my genius sister can be pretty dense.

I run my finger over the charm that used to be Mom's—a blue-and-white circle, smaller than a penny. It's this Greek thing, supposed to be protection against the evil eye. Mae would never wear something superstitious, but it makes me feel closer to Mom. I don't know why she didn't wear it in Malaysia. Maybe she was afraid it'd get lost when she was swimming. Maybe it would have protected her somehow.

"Mae, I know you're a scientist. I get that. But you can't tell me you don't believe there is something, *anything*, out there. People have pretty much proven the existence of ghosts. And Mom's intuition—I mean, how could she *know* things were going to happen before they did? And remember how Yia-yia would always know she was going to get a letter in the mail and from who and then it would be there, in her mailbox? Or, like, how the cards are *always right*? Something is behind all that. I mean, look how complex we are. You can't simply evolve into something that composes a symphony or choreographs a ballet."

"You're talking about 'God.'"

"Not God with a capital G. But a knowing . . . presence. Something so much more evolved than us that we don't even have words to describe it—you know?"

"Like colors?"

"Huh?"

She scoots closer. "There is so much we can't view with the naked human eye. We can't see infrared or ultraviolet—which means we only see a fraction of the colors in the universe, unless we have the aid of scientific instruments. But those colors—they're there, even though we can't see them."

"I guess that's what I mean. Yeah."

Mae's quiet for a moment. She's got her thinking face on. "Sometimes I think about how there are billions of galaxies in the universe—maybe more. And my mind short-circuits, just trying to imagine that. We'll only ever get to see the tiniest FRACTION of it. Or I think about how our individual lives seem so important, but we're just blips on the timeline of human existence."

"But blips *matter*. Think about the Butterfly Effect—how one tiny act somewhere on Earth can change the whole course of history."

Mae smiles. "You sound like Mom."

"You sound like Dad."

These were the kinds of talks that we used to have around the dinner table—never arguing, just passionate conversation and lots of questions.

I lie down, stare at the ceiling. This one doesn't have cracks.

"We'll never see them again," I whisper.

Mae lies down next to me and slips her fingers through mine. "No."

And I think, with her here, with the possibility of Something Else: Maybe I don't need the pills. After these ones, I mean. Maybe I can stop.

We fall asleep, hand in hand, curled against each other, like twins in a womb. When I wake up, Mae is gone.

So are my pills.

This right here, this is the Three of Swords card, each blade sticking into a heart: *Betrayal.*

Here I thought we were having a moment, and all she was trying to do was steal my fucking pills. Did she lie awake, waiting to make sure I was asleep?

I throw off the covers, ready to tear into her, but then I stop, because I can already see how this will play out. This argument in which I try to reason with the Queen of Swords—the embodiment of logic—about how it was wrong of her to flush her sister's stolen opiates down the toilet.

I'm tired of losing things: pills, pride, people.

There is no point arguing, defending yourself. Everyone just decides who you are—that you're a zero, a druggie—and nothing you do or say changes that. Once you get labeled an addict, that's it. You're fucked for life. That's why at meetings they don't let you say, *Hi, I'm Hannah and I WAS an addict*. No. You have to say, *I AM an addict*.

They never let you fucking forget.

At Al-Anon, where the parents go to bitch about us losers, I heard they have this saying, this fucked-up joke: *How do you know an addict is lying? . . . Because she's talking.*

So maybe it doesn't matter, the trying. No one's gonna believe me anyway.

13

Mae

ISS Location: Low-Earth Orbit
Earth Date: 2 October
Earth Time (EST): 21:30

t's cold in Boston.

And beautiful.

The leaves on the trees are russet, scarlet, gold. People wear scarves and wool coats now that it's getting colder, and they walk quickly, with a lot of purpose. They have stiff upper lips.

In Boston, sprinkles are *jimmies* and milkshakes are *frappes*. We don't take the train to Harvard Station, we take it to *Hah-vahd* Station. Every few blocks we pass a beautiful stone church. The graveyards here are so old the stones are crumbling, and the graves are filled with soldiers from the Revolutionary War. This place has roots.

I've always liked Boston more than LA. Maybe that's because, thanks to Harvard's Center for Astrophysics, there are more physicists here than anywhere else in the United States—except for NASA, of course. There's MIT, too.

People here read a lot. On the train, on benches, in cafes. Everyone looks like they've pulled an all-nighter, because they probably have. It's a town of universities, of *smaht* people. I really love it a lot. For the first time, I don't feel like the strangest person in the room. I hope Annapolis is like this, too. And NASA.

Nah hates it. *Hates* it. You take her anywhere below seventy degrees and she's miserable. She doesn't like wearing socks. She is suspicious of places without palm trees or green juice or sun all the time. She was already wilting in LA—even before the wave. One of those roses that needs very special fertilizer and gardeners who sing to them and the perfect balance of shadow and light. I am afraid she is going to shrivel up in Boston.

Aunt Nora lives in a two-story brick house in Brookline, on a quiet street lined with other big, old houses. I thought I'd miss the sound of the ocean, of skateboarders rolling by, and people cooking out all the time, Micah's surfboard propped up next to the front door, but I don't. I like the quiet here, how it wraps around you like a soft blanket. Sometimes in the morning I look out the window and see wild turkeys in the backyard. Actual turkeys. There is frost, and the air smells like autumn: crispy and smoky.

Sometimes Earth is an excellent place to be, if you can't orbit it.

We've been here countless times before—with our parents, on vacation. I can still see Dad holed up in a corner of the living room, reading in the leather wingback chair. Mom would always be in the kitchen, cooking while Aunt Nora worked on legal briefs at the table and kept refilling their wineglasses. Uncle Tony might kick them out to make his famous meatballs or lasagna if he wasn't working on his car. Nate would be showing me something insanely cool that he built for class. Hannah would be on the phone with Micah.

It's not like that now.

For one, it's been very, very quiet. Just me, Nah, and our aunt and uncle, all of us tiptoeing around, speaking in whispers. We've only been here a few days, so I'm sure that will change. I don't feel like a guest, exactly, but I don't feel like it's my home, either. They keep saying it is, but it's not. So far, Nah refuses to eat much of anything, so I end up alone with my aunt and uncle for meals. We don't know what to say, so we end up watching TV, which would have driven both of my parents mad.

My room is on the second floor, down the hall from Hannah's. It overlooks the tiny backyard while hers looks out onto the front yard, just like our setup in Venice. There's a huge sycamore tree taking up most of the backyard. Nate, Nah, and I named it Elvis when we were all really little. I like Elvis. He's here to stay, and it's nice to know that something isn't going to change.

All I have from home right now is a large suitcase and my telescope. I put my telescope beside the window, but I don't have the heart to look through it tonight. Instead, I drag the desk chair to my bed, and then— very carefully so I don't fall and break my neck—I tack my poster with the image of the Helix Nebula on the ceiling above my pillow.

But that only takes five minutes.

I wish I had homework to do. Calculus. Physics. But we don't start school for two more days.

I don't mind being far from friends at school. We all would have had to say goodbye in June, anyway, if I got into Annapolis. Plebe Summer begins on the first of July—navy hazing, my dad calls it. *Called* it. I do mind being far from Dad and Mom and Hannah, though. I didn't realize how much time we were all together until they were gone. Hannah's only technically here. We share oxygen. On occasion. It's been thirty-six hours since I took her pills, and every time I try to talk to her, she walks away. So.

I think my dad was my best friend.

Why did it take this long for me to figure that out?

This is not a line of thinking that is conducive to becoming an astronaut, so I lie down, put in my earbuds, and hit PLAY on my phone: "Starman."

When I wake up, the room is dark. I haven't taken a nap since kindergarten. Perhaps it's jet lag. Nate has texted me three times, and when I take out my earbuds, I can hear him laughing downstairs. Home from MIT for the weekend.

I think he might be my mission control now. The person who will answer if I say, *Houston, we have a problem.*

When I reach the bottom of the staircase, a boy I've never seen before is sprawled on the couch next to Nate, staring intently at a laptop on the coffee table.

"Yeah, but the aerodynamics are all off," Nate's saying. "There's no way I'm getting that past Paulson."

The boy next to him looks up, and I think I maybe gasp a little because MY FAVORITE MANGA CHARACTER IS IN MY NEW HOUSE.

It's as if Ichigo Kurosaki from *Bleach* decided to come over for dinner. This boy specimen even has the same messy orange hair.

"You, I don't know," he says.

"That's my genius cousin," Nate says. "Be nice to her and maybe she'll give you a shout-out on Twitter when she's up on the International Space Station."

The boy stands up. Dear god, he's moving closer to me and I have yet to introduce myself or vet his respectability as my cousin's study partner in any way, but I can't because I HAVE LOST THE CAPACITY FOR SPEECH. It's possible I'm having a lucid dream. This would explain any and all cognitive malfunctions on my part.

"I'm Ben," he says when he reaches the bottom of the stairs.

Something very strange is going on in spacetime. As in, I no longer know *when* I am or how long I have been staring at this Ben person and I should stop but I am becoming increasingly confused.

He looks exactly like Sôta Fukushi, who plays Ichigo in the live-action movie. If I saw him on the street and had no self-respect, I would ask him for an autograph. On my bare chest. I am losing my mind.

Maybe he *is* Sôta Fukushi, but is incognito and using the alias Ben. So he can study abroad in peace.

IS SÔTA FUKUSHI IN MY LIVING ROOM?

"Tamura's my roommate," Nate says. "I'm building a plane, and he's calculating the probability of it crashing." He leans toward me. "But he's a geophysicist, not an astronautics engineer like—ahem—some of us, so his calculus isn't up to snuff."

Ben—if that's even his name—flips off Nate before he takes my hand in his and this causes a medical emergency. I feel all melty and . . . weird.

"Mae," I say, but it's more a croak, so I have to clear my throat and say it again. "Mae. Is my name."

CODE RED, NASA, CODE RED. I grasp at the first thing that comes to mind—Dad always said, First thought, best thought.

"Nate brought you in on his project because your geophysics can help him determine the relative impact his plane would have if crashing on different topographies, right?"

Ben laughs, and it's a very nice sound, and something about it makes him real and not Ichigo. It's not the kind of laugh you give before you use a katana to banish a ghost monster from the world of the living.

"I think your cousin's just desperate," Ben says. "Besides, at the speed he's going, that plane's a goner whether it hits low-elevation desert or sedimentary rock."

And just like that, my flat spin is over.

At space camp one year, an air force test pilot came to speak and he said that when your plane's in a flat spin, the best way to know whether it's recoverable or not is if the nose is pitching down to Earth. And what's more down-to-earth than a geophysicist?

"The plane is not crashing!" Nate says. "Now both of you sit down and tell me everything you know about aerodynamics so I don't fail my midterm."

As we start toward the couch, Ben gives my vintage overalls a once-over. "Are those pineapples?" He leans in a little to study the pattern, and I catch a faint whiff of coffee.

"Yes. Pineapples make me happy." I glance at Nate. "Hannah says they're too much."

"Nothing can ever be too much." Nate gestures to the sequined head-band he's wearing. "Case in point."

It is one of the strangest nights of my life. I'm both in my body and entirely out of it. Maybe it's like going through the atmosphere—you're not on Earth anymore, but you're not totally in space, either. I see me and Ben and Nate on the couch, working on equations, and then I feel every centimeter of Ben's thigh touching mine. And then I'm hovering above us all again, watching.

When we finally make sure the hypothetical plane my cousin is building isn't going to crash, Ben turns to me. "I thought Nate was exaggerating about the genius part. You're intimidating as hell, Mae."

My cousin grins. "Believe the hype. We got a future Nobel winner here."

The words make me feel suddenly, utterly hopeless. How many times had I heard Dad say them? It's not like I forgot he died, but all this work hit the PAUSE button on my memory. Now it's on PLAY again.

"I still haven't done my Annapolis interview, so . . ." I wave my hand, like everything else—my entire life—is beside the point.

Nate stands. "Gravity's a bitch, Mae."

I should never have told him I cancelled my interview in LA. Or that I haven't rescheduled here in Boston. I should never have said, *I can't do this without him*. It was out of character for me. The thought of sitting in that interview and then not being able to talk about it afterward with Dad . . . No one but Nate knows. And I will reschedule. Of course I will. For him—Dad. And me. I didn't mean I can't ever do this without him. I just can't do it without him *right now*. I'm interviewing for a naval military academy. If something they say triggers my emotions, I could risk losing my place there. I need more time. I need more chances to practice telling people they're gone in a voice that can also say things like, *The nukes on our submarine are ready for launch, sir*.

I sigh. "I'm not an inert object. I told you, I just need time."

Ben leans his head back on the couch. "Okay, you two have just teleported into the spacetime continuum and I'm stuck on this rock. I'm a simple man of the land. Translation, please?"

I glare at Nate before turning to Ben. "My cousin is making a rookie mistake, conflating a Newtonian description of gravity with general relativity, attempting to use physics as a psychoanalytic tool to suggest I'm struggling with inertia—which I'm not, by the way. Gravity is not a force, it's a consequence of the curvature of space and time. Everyone confuses that, but I would have thought an MIT student wouldn't." I give Nate a look, he gives *me* a look.

Ben doesn't give me a look, he just looks at me. Which is a little disconcerting, but also nice.

"So Nate's suggesting gravity is going to catch up to you and force you into forward motion."

"Correct," Nate says. "Basic physics."

"Basic obnoxiousness," I snap.

Nate reaches over and squeezes my shoulder. "Make the call, Buzz."

My cousin shuffles off to the kitchen to grab us some chips, and Ben glances at me, his lips turning up in a smile.

"If it makes you feel any better, he micromanages my life, too."

"A little."

Ben rubs his eyes. "He's usually right, though. Bastard. A word of advice: If you ever become a barista and your best friend tells you not to agree to the opening shift, listen to him."

"So that's why you smell like coffee."

"One of the perks. Ha. No pun intended."

We're quiet for a minute, and then he turns to me and I can't help but think how good he would look fighting crime with that bleached hair and those dark eyes.

Observations like this are evidence that I'm running on fumes. I must maintain my focus. It's the only way I know I have a chance at Annapolis, at NASA. It's inconvenient, to meet the first person I've been genuinely attracted to since Riley at this particular stage of my life. It would have been nice to meet him in college or much, much later.

His eyes touch mine, then he looks away, throws his calculator into his backpack. "You should come by sometime. I'll give you free coffee and regale you with fascinating tales about my customers and, if I'm feeling particularly loquacious, mineralogy."

"Typical geophysicist."

"Please. I prefer *rock detective*. We're living on a mystery, you know."

I huff out a tiny laugh, and it feels good. "Please expand."

He rubs his hands. "Okay. We don't know what Earth's core is made up of—which means every minute of every day, we're, well, living on a mystery." He grips his hair a little, and I don't think he knows he's doing it, or how cute it is. "And we may never know! Like, we figure it's maybe eighty percent iron—debatable number, but we'll just go with it—but because of its lightness, that's not the whole story. But it's a third of our planet's mass! So is there a shit-ton of xenon in there, or silicate . . . Who knows? Then when you consider the periodic reversals in Earth's magnetic field, plate tectonics . . ." He throws up his hands. "It's a mystery."

"Plate tectonics." I never knew that term could become so personal. "So. You study earthquakes. Sometimes."

He hesitates before nodding, and in that moment, I know that he knows. Of course he does. Nate's his best friend.

"In regard to earthquakes . . . I'm sorry about your parents," Ben says. His voice goes soft, different. "That's really fucking heavy."

I bet they studied the wave in one of his classes. The underwater fault lines that sent it over my whole life. I bet he knows more about what killed my parents than I do.

"Could you . . . tell me about the wave?"

Ben looks at me for a long time, like I'm maybe under a microscope. "Will it help?"

I always thought that the more data I had, the more sense I could make out of anything. But maybe there are just some questions that can never be answered.

"I don't know."

He nods. "My three favorite words."

"My *least*-favorite words."

He smiles. "So what are your favorites?"

"Just one: *Why.* I even have a T-shirt that says WHY in huge orange letters. Ugly, but I love it. Hannah found it for me at a thrift shop in Venice." I glance at him. "I hate not knowing. It's why I science."

"I love it. It's why *I* science."

For the past two hours and forty-two minutes, my heart has been doing things I am not accustomed to. Hannah things.

It appears that Hannah feelings are not as enviable as I thought. They are questions and not answers.

I wish Ben didn't smell so good. Or look like Ichigo Kurosaki. Or wasn't smart enough to do advanced physics at MIT.

I am way out of orbit. I need to correct course somehow. I think that involves standing up and leaving the room, but I seem to be experiencing a gravitational malfunction.

"What's your favorite thing you don't know?" he says.

Suddenly I'm back in orbit. This I can do. I turn on my side, tuck my knees in.

"Dark matter, dark energy. Ninety-five percent of the universe is made up of this stuff, and we don't even know what it is," I say. "We know what it's *not*—a little, anyway. But most of the universe is dark matter, and it's a total mystery. A dark force pulling galaxies apart, causing the entire universe to expand. It's infuriating! And awesome."

He grins. "And you're gonna find out."

"I don't know. I want to be up there." I point toward the sky. "Most astronomy- and cosmology-based research is done on Earth. You don't need to get in a rocket to observe how dark matter affects the gravitational forces of distant galaxies." I swallow. "My dad was a theoretical physicist— you probably know that."

Ben runs a finger over one of the pineapples on my knee, and I like that very much. "I do, yes."

He's gone and I can feel it, like my space helmet's been ripped right off my head. Someone at the funeral said Dad was dancing with neutrinos now. I think they were trying to help.

"We had a plan," I say. "He was going to do all the research down here—subatomic particle stuff, you know—and I would be up there and fill in the blanks. They've got an instrument on the International Space Station right now that's hunting cosmic rays. It's called the Alpha Magnetic Spectrometer. It's measuring the subatomic particles in space, but also studying the Big Bang, formation of the universe—all the good stuff. It hasn't found anything my dad would consider significant yet, but it—or an instrument like it—might. Very few people have the ISS on their radar for dark matter research right now, but in ten years—who knows? If we could somehow get an axion magnetic detector on the ISS, that could really be something, but you need such a large magnetic field, and obviously that could endanger the ISS itself. So that might not be a viable option. Anyway, I figure that someone on the ISS has to make sure dark matter instruments are working properly and perhaps work with some of the data. Maybe by the time I apply they'll need me. Or a pilot, anyway."

"A pilot."

"To fly whatever Nate builds me to get to the ISS."

He stares at me. "I'm trying really hard not to be intimidated right now. Did you just tell me you're going to be studying the nature of the universe while also flying the rockets themselves?"

I bite back a smile. "I have a better chance of being an astronaut candidate if I've got naval aviation experience."

"Like . . . a fighter pilot?"

"Well, not *just* a fighter pilot. I'll hopefully get to be a test pilot, and obviously I'll do what Nate's doing—astronautical engineering. Dad says . . . *said* . . . I can sneak in a PhD in physics, but I don't know."

"Okay. Wait. You want to *test* the planes? Correct me if I'm wrong: That does involve forcing a fighter jet into uncontrolled spins at, like, Mach Two, and then hoping you can get them back under control before you land, right?"

I nod. "Mach Three, some of them. Depends on the model. It's not really much crazier than strapping yourself to a bomb and flying into space."

He laughs. "I dig your logic. Although, I feel the need to point out that there's no danger in your equation."

"Danger isn't a variable in any equation—the math would never check out. It's unquantifiable."

This makes him smile, which makes me consider the possibility that certain kinds of dangers, especially ones involving manga-character doppelgängers, actually *are* quantifiable.

"What's *your* favorite thing you don't know?" I ask.

"Right now? You."

I cover my face and groan.

"Too slick?" he says, and I can hear his smile getting bigger.

"Yes."

"Fair enough."

Nate should be back. I have a sneaking suspicion he's taking twenty years to look for chips on purpose.

I stop covering my face and look up at Ben, and looking at him makes me feel like I'm back at space camp, in the tank, weightless, all the air sucked out. But also like my feet are on solid ground.

"You know what's really crazy?" I say, because I can't stop myself, because I want to tell this mystery in front of me about the biggest mystery of all.

He scoots closer. "Hm?"

"That all the matter and energy that formed the whole universe as we know it was once smaller than a marble. The size of an *atom*. Doesn't it make your mind COMBUST imagining holding the ENTIRE universe in the palm of your hand?"

Maybe I would say more, except my eyes hit his eyes and for a second we just stare at each other.

"I'm in so much trouble," he breathes.

I blink. "What?"

Glass shatters in the kitchen, and I'm on my feet in a nanosecond as my sister's angry snarl cuts through the swinging door.

"Jesus *Christ*, Nate, get *off* me."

I bolt.

Toward my sister, away from—oh god, what just happened? What is *happening*?

I push open the door and stare. A supernova has exploded on the kitchen floor, an eruption of waves of hair and a red dress and bourbon and shards of glass, skin and flecks of chipped black nail polish.

Nate is staring down at Nah as though she is an equation he can't possibly work out, and maybe she is. My sister is a mystery I will never solve.

"Nah." My voice is faraway, tinny.

I took the pills away. How is this happening?

I can't move. I need to. I should. Mom would be on the floor already, cleaning her up, fixing this, but it's like someone's put weights in my shoes.

Gravity is a bitch.

She looks up at me. "I wish I were you."

Nah lets out a laugh like the lady on the boardwalk at home who sells incense and tells everyone she's Cleopatra reincarnated and also she knows who killed JFK and do we by any chance have some weed we can give her because she just needs a little something.

"You think you know everything, Mae, but you don't know—you don't *know* . . ." She breaks down, hacking sobs that echo throughout the kitchen. "People like me, like Mom—we're never enough. That counselor at the clinic lied, she lied, because we're not, we're *not*."

"What are you talking about?" I lean down, just outside the puddle of bourbon and miserable sister. "Nah, please. I know this is the most horrible thing, but you can't do this, you have to stop, you have to . . . to find *something* to keep breathing for—"

"I'm not like you, Mae," she says, her eyes so bright with fury that they look like the Helix Nebula in infrared: two bursts of green fire. Dad's eyes.

"I can't just forget them, put my head down, and get on with all my grand plans for life—"

"*Forget* them?"

I shoot up and, oh, that fight-or-flight response kicks in and I want both at the same time—how dare she, and maybe she's right, maybe I'm a terrible daughter, but Dad said, he always said I had to never give up and—

Nate pushes off the counter and gets in Nah's face. "Not cool, cuz."

I am being flooded with chemicals and my body responds to the increased adrenaline by shaking uncontrollably, because I thought I'd worked the problem, gotten us here, away from the pills on the board-walk, but our problems have followed us and now I don't even have Micah to help, and danger *is* in the equation, an X that ensures no matter how many experiments you conduct, it will never come out right. This addiction, this sister—how can I solve problems with variables like these?

Something warm and solid rests between my shoulder blades—Ben's hand. For just a second, there's quiet. I breathe.

It was so nice in the living room. Fixing Nate's project. Talking to Ben. I didn't realize I needed a break from my sister, from her weather system, until I had it. Every time I'm with Nah these days, it feels like liftoff will never happen. Like we'll both be grounded by the wave forever.

Nah starts to hoist herself up, and Nate reaches for her arms, but she pushes him away. "I don't need a fucking audience."

"Then maybe stop giving such heart-stopping performances," he says gently.

"The glass," I say. "You could get hurt, Nah."

"Well, at least I'm not dead at the bottom of the ocean."

I let out a breath. Ben's hand moves softly between my shoulder blades, up and down.

My sister's eyes fill, her face falling like an autumn leaf, beautiful—done. "I'm sorry."

"It's okay." I glance at the floor, sticky and littered with glass. "I'll clean up."

"I'm sorry," she says again.

I nod. "I know."

We watch her go. She floats away like space debris into the darkness of the hallway, up the stairs. Gone.

Nate grabs a mop from a closet by the pantry and starts filling a bucket with water. "It's a good thing my parents are still out. Mom would have blamed herself for this, I bet."

Aunt Nora has been at a loss, I think, when it comes to Nah. Annie died before she ever got close to being a teenager, and Nate's always been easygoing. For a minute, I almost tell Nate the truth about Nah, the pills and rehab last spring and all of it, but I can't. Mom and Dad were always clear: It's Nah's story to tell. But what if it's all starting again? I want her to be okay, and I don't want my aunt and uncle to regret taking us in.

"Your parents have been amazing. Nah's just having a hard time. I'll make sure this never happens again. I don't want us to be a burden—"

Nate glares at me. "Hush. *Burden.* You're ours. We don't want you anywhere but here." He glances at Ben, raises his eyebrows. "Do we?"

I *knew* he was purposefully staying out of the living room all that time.

"No," Ben says. "Who would make sure you don't fail out of MIT?"

He squeezes my shoulder as Nate cackles, then steps into the center of the kitchen and leans down to begin picking up glass.

I move to join Ben, but he holds up a hand. "I got it."

"You don't have to—"

"Mae, let the guy earn his keep," Nate says. "By the way, I figured out what's wrong with my plane's design."

"What's that?" I grab a broom and the dustpan.

"We don't have enough lift," he says. "You can have all the thrust you want, but that forward momentum won't get your plane off the runway or your rocket off the launchpad without proper lift."

"How do you get lift?" I cross to the puddle in the center of the kitchen and lean down to pick up the largest shards of glass.

Ben looks up at me, black lashes flicking over deep brown eyes. "By figuring out what's dragging you down."

i wish I didn't look like my dead mother.

Window on Train Car Door
The C Line
Boston

14

Hannah

I wait until we've been at school for two days before I start talking to the maybe-dealers. The headaches, my bones hurting—I can't hold out much longer. Withdrawal is probably worse than death. At least after you die, it doesn't hurt anymore.

They're not hard to spot. The dealers. They look grungier than everyone else at this fancy private school that my aunt's insisting on because Nate went here.

They're always looking over their shoulders. Their eyes have secrets. I go for the cutest one first because why not? Also, he's in my dumb-person math class.

I find him after school, leaning against the flagpole. Waiting. For someone like me.

"Hey." I stop in front of him.

"Hi." His eyes narrow, suspicious.

"Math class, right? Algebra Two with Stephens?"

He just looks at me. Right. I shouldn't expect my dealer to be sober.

"I'm Hannah. New girl. From LA?"

"Hi, Hannah New Girl From LA."

Fuck this guy. "This is the part where you tell me your name."

He smirks. "Drew."

"Okay, Drew, I'm not one for small talk, so this is the deal: I have a wad of cash in my pocket and I'd really love some pharmaceuticals. So what do you have and how much is it?"

"Why are you asking me?" A sliver of fear catches in his eyes. Good. I don't like his upper-hand vibe.

"Lucky guess. Now, are you holding or not?"

Drugs were so much easier to find in LA. All I had to do was walk two steps down the sidewalk from my door and I'd be on the Venice boardwalk, the real Boulevard of Broken Dreams.

"*If* I was holding—and I'm not saying I am—why would I sell to someone I don't know?" Drew says. "In case you aren't aware, Hannah New Girl From LA, buying or selling drugs here will get you expelled. They have a zero-tolerance policy at Saint Francis. And I'm on scholarship."

"I know the drill." What a little prick. Fucking standing there, toying with me. Even drug dealers are patriarchal assholes. It's always dudes that are holding, and they often get more than just money in exchange for their wares. Is that what he wants? "Look, I'll go ask someone else. Whatever."

I turn to go—one step, two—

"Wait."

I smile and turn around. "Yes?"

"What do you want?"

"Percs. Vicodin."

Oxy. Oh boy, do I want Oxy. But I don't deserve to feel *that* good. Although—

"I ran out of Vicodin. I have Percs. And, before you ask, I don't sell cotton to people I don't know. That shit's intense."

"Okay, whatever. I'll take what you have. How much?" I see Mae come out the front door, talking to some girl. *Shit.*

"Five for five milligrams, ten for ten. I recommend the ten—it's a great high. Five will get you there, though. Just not as quickly."

"I don't need to be schooled on what will get me high. Look, I have to go." I start backing away. "Can I get it from you tomorrow?"

"I might not have any tomorrow. But, whatever, it's your deal."

"I don't want my sister to see," I say, nodding toward Mae. "She's . . . not like . . . us."

His eyebrow raises just a tad. "Us?"

Losers.

"She's a good girl."

His mouth turns up a little. "Well, I'm certainly not one of those." His eyes flick up to mine, and I force myself to hold his gaze. "Tomorrow at lunch," he finally says. "Under the bleachers near the baseball diamond."

Diamond. Perfect.

I suddenly feel a rush of gratitude for this asshole. "All right. Thanks."

When I get to Mae, she's looking over my shoulder, craning her neck to get a better look at Drew.

"Who was that?" she asks.

"Dude from my math class. I forgot to write down the homework."

"He looks like the guy from that vampire show you like—the one with the brothers. The bad brother." She bumps her hip against mine. "Ohhhh, I'm telling Micah."

We're trying to do this, to be like we used to. But it feels like we're reading lines in a play. Even though I apologized for being a mess the other night, breaking that bottle in the kitchen, I'm still so mad at her for taking my pills.

I smile. "Shut up."

I can always not meet Drew tomorrow, just forget I ever had that conversation by the flagpole. Make another quit attempt. Come clean to Aunt Nora and Uncle Tony and Nate. I know telling would be the first step in really trying to get sober.

But then I remember my parents are dead and my boyfriend is on the other side of the country and also that I'm a fucking loser piece-of-shit junkie.

"What's wrong?" Mae asks.

Everything. Obviously.

"Nothing," I say. "Why?"

She shrugs. "Besides the obvious? I know you don't like it here. School. Boston."

"I'm cool, Mae. Just . . . don't breathe down my neck so much, okay? I'm a big girl. I can take care of myself."

"I know," she says, her voice quiet.

Fuck. Nothing comes out right anymore.

"I'm sorry," I say. "I just . . . you know. It's hard."

She takes a breath.

The kind before you jump into the deep end of the pool.

"Nora thinks we should talk to someone. A therapist."

"Oh God," I say. "That's a quick way to make us feel shittier. The last thing I want to do is talk about it. Any of it."

"It could help, Nah," she says in a small voice. "With . . . everything. You know. The pills—"

"Is this voluntary?" I ask.

"Not so much. No. I suppose you could go on a hunger strike or something, but she says we need to talk to someone. Who it is—that's our choice."

. ● . ●

When we get home, my fears are confirmed.

"So I have a list of the therapists in our area," Nora says.

"I'll look at it later," I say. "I'm really tired."

The next day, I make up an excuse to be late for lunch with Mae and her new friends, all confirmed nerds, and hurry over to the bleachers by the baseball field.

Drew is already there. He's wearing a black hoodie with a puffy vest, ripped jeans, a beanie. Total drug dealer chic.

"I kinda thought you might not show," he says, keeping his hands in his pockets.

"Well, I'm here."

"How'd you know I'd be able to hook you up?"

"You just look . . ."

"Shady?"

Most of the guys here go for the *I'm-applying-to-Harvard* look: dock-siders even though it's too cold to go boating, khakis, polos.

"Pretty much, yeah." I hand him a hundred bucks. "I'll take ten tens."

Money was never a problem for me, for anyone in my family. My life-long savings did get low in the worst months, but then my parents died and everyone felt bad and Aunt Nora put a lot of money in both my and Mae's accounts. Supposedly to get Boston wardrobes, since we're basically in Siberia and you can't wear jean shorts and flip-flops in places with negative degrees. When you're a privileged junkie, it means you don't have to stoop so low as to steal from the people you love or do all the things girls can do to get their fix. I'm the luckiest unlucky girl I know.

His eyebrows go up a little. "I've got fives if you—"

"Ten is good."

"Ten it is." He pockets the money, then takes out a bottle.

"Hold out your hand," he says.

I do and he pours ten blue little circles on my palm, then one more.

"A little something extra for my new customer," he says.

"Thanks."

"So, you're from LA?" he says, following me as I start for the caf.

"What do you care?"

He shrugs. "Just making conversation."

"I give you five stars for customer service, okay? You can go . . . wher-ever you go at lunch."

"I was just wondering what a nice girl like you is doing buying opiates."

"First, I'm not a nice girl. Second, it's none of your business."

"Fair enough."

We walk in silence for a while, and I can't stand it.

"My parents died in that tsunami in Malaysia. Both of them."

I see the weight of my truth settle on him. But instead of getting awk-ward, he looks at me—really looks at me.

"That is one of the most fucked-up things the universe could do to someone," he says.

The absolute most right thing to say. I'd give him six stars for that.

I nod. "Yeah."

"I shouldn't have sold it to you," he says quietly.

"Jesus. Don't give me your pity—trust me, I have enough of it. I just need something to get me through senior year. That's all. And if you tell anyone I told you—"

"That would be a violation of doctor-patient confidentiality," he says, with a half smile.

I give him a long look. "Are you actually a nice guy?"

"Total hardened criminal. But I have a soft spot for brunettes."

"My hair is actually black. And I have a boyfriend. In LA. In college, actually." It feels important that he know because he's flirting with me and I suddenly feel guilty because I want to flirt back. I miss Micah so much.

Drew whistles. "A college boy. Are your dates at the library?"

"Very funny." I point to the caf. "I'm gonna grab some food before sixth period."

He nods. "I'll see you around, Hannah."

I head to the bathroom and don't make eye contact with anyone as I hide in a stall. I gulp down a little blue pill with some water from one of the metal bottles Mom sold at her studio. It says ALL WHO WANDER ARE NOT LOST. This water bottle doesn't know shit.

I wonder if Mom and Dad can see me here, now. They'd be so disappointed. Ashamed, maybe. My eyes fill and I press my hands against my lips to keep the sob in, to hide it behind the gossip and the makeup sharing and the *I need a tampon*-ing of Saint Francis's largest female-identifying bathroom. I'm the last to leave when the bell rings, when it's quiet and no one will talk to me.

It doesn't take long for the Percocet to kick in. It's much stronger than Vicodin, and I went straight to my old dose, even though I haven't worked up to it. Rookie mistake, but I don't regret it because halfway through math I'm in my happy place. But remodeled. Warmer and fuzzier. Drew looks over at me a few times, and I smile, actually *smile* at him. I have no idea what's happening in class—there's a lot of shit I don't understand on the board. The teacher calls Drew *Mr. Nolan*, and I have fun making sounds in my head with his last name. Drew *Nooooo—laaaaan. Nohhhhhh. Lllllllllannnnn.* When the bell rings, I float out the door.

"You only took one, right?" Drew asks quietly as he comes up to me.

I nod. "I'm a lightweight. And you're a very nosy drug dealer."

"Good customer service, remember?"

He puts his hand on my elbow and guides me away from the pushing and shoving, from the hordes of people. A life raft in this wave.

"How good?"

He gives me a sideways glance. "What do you mean?"

"Like, good enough to ditch with me good?"

He hesitates for just a second. "Yeah, okay."

And, just like that, I'm skipping out on the rest of the school day with Saint Francis's resident drug dealer.

my father is a liar.

Hannah

**D**rew grabs my hand and leads me toward the closest exit. We're in the neighborhood across the street from Saint Francis by the time the bell rings. I notice we're still holding hands, but I don't move away. It feels good to have some kind of contact. I am the girl that still laid her head in her mother's lap when she was seventeen.

Also, his hand feels like warm sand—or maybe I'm just full of warm sand.

"My head feels like an hourglass," I say. "Like . . ." I stop and I show him. The sand that's falling, so slowly from the crown of my head, down, down. "You know?"

"I'm glad to see my product's working so well."

"Five stars."

He nods toward a Ford Fusion that's seen better days.

"This is precisely why I don't park in the student lot," he says.

"A good Knight of Wands move."

He laughs. "Um, okay, whatever that means. I like the knight part."

"Your cards. Tarot."

"Ah. Cool. So, where to?"

"I don't know. I usually go to the beach. But the beach here sucks. What do you recommend?"

"How about the Common?"

"All right."

Boston's most famous park. Right in the middle of the city, where we can hide in plain sight.

"Didn't they kill people there?" I ask as he starts up the car.

"Yeah. Public hangings."

"Fuck."

I sink into the seat and close my eyes. "Your car smells like ass lemons."

"Air freshener. Sorry. My cousin is always borrowing it and smoking his crappy cigarettes in here."

I peek at him. "You don't smoke?"

"No. That shit kills you. And they're wicked gross."

This is funny. It makes me lauggghhhhhhhh. My drug dealer is kind of a square.

"Says. The. Drug. Dealer."

It gets hot, really hot, and I start taking things off. "Can you roll down the windows?"

"On the door next to you."

I look at the knob-thingy. "This car is so *old*."

"Hey, it's a car. You wanna take the T?"

The thought of getting on the subway is, like, so horrible. People eating food. All that perfume. Talking on their cell phones. The way it makes those sharp turns and I can never keep my balance.

"God. No."

"Okay, then. Show Sunny some respect."

"You named your car."

"Fuck yeah, I named her. She's my pride and joy."

I smile at him, then pet the dashboard. "Good girl, Sunny."

"Oh my God. She's not a *dog*."

The look on his face. I burst out laughing again.

"I'll be here all night," Drew says.

I stare out the window as he drives us into the center of the city, not too far from Saint Francis. The buildings here are beautiful, like we're speeding through a picture book: brick with elegant molding; old, narrow streets.

I stop talking. I don't know if Drew's picking up my vibe or if he's normally quiet. He's got a local college station on—Emerson, probably—and it feels right, somehow, to be in a car with a drug dealer while Ben Howard sings along with his guitar.

Drew parks on a side street, then jumps out and comes around to help me.

"A gentleman drug dealer, eh?" I say when he opens the door.

He gives a bow. "At your service."

I follow him down the narrow street and out onto Tremont, past another old church. The sand in my head falls, falls. Boston is *so much better* when you're high.

"This place must have more churches than anywhere else," I say as we pass a large stone one. Puritans, man. "Except maybe Rome. Have you been?"

He laughs. "I'm a Saint Francis charity case, remember? The farthest I've been is an ill-advised trip to drop off product in Brooklyn."

I forget sometimes that my family has money, that things are easy for us. Except the staying-together-and-alive part.

"I've never been to Brooklyn," I say.

A massive gust of wind blows past us, and I shriek a little. Drew laughs.

"Gotta get your East Coast sea legs," he says.

"It's fucking freezing!"

He laughs. "Oh, Hannah. It's only the beginning of October. You just wait until February."

We start across the wide expanse of Boston Common, which is filled with people even though it's already cold as hell. I shiver, and he takes off his coat without a word and drapes it around my shoulders.

"You don't have to—"

"Shut up," he says with a soft smile.

"Thanks."

His warmth seeps into me, caught in the fibers of the wool coat.

I wonder what Micah's doing. He didn't call me back last night—the first time that's ever happened.

"It's okay, though," I say.

"What?"

"Am I talking out loud?"

"Yes."

"Oh. Never mind." I reach out my hands as the sun blazes out from behind a cloud and gives my face a big, warm kiss, so I kiss it back. "I am so much smarter than my sister!"

"Oh?"

"Yes. *Yes.* She's fucking sweating it out at that jail school place Saint whatever and *I* am in Boston Common with *you* and we know the secret of everything." I smile at him. "Mom told me I should never wear sensible shoes or business casual."

He looks down at my canvas tennis shoes, no socks.

"You took her advice."

The sad, it just swoops in and whispers, *Your mother is dead*, and I can't breathe.

"Hey," Drew says. "Hannah, hey. Let's do my favorite thing. Yeah? It'll be nice. I promise."

"She's dead."

"I know." He takes my arm. "I know," he says again, very soft, but not in a patronizing grief voice. He is actually *really* listening. Hearing me. No one ever does that.

We pass a pretzel cart and just the thought of it makes me want to hurl. A guy is selling balloons. Little kids on a school trip, all connected to one another on harnesses, like some kind of primary-color chain gang.

When we reach the grass, Drew pulls me toward the green blades. "Lie down. But close your eyes."

I lie down. I close my eyes. The grass feels prickly.

The sand falls faster, faster. The sun is warm, and all the sounds, it's all happening.

"It's all happening," I whisper.

Bright warm light, an opening wider and wider, I open, my chest filling with the sun, and oh my God, how did I not see this before, see all of this?

"It's all *one*," I say. "Holy shit, I AM the walrus. They put this secret in the song! *You are me and we are all together*—fuck. No wonder Yoko fell for him. John Lennon, man. John *fucking* Lennon. Wow."

I feel Drew squeeze my hand.

Everyone's peak looks different. Mine is like what Mae says being in a space camp gravity tank is like.

Z

E

R

O

Gravity.

But then I feel it go. After a while. Like bubbles popping. Such pretty sky water. Then: gone.

I open my eyes and turn to Drew. He reaches up and holds a hand over me, blocking the sun so I can see him better.

Mae's right: He kind of does look like a bad vampire.

"Peaked?" he asks.

"Yeah."

"Good?"

"So good. Thank you."

"My pleasure."

The sun goes away and it's immediately so much colder.

"Come on," he says. "Let's warm up."

Drew helps me stand and we cross back to the path and I don't even care that I'm leaning against him, I'm so tired.

I sigh. "I think my high is gone."

He reaches into his pocket and hands me another pill. "This one's on me. Just a five. A little top-up."

"Thanks."

In twenty minutes, I'll be me again.

"What about you?" I ask.

"That parking spot is only good for three hours. I have to take care of Sunny. You go ahead. I'm good." We near a pretzel cart and he stops, grabs his wallet. "You hungry?"

"God, no. Food and opiates do not mix."

"Just one for me," he says to the guy as we walk up. "Salt, please."

Please.

"What kind of drug dealer are you?" I ask once we've left pretzel guy behind.

"What do you mean?"

"You say *please.*"

Drew has a shy smile, and it's cute.

"I mean, you don't have to be a dick to deal."

"Tell me, *please*, how does someone become a dealer?"

He shrugs, pulls off a bit of pretzel. We walk along a path and it's nice. Walking. Being in the sun.

"It just kind of . . . happened. After I came to Saint Francis, people started asking me to hook them up. They figured since I came from Dorchester, I'd have a way to get product."

The neighborhood Mom grew up in, when she was really little. Rough around the edges, she called it. Dad was the one with the *Mayflower* money, but what Mom's family did, getting out of Greece and making a life in America even though they hardly spoke the language—that was always more impressive to me.

"So you had a way to get what they wanted, or you, like, signed up with a cartel?"

He laughs. "My cousin has a thing going with pills."

"Must be good money. That's why you do it?"

He shrugs. "Yeah. Mostly. Rich kids at Saint Francis are gonna buy this shit from someone, right?"

"Like me."

"You're not like them."

I roll my eyes. "Whatever."

"Hey," he says. I look at him. "You're not. Like them. They just want to party. You . . . you know. There are extenuating circumstances."

"I told you, I don't want your pity, Drew."

"You don't have it."

I reach out and pick a thick grain of salt from his pretzel, rub it between my fingers. I miss the smell of the ocean.

"You said you *mostly* do it for the money," I say. "Why else?"

"Are you always this curious?"

I think about that. "It depends on the thing. Or the person. You're very interesting."

"I am?"

"Obviously. For one, you don't wear boat shoes." I smile. "But I think you're stalling. So. Other than money, why do you deal?"

He shrugs. "It's nice to have a . . . a *role*. You know. Like, I'm not a jock or a nerd or whatever."

"That's just sad, Drew."

He balls up the paper from his pretzel and lobs it into a nearby can. "Someone's gotta provide the good times. It might as well be me."

My phone buzzes—a text from Mae. School must have just gotten out.

"My sister's checking up on me." I shove the phone back into my pocket. "I'll make up a good story before I get home."

"She's not into this scene, huh?"

I snort. "No way. She's crazy smart—wants to be an astronaut, like, literally a rocket scientist. My dad taught physics, so . . ."

"Wow. I don't think I've met anyone that wants to be an astronaut who's over the age of, like, ten."

"Right?" We veer toward the Public Garden, past rows of red and orange trees. The fall colors are so bright—straight out of Dr. Seuss. "What do you want to be when you grow up?" I ask. "Pharmaceutical industry bigwig?"

"Nah. A respectable citizen," he says, with that half smile again. "I like to draw. Maybe something with that." He looks away. "Though who am I kidding? I'll probably just end up joining the union like my dad, working construction."

"That would be a waste of your entrepreneurial talents."

He laughs. "What about you?"

"No idea."

I'd planned to live with my parents until Micah and I saved enough money to move out on our own. I thought I'd just figure life out as I went along. Now that I don't have them, it suddenly seems really important that I have a Plan. I can't mooch off of my aunt and uncle forever. I can't work part-time at Mom's yoga studio, like we were talking about.

"I just want . . ." I glance at him. "Never mind."

"Nu-uh. You just want what?"

"My sister has all these huge, planet-sized goals. I think it'd be nice to be like my mom. She taught yoga, had us, made soup, kicked around in her garden. Just had a life."

"Sounds good to me," he says.

"It was all about the Something Else for her. Finding . . . the source, or whatever, every day. Connecting to it. To us. Like we were this big spirit soup she was making." I frown. "But for that to work, you need other people. People you can depend on."

A husband who doesn't fucking leave you for his hot young research assistant, for one.

"Your sister?"

"Hard to depend on someone when they're in outer space."

I stumble a little—it's hard to walk and float at the same time—and he reaches out to steady me.

"Thanks."

I lean into Drew, just a little. He smells like tea tree. I take a deep breath and he laughs softly.

"Are you . . . smelling me?"

I nod. "I love tea tree."

"Yeah, my ex got me this bougie soap and I'm kind of hooked on it."

"It's nice." I take a deep breath of cold, fresh air. It clears my head more than I want it to.

"Do you have a girlfriend, Drew? Or just an ex with good taste in soap?"

"Nope. Just the ex. Why?"

"You're cute and nice and have wonderful little pills. What's not to like?"

"What, indeed?"

"I'm not hitting on you," I say.

"I know. College boyfriend—got it."

We pass under an enormous tree that's beginning to turn, bright red and orange creeping onto the leaves, like spilled paint.

"We don't get this in Cali," I say. One of the leaves floats down and Drew reaches out and grabs it, then holds it out to me. Bright red.

"A genuine Boston souvenir," he says.

I smile, take it. Some things are pretty when they die.

"I love it," I say. "Thank you."

"It's just a leaf," he says, laughing.

"Don't be mean to my leaf. She's beautiful."

He runs a finger over one of my leaf's dark veins. "She is."

We start walking again. "You miss LA?" he asks.

I nod. "I mostly hate it here. No offense."

"Hey, if I had to leave paradise, I'd be pretty pissed, too." He frowns a little. "So you're going back? After graduation?"

"My boyfriend and I . . . We had this plan. I'm supposed to move in with him. Next summer."

Drew raises his eyebrows, two dark slashes. Very dramatic, those eyebrows. I like them.

"Supposed to?"

I shrug. "We'll see."

It's all mixed up now. He wasn't at the clinic, but he was there, almost every second, after the wave. And I miss him. But I also don't. It's nice not to have someone look at you with a question in their eyes all the time.

"What about your sister?"

"She'll be in school. Annapolis. MIT if she has bad luck. Harvard. Whatever."

"Damn."

"Yeah. We aren't as close as we used to be. The older we got, the more—she's like this intergalactic being, you know? And she's always on my ass. Watching me. I don't know. I love her. She's just—if you ever meet her, you'll know what I'm talking about. And then our parents . . . It's all fucked. Just fucked."

"I bet it's a lot to process."

"A lot. Yeah." I shake my head. "I can't talk about this anymore. It's killing my buzz."

"Well, we wouldn't want that." He steers me toward the side of the path. "Come meet my friends."

And I get nervous until my eyes catch a line of little bronze statues on the ground at my feet—ducks.

I crouch down to pet one of them.

"Hi," I say to them. I look up at Drew. "They're so cute."

"These guys are famous." Drew squats down beside me. "Ever read the kids' book *Make Way for Ducklings*?"

I can almost hear Mom as she turns the page, making the *quack* sounds of the ducks. Mae and I are in matching nightgowns, our toenails painted pink. I nod, feeling teary all of a sudden. I stand, blinking hard so they don't fall.

Drew slips his hand into mine. "Jesus, your hands are freezing."

I shrug. "We don't need gloves in LA."

I can tell he knows I'm about to cry, and it's nice that he doesn't get weird about that.

He tugs on my hand. "Come on, let's warm you up."

I should take my hand out of his, but I don't. It's so *warm*. We hurry through the gardens across from the Common, but I stop as we reach a bronze angel statue tucked into a corner at the far end of the gardens. She's in the middle of a fountain, on a pedestal, holding a basket. Her wings cut into the bright blue of the sky.

"Oh," I breathe.

Something about her fills me up. Her face is so calm. Serene. For a minute, that peace washes over me, too, smoothing over the anger and sadness. The Judgment card in the tarot. Waking the dead.

Drew's hand tightens around mine, and when I look over, he's watching me with the strangest expression.

"What?" I say.

He clears his throat. "Nothing."

His eyes are gray with little flecks of gold, which somehow the charcoal beanie he's wearing brings out. I suddenly have an almost overwhelming urge to kiss him, to have his arms around me, to be held, and I know it's only because I'm needy, but it freaks me out, how close I am to rushing through the space between us.

I let go of his hand. "Coffee?"

"Er. Right." He puts that hand to the back of his neck and looks down for a minute. "Yeah. There's a Dunkies on Newbury."

"What is the obsession with Dunkin' Donuts in this place?"

It seems like there's one on every corner. Not that I'm complaining.

He grins, and it looks good on him. "We Bostonians have very discerning taste."

I follow him down a street lined with brick town houses that have been turned into fancy boutiques and upscale stores that feature expensive winter coats in the windows. Halloween decorations abound. A few Christmas displays are already up. It's the loneliest thing, maybe, knowing that this year will be the first one we don't bake cookies with Mom or help Dad put lights around the tree.

The Dunkies is in what once would have been a garden apartment, tucked beneath a toy store. We get our coffees "regular," which is Bostonian for lots of cream and sugar. Then we head over to Copley Square and sit on the steps of the library, which looks like it should be in Paris or Berlin, maybe, with its statues and decorative iron lamps. I stretch my legs out and sigh as the warmth of the coffee burns my hands, as that pretty little Perc finally kicks in. More mellow. Takes the edge off. I have to remember how functional I can be on fives. Tens are like, *Byyyyye, world.*

"Better?" he asks.

I nod. "I feel warm and fuzzy again. Thank you."

"You're very welcome."

"What do you do when you're not selling drugs or ditching with me?" I ask.

"I play guitar," he says. "Read. Go out."

"A drug dealer who reads for fun?"

"I'm not *just* a drug dealer," he says.

"What do you like to read?"

"Fantasy. *Lord of the Rings, Game of Thrones,* that sort of thing."

I raise an eyebrow. "You love *Harry Potter,* don't you?"

"Hell yeah, I do. I have a Gryffindor scarf."

"Not Slytherin?"

"The Pottermore quiz doesn't lie: I know it's hard to believe, but I'm one of the good guys."

I think I kind of believe him.

"I'm a Hufflepuff," I say.

He laughs, soft. "I like Hufflepuffs. They're sweet."

"You just don't know me yet."

"Guess I'll have to change that." I can hear the smile in his voice, but I can't look at him because I like looking at him too much, I think. "So, Hannah From LA, what does a Hufflepuff do when she's not ditching school and popping pills?"

"I used to hang out with my boyfriend. Go to the beach. Work at a coffeehouse near the boardwalk. Yoga. Tarot."

"So I read fantasy, but you live it," he says.

"I guess so." I smile a little. "Maybe I have magical psychic powers."

"I'd love to see those in action."

"I'll read your cards sometime."

"It's a deal," he says.

The square between the library and Trinity Church is filled with people. Tourists, maybe, but lots of locals hurrying around with briefcases and backpacks.

"Everyone here seems like they have somewhere to be," I say. "Why do they try so hard?" I watch them go, go, go. "It clearly doesn't make them happy."

"East Coast hustle," he says. "Big dreams, big money. They're trying to get to happy." He shakes his head. "Like it's a place. But they're trying to get out of the cold, too. Not like in LA, huh?"

"I lived five seconds from the beach. You don't hurry in Venice, unless it's to catch a wave."

"You surf?"

"My boyfriend does."

Micah with his shaggy sun-bleached hair and tan skin. The thought of him makes me anxious.

"Do you think your boyfriend would be mad that you're hanging out with some dude who sold you pills?"

"He trusts me," I say.

"What's he like?"

I smile a little. "Fun. Pretty chill—surfer, you know. I don't know how I would have gotten through the past month without him. He and my dad were really close, but he kept it together, you know? For me. He's loyal like that." I take a long sip of my coffee. "Usually."

"Usually?"

I shrug. "It's a long story. What happened with you and your ex?"

He grimaces a little, rubs his palm against the back of his neck. "Just too different. We broke up at the end of last year."

"Miss her?"

He frowns. "Sometimes. But not really. We weren't right for each other. She's the captain of the soccer team, goes to church."

"Were you dealing at the time?"

"Yeah. That's part of why it was never gonna work out," he says. "But I also felt like . . . I couldn't be *me* with her. Like I had to be this version of me she wanted, but the real me—she didn't want that." He runs a finger around the rim of his cup. "I want to be all in with someone. You know?"

And that's the thing about Micah. He's not all in. Not anymore. And I don't think I am, either.

I nod. "Yeah."

We get up and head back toward the car. We're waiting to cross the street when I notice a woman with a tiny belly rest her palm against it, almost protectively. Something about that gesture stops me cold. Then it hits me, a sudden knowing, like the kind Mom used to get. My body floods with heat, and I'm so angry I can hardly breathe.

I grab Drew's arm because for a second, it feels like the earth opens up beneath my feet and if I don't hold on to something, it'll pull me down.

"Hannah? What's wrong?"

There's a reason we can't wait.

Rebecca Chen, when I met her at the funeral, before I read the emails: resting her hand on her belly and saying, *I'm feeling a little under the weather.*

"She's pregnant." The crosswalk signal goes green, but I just stand there. "Holy fucking *shit.*"

"Who?"

"My dad's . . ." I don't know what to call her, but I look up at Drew, and he gets it.

His eyes widen. "Shit."

And just like that, things get worse.

16

Mae

ISS Location: Low-Earth Orbit
Earth Date: 18 October
Earth Time (EST): 13:05

The way to survive space is to keep asking yourself, again and again: What is the next thing that can kill me?

It's not paranoia. It's good common sense. Chris Hadfield, ace astronaut, swears by this question. It's what's saved him countless times in space.

By always thinking about what could potentially end you, you're staying one step ahead of death. Sure, it will find you eventually—that's just the law of nature. But it doesn't have to be today.

The problem is, of course, that there are a lot of things that can kill you.

Faulty jets in flat spins going Mach 3.

Waves.

Your sister shutting you out of her life entirely.

Nah hides in her room all day, and she purposefully avoids eye contact with me or wears dark glasses so I can't check her pupils. I don't need to. Every time I see my sister, she is on something. I wouldn't have known the difference before because I don't do stuff like that—however, this past year has been an excellent education in drug addiction. But I can't talk to her about it. There's a wall between us now.

I don't know how to tell her that she's all I have without it sounding like a trick to get her sober. All that's left. But we aren't in the same orbit, anymore.

My sister spends most of her time in bed, curled onto her side. She thinks I don't know about the other pills, the new ones, but I do. Her purse was in the hallway after school yesterday, open, and I saw a mini Altoids tin and she hates those mints, so I knew there must be pills in there. I was right. Different pills from the ones I already took. Percocet. I was going to take them, but then Aunt Nora came up and I couldn't. The next time I was in the hallway, the purse was gone.

Where is she getting this Percocet? Dad had Vicodin. Did she steal the pills from my aunt and uncle? Because if she did, they are going to find out, and when they do, they will have to deal with this, and they already have enough to do, taking us in. I mean, that is a real violation, stealing someone's medicine. Uncle Tony said the vodka is missing, in addition to his bottle of bourbon. Nate took the blame for that, but he said it's the last time he'll cover for Nah. And then I had to lie to Nate when he asked what was going on with her, the drinking. I made it sound like it's a new thing.

When I told her I knew about the new pills, the old Hannah—sober Hannah, who is sweet and likes to dance around the kitchen with Mom— was gone, and *this* Hannah told me to mind my own fucking business and leave her the hell alone.

And I can't do that, obviously. But the way I'm going about it is all wrong, I think. I don't want to push her away even more. Then we'll never get back to each other.

Her grief, it's an ocean. It's a wave. Mine, I think, is a glacier, floating in that water. I can feel it in my chest, this ancient, cold mountain of grief. It's all in one place, but you can only see the tip. It's so much bigger than people realize.

I spend most nights on the trampoline in the backyard, staring up at the stars, wrapped in a sleeping bag. It hurts too much to use the telescope Dad bought me for my birthday last year. It seems wrong to look through it without being able to tell him what I see. It's strange, how instinctual it is to search for dead people in the sky. Perhaps it's a biological imperative our psyche needs to make sense out of the sudden disappearance of the people we love. I always knew my parents were not going to live forever. But my brain never told my heart that.

They're not up there, gazing down on me. But I can't stop looking.

I don't remember what it was like being in foster care—I was too young. But my bones know what it's like to be abandoned, and I feel that deep inside, like you'd have to give me an MRI to see it. It's an ache that won't go away.

Everyone I love leaves me. I don't know why.

I wish there were math for that. To figure it out. Or an abandonment supercollider, where you could take all the leaving particles and throw them in there and understand how they work, why they work. Maybe abandonment is necessary for certain species to thrive. Such as astronauts. Being alone is a big part of the job. You can't relocate your whole family to the ISS just because you have a job there. And then, of course, that job site is four hundred kilometers away from most of the human species.

Dad always said that our greatest hardships end up giving birth to our biggest strengths. Maybe everyone leaving me is a sim. Getting me ready for being alone in those fighter jets, alone outside the ISS in my space suit, fixing a broken part. Maybe it's a good thing.

But.

If I don't die on a mission, if I die when I'm old, then I don't think there is any way to prepare for that. I will be all alone because everybody leaves, they all leave, and it will take ages for anyone to find me, to know I'm dead. And the paramedics will open the door of my house, my orphan house, and the smell will be horrific.

This loneliness, a deep pit. A grave.

It's the thing that will kill me next.

I have to work this problem. And this means keeping my sister alive. Because I want to be an old lady with her. I think that would be fun.

By Friday of our second week at school, I decide it's time to stop being afraid of her pushing me away. Better to have her mad at me than be dead from an overdose. I will confront her. If this doesn't work, I will have no choice but to enlist the help of others.

The bell rings at the end of the day, and I find her waiting for me in her usual spot, sitting on the low wall in front of the brick-and-ivy building. She's talking to that vampire-looking boy, and when he sees me, he squeezes Nah's shoulder, then walks off.

"He's the guy from your math class, right?" I say.

"Yep."

"What's his name?"

"Drew."

"Like, Andrew or—"

"Just Drew, Mae."

She tilts her head up, looks at the sky. Blue, not a cloud. My favorite kind of day because it means great visibility for stargazing once it's dark.

"It's good. To make a friend," I say. "Maybe he can come over sometime and—"

"Yeah, no. We're not friends. Just friendly."

It's not fair, her being angry at me. It wouldn't even be fair to be angry at the wave—even though I am—because the ocean can't help what it does when there's an earthquake under it, but if she's going to be irrational, I'd prefer her to channel her anger in that direction.

"Good day?"

Nah's wearing sunglasses, but I can tell she's rolling her eyes. "Sure, Mae. Fantastic."

I sit next to her on the low wall, but I'm quite short, so my feet dangle, whereas her long legs stretch onto the sidewalk. We are quiet. She doesn't move, and so I don't either, which is just as well because what I have to say to her isn't really a conversation for home. It doesn't take long for the students to clear out, and soon it's just us.

"Nah, are you . . ." I never have the right words for her. I know I can't be too exact. That will make her angry. If she's using, she could get mean and call me *professor*, which really annoys me. "What I mean is, right now, are you currently—"

She knows what I'm asking, but makes me say it. "Am I *what*?"

My sister shoots me a truly ferocious look, as though we're not on the same team, the same side, anymore. If she'd take off her sunglasses, I bet her pupils are tiny specks, like extremely distant stars across the galaxy. She's taken a pill today—I don't know what, but it contains opiates. At lunch, all she did the whole time was stare at a spot on the floor. She wouldn't eat—of course, the pills make you nauseous. But people were around, and I couldn't say anything. A high school cafeteria really isn't an appropriate location for an intervention.

"Are you on something?"

There are other ways to express this—the vernacular particular to drug use is quite varied, and you really could write a linguistics paper on it—but I choose this general, less loaded term (*loaded*, of course, being a colloquialism favored by many). The whole situation is crass enough.

"No, I'm not, actually." She stands, towers over me. Her jeans and sweatshirt—one of Micah's old surfer ones—hang too loose on her tall frame. "Are you *trying* to make me feel like a piece of shit?"

"Excuse me?"

"I was just sitting here, waiting to walk to the train with you, and you come up and make all these accusations—"

I throw up my hands. "It's a fair question, Nah!"

"No, it's not. When you don't trust me, it makes me feel like shit. And when I feel like shit, I use. So I need you to trust me, Mae."

This manipulation technique worked on me last year, and it took a family therapist to explain what was happening. My own sister is gaslighting me. Just because I don't get vibes like her and Mom doesn't mean I don't know when someone's lying to me.

"Your logic's faulty," I say. "It sounds like you're reasoning that if you use, it's my fault."

I stand up and I try to take her hand, but she backs away, this tide of her always receding.

"You're lying to me." I say this very nicely, but her reaction is immediate, as if she's cesium—one of the most reactive alkali metals—and I'm water.

There is an explosion.

"Wow. *Wow*, Mae. Well, you know fucking everything about every-thing and I'm just your dumb sidekick, so, yeah, sure, you're probably right. I'm lying to you. That's all I do, right, because I'm an addict and I'm opening my mouth, so I *must be lying*." She throws her backpack on. "I wish I could get tested right now just to see the look on your face when you find out I'm *not fucking high right now* and you're actually, for once, wrong about something."

She's shaking, and her voice carries on the breeze so that her anger surrounds us completely, a whirlpool. I could stop right now, stay on Hannah's good side, apologize. But Mom and Dad would never forgive me if I let her do this to herself. *I* would never forgive me.

"Maybe you're not currently high, as you say, at this moment. But you were at lunch." I step closer to her. "You're lying to me. Every day. I know you are. I know you have more pills."

"And why is that, Mae? Hmmmm. Could you have reached that con-clusion because you stole the ones I did have from *under my goddamn pillow* after pretending to have a sister moment with me?"

"No. I reached that conclusion because you didn't say a WORD to me after I threw those pills away. Which was very suspicious." I cross my arms. "You would have been a lot more mad at me if you couldn't have gotten more."

"Oh, so now you're Sherlock fucking Holmes. Whatever, Mae. Also, for the record, trust me, I *am* a lot more mad at you."

Sometimes, trying to talk to Hannah is like attempting to solve the Riemann hypothesis. My sister is a pure mathematics conundrum.

"You have to stop this, Nah. It'll get bad again—it already is! I know it's so, so hard. Everything is mostly horrible right now. No one understands more than me! But, Nah, what would they say if they knew—"

As soon as the words are out of my mouth, I regret them.

Hannah looks at me like I am a waste dump being sent back to Earth. She looks at me like she *wants* me to disappear.

"Fuck you, Mae."

Abort mission. *Abort.*

"Nah, I didn't—I'm sorry. Sometimes I don't say things in the most helpful way. I know that. I'm sorry. I'm trying to keep you safe."

Hannah turns around, starts crossing the parking lot in the direction of the T. Her legs are so long, I'd have to run to catch up to her. I want her to choose to stop. To not make me always have to run after her.

"Hannah!" I yell.

She doesn't turn around.

I watch my sister stomp away, arms wrapped around her against the cold, and I think I know what it would be like to be on a space walk and have your tether break.

All you can do is float in the darkness, watching the light slip away.

• • •

If my sister were a weather system viewed from the ISS, she would be great big storm clouds sweeping over the face of Earth, covering whole landmasses, blocking out the sun.

More and more I keep thinking about the Little Prince's rose and how he left his planet, Asteroid B-612, even though he loved her, because she was impossible to live with. No matter what he did, it wasn't enough. And she was always waving her petals, so to speak—saber rattling, raring for a fight. Snapping at him. Refusing to accept his help. Totally self-absorbed.

Sometimes I feel like I'm stuck on Asteroid B-612 with Hannah.

Honestly, I am growing very tired of it.

And I don't like being cursed at.

Or walked away from.

And I don't like being lied to.

I found a postcard. I don't know when it came in. Why she didn't tell me. And I can't even say anything because I found it when I was going through her stuff, looking for more pills to throw away. Why would she keep that from me? Their last words to us. As though, by rights, they belong to her more than they do to me. She is part of them. She is made up of their genes. So maybe they are more hers.

But maybe the worst part of finding that postcard was: What was the joke Dad was going to tell me?

It might make me insane, never knowing.

I don't need to be the center of attention—I never have been, and it's not a place I like to be. Nah always needed that, needed applause and *good job*s and people blowing kisses. And that's fine. But right now, when we're all trying to figure out how to deal with Mom and Dad being gone, suddenly it's become about keeping Hannah okay. Everyone tiptoeing around her, worrying about her depression (because that's what they think the whole problem is), knocking on her door, wringing their hands. Uncle Tony trying to ask about school, meeting with Hannah's teachers. It's the Hannah Show, and we all have front-row seats. And I want to stop going.

Aunt Nora keeps trying to do all this nice stuff for us, and she has no idea we're both lying to her face every single day. Hannah, because she's using, and me, for not telling my aunt and uncle what's going on. Not telling them there are drugs under their roof and a drug addict sleeping on their bed. They deserve to know, but I've got one more card to play. And then, I don't care if it's disloyal and Hannah never talks to me again, I'll confess. Everything. I'm scared that they'll send her away somewhere, that her life will be even worse, but I have to take that chance. For her.

I want her to make Mom and Dad proud. Not turn into my bio mom.

Because that's what she is going to become, maybe for life, isn't she? Isn't that what happens when you can't ever stop? And how am I supposed to deal with that? What am I supposed to do?

So I have to fix this. I have to fix her. I have to work the problem.

But how do you fix someone who has broken into a thousand pieces?

The data is terrible. My sister is refusing to go to the counseling sessions; the school has called about her ditching. After I confronted her today, she shut her door and refused to come out.

So I do the only thing I can think of: I call Micah.

"Hello?"

A girl's voice. I look at the screen, thinking—but, no, definitely Micah's number.

"Hello. Can I please speak to Micah?"

"What?"

It's loud in the background. A party, probably. It's Friday night, after all. Well, it's only four in the afternoon there, but surfers get started early.

"Micah. I need to talk to Micah?"

"Oh, right, yeah, uh—he's kinda . . . busy." Laughter. Hers. "Hold on."

Even though I'm not there, I want to go stand in a corner and hide, or see if they have any good books on their bookshelves. I have been to three parties in my life, these kinds of parties, and I did not like them at all. Sometimes it's very clear I do not belong on Earth.

The longer I wait, the more it occurs to me to wonder what it could be that Micah is so busy doing. What her laugh meant. A knowing kind of laugh.

Oh god.

"Hello?"

Micah is out of breath.

"It's Mae." I don't feel like greeting him properly right now.

"Hey. Hey. Uh. Hold on." The sound of the party fades a bit, like he's gone into another room. "Sorry. Is everything okay?"

I am feeling weird.

Nah is the one who gets . . . vibes. She calls them that. Very unscientific. But I am feeling—Mom says it's like someone's walking over your grave. And I am feeling not good about that girl who answered the phone. Her laugh.

"Mae? Where's Nah? Is she okay? She hasn't been calling me back the past few days."

I take a breath. This is Micah. My big brother. Who is like a moon that revolves around my sister, lighting her up, Nah the center of his world. Vibes are not hard science, and I am going to go with what I know. And what I know is that Micah loves my sister more than anyone in his world. At least, that's my working hypothesis based on previous evidence.

"She's in her room," I say. "Listen, Micah, Nah would kill me if she knew I was calling you, but I need your help."

I tell him everything. The pills, the night with the broken bottle of bourbon. The ditching.

"You're wrong about the pills," he says. "She only had a few left. And she said that was it, she just needed to take the edge off—"

"These are new ones. Percocet."

He curses. "Did you check your aunt and uncle's cabinet?"

"There's nothing there. And I can't ask if they're missing anything."

"She probably just asked your cousin to hook her up if she didn't take it from them. I know you're worried because of all that shit from before, but this is different. She's had a rough time. Go easy on her, and if she starts screwing up at school, then worry. She just needs to chill, and this helps."

I am not a person who throws things, but I'd really like to now. At him.

"How can you say this—you saw how it was before! This is *exactly* what it was like before she went to detox and all that."

"Look—I know you two are close, but she doesn't talk to you about this kind of thing. She told me she just needed to get through these past few weeks—"

"Wait, you *knew* and you didn't tell her to STOP?"

"Whoa. Hold on. Yes, I know. I'm her boyfriend. And I'm not going to, like, tell on her to her sister. She's okay. I'm checking in. She's just sad, Mae. You gotta lay off her."

"I'm certain she's on something every day. She had—has—a serious addiction, and you're being extremely irresponsible in your logic right now. Nah's becoming reclusive, temperamental, she won't eat, she's making very bad choices—"

He blows out his breath in a frustrated way, which I resent, I really do.

"Mae. Dude. Chill. Your parents just died in a really fucked-up way. You've had to move to a new city across the country. Nah and I are going to be apart for months." He sighs. "And she's still having a hard time about . . . you know. What happened in March."

What happened in March. We use all these euphemisms, as if not saying *abortion* somehow makes Nah hurt less. I think everyone just wants to pretend it never happened. But it did. I think it's part of why she can't get better. I don't know how to make him understand. Mom said that part of why people are sometimes intimidated by me or don't understand me is that I need to be more vulnerable. She said even astronauts have to wear their hearts on their sleeves sometimes. I told her that would medically disqualify me as a candidate, but I know what she meant.

I take a breath. I tell him my greatest fear for my sister. "She could turn into my bio mom, Micah."

He knows about the meth and social services, about the way they found me in a crib covered in excrement. Dad let me read my file when I turned sixteen. That was our deal. It was a difficult night.

"This time, Hannah chose to have an abortion," I say. "But what about next time? What if she doesn't, and then you guys have a baby that's all messed up, or you get lucky and have a healthy one like me, but then she forgets to change its diaper because she's too high? She'd never forgive herself. *I'd* never forgive her."

I'm grateful I exist, grateful that when my birth mother recognized that she wasn't able to care for me, she gave me a fighting chance to have a better life—which I got. But I'm also grateful that Hannah doesn't have a baby right now. I'm glad she made that choice. I don't really know how to reconcile those two things.

"What the fuck, Mae? That's not gonna happen. She's not your bio mom—*Jesus*."

"Really? Because the woman who gave birth to me was the kind of person whose entire life was defined by the drugs she couldn't stop taking." And then I say the thing I probably shouldn't, but I can't help it. Micah's being incredibly dense right now. "Listen. I don't know what Hannah would have chosen to do if she hadn't been on drugs. I really don't. And I'm not sure she does, either."

He's quiet for a long time. Then he says, "I can't even believe you're saying this right now. She's *seventeen*, Mae. We didn't want a kid."

"*You* didn't want a kid. Don't put words into my sister's mouth."

"Oh, so if *you* got pregnant right now, Mae, you'd have it? You'd give up NASA?"

"No. I don't want a kid now or ever, and I wouldn't give up NASA."

"You'd have an abortion."

"Yes."

"But you're judging Hannah for having one?"

"*No.* Are you even listening to me? I'M NOT HANNAH. We want different things in life! Micah, you scored a fourteen-ninety on the SAT—why is this so difficult to understand?"

He lets out a frustrated growl, which alerts me that I am now having to reason with a caveman.

"This is all beside the point," Micah says, after a minute. "The pills—she's just . . . dealing, Mae. In the only way she can right now. I know you're not into that scene, but, trust me, her problem is not a problem anymore. This is different. I trust her."

"She's *not* dealing, Micah, that's what I'm telling you," I say. "And if she's telling you that and you trust her, then she's manipulating you and/or lying to herself. You should trust ME, the person who occupies the same physical SPACE as her. The SOBER PERSON on the ground."

"Look, I bet it's just your cousin hooking her up. Tell him to stop giving her pills. Problem solved. If her supply runs dry, then she'll—"

"Nate would *never* give her something like that," I say. "Plus, he's not into that crap. He's an actual rocket scientist. He has better things to do than get high."

He's rolling his eyes. I can tell. I can *hear*. "Then someone at school gave them to her."

"She doesn't know anyone."

"Look," he says, "she's got some kind of hookup, Mae—someone is dealing to her. That's the only way to get pills like that."

"A dealer? Like, a *drug dealer*? No. That's . . . No."

That weird circus girl on the boardwalk is one thing. She and Nah were friends. Dealers make me think of guys in leather jackets and alleys and knives and, oh my god, CARTELS—

"This could be like that show on TV you guys like!" I say. "The one where everyone is on meth and then those scary guys from Mexico come and—"

"Mae. Just . . ." He sighs. "I know you are super . . . You're a good girl, and that's cool, but please trust me when I say that whatever it is you're imagining is not at all true. Okay? Some kid at school is helping her out, and that's it."

"But that is totally out of my control! How can I find this person, how can I stop them—don't you see this is a total all-systems fail?"

He's quiet.

"Micah! You have to help me fix this. She's drowning."

"Just give her time, Mae. I'll be there at Christmas and I'll talk to her in person about all of it. I promise." The background noise on his end gets louder. "Hold on a sec."

I hear a girl's voice, soft. "Hey, you. We're gonna head down soon. You almost ready?"

A tingling sensation spreads across my fingers. The last time I got this feeling was the wave, and before that, it was when Riley came over and had this look on his face and then he told me his family was moving to China and that he didn't want to do a long-distance relationship.

Vibes. Bad ones. Maybe this is data I should consider more seriously.

"Yeah," Micah says to the other voice. "Five more minutes." A door shuts. It's quiet again. "Mae? Look, I have to go. I'm coming for Christmas, right? And it's already October, so I'll be there before you know it and I'll sort it out. Okay? Just hold tight."

"I'm sorry, Micah, do you have something better to do right now than discuss the fact that your girlfriend whose parents just died is maybe suicidal?"

"Whoa. What the hell?"

Finally, I can't stand it.

"Who was that girl?"

"Huh?"

"That you were just talking to. Just now. That girl."

A pause, then: "No one. Look, is Nah around? Maybe I should just check in with her for a sec. But then I really have to go."

No one.

No one isn't *no one* unless they are someone.

"Are you cheating on my sister?"

Another pause. One that is long enough for me to enter the quantum realm, where particles do not follow the natural laws of physics, where anything can happen. Quantum leaps. Where you can suddenly jump from one place—the land of having a big brother who loves your sister and is part of your family—to another: the land where this big brother is a lying, cheating bastard who just might be the death of her.

Unless I can somehow fix this, my sister just lost her real-life version of the Little Prince.

"You're so lucky my father's not alive, Micah." This voice, this cold, hard voice, is not my voice. It is the voice of Commander Mae Winters, who is reaching Mach 2, about to put a two-million-dollar plane into a forced tailspin. It is me, suddenly, right now, getting ten years older.

"Because if he were, he would tell you to your face what a sorry excuse you are for a human being."

Micah loved my father. His dad is a total loser who lives in Michigan and calls him once a year. My dad wrote Micah's letters of recommendation, checked his trig homework almost every night, and took him hiking up in Malibu Canyon, just the two of them, every Father's Day. It is the cruelest thing I could possibly say to him.

He breaks down. Huge, heaving sobs tear through the phone.

And I don't feel a damn thing.

I hang up.

I don't have time for his grief.

17

Mae

ISS Location: Low-Earth Orbit
Earth Date: 23 October
Earth Time (EST): 18:00

Nah is holed up in her room. I knock, then try the door—she keeps it locked now. She doesn't answer. She hasn't been eating lunch with me for the past week at school, either. I don't know where she goes. We're strangers now. I know my lab partner better.

I wonder if Mom would say something about energy. She was big on that. Mom would assert that not telling Nah Micah is cheating on her is manifesting as negative energy, affecting my energy field. She would say that Nah is picking up on my deceit on a psychic level and responding by throwing up her own protective energetic barrier.

I'm starting to wonder if Mom was on to something.

I also know that, because I can't rely on Micah to save the day, I need to get my family's help. It's time.

"I'm going to Castaways," I say through the door, through the atmosphere and debris that separates us all the time now. "Do you want to come? Free coffee. Brownies."

Nate has invited me to come study with him tonight at the coffeehouse Ben works at—more accurately, he has *ordered* me. He thinks I worry too much about Nah and that I need to get out of the house. He has no idea. Ben has the closing shift and is promising free coffee and whatever we want from the pastry case. Sugar and caffeine are excellent motivation for crossing the Charles River.

If I am being completely forthright, *Ben* is excellent motivation. It's been three weeks since that night in the living room, and I haven't seen him since. The timing isn't right. But I want to. See him. And my resolve to stay completely focused is wavering.

I press my ear to the door. It is silent.

"Come on, Nah," I say. "How can you say no to brownies? They're your favorite!"

I know what would get her to open this door. All I have to do is tell her the truth about Micah.

I have never missed my mom as much as I do right now.

"Nah, please. Talk to me."

There's a *thud*, then shuffling, the lock clicks, and the door opens. My sister stands before me, a wraith.

I try my best to smile. "Hi. Did you hear anything I—"

"I'm tired, Mae. Okay? I just want to be alone."

Micah is cheating on you.

"Oh—okay." I slide my foot past the doorway, in case she tries to shut me out again. "I don't think that's a good idea, though."

"I do."

Hannah. Our rose. She needs Mom's soft voice—*grow, grow, grow*. But if you're anyone other than Mom and you say *grow*, she'll wither, just to defy you. Stubborn blood, that's what Yia-yia used to say. Karalis blood. Can't push her. You do, she'll go the opposite way.

I need a Hannah whisperer.

"What if . . . I just hang out with you instead? We don't have to talk. Or go anywhere. I can do my homework—"

"We have to get used to it, Mae."

"Used to what?"

"Being apart. You're leaving at the end of June. Plebe Summer. Annapolis.

Then the military. Five years, right? That's what you give in exchange for school?"

"Yes." I overcame my inertia and rescheduled the interview; it's in two weeks. My study session with Nate tonight is to prep for it. "But I'll visit—"

"And then you'll go to Florida or Houston or Russia or wherever NASA sends you. And then the moon. Or whatever." She shrugs. "Let's face it, Mae: Our family—it's done."

I stare at her. *"What?"*

My vision turns spotty, like the room has suddenly been infested with gnats.

Our family—it's done.

"Besides, I'm going to LA soon. Micah and I are getting a place, you know?"

But he's cheating on you, I want to say. *You can't live with both of them. All three of you.*

"We still have a family, Nah. Me and you . . . and Aunt Nora, Uncle Tony, Nate, Gram, Papa . . ."

She backs away, toward the bed. "I'm tired. I'm going to sleep now."

"It's only six! Come on, *brownies—*"

"I don't want a *fucking brownie,* Mae." She lies down, her back to me. "Shut the door." She sighs. "Please."

I walk outside, in the dark, in the cold, my coat buttoned, holding on to the straps of my backpack, which is carrying too much. There is no moon tonight. Too many clouds covering the sky.

I cannot see the stars.

. • .

Trains are good for thinking.

On the Red Line to Harvard Square, which is where Castaways is, my brain begins working the problem of Hannah. I think it's possible when one decreases distance to Harvard you get an increase in intelligence. Just a theory.

And here is another theory:

The radius of separation between my sister and me is growing, which shouldn't be scientifically possible, if you consider Coulomb's law.

In physics, two charged objects of opposite charge are attracted to each other—they move *toward* each other, thus decreasing the distance of separation. This is why, historically—before the pills—my sister and I got along so well.

For this equation I'm categorizing Hannah as "negative" and me as "positive." When one considers psychic energetic fields—not sound science, but this is a thought exercise, like string theory—it would make sense to use traditionally considered notions of what positive or negative is. Sad and Addicted = Negative, whereas Relatively Well-Adjusted = Positive. (Please note that "positive" is not a value judgment in which the positive quotient is better.)

Ergo: Hannah = (-) and Mae = (+)

Opposites, as they say, attract.

Not so anymore.

I'm really beginning to wonder if Mom was right. Perhaps humans really do have a quantifiable energy field and you can actually apply the laws of physics to relationships.

(!!!!!!!!!!)

I'm not suggesting that this experience actually disproves one of the most basic theories of physics, as my sister and I are not objects. However, if my mother's belief in psychic energetic fields were ever actually proven and shown to be sound science, then the increased separation between Hannah and I would directly challenge Coulomb's law.

As we know, when *distance* increases, the forces and electric fields between the two objects decreases. More distance = less connection. Simple, right? Forces between objects (sisters) become stronger as they move together and weaker as they move apart.

According to Coulomb's law (see below), it should *not be possible* for Nah and me to be moving apart BECAUSE WE HAVE OPPOSITE CHARGES. Opposites attract! But according to the work I've done, THE LAW DOES NOT APPLY TO HUMAN ENERGETIC FIELDS. (If they exist, which we don't have enough data on yet, but I'm beginning to think they do. I should not mention this fringe theory in my NASA interview.)

BUT WAIT. It IS possible for us to have opposite charges and move apart because even though there is an attractive Coulomb force, our velocities could be moving us away from each other faster than the attractive force can bring us back together. Which means WE ARE GOING TOO FAST IN OPPOSITE DIRECTIONS. It's like the wave has thrown Nah and me into separate, fast-moving currents that are moving away from each other. Well, I'm not an oceanographer and actually know nothing about currents, but YOU GET MY DRIFT. (No pun intended.)

My math checks out.

Coulomb's law is $F = kq_1q_2/r^2$

Or:

F being the force of our sisterly bond = Hannah's negative charge as a result of being very sad multiplied by Mae's positive charge of working the problem and eliminating things that can kill her next, divided by the radius of separation squared, which in this case is the psychic distance created as a result of grief, depression, and addiction squared . . .

Clearly we should be moving *closer to each other*.

I must consider the possibility that the radius between us must be so much greater than I thought. Maybe the relative distance is so vast that even though we're opposites, the charges can't pick up on each other.

I could have stayed in that room with Hannah. Lay down on the bed with her, or sat at her desk to do my homework. But I didn't.

Turns out I can be as stubborn as her, when I want to be.

I should not be going to Harvard Square, to a boy with a magnetic force field. She will take another pill. I know it. She wouldn't be able to, if I were there. But:

Our family—it's done.

She is a *rosa sericea*, a winged thorn rose. Known for their huge thorns.

Would she have said that to me if she knew the truth about Micah?

Maybe fourteen years of being told we are sisters isn't enough. Maybe it does matter—blood. Maybe she feels like her family is done because the other blood members are gone, and she is the only one left.

No.

She's just depressed. And scared. She thinks I'm leaving her. I *am* leaving her.

Work the problem.

I stare at the floor of the train, where people have tracked in autumn leaves. Time is going by so fast. Just a month ago, I was wearing shorts and sandals. In LA, but still. Time is running out. I will be leaving soon. And what will happen to Hannah? She won't be better by June. That's not possible. That's not how addiction works. Or grief.

This is why my sister said our family is done. She's increasing our radius of separation on purpose, because she's trying to say goodbye. Trying to get used to being alone. Hannah doesn't practice being alone like I do. She's not used to it. She hasn't *trained* for it. She's treating these months like a sim for loneliness, and she's failing every day.

Work the problem.

The train takes a sharp turn, and everyone's bodies—all the people in here with their coats and scarves and hats—sway in this new direction.

New direction.

Me leaving is a variable. A changeable variable. I've been acting like it's a theory you can't disprove. But it's not.

A good astronaut is able to pivot. To work with the situation that's happening, regardless of their expectations. If you have a flight trajectory set, but something happens to someone on your crew, you're going to have to make changes. Even if it affects all your hard work. Even if it sacrifices the entire mission. Because the safety of the crew comes first. Always.

So many things can die in just one month.

18

Mae

ISS Location: Low-Earth Orbit
Earth Date: 23 October
Earth Time (EST): 19:17

When I get off the train, I stand on Mass Ave and lean against a streetlamp, facing Harvard. A few decades ago, my dad was behind those wrought-iron gates, having no idea that someday I would be standing here, wishing him back from the bottom of an ocean across the world. Wishing I didn't have to make the choice I think I have to make.

A gust of wind howls down the avenue like a Hollow from *Bleach*, a soul turned bad from unrest. Ichigo Kurosaki would have to defeat it.

Ben.

I didn't think this sudden coldness inside me would ever go away, but the thought of him disproves that assumption.

I start walking up Mass Ave, past J.P. Licks, where people are eating ice cream and laughing and smiling and I wonder what that is like, because I don't remember. It's also very cold to be eating ice cream. Maybe that's normal here.

Students run around with scarves wrapped up to their noses, on their way to Wednesday night study sessions or dinner, rushing past boutique windows filled with cobwebs and skeletons. That is my family now. Cobwebs and skeletons.

Cambridge is bricks and ivy and wrought-iron gates. You don't even feel like you're in America anymore. If someone told me I was in England, I'd believe them. I know Nah misses the sunshine and the palm trees, but I don't. I like the cold. I like places you have to work a little harder to survive in.

Castaways is across from Harvard, tucked off a side street behind the Harvard Book Store and Grolier Poetry Book Shop, Mom's favorite. I pass a guy and his dog hunched against a brick wall with a hand-lettered sign, and I drop a dollar into his hat before pushing through the metal door, which has a porthole in its center.

The coffeehouse is large and cozy, with a small anteroom for ordering your things and then an entryway that leads into the main room, which is filled with thrift furniture and Cambridge's weirdo hippie types mixed in with students hunched over books and laptops. The chairs and tables are mismatched, and the whole place has a nautical theme: old paintings of ships, anchors, a mermaid masthead that looms from behind the bar. It feels lived in, the hardwood floors dark and splintery.

For a second, I just breathe in the heavy scent of coffee and let Vampire Weekend wash over me. It's very strange, to feel, at the same time, both utterly devastated and totally relaxed. I'm not sure how that's possible. I think I need to take more biology courses.

"Welcome to the Sanctuary of the Holy Bean."

Ben's standing behind the scarred wooden counter, watching me. I smile. He makes me smile. This is so many fantasies coming together at once: a coffeehouse in Boston filled with people who might have read the same books as me, a boy that looks like he stepped right out of *Bleach*, free caffeine at my fingertips . . .

I've been on planet Earth a long time, but this is the first place that's felt like home. Maybe it's a sign, the kind Mom is always talking about. A sign I'm not meant to leave Boston or Hannah any time soon.

Ben has texted several times since that night Hannah broke the bottle of bourbon. Save him from these Harvard Square douches. Rescue him from the boredom of a Monday-night closing shift. Come see the cool space-inspired latte art he's been perfecting.

I've always said no.

I wanted to say yes.

But his eyes are the exact shade of brown as my mother's.

This bothers me less tonight. I like seeing her eyes in his face. They fit together.

"And you're the high priest of this establishment?" I say.

His lips turn up. "Merely a lowly altar boy." He wipes the counter off with a towel, then throws the towel over his shoulder. "What'll it be? Anything you want. Go crazy. It's on me." He grins. "Least I can do for someone who just spent the better part of their evening on the Green Line."

The line my aunt and uncle live off of is notoriously slow, a trolley more than a metro of any kind. Once you transfer to the Red, you're back in the modern world. It takes an hour, sometimes more, to get to the other side of the Charles River.

"Just coffee. Black."

"This isn't *just* coffee," he says. "It's organic free-trade earth magic made by genies."

I laugh. He makes me smile *and* laugh. And that adds up to something, I know it does. I'm good at math.

"Well, then I'll have a *magical* cup of coffee."

"Coming right up."

I glance over my shoulder at the large main room behind me. "Nate here yet?"

"He's on his way. Got caught up in a lab."

I slide off my backpack, then shrug off my wool coat—a recent gift from Aunt Nora, since there is no need for an Angeleno to ever own one. She took me to a vintage store here in Cambridge, and even though it smells like an old lady's closet, I love it.

Ben turns around and sets the coffee down, then gives the thick striped turtleneck I got at the dollar sale in the Jet Rag parking lot in Hollywood an approving look.

"I like your style, Mae."

I glance at his faded tee and fitted sweats. "Thanks. I appreciate your nod to disgruntled scholars everywhere."

He laughs. "Usually I make more of an effort, but I was at the meditation center before my shift—can't sit on a cushion in skinny jeans."

"Meditation?"

My world tilts just a little, which I know isn't possible because we're spinning, which is an entirely different—my point is: Ben Tamura throws me off balance. For just a moment, I see Dad sitting on his cushion. He'd like Ben. I really wish they could have met each other.

"I'm not a Japanese American cliché, I promise." He huffs out a laugh. "I don't do karate. Or eat sushi."

"Manga?"

"Okay, yeah, you got me there. You?"

He must know he looks like Ichigo. He *must*. "A little."

He grins. "It's actually pretty funny, messing with people's heads. Like, I tell them I meditate and then they feel all weird because they don't want to stereotype me as an Asian, so then I get this whole spectrum of awkward questions and I'm, like, dude, I learned how to meditate from a Mexican across the street from MIT." He shakes his head. "When I told my parents I started meditating, they were kind of horrified. It was pretty adorable, actually. They're Christian. As if it weren't bad enough that I'm a scientist."

"What kind of Christian?" I ask.

Gram is Catholic, but she believes in evolution—because she's a rational human being—and she advises Nate on which celebrity men she would prefer as grandsons-in-law, because she understands that he was born the way he is and that there is nothing wrong with him. Simple biology. Science and faith, as Dad said, do not have to be mortal enemies. But sometimes they are.

He frowns. "They protest at abortion clinics."

"Oh, wow."

"Yeah. Meditation helps with . . . that." He rolls his eyes. "My ancestors were Shinto. I think I'm the only Buddhist in my family's history on either side. Isn't it funny? I'm third-generation, but still. My grandparents immigrate to America, and I wind up on the cushion."

"That must be really great, though," I say. "Knowing about your family's history. Where you came from." I take a sip of my coffee. "I'm adopted, so . . ."

"You don't know anything?"

"I could take a DNA test, of course, but I don't want my birth family to track me down. Once you take the test, that information is out there, even if you check the privacy box. Who knows if it's actually secure? This girl I know found her birth mother that way, and I . . . don't want that. Maybe I'll do it someday, but right now, I'm not sure what the benefit of knowing my ethnic makeup would be. It wouldn't change anything. Or mean anything. The stories and culture I grew up with, that's what feels real to me. My mom—my *mom* mom—is, *was*, Greek American. My yia-yia and pappoús immigrated to America after World War Two on this creaky ship. Went through Ellis Island. My dad's family came on the *Mayflower*, if you can believe it."

"Boston's so weird."

"Right?"

"So are you into Greek culture and stuff?"

"Yes. I love it. It's strange, though. Ever since my parents died, all of this has been—it's been bothering me."

Ben leans his elbows on the counter, and, I must admit, I like this decreased radius of separation.

"How so?" he asks.

"I grew up being told I'm a Karalis woman, and we went to Greece and everyone treated me like I'm one of them and I can make avgolemono . . . I grew up with it all; it's my family's culture, so I *think* it's mine, too, but I don't know—is that appropriation? It's all very . . . confusing. And I don't *like* being confused. I wish there were some way to determine the right answer."

"An identity formula?"

"Yes. EXACTLY."

I grip my cup. The words are spilling out of me, and I can't stop them because there is something else about my parents being gone that has been bothering me, something I haven't even been able to tell myself.

"Everyone's talking about race and culture all the time," I say. "Owning what you are, who you are. Shouting it from the rooftops. More and more, it's all about your heritage. But what does that mean for someone like me? I love avgolemono. And *My Big Fat Greek Wedding*. And, even though I don't believe in it, I really liked all the evil eyes my yia-yia hung around the house. And I want them to be mine—my culture, a part of me. But they're not. The problem is, if I got a DNA test and found out I was Norwegian or something, I wouldn't be *that*, either. Because blood isn't culture. I don't have any connection to Norway at all!"

"You're American. That's a culture." He smiles. "Playing devil's advocate, by the way. I get what you mean."

"No, you're right. I am American. But. American culture is immigrant culture. Everyone has these culturally identifiable last names. These stories about ancestors immigrating. Family recipes and language and all that. Everyone! Only Native Americans don't have immigration stories, but they have their own stories. Migration stories, obviously. They have *tribes*. My dad's family *loves* talking about the *Mayflower* and showing us graves in the old cemeteries here—we have Revolutionary War soldiers in the family, Civil War soldiers. There's this line—of people and stories—that connects everyone in the Winters and Karalis families, and I don't have *any* of that."

"But you do," he says. "Having Puritan weirdo ancestors and Greek grandparents who came over after World War Two is your family's story. And *you're* part of your family. Ergo, I think all that stuff *is* yours. Those are your stories. Your culture. I really don't think people have a right, at least in your situation, to say otherwise. I don't know, I'm not Greek, so maybe some fully Greek person might not agree, but that'd be pretty harsh."

Our family—it's done.

"When I was little, I got a black marker, tried to make my hair like Hannah's and Mom's."

Ben reaches out and tugs on a strand of my chin-length blond bob. "For what it's worth, I like your hair. And your blue eyes." He rests his hand, the color of wet sand, next to mine. "Culture, heritage—you're right, it's about more than blood. It's more than a DNA test. So is family. Nate's my family, even though we don't share a drop of blood. Know what I mean?"

I nod.

"You'll figure it out," he says. "You don't have to label yourself. I don't go around being all, *I'm Japanese American*. I've never been to Japan. I'm from Brooklyn. I'm just me. You're you. Fuck labels and the people who insist on them. If a label society wants to give you is helpful to you, makes you feel connected to the world—gender, race, religion, nationality, whatever—cool. Use it. There can be awesome community there. But if it's not, if the label makes you smaller inside: *Fuck it.* My lab partner refuses to share their gender with anyone. They told me that they've decided what they are, but it's no one else's business. They're like, *Fuck all your assumptions about what or who you think I am if I say I'm male, I'm female, or even nongendered. I'm just me, and that's all you need to know. Hello, nice to meet you.* You feel me?"

I cannot wipe the smile off my face. No one, *no one* has ever made so much sense to me in my whole life, not even Dad explaining his dark matter quintessence theory.

"Wow, Ben. WOW."

He laughs. "If there's one thing meditation has taught me, it's that there's a place beyond all that. It's big and wide, and has no borders or labels or systems. It just *is*. That's where I live."

"I want to live there, too. But not everyone can. Even if they'd like to," I say. "I mean, you said so yourself: People get weird around you when you say you meditate. About the Asian thing. You still have to deal with that."

"But not on *their* terms. That's my point." Ben takes my mug and refills it, sets it down in front of me. "*Homo sapiens*, man." He sighs. "We complicate the hell out of everything, huh?"

I laugh. "Yeah. But we figured out how to walk on the moon, so we're not so bad."

"Facts."

I wrap my hands around the mug. Mom loved this kind—diner mugs. Thick. Indestructible. It was all we had at home.

"My dad was a meditator."

I can picture him so clearly, sitting on his cushion in the corner of his office, eyes closed, that slight smile on his face. The sound of the bell when he was finished, pulsing through the whole house.

My eyes prick, and I take a sip of the coffee. It's good. Bitter. It burns. When I set my mug down, Ben rests his fingers, very lightly, against mine. He doesn't say anything. Today his nail polish is dark metallic blue.

I am in so much trouble.

I have run his words through my head so many times. What did he mean, exactly? I haven't seen him since that night Nah collapsed on the kitchen floor, three weeks ago. But we've texted, emailed. He likes me. I know he does. Nate certainly teases me enough about it.

I thought I didn't have time for Zen masters who make me feel like I'm in zero gravity. I need my feet on the ground. But if I stay in Boston, then maybe, when Hannah's okay and I know for sure I'm staying . . . maybe I do have time. Later. Not now.

I pull my fingers away. "So . . . you just, what, sit in your dorm room? Close your eyes?"

"Most days, but a bunch of us got a group going—the Dharma Bums. Students, most of us. We sit, talk. It's pretty cool."

"What do you talk about?"

He grabs the biggest brownie in the case and slides it onto a plate, then pushes it toward me. "Oh, you know, the usual: the nature of reality, impermanence, death, and nirvana."

"Casual conversation." I take a bite of the brownie. It is a four-by-four-inch portion of heaven.

"Totally." He leans on the counter. "So. We've warmed up with race, gender, and culture. Before we get to politics and the sciences, you gonna tell me why you're having a bad day?"

I frown. "Is it that obvious?"

"You're less sparkly."

"I sparkle?" This, I did not know.

"Like Christmas, but not tacky." He smiles a half smile that is so cute I have to smile back. "Aha! I knew I could make you smile—I used the sly one on you."

"You categorize your smiles?"

"Of course. I have a whole periodic table." He gives me a wild grin. "Helium."

I shake my head. "Geophysicists have way too much time on their hands."

And then I get a flash—just a second, and it's gone: me, Mom, Dad, Hannah, Micah, and Ben eating avgolemono, laughing.

"Hey . . ." Ben squeezes my shoulder. "You okay?"

Compartmentalizing is a key skill for astronauts. Neil Armstrong could simultaneously go to the moon and be the father of a dead child. Maybe Mom's right and astronauts need to wear their hearts on their sleeves, too, but only after they know they're not going to become blubbery messes.

I nod. "There's a lot going on at home."

"Wanna talk about it?"

I shake my head. "I tried to do that the other day with someone, and it didn't go well. I think I should stick to my general policy, which is to talk about a problem after I've solved it."

I've been refusing to take Micah's calls. I bet he's terrified I'm going to tell Nah. I prefer to make him sweat a little. He deserves it. And I need to figure out what to do.

"Well, I'll go through the whole table, if you need me to. All one hundred eighteen smiles. I might need an espresso shot or two to do it, but I'm ready."

I really like him. But I don't want that to influence my decision. If I stay in Boston, it will be for Nah.

"That won't be necessary," I say. "Though I bet you could charge for that performance. Besides, as soon as Nate's here, I'll have to get to work."

"Fair enough. Offer still stands, though. If you need it."

A customer comes in from the main room and Ben gives him a refill, then turns back to me. "So. Annapolis interview prep? Nate said it's coming up—after Halloween, right? First week of November?"

"Yes. About two weeks from now. Keeping tabs on me?"

"I'm a curious fellow, is all." There is a wink in his voice.

I run my finger around the rim of the coffee mug. "Do you remember when Nick Hague's mission got aborted? It was all over the news."

Ben nods. "They crash-landed, right?"

"Yes. The cosmonaut he was with had to bail on their rocket just after launch. It was supposed to be Nick's first mission in space. He waited five years after completing NASA's astronaut candidate program to go up there. That's how long he trained."

"Sucks."

I nod. "He got lucky and hitched a ride a few months later and took all these great photos from the ISS, but there are astronauts who have to abort the only mission they'll ever have a chance to go on. Funding, timing, problems with your crew, getting sick—anything can keep you on the ground."

Before the wave, I thought that was my worst nightmare. My worst-case scenario in all of life. It's not. I know that now.

Ben crosses his arms, tilts his head. He's observing me like I'm a faceted geode he's checking out in the field. Or whatever geophysicists spend a long time studying.

"Mae. Can I say something?"

I think I will not like what he has to say. "Of course."

"I didn't know your parents—obviously. But I think they'd be really happy for you, if you got Annapolis. It's your dream, right?"

"Can we talk about something else?"

His eyes skim mine for a moment before he turns to the espresso machine, throws a mug on the metal grate, and pulls a shot. "What are your thoughts on Mars? To colonize or not to colonize?"

I am in so much trouble.

A laugh falls out of me and, just like that, the world hurts less.

"Because, I don't know, Mae, I gotta say that as exciting as it sounds, I kinda like our little rock here." He takes his finished shot and leans his elbows on the counter, his eyes on mine. "So many things on Earth to recommend it, wouldn't you say?"

I take a breath, eat my brownie, and studiously ignore his eyes. "Well, there aren't brownies on Mars. Yet."

He leans forward a little bit more, and I look up at his bleached hair sliding by those warm brown eyes, and I am instantly invaded by an army, an entire *cavalcade*, of lusty chemicals.

"Was the brownie worth the train ride?" he murmurs.

"It . . . the . . . what?"

WHAT IS HAPPENING? How have I lost capacity for speech, and why is my oxygen supply running low? WHAT IS HE DOING TO ME?

He leans closer. Oh, that smile. Ben Tamura is a threat to the mission—and he *knows* it. "The *brownie*, Mae."

I push back from the counter. "You—just. Stay there. Dopamine."

He raises his eyebrows. "I've been called worse."

"Serotonin *and* norepinephrine."

That's all this is. Chemicals, hormones. My body just being a body. A stupid, human body.

He grins. "When do I get to be oxytocin and vasopressin?"

The attachment chemicals. I don't smile back.

"I . . . I can't, Ben."

I don't like how he overwhelms me. How I can't think straight. His presence makes me waver. Doubt my choices. And besides, oxytocin is the kind of stuff Nah used to buy from the boardwalk—everyone's favorite opiate, apparently. But people can become drugs, too. I don't want to ever need something that much.

The playful glint in his eyes gutters. "Mae—"

"Listen. My sister is sick. My parents are dead. Everything in my life is up in the air. I can't take on anything else."

"I'm not something to take on. I can help."

"I don't need help. My sister does. I'm sorry. It's not a good time."

He hoists himself over the counter in one astonishingly fast move, one worthy of Ichigo, and takes my hands in both of his. They are so warm, and that's nice, but then an electrical charge goes through my whole body and I feel myself lean toward him and I don't stop. I need to stop. Why can't I stop?

"*Everyone* needs help," he says.

I'm saved by the couple who pushes through the door, bringing in a gust of frigid air. I pull my hands away, grab my bag and my coat. I'm halfway to the warm inner room of the coffeehouse when he calls my name.

"Mae."

I turn. I shouldn't, because I know those chemicals will rush through me even harder when I look into his eyes, but it'd be rude to ignore him, and I am a polite person.

"One of the benefits of meditation is that it helps you develop patience. A lot of it." He smiles. "Just so you know."

"Astronauts have a lot of patience, too."

His eyebrows go up, and the light comes back in his eyes. "May the best nerd win."

I don't have to come up with a clever response to *that* because he has to help his customers and because Nate walks through the door. As soon as I see my cousin, I nearly collapse with relief. I don't think I could have held out against Ben Tamura much longer. He's a formidable opponent.

My cousin gives me a quick once-over and shakes his head. "Fill me in on whatever has produced that look on your face."

I drag him into a corner booth. Ben's right. I do need help. Just not his. Nate leans back, watching me.

"So . . . you and Ben."

"At this precise moment, I don't care about Ben. Table that topic."

He leans forward. "Listen, he's not *quite* as good at math as we are, but he's pretty good, Mae. And his physics—spot-on. In fact—"

"Put your serious face on, Nate."

He sighs. "Okay. What did he do?"

"*He* didn't do anything. He's perfect. It's Micah."

"Micah?"

"You can't tell her, okay, because it will be so bad and I don't—Micah's cheating on Nah. If I tell her, she will . . . I don't know, but I'm scared what she'll do. And also she has some drug dealer or something and—"

"Wait, *what*?"

I am betraying my sister, but I don't have a choice. I really don't think I do. If I'm going to do something as extreme as possibly give up Annapolis, there will be questions. Dad always said, "Let's put more brains on this business," when there was a problem he couldn't solve. I need more brains on this business.

"I know this is Nah's story to tell," I say, "but it's an emergency and I can't—I *can't* do this on my own anymore, Nate, and—"

"Hey, *hey*." My cousin rests a hand on my arm. "Buzz. It's okay. Whatever it is—I got you. Just give me the data, yeah?"

"I found Percocet in her bag. Your parents didn't have any, did they?"

"Not that I know of. Is this the only time she's messed with this stuff?"

"No. She was . . . she was in an outpatient rehab earlier this year. It was bad. She was doing better, sober for five months, but then the wave happened."

"Fuck." Nate's frown deepens. "And Micah—how do you know he's cheating on her?"

I tell him.

When I'm done, Nate takes a breath. Undoes the little pearl buttons on his blouse. Rolls up his sleeves.

"Okay. I need coffee. And some graph paper."

"Graph paper?"

Nate shrugs. "We have a problem. Problems require graph paper."

He stands, takes a step toward the counter, then turns to me.

"I'd like the record to note that you said he was perfect."

"What?"

"Ben. You said he was *perfect*." He leans forward and chucks me under the chin. "You know, Buzz, for someone willing to strap herself to a bomb and blow her body into outer space, you're kind of a wimp."

Maybe he's right. But I'm looking at the math on this one. If a girl is left by everyone she loves, what is the probability that the next person she loves will leave her? You don't need to be a statistician to figure that one out.

i wish angels were real.

Bench
Public Garden
Boston

19

Hannah

reach into my purse for a pill, but the Altoids box I keep them in is empty. Panic slices into me, the same flavor as that time I thought I'd left my wallet on the D Line. I didn't realize I'd gone through them so quickly. How could I have—

No, that's impossible. There were six in here yesterday. I know it. I counted.

Mae.

The four corners of my bedroom—my new bedroom with its bare walls and unpacked boxes—slide in, closer and closer.

I'm off my bed and in the hallway, down the hallway, throwing open the door of her room before I even think to do any of it.

"Who the *fuck* do you think you are?" I say. Snarl. Growl. Spit.

She is not surprised to see me. My sister sets the huge book on her lap aside and clasps her hands together over her knees. Just like Dad.

"I'm sorry," Mae says. "I had to."

I let it go that first time. Tried to be sneakier. Didn't want to get into it with her. But now: We're fucking getting into it.

"No, you didn't. You have no right to go through my things—"

"Where did you get them?"

"It's none of your goddamn business," I say. "Give them back."

She looks at me, the smooth surface of a dark lake.

"I flushed them down the toilet."

Someone—not me—reaches for the nearest thing and throws it at her. As it flies toward her, I see what it is and I stop breathing.

Mae reaches out to catch it, not to block herself but to *catch* it, but the model falls on the hardwood floor and shatters.

Mae stares.

Hundreds of shards—wood and plastic and bits of metal—are scattered at our feet. I see them now as they were all those years ago, when Mae and Dad took over the dining room table to build the International Space Station and a shuttle docked against it. It took several weekends. Their fingers, painting and fitting and gluing. Dad, building her dream right alongside her. His hands, shaping her world.

"Mae."

My sister doesn't make a sound as she slides off the bed and onto her hands and knees. Crawls.

"Mae, I'm—"

"Get out."

This. Right here. This is why my parents wanted another baby. They must have known, even then, what a mistake they'd been stuck with when they had me.

I don't remember to grab a coat when I leave. I didn't ever wear one in LA. Sweaters. That's all I ever wore. I hear Aunt Nora call my name, but I hurry away before she can grab me. Run to the T.

I call Drew before it goes underground. He picks up on the first ring.

"Drew's Pharmaceuticals, how may I direct your call?"

"I could use some more of your pretty little pills, Drew. Can we meet somewhere?"

He's quiet for a moment.

"Drew?"

"You're out of them already?"

I sigh. "Oh, Jesus, not you, too."

"Not me, too?"

"Look, sell to me or don't. I can find someone else who will—"

"Where do you want me to meet you?"

I am so grateful. It's sad how grateful I am that I don't have to spend the night looking for someone who feels as desperate and sad as me, someone who might know where I can find more.

"You remember that angel statue in the Garden?" I ask. "On the corner of Beacon and Arlington, but kind of hidden?"

"Yeah."

"I'll be there in half an hour."

"Okay."

This evening my angel looks especially fierce. Dark storm clouds are gathering behind her, and leathery leaves the color of my mother's spiced pumpkin soup swirl around her every time there's a gust of wind. We are alone in our little corner of the Boston Public Garden. Just past the wrought-iron fence are the elegant stone buildings of Newbury Street— hotels and shops and cafes. Places for the living.

"Hello," I whisper to her.

She says nothing, just stares beyond me, one arm uplifted, scattering crumbs from her bronze bowl.

The way her wings cut into the sky—she makes me want to pray. The angel on Mom's Judgment card is in the sky, too, hovering over three open caskets with a mom, a dad, and a child. She's woken them up with her trumpet. In front of them is a body of water, but it's not scary, not the wave.

"Wake us up," I whisper to her.

From this nightmare of them being gone. Of me being here, buying more diamonds.

"Tell me not to do this."

But she's silent.

I sit on the stone lip of the statue and, because no one's looking and because I can't help it, I pull out my Sharpie and write a little acorn.

I slide to my knees when I'm through, stare up at her like she's one of the icons in Gram's church. I wish I could light a candle. Or conjure my mother's ghost. Read her death yoga like cards or tea leaves. I don't know why she hasn't visited me in Boston. Maybe it's too cold here. Or maybe Mae's right, about how disappointed my parents would be if they saw me now. Maybe Mom knows, and she can't stand the sight of me.

At some point, Drew kneels down beside me.

His eyes slide over my face when I turn toward him. "Does she talk to you?"

Everyone is always trying to figure me out, but for some reason, it doesn't bother me when Drew does it. Maybe because I'm trying to figure him out, too.

"No." I look back at her. "Maybe someday she will."

He hands me a cup of coffee from Dunkies. "Thought you might need this."

"You go the extra mile like this for all your customers?"

"Just the pretty ones." He stands and reaches out a hand to help me up. He doesn't let go right away. "You're freezing. Again. Where's your coat?"

I shrug. "Forgot."

He sets down his coffee and starts to take his off. "Drew, I don't need—"

"I'm only doing this for the favorable review," he says. "Five-star dealer service."

He lays it over my shoulders and, oh God, it's so warm. He's so warm.

"Thank you."

"You're welcome." He picks up his coffee. Takes a sip. Watches me out of the corner of his eye. "I'm sorry about . . . I'm not trying to be a dick. About you running out."

"Okay."

"It's just, I sell them for recreational purposes and, I don't know, I feel like maybe—"

"Did you just come here to lecture me? Because if that's the case, you can take your coffee and—"

He rests a hand on my arm. "Consider what I have to say the warning label on the packaging. I know it's hard, with your parents and—"

"I'm leaving," I growl.

I turn, but he grabs my hand.

"Hannah."

His voice is soft and gentle, and I hate him for that, for his kindness that might be pity, but might not be. I try to shake him off, but he holds on.

"What the fuck, Drew?"

"I'm just trying to watch out for you. I have to be able to sleep at night."

"Me, too," I say. "That's why I want the goddamn pills."

"Let me help," he says.

"This—the pills—this is how you help me, Drew. Okay? You said you wanted a role, right? That's why you do this. Tell your Jiminy Cricket to shut up."

"I don't—I think I should . . ." He takes off his beanie, runs a hand through his midnight hair, a mess of waves.

He's not going to give me the pills.

I will spend the rest of this freezing-as-fuck night looking for a dealer in a city I don't know and I am so sad and I hate myself and I broke the entire International Space Station and—

I burst into tears. I can't help it.

"Hannah, no," Drew says, eyes wide. "Hey. We can . . . Please don't cry. I'm sorry." He takes my coffee and sets it down on the ground, then wraps his arms around me. For some reason, this makes me cry harder. "I'm really sorry. I'm just worried about you."

I hear Micah: *I can't carry you.* Drew will realize that soon enough, too.

I push him away.

"I have to go." The first raindrops begin to fall. And of course I don't have an umbrella because, where I come from, rain doesn't exist. "You know, you should find a new role, because this one? You suck at it, Drew."

He pulls an umbrella out of his back pocket. "Here."

"I don't need your umbrella."

He bites back a smile. "Yes, you do." Then he looks at my feet—a pair of flats, no socks. I can't feel my toes. "Hannah."

It starts raining harder now, but *I can't carry you.*

"I can take care of myself."

Let the tigers come with their claws!

He opens the umbrella and holds it over me. "Just so you know, I find your stubbornness really attractive. So you might want to tone it down." He wraps an arm around me. "Come on. I'll walk you to the T."

We walk. Through the garden paths, onto Beacon. Past the pretty shops and old stone churches. I am so cold. He is so warm.

"My sister found them," I say. "She flushed them. And I—I got so mad and I . . ." A sob breaks out of me. "I did something horrible to her. And I can't fix it."

Drew stops. It's raining harder now, the drops playing a soft, insistent song against the umbrella we're squished under.

"Hannah?"

It's dark now, and he is a smudge of charcoal above me, soft and shifting.

"Yes?"

"You're alive," Drew says softly. "And she's alive. You can still fix it."

But that's the problem: Mae's the one who knows how to fix things. I just know how to break them.

When we get to the train station, Drew slips something into my pocket.

"Ten Percs. That's all I'm giving you. Then we deal with this the good old-fashioned way."

"What's that?"

Drew smiles. Doesn't say anything. He wraps my fingers around the umbrella handle. His eyes find mine for just a moment, and I forget all about the pills and the rush of people around us and the rain and the everything. Then he backs away, into the storm. He's instantly soaked, black hair slicked down, gray eyes bright in the streetlights.

"Wait. I have money—"

He shakes his head. "You want to get lunch tomorrow? The burger place down the street from campus is pretty good."

"Okay."

I surprise myself with that. Him, too. Maybe he thought I'd say no. Drew grins, a sudden flash of brightness across his face, then nods once to himself before turning away, his shoulders hunched against the rain. In a T-shirt, because he gave me his coat and umbrella.

When I get on the train, I reach into my pocket, grip the packet of pills in my fist. Ten little lifeboats.

But.

I don't need one as much as I thought I did. Not right now. Maybe later.

Sometimes you don't need a lifeboat. Sometimes you just need someone to lend you their umbrella.

Mad Matter Magazine Vol. 4, No. 12

Mad Matter: You often talk about the Zen concept of "beginner's mind" in regard to your research methods. Can you elaborate on that a bit?

Dr. Winters: If there's one thing I've learned from meditation, it's that the more demands are placed on you, the more you need to sit in the silence.

Mad Matter: Is that where you find your answers—the silence?

Dr. Winters: Always. You know, there is no sound in space. In order for sound to travel, there has to be something with molecules for it to travel through. Here, on Earth, sound travels to your ears by vibrating air molecules. Our air is the conduit for sound. But in deep space—no air, right? All those miles between planets and stars, all that vastness. And not one. Single. Sound. The secret of the universe itself is held in utter silence. So we have to make ourselves quiet. Find a new way to hear the secret.

Mad Matter: Would you say that science is the language of secrets?

Dr. Winters: I don't think science has the corner on that market. I wouldn't be surprised if our friends in genetics find secrets embedded in our DNA. The whole universe is a secret. And so, in turn, are we. Each and every one of us is a secret. I used to only want answers. Truth. As Hawking said, "My goal is simple. It is a complete understanding of the universe, why it is as it is and why it exists at all." And while I still feel this way—the search for the truth of the universe *is* my life's work—I'm getting more and more comfortable with not knowing. It's a cool place to hang out. There's so much possibility there. You start getting answers, you lose some of the mystery, right? And the mystery is magical, fascinating. So many people want—*need*—absolutes. They want proof. Does God exist or not? Are ghosts real or imagined? Is there an afterlife, or nothingness? But—and I say this as a devout scientist committed to the search for truth in all things— the answers don't always matter. They're not the What.

Mad Matter: The What?

Dr. Winters: "The What" is a phrase I use as shorthand for "what it's all about." The point of everything. My, your, our raison d'être—our reason for existing at all.

Mad Matter: So what's your What?

Dr. Winters: Whitman's "When I Heard the Learn'd Astronomer." You know the poem?

Mad Matter: No.

Dr. Winters: At its heart, it's a poem about ditching the scene. The noise. Being a brand. All that bullshit. This is my favorite part, the end:

> . . . *I wander'd off by myself,*
> *In the mystical moist night-air, and from time to time,*
> *Look'd up in perfect silence at the stars.*

That moment—of remembering what matters and not having to telegraph it to the whole world so you can get your daily ego boost—that's my What. I hope I can figure out what dark matter is in my lifetime. But the journey, the conversation I'm having with the universe, the stars, the fabric of existence—that's enough for me.

Mad Matter: I couldn't help but notice that in your Whitman poem, he, too, sought silence.

Dr. Winters: That's where the magic happens.

20

Mae

ISS Location: Low-Earth Orbit
Earth Date: 25 October
Earth Time (EST): 17:43

I have been kidnapped by a Zen master who wears sky-blue nail polish.

I wish that did not make me a little happy.

I wish we were going farther than just across the Charles River.

I wish we were going as far away from my sister as possible. Preferably entirely different planetary systems.

No.

I just wish she were here with us. Wanted to be with us. Instead she's off who knows where, with who knows who.

"I'm only coming out because it's Uncle Tony's poker night and it's impossible to study with a bunch of drunk Italians in the kitchen," I say. "Just so you know."

"Noted."

Ben steadies me as the train swerves, the driver taking the curve a bit too fast, if you ask me, and I grip the metal pole in the center of the car tighter. Halloween's next week, and people are wearing costumes. We are traveling with a ghost, a sexy maid, and one of the Ninja Turtles.

Humans are strange.

I look up at Ben. "What kind of name is Dharma Bums, anyway?"

"Stole it from a Kerouac book. Didn't actually like the book, but it's a cool name. *Dharma* means *truth* in Sanskrit."

"So we're going to . . . a religious thing? I thought you were a self-respecting atheist."

He rolls his eyes. "I'm a card-carrying atheist, don't worry. We just sit. Talk. Get food after. It's nice."

"My dad tried to get me to meditate once, and it was a failed mission."

He laughs. "Isn't everything, first time around?"

And the way he looks at me, I know we're not talking about meditation. Ben is like the sediment he studies in geophysics. Many layers.

I decide that now is a good time to inspect my shoes. Boots. I have boots now. Warm ones with fuzz inside. Very strange. I miss flip-flops, but these are good practice for my space suit.

"How's Hannah?" he asks.

"Why? Did Nate say something?"

It's only been two days since we hatched our plan at Castaways, with phase one being me throwing her pills down the toilet (again) and her breaking the ISS.

I don't want Ben to only see Hannah as this messed-up science fair project. I want him to see the real her, the non-addict her. The one who sings and dances in the kitchen and does cartwheels on the beach and laughs so hard at dumb shows that she cries.

"No. Why?"

"Nothing. She's . . . really great. Usually."

"I know. I can tell."

"How?"

His eyes find mine. "Because you are."

He's really too much.

I shake my head. "Nate and I had this plan. To . . . fix her. I don't think it will work." He smiles a little. "What?"

"Well, that was your first mistake, Mae. You can't fix anyone."

"Everything can be fixed. I just have to work the problem."

"No problem to work, Commander." He leans closer. "She's not broken. No one is. She just has to figure that out."

I stare at him. Ben smiles, makes a little explosion sound as he flares his fingers. "Dharma Bomb."

He doesn't get it.

"Maybe you should change your major to philosophy," I snap.

"Not nearly enough homework. I couldn't take myself seriously."

"*This* is serious. What's happening with Hannah. You saw her that night in the kitchen. And there are . . ." I lower my voice. "It's not just my parents she's upset about. There are other things, things you don't know about. That *she* doesn't even know about. Yet. I have to *do* something, Ben. She could die. She *will* die."

The longer I keep the Micah secret from her, the more our radius of separation increases. I can feel it, the force field between us getting bigger and bigger. It's the size of an airplane hangar now. One big enough to fit a rocket.

He gives me an inscrutable look. "Yes."

"Yes, what?"

"Yes," he repeats. He reaches out, tucks a strand from my bob back behind my ear, where I like it.

I am about to attack him for lacking proper conversational technique when I realize what he's saying:

Yes, she will die. Because we all will. Someday. But I don't think Nah has until *someday*.

Hannah will die.

Possibly soon.

This was a terrible idea. I'd rather be home with earplugs in, teaching myself Russian so I can keep up in Star City if I launch with a Russian team.

"I think I prefer the drunk Italians," I say.

"Close your eyes," Ben says.

"What?"

"Just do it. Please."

I do. I don't know why I let him boss me around.

"Now," he says, so close I can feel the heat of his breath. "Just breathe. And listen. Don't think, Mae. I know that's impossible for you, but try. Just listen. Be here. Really be here. With me, with all of us."

I open one eye and he smiles. "Mae . . ." I close my eye.

The train's wheels clack on the rails. A baby is cooing and gurgling. Someone laughs, high and long. A newspaper rustles. A person behind me cracks their knuckles. Ben sighs. Low and soft. I lean into him, my eyes still closed, and he wraps an arm around me.

The train lurches, the brakes squeal, and my eyes snap open.

"Our stop," Ben says.

He takes my hand and pulls me out. Everyone on the car wearing MIT sweatshirts spills out behind us. The university's just a block away. I follow Ben, dazed.

"What *was* that?" I say.

He glances at me. "It was."

This takes me a minute.

"Is that some weird Zen shit?"

I sound like Hannah. He brings out the Hannah in me. I'm all over the place.

"It is, indeed, some weird Zen shit."

I *told* myself I was going to keep some distance with Ben, but that was only two days ago, and here I am. I used to be so certain about what I wanted. Maybe Mom and Dad were part of that process. Maybe I got more advice from them than I realized.

We are part of the school of fish, the bodies flowing out of Kendall station and up into the cold October night air.

"You didn't have to come get me, you know," I say as we reach the sidewalk. I have been possessed by a grouchy old lady. "I could have just met you here."

"I was in your area."

"No, you weren't. It took you an hour to come to my house, pick me up, and bring me all the way back here." I stare him down. "This isn't a date."

"Okay." But he smiles.

I hate how all the particles in me rearrange themselves when he does that. I pull my hand out of his and slide on my gloves and shove a hat on and stomp ahead until Ben calls, "You're going the wrong way."

Right. I am in entirely new territory. *His* territory.

Ben keeps smiling as we pass Lafayette Square. He gestures toward a nightclub and restaurant on the left.

"We usually get dinner at the Middle East after. You'll like it. We could go to a show there sometime, if you want."

"A show?"

"Like, a concert."

"Oh." I've never been to a concert before. That's Hannah's thing. I glance at the marquee. "Who are the Dresden Dolls?"

"Only my favorite band. *And* I might just have an extra ticket." He glances at me. "Nate's coming. I promise I'll only try to kiss you three times. Four if I'm feeling especially bold."

"You are—" I throw up my hands. "I actually have no words."

"Just *yes* will suffice." He stops. "We're here, by the way."

Ben steps inside the doors of the yoga studio his group uses on Friday nights, and I don't have a choice but to follow him in. It's cold outside. And, despite the fact that Ben talks about death like it's the weather, I want to sit beside him and breathe his air.

But the last yoga studio I was in was my mom's.

I stand on the sidewalk for a minute, lost in a spacetime bubble.

"Mom, I can't twist like that!"

She laughs. "Mae, honey, just put your head—no, put it under your arm. Yes, like that."

I glare at her. "This is harder than advanced calculus."

"How are you going to get around a space station without bending, hm?"

"I'm going to float through it. Obviously."

I give up on the pose and lie on my back. Corpse pose. I point to myself.

"You're killing me."

Mom laughs, then lies next to me, the tips of our fingers touching. We stare at the ceiling, which I helped her paint a long time ago to look like the night sky.

I stargaze with both of my parents, just in different ways.

"Mom?"

"Yes?"

"Did Riley give up on me because I'm so . . . inflexible?"

An astronaut needs to be disciplined, but not everyone understands that.

My mother reaches out and brushes back my bangs. The sunlight streams through the window behind her and turns her hair into melted chocolate.

"Someday, Mae, you will find your person. Or they will find you. And they will love you for the driven, intelligent, shoot-for-the-moon girl you are. You hold out for them. They're out there. I know it."

I smile. "Like you and Dad?"

She leans forward. Presses her lips to my forehead. "Riley's not your person. But I bet you'll always be the one that got away."

It's not until now, standing outside this Boston yoga studio, that I realize: She didn't answer my question about her and Dad.

•   •   •

Ben sits next to me, and the weight of my body on the meditation cushion and the weight of his body on the cushion next to mine and the distance between us, which isn't very much, gets me thinking about Newton and how, maybe, attraction is an expression of the universal law of gravitation.

Everyone who has ever felt something for another person is really just playing out

$$F = Gm_1m_2/r^2$$

The force (F) due to gravity between two masses (m_1(me) and m_2 (Ben)) which are a distance apart (r)—in this case, I'd say about six inches. G is the gravitational constant, which is 6.67408×10^{-11} m^3 $kg^{-1} s^{-2}$.

So the reason I can't move away when he's around is simply because of gravity. Just the force of masses.

Ben's only a math problem.

"It's just physics," I say.

He looks at me. "I'll buy in if you catch me up."

"I said that out loud?"

He nods. Smiles.

I'll buy in if you catch me up. No one ever wants to buy in on my thoughts or be caught up except Dad. Mom would try, but her eyes would glaze over as soon as it got too sciencey.

"Ignore me." I put my eyes on the front of the room. Looking at Ben makes me wobbly. "I'm just on a mental EVA—an Extravehicular Activity, better known as—"

"A space walk—I know. I may be a geophysicist, but I'm not totally clueless." And then he winks. WINKS!

"Well. That remains to be determined."

All around us, people are talking quietly on their cushions, but I'm sure their conversations are more normal. I don't know how to have normal conversations. I try, but I never get the references. Who has time to watch all those videos and memes? How do people keep up?

The room is small and warm and smells like cedar. I thought places like this were only for Mom and Hannah. There are seventeen people here. All college-aged, a mix. Most of them have arms covered in tattoos, but some are pretty clean-cut. I am certainly the only person wearing a vintage eighties polka-dot sweater, complete with shoulder pads.

"So." Ben scooches closer. "You go on mental space walks?"

"Yes. Well, that's what my dad calls it."

"So catch me up."

$$F = Gm_1m_2/r^2$$

I pretend to adjust my cushion, but really I'm turning six inches into twelve inches. "Usually people just let me go on them. By myself."

Hint. Hint.

He shifts his cushion closer, ignoring all obvious hinting. "But I want to come with. So."

He takes my hand. It is warm. Thermodynamics. I'm not great with those equations. Yet. But that's all it is. Heat is an energetic exchange that's—

"Where are we going?" he asks, soft.

Ben Tamura is relentless. Typical scientist.

"I'm . . . I'm working on a theory. That . . . that . . ." I pull my hand away. I can't tell him about gravity because this is NOT a date. "Human interaction can be expressed mathematically. I've applied Coulomb's law to Hannah and I—the results were surprising. And it's making me wonder if there is an equation for other things, like emotions. Grief. What is the mathematical expression of grief? Can you quantify it? And if so, can you solve it?"

He looks at his hands, frowning. At first I think he's disappointed in this particular space walk, but I realize this is Ben's thinking face, and I like it. I like his face. All of his faces. The whole periodic table that plays out across the valley beneath the ridge of his nose and the planets of his eyes and the craters beneath them, dark circles from late study nights and early mornings at the coffeehouse. I want to be the Neil Armstrong of Planet Ben, plant a flag.

I AM IN SO MUCH TROUBLE.

Oxytocin and vasopressin. Attachment chemicals. This is what this is. He is an evil genius, convincing me to come here, to be around him more, and now he's not just dopey dopamine, which I could have handled, now it will hurt, it will *hurt*—

"You could maybe look at an equation for the moment of inertia," he finally says. "Does grief feel like that? Like not moving?"

Wow. He . . . *wow*.

But his hypothesis is incorrect.

Losing and the fear of loss—they feel the same. So fast. Rushing. Rising and cresting until it covers you completely.

"No," I say. "It feels like a wave." I grab my purse. "I have to go."

I try to stand, which is difficult when your foot has fallen asleep, and Ben is looking up at me, stricken. A question forms on his lips, but before he can ask it, before he can ask *my* question—*Why? Why?*—and I can give him *his* favorite words—*I don't know*—a bell rings, clear and bright.

It is the sound the sun would make, if it could make a sound, when it is coming up over the horizon. *Hello, Earth. Good morning. Good morning.*

I am half-crouched, uncertain. I can hear my father ringing that bell in his study. It meant he was done meditating, that it was okay to knock on the door, to come in, to be together again.

Gravity expresses itself in its most familiar way: It pushes me down, back onto the cushion.

The room quiets, a quiet that thrums with expectation. Readiness. How it feels when Dad is about to lecture, and he looks out over the auditorium. Pushes up his glasses.

I pull my knees up to my chin. Ben reaches over and—just for a moment—rests his hand on my foot, on my *Doctor Who* sock, and squeezes. Then he lets go.

A woman is now at the front of the room, sitting on the cushion. She has the most beautiful Afro I have ever seen, like a star system, and wide-set eyes that know things. I think you only get to sit on that cushion if you know things.

Like almost everyone here, the woman is covered in tattoos. Her hands, even. When she puts her palms together, the sides read: ONLY LOVE.

"Hey, everyone. I recognize most of you, but for those of you I haven't met, my name is River. Yes, that's my real name, not some shit I made up to sound enlightened."

Oh, I like her.

There is soft laughter, and she smiles. For just a moment, her eyes meet mine, and she gives me a nod.

"So, here's the deal. We're gonna sit. Simple—but not easy." She shakes her head. "Contrary to popular belief, we don't sit here to relax. To have a little time-out from our lives, do some deep breathing, and call it a night. Nope. You want that, you motherfuckers came to the wrong meditation class." Now there's some real laughter. "We are going to sit here with all our shit, with ourselves just as we are, and accept whatever is happening. We are going to just *be*. Right here, right now. Not in yesterday, thinking about the past. Not in tomorrow, thinking about the future. We are going to be here. Right now. This moment. This breath.

"You might be bored as fuck. Sit with that. You might be scared at what you see in yourself, what you feel. Sit with that. You MIT nerds among us might figure out the cure for cancer. Sit with that—and don't write anything down until we're done sitting." More laughter. "Why do we do this? It's Friday night. We could be at a party, could be binge-watching something stupid, could be kicking our roommates out of our rooms so we can study anatomy . . ." Ben laughs softly, and I do not like what that does to certain regions of me that shall go unnamed for reasons of discretion.

"We do this," River says, "so we can wake up from the trance. You know what I mean, right? The trance of thinking that this"—she waves a finger around the room—"is for keeps. It's not. *It's just a ride.* Amanda Palmer said that. And it's true. It's just a ride. And we are missing it because we are too lost in all the shit we want to have or do or be. We miss it because we're too busy updating our social media status and reading another article online and watching another video. And this ride? You only get one ticket—one go. Unless you have really fucking fantastic karma, if you believe in that. Most people, they get on this ride and instead of buckling in and *doing this thing,* they check out. Buy shit they don't need.

Live on their phone. Not us. Here, we sit so we can rock the shit out of this roller coaster."

For just a second, the room dissolves. Explodes, maybe.

This, I think, is what Ben would call a Dharma Bomb. A truth bomb. I have been living my entire life in the future. The present has always been a means to an end. But what if my end is a wave, too? I've been living for a life that might never happen. What did I miss with my parents that I can't ever get back?

"All right." She smiles. "Let's ride."

We close our eyes. She rings the bell.

Almost immediately, I want to bolt.

My back hurts. Am I breathing right? Can Ben hear me breathing? Why does Bowie say "ground control to Major Tom" and not "mission control"? Maybe it's like how in England they say jumper instead of sweater. So in England it's called ground control. But they're not controlling the ground, that's bonkers, they're trying to control a spaceship in the sky, and they're obviously not doing a good job of it, because Major Tom is not going to be making it home. Are there even English astronauts? I think there are. Chris Hadfield's Canadian, and that's part of the Commonwealth, so I guess technically England is represented, but maybe there are actually British—

"You're going to have thoughts," River says, soft and gentle. "But don't hold on to them. Let them be like clouds passing across the sky of your mind: Don't cling to them, let them go. Focus on your breath. When a new thought comes, let that cloud go. Tibetans call this 'sky mind.' Thoughts, feelings, images, urges, sensations in the body—all of it is just weather."

Okay. Breathe. Breathe.

I can't hear Ben breathing. Is he alive? Of course he's alive. But maybe

I should open my eyes and look at him, to check, but then River will see me do it.

Sky mind. Sky mind. Weather.

"Just breathe," River murmurs.

My back hurts. I can't believe Dad did this every day. He never said his back—weather. Sky mind. Cloud. Cloud. Hannah breaks the ISS and Mom brushes back my hair, whispers, 'We are responsible for the things we tame,' and Dad says, 'Would you look at the Milky Way tonight!' I miss him. I MISS HIM. I MISS HER. I MISS. I MISS.

Oxygen levels low. Very low. Breath is fast and ragged, can everyone hear me? Is the whole room sounding like my breath and they're all looking at me? No. Paranoia is setting in. Breathe. Sky mind, sky—I MISS I MISS I missed so much of the ride with them, and now they're gone—am I going to faint? Or cry? Not here. NOT HERE.

This is a tailspin, that's what this is, and see, this is what happens when you lose control, when you let your subconscious take over. A bad idea, a HORRIBLE idea, what sick game is Ben playing? Sky mind. Ground control. Ground control. Grip my knees—yes. A coping mechanism is key in life-threatening situations. Hold whatever is building in me at bay. Work the problem. Calm under pressure. An astronaut stays calm under pressure. When is she going to ring the FUCKING BELL because I can't breathe. Calm. Calm. NO.

My eyes snap open.

The room is dark and quiet, a cocoon. Not a jet plummeting from the sky. Everyone's eyes are closed. River's, too. Ben's. A sigh falls out of me. He is so beautiful. Dark crescent moon lashes. Would it be weird if I just laid my head in his lap for the rest of the meditation? Would he be okay with that?

"You don't have to do anything," River says into the dim room. "All you have to do is take this breath. All you have to think about is this breath. That's it."

I close my eyes. I take this breath.

Then the next one.

Then the next one.

For a sliver of that breath, I feel something. I touch . . . *something*. It is wide and deep, dark and light. It is quiet here. Still. It is like shrugging off yourself. Like yourself is a too-heavy coat and you don't have to wear it anymore.

Silence.

The bell rings.

Good morning, Earth.

My eyes peel open.

I turn to Ben. When he looks at me, that something, that quiet place, it's there, in his eyes. He smiles. I smile back.

"So," River says, "this is the dharma according to James Baldwin." She glances at a piece of paper in her hand.

"Love takes off the masks that we fear we cannot live without and know we cannot live within. I use the word 'love' here not merely in the personal sense but as a state of being, or a state of grace—not in the infantile American sense of being made happy but in the tough and universal sense of quest and daring and growth."

She looks out at us. "This is what the ride's all about, my friends. Why we take it in the first place. Love. You've never been on a roller coaster that didn't require some bravery. Right? Like Baldwin says, we need *daring* and *growth*. That's what we're doing here. We're daring brave." She places her palms together. ONLY LOVE. "Now go out there and don't be assholes to yourself or anyone else. I'll see you next week."

Everyone laughs—even me. This is certainly not Midnight Mass with Gram.

"What did it feel like?" Ben asks later—much later.

We are at the Middle East and our bellies are full and he has pulled me into a corner. It's so crowded here you can't even see the floor. The room smells like old beer and good food. I suspect we are the only people drinking smoothies.

I think about it. "Like . . . finding zero gravity while on Earth."

"The geophysicist version of that is *grounded*." He takes my drink out of my hand and sets it on the counter beside us, then takes my hands in his.

"What are you—"

"Do you remember that night on the couch, how you told me the universe was once so small we could hold it in the palm of our hands?"

I nod. "And you . . . you said . . ."

"*I am in so much trouble*," he whispers. "Do you know why I said that?"

I shake my head. Even though I know. This would be so much easier if he didn't feel like a deep breath, like that bell, ringing: *Good morning, Earth.*

"Because, Mae, you hold me. Just like that. You hold me in the palm of your hand."

He brings my palm to his lips. I don't have an equation for turning into starlight.

It is the seventh time I cry in my life.

"Oh god," he says, panicked. "Tell me this is good crying."

"I don't know!"

Ben smiles. His favorite words.

I shake my head. "I have felt everything, *everything* on the human emotional spectrum in the past seven weeks. I can't . . . I just—"

Ben pulls me farther into the corner as a group of people push through the tiny space. Someone turns up the music and turns down the lights. He has to shout over the Arctic Monkeys.

"Mae, I'd like to join your crew. Now, before you say, *no, no, you're a geophysicist, and we don't need a geophysicist,* hear me out. Every team needs a mission specialist. And I am *specialized.* I didn't realize this until, well, until I met you, but I have been training long and hard to be *your* person."

"My person?"

He couldn't know. What Mom said to me at the yoga studio. *Did you hear him, Mom? DID YOU HEAR THAT?*

I stare at him. Stare and stare. How, HOW is this possible? It's like . . . magic. This is completely unscientific.

He nods. "*Your* person. I believe that as a member of your crew, I can help you on your mission—which is, you know, *life*—not just with copious amounts of free caffeine and meditation instruction and other—er—fringe benefits, but because of . . . quantum mechanics."

"Ben. Are you trying to convince me to be your . . . person . . . on the basis of *quantum mechanics?*"

Because, if so, I am a goner.

"Yes."

Goner. Pilot down.

"So, you're familiar with Werner Heisenberg?" he says.

Mom, my person. Did I find him, is he my person? Because my person would know who Heisenberg is. Tell Dad. Tell him to come quick and LISTEN TO THIS, OH MY GOD.

"Yes," I say. "I'm a fan."

I look everywhere but at Ben, because it is not safe, categorically NOT SAFE, to look at Ben.

"You seem distracted."

"I'm not . . ." I look at him. *Oh.*

This is what it will feel like, I think, to have my hand on the parachute lever in a plane that's going down, to be about to pull when I suddenly figure out what's wrong and recover. I won't need that parachute after all.

"There you are," he murmurs.

"Here I am."

Not in the future. Not in the past. I'm in the now.

It's nice here. I might stay awhile.

"Tell me about Heisenberg," I say.

"Okay." His eyes catch the light above, fill with little sparks. "So you know how Heisenberg was dealing with the nature of reality and how the quantum world is the Wild West of reality since not all the usual rules apply and how basically he was all like, *guess what, electrons only exist when they're interacting with something else*, right? And when nothing is disturbing the electron—trying to get it to go to a meditation class, for example—then it's not in any place at all."

"So you're saying I only exist in relation to you?" I frown. "Hello, Patriarchy."

"No. I'm *saying*, that according to the principles of quantum mechanics, okay, no object has a definite position except when colliding with something else." He leans his forehead against mine. "Ergo, *I* am lost without *you*."

"Jesus," I breathe. "You're good." I look down. "Ben, I have so much going on right now. I won't be a very good—"

"Kiss me," he says, "and then decide. Let's put quantum mechanics to the test. If you don't feel like you have a . . . definite position . . . in the universe when you kiss me, then okay." He leans in. "We're just two scientists with a question. We should test the hypothesis. Isn't that how everything starts, anyway?"

"That is . . . a reasonable assertion," I mutter.

Two days. I held out against his wiles for only TWO DAYS. Maybe I'm not commander material, after all.

Ben takes me to the banks of the Charles. Across the dark slip of water, Boston glows. The moon is a sliver, sly and winking.

I haven't kissed someone for over a year. I'm not sure if I remember how. Riley was my height, and now the spatial logistics are all off because Ben has to bend his head to get within striking distance. *Striking distance* is not a very romantic term.

"Ben?"

His lips are so close. He smells like freshly roasted coffee beans and the wind.

"Yes?"

"What if . . . we both just get lost?" I say. "If the quantum realm is the Wild West, then we must consider how the Wild West was incredibly DANGEROUS. We could collide with *other* electrons and then, you know, quantum *leaps*, and then, I don't know, WORMHOLES or something and—"

"It's a metaphor." He smiles, and it's kind and a little bit wicked and my body moves closer to his and my hands grip his arms. "Can I kiss you, Mae?"

"Okay. Yes. For science."

He looks up. "I owe you one, Heisenberg."

And then:

There is no other word for it: *collide*. We collide.

Particle acceleration, more and more and Ben and his breath in my lungs and the taste of him and I had no idea, no *idea* that another person could be your oxygen supply.

I am not lost. I am utterly, utterly found.

Some spacetime insanity happens, because when he pulls away, I honestly have no idea how long we've been here. Maybe my hair is completely gray. Maybe there is now a colony on Mars.

If I wanted to fly solo, I should not have let Ben Tamura kiss me.

He watches me, eyes filled with nebulae.

It's just a ride.

One ticket. One go-around. This boy.

I take Ben's hand. Press my lips to the palm. A whole universe, beginning right here.

"Welcome to the crew," I say.

i want to kiss someone I shouldn't.

Solo Cup
32 Perkins Street
Boston

21

Hannah

The only parties I ever go to are surfer parties, but I'm making an exception tonight. Some girl named Jackie who goes to our school is throwing one because her parents are out of town, and Drew has asked me to come along. I need one night off from my sister's X-ray vision, so I say yes.

"Is this you mixing business with pleasure, or would you have gone to the party even if you weren't holding?" I ask as we walk toward one of the fancy Victorian homes Jamaica Plain is known for. This one looks particularly imposing, with a large porch and three floors, the windows blazing with light.

"I probably wouldn't have gone, but since I've got company *and* I'm holding, it was a no-brainer. Unless you want to go back to my place and play video games."

I wrinkle my nose. "No, thanks."

He laughs as he heads up the walkway.

We get inside, and it's already packed. The house is very Saint Francis, all grandfather clocks and heavy drapes, real art—not some shit you buy at a home store. Drew grabs my hand and pulls me toward the kitchen, where there's an impressive assortment of bottles on a counter—good stuff, too.

"Let me guess," he says, giving me a once-over. "You're not a rum-and-Coke kind of girl. Whiskey?"

I nod. "Straight."

He raises his eyebrows. "You came to play."

Drew gets me a cup, and I've barely taken a sip before someone is pulling on his hoodie and palming cash. Drew looks at me, and I make a *go on* motion.

"I'll be right back," he says, and follows the guy upstairs.

I push through to the open sliding glass door that leads to the patio. It's quieter out here. It's a pretty big backyard, and it's filled with people I don't know. There's a fire pit and s'mores. Someone has a guitar. Someone always has a guitar. Nobody talks to me and I don't talk to anybody. I just drink my whiskey, then go back into the kitchen for more. I notice Drew coming down the stairs, and it occurs to me that Drew Nolan is hot. Like, really hot. Maybe I haven't been sober enough since I met him to notice that.

I feel a twinge of guilt and slide my phone out of my pocket. I send Micah a text, but he doesn't text back.

"Skittles?" a boy asks, holding out a heavy crystal bowl toward me, the kind in Gram's fancy hutch.

"Uh, sure?"

But then I look in the bowl—*not* Skittles. Pills. All kinds.

"How do you know what's what?" I ask.

"You don't," he says. "That's the fun."

"Yeah, no," Drew says, pushing the bowl away. "She's good."

I glance at him. "I am?"

"You are."

The boy shrugs, sidles away to offer pills to the group of girls lounging on the couch.

"It's a thing," Drew says. "Everyone raids their parents' cabinets, throws the pills in the bowl. Don't mess with that, okay? You have no idea what's in there. Mixing shit—that's how you end up in the ER, you know? Fucking idiots."

My mouth turns up. "Well, I don't need that bowl, since I have my very own private dispensary, anyway."

He throws me a hooded glance. Maybe he really meant it when he said he wasn't going to give me more than that last set of ten.

"The boyfriend?" Drew nods toward the phone in my hand as he reaches past me for a cup and the bottle of Maker's.

I nod. "He's MIA. Probably screwing some girl from his dorm or the surf club."

I say this as a joke, but it suddenly occurs to me that it's possible. Maybe he's with someone like I'm with Drew and he sees her come down the stairs and he realizes she's hot. Maybe that's how it starts.

"Then he's a fucking idiot." Drew keeps his eyes on mine as he says it.

"Whatever."

"Hannah. You're gorgeous and smart and cool. If he's fucking someone else, he's an idiot."

I don't like the way his words fill me up. Also: No one has ever called me smart before.

"This isn't a date," I say.

My voice trembles a little, and I hate that.

"I know. If this were a date, this would be the last place we'd be."

"What are you, a moonlit-walk-on-the-beach kinda guy?"

He shrugs. "Sometimes."

I shake my head. "You're an enigma."

Every time I try to put Drew into the dealer/druggie box, he hops out.

"I think I'm okay with that," he says, with that small half-smile.

I'm starting to get a nice buzz, a warm-all-over kind of feeling. I'm annoyed by the people around me. How loud and dumb they are. How they keep jostling me.

"Drew?"

"Yeah?"

"This party sucks. Let's go."

He steps back. "After you."

We end up going to his house and liberating beer from his dad's fridge, then stand around the kitchen drinking it, because couches and beds are for dates. And this isn't a date.

"So, you packing tarot cards tonight or what?" Drew says as he pulls another Sam Adams from the fridge. "Because I distinctly remember being promised a reading."

I laugh as I grab the Rider-Waite-Smith deck Cyn gave me out of my purse. "I guess having tarot cards is like packing heat, but I never heard anyone say it quite like that."

His lips turn up a little. "How so?"

"They protect you." I slide the worn cards out of their velvet bag, the colors beautifully muted, the images iconic, archaic.

"From, like, evil spirits?"

I shake my head. "From yourself. They show the truth about the world, other people, your life—and so it protects you from going down the wrong path." I roll my eyes. "If you listen, of course. Obviously I ignore them on the regular."

Just this morning I pulled the Devil: temptation. Addiction.

I shuffle the cards, pushing my energy into them.

"So how does this work?" he asks. "You gonna tell me my future?"

"No, it's not like that. My mom always said tarot is basically just a friend who tells it to you straight about your life. No predictions—it's not magic in that way. It's magic because it helps you get what the fuck is going on. So." I shuffle again. "Think of a question. You don't have to tell me what it is. A question about something in your life you need some clarity on. *How* and *What* questions are best."

"So not *Will I be rich someday?*"

"No. It's not a Magic 8 Ball. Like, okay. *How can I expand my entrepreneurial skills outside the pharmaceutical industry?*"

He laughs. "Got it. Okay, I have a question in mind. It's kind of . . . private."

"You can keep it to yourself. The cards know all."

"So it *is* magic."

"It's Something Else." He's something else, too, but I don't say that. "Okay, keep thinking the question as I shuffle."

He closes his eyes and gets this very serious expression on his face, which is so cute.

I shuffle, trying to focus, breathing deep like Mom as I channel my energy, my Something Else, into the paper between my palms. After three shuffles—I don't know why, this feels like the right number—I divide the cards into three little piles.

"Okay. Pick one."

Drew opens his eyes and, for a second, we just look at each other. When my face goes Karalis on me, making it look like I've been a little too heavy-handed with the blush brush, his lips twitch and he looks away.

Drew points to the center deck. "That one."

I pick it up, and my fingers are shaking a little. I shouldn't like how he looks at me—*Micah, Micah*—but I do.

"Okay, I'm going to lay out three cards: past, present, future. So we look at how your whole life is in conversation with this question you have."

This is my favorite part—the story the cards tell, how it's all connected.

I lay the top three cards from the center pile facedown in front of me, then, one at a time, turn them over.

"Ten of Wands for the past," I say. "Page of Wands for the present. The Chariot for the future."

"They don't look scary," he says, coming to stand by me. "That Chariot one's cool. What do they mean?"

"Is your question about something you want? Something you're trying to get?"

"Yes."

"Makes sense." I wonder what it is. He is such a mystery to me. And I wish he weren't. "You have two Wands cards, and the Wands are all about passion, taking action on something. Fire energy. And the Chariot is interesting because it's a water card, meaning a different energy. So, like, right now and in the past, you had all this fire energy, but now you need water. More emotion, more intuition. Feeling."

I can't look at him because I keep thinking about how Micah was my Temperance card, his water balancing my fire.

"Okay. Uh . . ."

His face is all scrunched up, and I laugh. "So, the Chariot is about perseverance. To not give up on this thing you want, even if it seems impossible. It's all about creating a big change in your life. So whatever this thing you want is, you're going to have to be all in because this card is kind of a bitch slap in the tarot."

"Why?"

"Well, it's basically saying that you can get this thing you want, but you've got to, like, man up. That sounds like toxic masculinity or whatever, but just—be brave. Don't give up."

"Okay." He smiles a little. "Worth it. So, what's the deal with the other cards?"

"Well, the past—Ten of Wands—is a card about shit being hard. Like, in the picture you see this guy is carrying all these sticks, but his back is bent and they look heavy as fuck. His view of everything is blocked by the sticks, so he can't really see the future. There's something from your past you need to let go of. It's weighing you down. Does that . . . ring a bell?"

He lets out a heavy sigh. "Yeah."

I point to the Page of Wands, his present. "And, as you can see, if you let that shit go, you'll be ready to take on the world. The Page is this character in the tarot who's like, *Let's do this thing*."

"The picture makes me think of Gandalf holding his staff."

"Uh . . ."

"*Lord of the Rings*. Told you, I read fantasy, you live it."

"Oh, right. That old dude. He was a magician or something, right?"

"Not a magician—*the* magician. Arguably the best one ever, with Dumbledore as a possible exception."

If he were Dad, I'd have to nerd alert that.

"Okay, so channel your inner Gandalf and make some magic happen."

He's quiet, arms crossed, his thinking face on as I gather the cards up.

"No one's ever done something like this for me before," he finally says. "Thanks. It helped. A lot."

I think about how his dad is at the pub, his mom just a memory. My parents got taken from me, but his parents chose to leave him. I suddenly get why he deals, why he wants a role. He's like me—he just wants someone to see him. I hand Drew the Chariot card, and a little jolt goes through me when his fingers brush mine.

"Keep it," I say. I'll have to find another card to replace it, but this is the kind of stuff I've seen Mom do, and it feels right. "Whatever this thing you want is, Drew—go for it. You told me that day we ditched that you're going to end up like your dad, but I don't think so." I hold up my velvet bag of magic. "The cards see what you can't. And I agree with them— you're passionate, driven, creative." I smile. "Entrepreneurial. Someone like you can do cool things in the world."

He blinks. Looks around his kitchen like he's never seen it before.

"Did I blow your mind or weird you out?" I say. "Because I'm thinking this reading could go either way."

Drew slips the card into his front pocket, then reaches back into the fridge and pops the cap off another bottle. He slides it toward me across the counter.

"Definitely blew my mind." He takes a long swig of his beer.

"Is your dad gonna notice all this beer disappearing?" I ask.

Drew shrugs. "Doesn't matter. We Nolans, we take the whole drunk Irish stereotype pretty seriously. My uncle owns a frickin' pub. I've been drinking since I was eight. Come to think of it, I think it was my father who gave me that first beer."

"Damn. I cannot imagine my dad ever letting me—"

I stop, the word stuck in my throat. I couldn't have imagined Dad cheating on Mom, either.

"I'm sorry," I say, as my eyes fill. "I'm a lousy drunk. I always get emotional. Either I'm too happy or I'm too sad."

Drew reaches out and wipes away the tears that spill down my cheeks with the backs of his fingers. I really like when he touches me, and that makes me cry more. I am such a piece-of-shit girlfriend. And sister. And daughter. All I've done since the wave is get wasted and sleep and yell at people and want to cheat on my boyfriend.

"Nothing to be sorry about." He leans against the counter, blows out a breath. "So . . . tonight was my last night as a dealer."

I pick at the label on my bottle. Try not to panic. He'd said he wasn't giving me any more anyway. I shouldn't care.

"Why?"

He looks down at his scuffed-up leather boots. When he speaks, it's so soft, I almost don't hear the words.

"I want to do right by the miracle."

"What . . . what does that mean?"

A ghost smile. His eyes, those gray-and-gold swirls, meet mine. "This famous scientist was giving a talk a couple years ago—I saw it online last night. And he said that we have a responsibility to be the best version of ourselves we can be. Whatever that is. Because it's so insane how a very specific set of circumstances brought the atoms that make you together. All the things that had to happen for you to exist. You know? And he said, 'We have to do right by the miracle. The miracle that is us.'" Drew shrugs. "I looked at the pills on my desk and . . . I was done."

"My dad would have really liked you," I say. His eyes widen, and this expression I can't make out flies across his face, but it's gone before I can name it. "Apart from the selling-me-drugs thing."

He nods. "Yeah. I'm a bastard for that."

"Drew. No. *No.* It's been my choice. I've practically forced you to sell to me." I try to smile, to not look shattered. "So your question. For the tarot. I'm guessing it was about, like, the rest of your life, right? Life after dealing."

He takes in a shuddering breath, then his eyes slide to mine, hands gripping the counter. The way he looks at me—suddenly I know his question. The shape of it. What he wants.

"Hannah, I—"

Micah. Micah.

"I should go soon." I glance at the clock on the stove. "It's . . . late."

He watches me for a moment, then nods. "So this is the last time we hang out."

"What?"

"Because I'm not, you know. Fulfilling my role. This is it, right?"

The vacuum No Drew suddenly opens up inside me is like being held in a glacier's hand. And I realize: He is the only deep breath I take.

I close my eyes, squeeze away the new set of tears. "Yeah. Totally. I mean, I knew that."

Drew starts forward. "Wait. I didn't—"

"Thanks for . . . I'll see you. Around."

I burst into tears. Jesus fuck, can I just be emotionally stable for once in my stupid, pointless life? I reach, blind, for my coat, my purse.

"What did I do? Just. Hold on—*Hannah*."

"I'm fine! The beer—emotional. Ignore me."

"Ignore you." He's standing there, looking at me like Micah looks at me, like I'm too much, too much.

I can't carry you.

I nod. "I get it, Drew. I do. You want to . . . be the miracle. Do right by it. Like you said. And I'm just. *Just.* Just Hannah. Right? You want to, like, *be* something now." I start laughing, I don't know why. "Not the kind of person who'd steal their dead father's Vicodin."

"That's not—"

"You can't carry me. I get it."

My fingers are numb and it's impossible to get my coat on and I drop my purse and now everything's on the floor fuck and I get on my knees and then Drew is there, surrounded by lipstick and tissues and pens and gum wrappers, and his arms are around me and he is holding me together.

"I wish you could see what I can," he whispers. "You're great. Just Hannah is my favorite Hannah."

"That makes zero sense. All you've seen me do is get high and ditch school and buy drugs."

"No. That's all *you* see. I see someone who's keeping a horrible secret about her dead father so that her sister doesn't have to hold that. Someone who is delighted by the world, when she lets herself enjoy it—who sees how beautiful a leaf or an old statue can be. Who isn't afraid to say a party is lame. Who is like some tarot sorceress. You don't pretend to be someone you're not and couldn't care less about your fucking brand on social or what anyone thinks of you. You're basically a revolutionary in the making! Do you know you're the only person I sell to who actually *talks* to me? Sees me as a person?" He tips my jaw up with his fingers and I look into his eyes and I know he's telling me the truth. "You're fucking awesome."

I never knew a dirty kitchen floor could feel like a temple or that a boy wearing a faded Dropkick Murphys shirt could be its high priest.

I tighten my hands around his shoulders because it feels like the planet is off balance, which Mae would say is impossible, but I can feel it, I can feel the center sliding away. "I don't know what to say."

I think he really means what he said. But that doesn't sound like me at all.

"You don't have to say anything. It's bullshit that you had to wait seventeen years to hear it. From me, of all people."

"Right now, you're all the people." I swallow, the right words stuck in my throat. "I think you might be the only friend I have, Drew."

He sucks in a breath, and I sag against him, and I say the thing I haven't been able to say to anyone, not ever. Not even to myself.

"I had an abortion in March, and I didn't want to."

Drew looks down, his eyes dark, like what I said has filled them with midnight-blue ink.

He looks *in* me. Not at me or through me. He sees all of me, and he doesn't turn away.

He keeps looking.

And that look is medicine.

Not a pill. So much better.

He sees me.

When I start to shake, Drew slides an arm beneath my knees and sweeps me up into his arms as he stands.

"What . . . what are you doing?" I say.

"Carrying you."

some people are mirrors that
let you see yourself

Junk Mail
Nolan Residence
Dorchester

22

Hannah

We go upstairs. To his room. It isn't the room of a drug dealer. There are two bookcases stuffed with books, the bed is made, the desk free of clutter. There's a Miles Davis poster.

He eases us down on the floor, so we're leaning against the bed. He takes my hand in his.

"Do you want to talk about it?" he asks quietly.

"Drew, you don't want—"

"I do." He curls his fingers around mine.

I can't look at him while I talk. I trace the half-moons of his neatly trimmed fingernails. Mae would approve of his unexpected tidiness.

"In the waiting room, my mom, she asked if I was sure. Said she and Dad would support whatever I chose. I mean, really, they would have. Whatever I wanted. I know that. I knew it then, too. There was no pressure or judgment. Totally my choice. You know? And the counselor, she was great, she said I could do what I wanted, said it was possible things were okay, that maybe the pills hadn't—like, I could get some tests, if I wanted, to be sure, but . . . I knew it wasn't fair, to any of us, to not do what I did. I mean, yeah, Mae turned out okay even though her mom was . . . but, like, what if she hadn't? Had had brain damage or . . . I mean, how fucked-up would that be, to do that to a person, from day one of their life, you know? And the look on Micah's face when I said that maybe we should think about it, not rush the decision . . . He didn't want that. Not yet. And he said, you know, the pills, he said I should . . ."

I take a breath and Drew tightens his hand around mine. "I don't think it was *wrong* of me to do it. I'm seventeen. Way too young to be a mom. And, Jesus, I can't even imagine right now, with a kid—after the wave. You know? And I was on a lot, I mean *a lot*, of stuff. I just think if I hadn't been fucked-up, maybe I would have—considered it. Having a baby. I don't know. It was earlier than I planned, but I wasn't going to do the college thing. I really do just want to be a mom and a yoga teacher, which maybe makes me basic, but . . . it's totally possible I maybe would have been like, *no, I'm not ready to have a kid and that's that*. If Mae got pregnant, it'd be such an easy decision. To go to the clinic. And I would have totally supported that. But it's all so fucked-up for me because *I wasn't certain*. It isn't simple, like, no drugs equals baby. Drugs equals no baby. If I were sober, I still might have done it.

"The worst part is *I don't know* because of where I was at, at the time. I was so depressed—Dr. Brown said that's part of why I started using in the first place. I mean, fucking duh, right? And because for Micah there was just no discussion, none. Maybe he would have left. And without him, by myself? How would I . . . ? He should have come. Maybe if he'd been there, he would have, could have seen, could have felt . . . I know we're young, but . . . He should have *come*."

"He let you go there alone."

His voice is so soft I almost don't catch how deeply fucking pissed he is. Horror and anger mixed together, like he took my feelings and made a sound with them.

"Maybe he felt, like, since my mom was there I didn't need him to be, too. I don't know. It's my . . . body. My choice." I chanted that at the Women's March with Mom and Mae. And I believe that.

"But it's your heart, too," he says quietly.

Right when he says this, some of the ragged parts inside my chest, all those frayed pieces of my heart, start to fuse back together.

He smiles, like he can hear that stitching happening. "This is probably the weirdest conversation you've ever had with your dealer, huh?"

"*Former* dealer."

"I like the sound of that."

We are staring at each other in the way you do when you've just hiked to the top of a mountain you thought you'd never be able to climb. It's hard to breathe. But the view—it's magnificent.

"Does Micah ever tell you how beautiful you are?"

His eyes follow the blood that blooms under my too-pale cheeks. My skin, it can't keep a secret to save its life. The Karalis curse.

"Sometimes."

"He should tell you all the time. Because you are. All the time."

The words come out of me like an acorn, a compulsion. I have to say them.

"You're beautiful, too."

He is. That wild, raven hair, a face sketched by a sure hand, and those eyes like the stars in Mae's posters.

Drew blinks. "No one's . . . no one's ever told me that before."

"Well, people should. All the time." I lean my head on Drew's shoulder, afraid to look at him anymore. Afraid because I want to kiss him. All over. And I want him to kiss me back.

I think I have wanted that since the beginning, since that day on the baseball diamond, beneath the bleachers.

Drew shifts so that his arm is around me, then he gently runs his fingers through my hair.

"That feels good," I mumble. We stay like that for a long time.

Until I remember Dad. And Becca Chen. Like father, like daughter. I pull away, abrupt, cold air rushing between us.

"I can't," I say, more to myself than him. "Micah."

"Okay."

"My dad . . . he . . . I don't want to be like him. What he did to my mom—"

"We're not doing anything wrong," Drew says gently.

"But I want to," I whisper. "That's the problem, Drew. I want—" I scramble away from him. Because I don't trust myself. I don't know how to say no to a high.

His eyes flare, and he inhales, a long, deep breath, then he reaches over and intertwines his fingers with mine, our palms pressed against each other's. He squeezes my hands once, then lets go.

"I'm just your friend," Drew says. "For now. But . . ." He leans in, his forehead touching mine. "I want to be more. When you're ready, Hannah. And if you're not, okay. That's okay. Either way, I'm here."

And suddenly there's a choice to make.

"What was your question—for the cards?" I breathe.

"*How can I be with Hannah?*" His fingers trail down my neck. "But I think you knew that already."

"Everything's changing so fast," I whisper. "It's . . ." I shake my head, suddenly overwhelmed. "I'm so scared, Drew. I'm so fucking scared." My eyes fill again. "I'm so tired of being scared."

I thought my problem was that I was invisible to the world. But Drew's shown me it's so much bigger than that. *I* can't even see me.

"Hey, I'm here. There's nothing to be—"

"Don't say it." I pull away from him. "There's *everything* to be afraid of! Outer space, for one. Like, the entire cosmos all around us. And if I start thinking about it all, about Dad, and not telling Mae about him, and Becca Chen being pregnant, and did Mom know, did she know about Dad, and then you and Micah . . . and Mae going to school, and never seeing Mom again, and maybe she's stopped visiting me because I'm such a fuckup, and the . . . the b-baby . . . and the *ocean*—"

"Okay, okay." Drew draws me close. "You're right. There's a fucking lot to be afraid of."

"I just want it all to go away. For a little bit. I just need a *break*. It's been so hard, Drew. I'm so tired."

"I want to help." His lips move against my hair, hot breath running along my scalp. "Hannah, let me help."

"There's nothing you can do." I look up at him. "I think it will always be this way. I don't think I'll ever be happy again. Maybe I never was."

Drew watches me for a moment, and I pull away, thinking I must be crushing him, because his face suddenly pinches with pain.

"We're going to change that," he says. Then he reaches into his pocket and holds up two pills. "This is all I've got left." He hesitates. "It's . . . stronger than what you're used to these days."

"Oxy?"

He nods. "And, Hannah, if we—you have to promise me, this is it. We do this together, and then that's it. And we find another way to make it better. Okay?"

I nod. Just one more time. I can do that.

"Promise me," he says.

"I promise."

I take one of the pills. "You've never gotten high with me before."

"I want to be where you are." Drew slides the pill between his lips.

It's not too long before we are floating on a beautiful cotton-candy cloud. A forgetting cloud. I am lighter than the cloud. Lighter than the moonbeams that pass through it.

I am the moonbeams.

I am No More and Nothing and Everything and Good.

Everything is perfect.
Everything.
No More.
Nothing.

Everything.
Good.

I am getting to go to space before Mae.

I pull my eyes open and look over at Drew. He's beside me on the cloud, his eyes half-closed, one hand curled around my ankle.

"I want to do right by the miracle, too," I say.

Or maybe I just think it.

"You *are* the miracle," he breathes.

Or maybe I just imagine it.

23

Mae

ISS Location: Low-Earth Orbit
Earth Date: 31 October
Earth Time (EST): 13:07

You don't need dark magic to bring the dead back to life: You just need a freshly carved pumpkin.

I run my hand over the blood-orange five-pounder Nate hacked into before going in search of better knives. Its tangerine guts have been laid bare, filled with white jewels. I don't know why pumpkins make me poetic, but they do.

The sour, earthy scent hits me, and suddenly I'm in the quantum realm, leaping into the past. No rules here in Quantum Land, remember? One minute I'm in Nate Russo's dining room, the next I'm back in Venice.

Joni Mitchell is playing in the kitchen. Pumpkin spice soup. Mom humming along.

"I'm thinking Einstein." Dad holds up a knife. "And we use the leftover cobweb decor for the hair. I bought mini battery-powered fans so it'll blow constantly. What do you say?"

"That'd be sick," Micah says, approving. I nod.

Mom sticks her hand into the gourd, pulling out seeds. "Ambitious, Professor. You think you've got what it takes?"

Dad glances at me. "We've got a naysayer, Winters. Help me out here."

"It can't be harder than researching extreme particle acceleration."

He grins. "Girl after my own heart."

Mom rolls her eyes. "You two."

"Someone did Einstein for the NASA pumpkin-carving contest last year,"
I say. "The Jet Propulsion Lab doesn't mess around. I could look up some
stuff and see how they—"

"Amuck! Amuck! Amuck!" Hannah squeals from the living room. "Why
is no one watching this with me?"

I glance into the living room. "Because we've seen it ten thousand times!"

It's quiet, and then I hear the beginnings of Nah's favorite part. She's
fast-forwarded. We all know what's coming.

"Don't do it!" Micah yells, already laughing.

"I put a spell on you, and now you're mine . . ." Hannah slides across
the hall's wooden floor, wearing the witch's hat that had been sitting as a
decoration in the living room window.

"Oh God, she's gone full Hocus Pocus on us," Mom says.

Hannah strikes a pose, more Lady Gaga than Bette Midler, but it works.
"You can't stop the things I do . . ."

Mom grabs the broom leaning against the fridge and uses it as a mic,
and now it's a duet. "I ain't lyin' . . ."

Dad holds his hands up, trying not to look amused. "Ladies, please. We
have serious work to do if we're going to get this thing in by the deadline!"

"Hello, Salem!" Nah shouts. "My name's Winnifred. What's yours?"

Mom does a snazzy—

Coffee.

Bitter and sweet.

And boy.

And wind.

I leap back through the spacetime continuum. To now. To a boy who
watches me, concerned and curious.

"You're here," I say.

"I am. Got off an hour early for good behavior." Ben is studying my face very intently. "Is your olfactory bulb messing with your hippocampus and amygdala?"

I blink.

Sense memory. He's talking about sense memory.

"Yes."

"I hate when that happens."

My cheek itches, and he reaches out and brushes it with the pads of his fingers. They come away glistening.

"Oh." I stare at his skin. Tears. Actual tears.

That's eight times.

"Lacrimal ducts are a bitch," he says. "I'm taking an anatomy elective right now, so I know words like *lacrimal ducts*. You impressed?"

"With you?" I say. "Always."

I've been his girlfriend less than a week, but it's very strange because I keep thinking, haven't we always been together? For years and years?

"That's my girl." He holds up a to-go cup of coffee. "A Castaways re-storative. Dirty chai latte, heavy on the dirty. Made it myself. Might not be too hot since it took me ten years to get here after my shift."

I reach out, my hand unsteady and a bit slimy with pumpkin. "Thanks." I take a sip. Spicy and bitter and sweet. "Chai and coffee?"

He nods. "Good, right?"

"Yeah."

He smiles down at me, very messy and sleepy-looking from an open-ing shift. Coffee stains on his sweatshirt.

He leans close and tucks back a strand of hair that has slipped from behind my ear. My olfactory bulb is taking notes. "I had a dream about you last night."

"You did?"

"You were on the space station, and we were video chatting—can we do that?"

"Yes," I say. "The satellites are pretty good."

"Okay, well, you were doing somersaults for me. It was awesome."

"Really?" Just the thought—the thought of that reality. I can hardly breathe.

It feels so far away now. Six more days until my Annapolis interview. I haven't cancelled it, but I haven't decided *not* to cancel it, either.

Ben nods. "Really. You looked totally at home in zero gravity." He leans in and presses his lips against mine. "More where that came from," he murmurs as footsteps in the kitchen get closer.

"Ah, Ben, you're here," Nate says, trooping in. He dumps a new set of knives on the table. "Where's my coffee?"

"In Cambridge," Ben says. "Go get it."

"Bastard." Nate glances at the cup in my hand, eyes narrowed. "So. This. You two. I refused to believe it until I saw it. It's go for launch, then?"

"Oh, it's launched," Ben says.

I roll my eyes. "Last Friday, Ben here used quantum mechanics to tell me he was lost without me." I take a sip of my chai. "What could I do?"

Nate barks out a laugh. "Heisenberg?" Ben nods. "Nice."

My cousin hands me a large metal spoon and gestures to the five-pounder. "Get in there, Mae. I've got some serious nerd ass to kick. First prize gets honor, glory, and—most important—two tickets to the first home game between the Sox and the Yankees."

My mother's scent hits the room, so strong I can hardly breathe. A summer rose garden. For just a second I hear her singing along to Joni Mitchell.

"I thought you science guys were above stupid things like sports," Hannah drawls.

My sister floats in, already a ghost. Moondust pale. She doesn't even need a costume to hand out candy to kids tonight. I try to catch her eye, but it's like studying the night sky in LA: It's impossible to get a clear picture when there's so much stuff between you. Ever since she became a supernova on the kitchen floor, single-handedly smashed the ISS to smithereens, and told me our family was done, she's been avoiding me even more. Holes up in her room like she's in quarantine. But her pupils are normal, so she's sober. This afternoon, anyway.

"Hey, we may be atheists, but baseball is religion here." Nate digs into another pumpkin with a knife that would have made Mom nervous.

There is less breath in me when I hear Mom say, *It's sharp—be careful!* My mind is a time capsule. A golden record that reminds me what we were, what was.

"You know what we call Fenway Park, where the Sox play?" Nate's saying.

"A good waste of a Saturday afternoon?" she says.

Nate stares. "I *cannot* believe we are related."

"The cathedral." Ben spreads his hands like Gram's priest standing under the crucifix, but his are slimy with pumpkin bits. "Holiest place on the Eastern Seaboard."

Nah groans. "That is ten kinds of wrong."

"You, too, huh?" I say.

He nods. "My family is deeply ashamed that a Brooklyn boy loves the Red Sox. I have your cousin to blame for that."

"*You're welcome,*" Nate sings, in full *Moana* mode.

Ben rolls his eyes and pulls the guts out of the gourd, his fingers tangling with mine. Deliberately.

I stare at him. He stares back. The force field here is so strong I'm sure we could suck in entire star systems.

The doorbell rings, and Hannah drifts toward the front of the house. "That's for me."

As soon as Nah's out of range, Nate leans close, his voice low. "I'm gonna put this in Mae-speak, okay?"

I nod.

"She's out of orbit. Understand?"

I nod. He's right. I know.

When satellites and other objects in space orbit Earth, they're able to maintain their path through a perfect balance between the object's inertia and its forward momentum, and the pull of gravity on it. If any of these things is changed, the satellite will either crash down onto what it's orbiting or spin off into space. The change usually happens if the object collides with something in space—a meteorite, something like that.

A tsunami.

Mom, Dad, Micah—they all kept her in orbit. Now she's spinning.

"She won't talk to me." I throw my hands up, and pumpkin guts fly everywhere. "Flushing her pills only made her hate me more. I need to do something more drastic."

Ben's eyebrows go sky-high. "Pills? Not just booze?"

I nod. "I didn't say because—"

"I understand," Ben says.

Nate brushes goo off his hands. "We gotta tell my parents. Have an intervention—"

His face suddenly turns bland and cheery as he looks over my shoulder, toward the front room.

Nah's with the only person I've ever seen her talk to at school in the month we've been there. The cute guy from her math class who looks like that vampire on TV.

"This is Drew," Hannah says.

Nate, despite wearing a pink top that says *Rosé All Day*, still somehow manages to present as a very intimidating older brother.

My cousin pauses, knife held aloft. Drew raises his hands.

"I come in peace," he says gravely. His eyes swivel to mine. "Mae. Nice to finally meet you."

"Finally?" I say.

He glances at Nah, but she's spinning off into some other galaxy, looking at one of the pumpkins with a frown. I wonder if she's remembering *I put a spell on you*, Mom using a broom as a mic.

"Er." Drew frowns, his hands digging deep into his pockets, like he's going to find the origins of the universe down there. "Just . . . heard a lot about you."

I grab my chai, take a sip. I thought they weren't friends. I can't believe how little I know about my sister's life now.

Nate studies him, like Drew's a plane with a problem. "You go to Saint Francis?"

He nods. "Senior."

"Where are you applying?" Nate asks, which, admittedly, seems like an aggressive question.

Nah looks over her shoulder. "Is this a police interrogation?"

Drew's eyes flick to Ben's MIT sweatshirt. "Not applying anywhere, actually."

"Military?" I ask. I'm trying. We could connect on that. He looks like maybe . . . army? Not intense enough to go marines, but you never know.

"Mae's gonna be a naval aviator," Ben says, smiling at me.

"So I hear." Drew's hands push deeper into his pockets. "That's really cool." He hesitates. "I'm afraid you're oh-for-two on me, though. I'm probably gonna join the union, work on a crew. Like my dad. Or help out at my uncle's bar."

"Which bar?" Nate asks, as though this is going to determine everything.

"Nolan's," he says. "In Dorchester?"

From the look on Nate's face, this must be a dodgy bar. But, really, his standards are quite high.

"Not everyone's like you guys," Hannah says, glaring at me.

"What? I didn't—what?" I look at her, then at Ben.

Drew laughs. "It's cool. I know it's kind of . . ." He pulls off his beanie, runs his hand through his hair.

Hannah comes to his side and loops her arm through his. A surprised smile flits across his face.

"Let's leave the brainiacs to the pumpkin carving," Nah says. "It's going to turn into this whole engineering project and—"

My phone rings, and I don't hear the rest of what she says, because when I turn to look at the screen, I see it's an unknown number.

Ben notices. Grins. "Think it's Annapolis?"

"I don't know why it would be—but I better take it, just in case."

Nate throws me a towel and I get as much goo off my hands as I can, then grab the phone.

I turn away, into the kitchen.

"Hello?"

"Hi, yes, I'd like to speak with Mae Winters?"

"This is she," I say.

That's how Mom answered phones, and I always thought it sounded very professional.

"Hello, Mae." There's a pause. "This is Marilyn Cole from the Red Cross."

All sound fades. There is just the pounding of blood in my ears. The ocean in my body. Surging. A wave. *The* wave. In me.

"Miss Winters?"

"Yes. Yes?"

Someone touches my elbow. Ben. He looks down at me, concerned. Perhaps I am not hiding the panic in my voice very well.

"I see here that you're still a minor and that your guardian is . . . Nora Russo—your aunt, is that correct?"

"Yes."

Nate is there now, saying something to me, but I wave him off.

"Would it be possible for me to speak with her?"

"Anything you have to say, you can say to me."

There's a pause.

"I'd really prefer if there was an adult present."

I look at Nate. "My cousin's here. He's an adult. Is that okay?"

"All right. Can I speak with him?"

Now Nah is in the doorway, the guy—Drew—just behind her.

I hold the phone out to Nate.

"It's the Red Cross. They want to speak to an adult. I don't know why they won't just let me—"

He takes the phone. "Hello? Yes. Yes, I am. I understand."

I watch my cousin's face as they talk. It goes from concern to a collage of hurt.

"Hold—can you hold on a moment? Thank you."

I grip Nate's arm. "Did they find them? Did they?"

Nah walks farther into the kitchen. Stands on the spot she'd been lying in a few weeks ago. A pool of bourbon. Grief whiskey. "What? Who is that?"

"It's about your mom," Nate says.

"They found her," Nah breathes.

Nate's eyes flick to mine. He nods.

"Dad?" I ask.

He shakes his head.

I hold out my hand and he puts the phone in it. The woman talks to me. I hear *mass grave*. That's all I hear. Nate takes the phone from me when I lower it. The woman is still talking. The word *sanitation* flows into the kitchen.

Hannah looks at me. Mom's face and hair and smile. She is Mom incarnate, and it hurts so much to look at her.

"A . . . mass . . ." I take a breath. "She was in a mass grave."

Hannah crumples, and Drew holds her up, gets her to the couch in the living room.

The only mass grave I ever saw was in a history book. Of the Shoah. Jews, in Dachau. My mom was in something like that. A body that had DNA samples collected from it by people in HAZMAT suits, maybe, then was tagged for later identification before being placed in a black or orange or white body bag.

Is she still in the bag?

I know she's gone, but I keep thinking how hard it will be for her to breathe in there.

233

Ben's arms go around me, and I hide in him. I want to stay here forever, in this place of coffee and wind.

"I don't know why I'm feeling so . . ." I push my forehead into his chest. "I thought—I'd hoped she'd just floated on the sea. With him. And he's . . . *Where is he?*"

I knew it wasn't possible, wasn't likely, that they would be together. But knowing they weren't . . . I suppose I had engaged in magical thinking. Or a suspension of disbelief. If you don't know for certain, you can imagine the best outcome of the worst situation.

I look up at Ben. "I didn't let myself imagine them dying. I wouldn't. And now—my mind won't stop. They weren't together, Ben. They died alone."

He rests his forehead against mine. He doesn't say anything, but he is like the rocks he studies, so solid and warm.

The garage door shudders, then the back door opens and Aunt Nora comes in with grocery bags. Uncle Tony is behind her. They stop talking. They stare at us.

Nate hangs up the phone. "They found Aunt Lila," he says, so soft, so gentle.

But still, Aunt Nora drops her groceries and the eggs break.

There's crying.

She is pulling me to her.

Later—I don't know when; I have lost the ability to organize time or anything, but at some point, Ben materializes from a corner, says something to Nate, crosses to me.

"Mae. Should I go? I don't want to intrude. Whatever you need—"

I slide my arms around Ben's waist and rest my cheek against his chest. His arms immediately come around me. Oxytocin and vasopressin.

"Don't go," I whisper.

"I think those might be my favorite words now," he says.

Mom would have liked him. So much. She would have figured out what his favorite soup was and then would have devised an elaborate explanation about what this said about him.

"What's your favorite soup, Ben?"

"I've always been partial to Italian wedding."

I go still. Dad's favorite. I look up toward the ceiling, even though that is not at all where my mother is because she is nowhere, not even in a body bag in Malaysia.

Did you hear that? I want to say.

When the space shuttle *Columbia* exploded in 2003, I was only three years old. Just out of foster care, a brand-new member of the Winters family. I don't remember *Columbia*, though I'm sure Dad, in a rare moment for him, had the TV on nonstop, watching the coverage. Seven astronauts died when the shuttle exploded on reentry into the atmosphere. The whole apparatus disintegrated, the pieces scattered over two states. The remains of the crew were found in the nose of the shuttle.

It's good to find them. Even if they are gone. I'm beginning to realize this now.

When an astronaut signs up for a mission, she knows she can die. It's a dangerous job, to say the least, and any number of things can go wrong. The *Columbia* wasn't the first disaster in the field of space exploration, and it won't be the last. This is the price we pay to know where we came from, how the universe works, and where we're going.

When you're up there and it's no longer a sim, but a real-life bad news disaster, you do everything you can to science the shit out of your situation. To stay alive. You don't give up.

But if you're an astronaut on the ground, supporting the crew, there's only so much you can do. You work with the data you've got. You do everything you can to stay in touch with the crew, to give them whatever support you can. But in the end, they're the ones up there dealing with that rocket, that atmosphere, that universe that is hostile to life. They're in the suit.

They say that mission control messed up with *Columbia*. That the *Atlantis* shuttle was ready to launch, and could have potentially saved the *Columbia* crew. Maybe. In the end, the astronauts lost consciousness. The restraints didn't work on reentry, so their little bodies were being thrown around, bludgeoned by the capsule. The shuttle went into a flat spin and some of them died of asphyxiation before they could get their helmets on. A terrible way to go.

Like drowning.

You'd think mission control would be in complete chaos, right? Phones ringing, data shooting out of computers like lasers, people running around and barking commands. But it's really quiet. I've seen the footage online. *Columbia*'s reentry and landing CAPCOM, Charlie Hobaugh—their point person on the ground, like Ed Harris in *Apollo 13*—he's so calm. As an astronaut himself, he knew that panic is the last thing the crew needed. You can hear him trying to talk to the pilot, Rick D. Husband—*"Columbia, Houston, comm check"*—even though the radio transmission had long since burned up. He kept trying. And on the video, you see the moment, the moment when he knows. He covers his eyes with a hand. Takes a breath.

And then issues the next command.

Send out the ground crew. The rescue crew. But everyone knows it's not to save the astronauts. It's to take care of what's left of them.

One detail that has always stayed with me about the *Columbia* tragedy, beyond the horror of that moment when those astronauts knew something was wrong and that they were never going to stand on Earth again, is this: In the shuttle, there was a copy of a drawing that had been done by a boy, Petr Ginz, while he was in the Terezín concentration camp—an image of what Earth would look like while standing on the surface of the moon. It's a charcoal sketch, or maybe pencil, with lots of spiky rock in the foreground and Earth floating beyond. The boy who drew that knew death was close. Maybe just around the corner. But he kept looking up. To that light.

Petr Ginz was murdered in Auschwitz when he was sixteen.

Ilan Ramon, one of *Columbia*'s crew, had brought Petr's drawing with him. He was the first Israeli in space.

Today, I picture Petr, looking past the barbed wire, gazing up at the moon. And that man, decades later, flying *away* from it. With that dead boy's drawing in his pocket.

What we need, I think, is a grief sim. But I've never heard of one of those.

24

Mae

ISS Location: Low-Earth Orbit
Earth Date: 31 October
Earth Time (EST): 19:45

The Celestron CPC 1100 telescope cost my dad over three thousand dollars. We named her Lucy, for Lucy in the Sky with Diamonds.

She's one of the best telescopes money can buy: an eleven-inch diffraction limited Schmidt–Cassegrain telescope with an aperture of 280 millimeters, which means I can see craters on the moon. And the rings of Saturn. The bands on Jupiter, and its great red spot. The Orion Nebula.

Since we're in an urban landscape, my images will never be as clear as they would be if I were in true darkness, somewhere like the Cape at night. Still, Venus is gorgeous tonight—bright and huge (with a surface temperature of 750 DEGREES!). The Big Dipper traces the sky with its ladle line of stars. Somewhere out there, past our atmosphere, stars are colliding and exploding and black holes are swirling all while Earth spins at 1,040 miles per hour. (This speed is at the equator. Here in Boston, at forty-two degrees north, it's roughly 770 miles per hour, which seems fast—except Earth's orbital velocity around the sun is 67,000 miles per hour. Which ALSO seems fast until you realize that the whole solar system—of which we are, of course, a part—is orbiting around the black hole at the center of the Milky Way galaxy at over 500,000 miles per hour. Which means all the humans on Earth are ACTUALLY moving through space at 140 miles per *second*. WE ARE SPEED DEMONS.) We spin and we spin, like whirling dervishes, swirling in our little pocket of the universe.

But no matter how hard I look, I'm not going to find my parents up there.

I wish I could believe in heaven, in a kingdom in the sky where Mom and Dad are staying at a resort, waiting for us to join them someday. I wish I could see them from my telescope. But I can't. Actually, I don't wish I believed in that. Because then that would mean that some god had *allowed* my parents and all those other people to die a horrible death. And, somehow, that seems worse than total annihilation.

My mother's body is in a mass grave.

We don't know where my father's body is.

They were hurt. And scared. And alone.

These are the facts. I can't change them, no matter how much I want to.

I close my eyes.

Sky mind. Sky mind. Breathe. Thoughts are weather. Sky mind. Breathe.

I wait until my mind is not swirling, and then I open my eyes, adjust the telescope, zoom in on the moon. Its incandescent light reaches us from 1.3 light-seconds away. It's by far the largest satellite body in the solar system and the only one astronauts have set foot on. But I bet we'll be on Mars soon. Dad said if his next book hit the *New York Times* bestseller list, he'd buy tickets for us to orbit the moon. Mom had said she could think of better things to do with half a million dollars, but when pressed, she couldn't come up with anything cooler than the moon, so she gave us her permission to go.

But he will never write that book. So I will never orbit the moon with my dad, or call him from the International Space Station wearing a NASA flak suit. When I'm on a rocket filled with over seventy-six thousand gallons of fuel and thinking about the *Challenger* blowing up, he won't be down on Earth, hoping I make it into orbit in one piece.

"Visibility is good tonight, Dad," I say.

I'm grateful Uncle Tony "accidentally" broke the streetlamp right in front after we moved in. He reported this accident to me while handing me the box labeled MAE'S TELESCOPE.

- Mars—perfect visibility
- Venus—fairly good visibility
- Saturn—average
- Uranus—average
- Mercury, Jupiter, and Neptune—slightly difficult to see
- Mom and Dad—zero visibility

Tonight, all I want to do is look at the moon.

I zoom in on the craters. Imagine the moon mansions I would build on them. This is something Dad and I would do. Moon mansions. Dad's had a Zen rock garden in the back, the most intricate and beautiful Zen garden ever, made with moon rocks and moon sand.

Mom said she didn't want a mansion, just a wide expanse where she could do yoga, so I always made sure to have a nicely tended patch for her. I zoom in on a plain beside one of the craters, half expecting Mom to be up there, doing sun salutations. Or would they be moon salutations?

I can't believe they threw her body in a pit.

Down below, I hear laughter and shouts. The sidewalks are full of goblins and witches and maybe some astronauts. We had plans to hand out candy and line the driveway with jack-o'-lanterns, but our porch light is off and the pumpkins are in the trash. Tomorrow is the Day of the Dead, and I suppose it's fitting, getting this call when we did. In Mexico, they go to their loved ones' graves and light candles. Gram will go to her church in Florida and light candles in front of saints. Even though Dad was an atheist, I bet he would like that a little. If only because it probably makes Gram feel better.

"Hey, kiddo."

Uncle Tony stands behind me, his eyes heavy. He's wearing his favorite Red Sox jacket and carrying a blanket and a thermos.

"Figured you'd be a little chilly up here," he says.

I reach for the blanket, throw it over my shoulders. "Thanks."

"Now, this hot chocolate has some peppermint schnapps in it," he says. "Don't tell your dad."

I smile. "You were Dad's favorite. In the family."

He nods. "He was mine. We had some good times, him and me." He sits next to me and pours me a little cup of spiked hot cocoa. I never drink, except for a glass of champagne on Christmas, but this is a special occasion, I think. "He was so smart, but he never made me feel stupid. You know?"

I nod. "Me, too."

He runs a hand over his head. "Your sister and me. We're the only nongeniuses in the family." He leans closer. "Sometimes that's hard. On her. You know what I mean?"

"But I don't care. Mom and Dad never did, never treated us differently or—"

"I know." He shrugs. "Food for thought."

I almost tell him about Hannah, but that would be too much, after today's news. It wouldn't be fair to him and Aunt Nora. Or Nah. Today is about Mom.

We look at the sky for a long time. Quiet. Peppermint schnapps is good. I can see why people drink alcohol. But it makes the stars blurry.

"What if they never find him?" I whisper.

The finding matters. I didn't know how much it would, but I should have. I want to find *everything*: the origin of the universe, a cure for my sister, the answer to every problem ever put before me.

"He'll get where he needs to go," Uncle Tony says. "That man, he's not the type to be lost. Know what I mean?"

I nod. Maybe I'm not giving Dad enough credit. He was like Ben, a Zen master. Maybe he rode the wave until he reached enlightenment, then welcomed it with open arms.

"Mae." Uncle Tony clears his throat. "I would never try to replace your pops . . . and you can never replace my Annie. But . . ." I remember him holding her little body. Her shallow breathing, his lips kissing her bare head. "It occurs to me that I'm a dad without a daughter, and you're a daughter without a dad. On this plane, I mean. They're still ours and we're still theirs. Always. But. I'm here. If you or Hannah need me. Okay?"

My throat grows thick. I nod.

"Okay." He smiles. "I'm freezing my balls off out here. I'm going inside."

I laugh. "I'll be down soon."

"All right, kiddo." He lays a hand on my shoulder, then heads for the dormer window that leads into the attic.

I turn. "Uncle Tony?"

"Yeah?"

"Thanks."

"Anytime, kiddo."

I stay outside for a while longer, until the schnapps makes the moon's craters turn into pools.

When I'm back inside, I peek in the kitchen. Nah has Mom's soup pot on the stove.

"What are we making?" I say.

She looks up from the cutting board. Her eyes are puffy and red.

"I just want to be alone."

"Oh." We've never not made soup together. "Okay."

In the middle of the night, I get up. Can't sleep. Keep thinking about the weight of dirt. Mom hated being dirty. Every time she got out of the shower she'd say something like, *God, I love showers*.

The kitchen is dark and smells like lemons and onions. I check the fridge, peek inside the container of soup sitting on the top shelf. I already know, though. What it is.

Avgolemono.

Mom's favorite. And the soup she made when Yia-yia died. Secret Karalis family recipe.

My sister didn't make a goodbye soup for Mom with me. Because she has decided I am leaving, too. Maybe she already knows what soup she'll make for me when I go to Annapolis. Except.

I'm not going.

I grip the counter. "I'm not going, Dad. I'm sorry. I know you understand."

Hannah will not be all right by June. And I won't be a second wave in her life. Not making soup together was the sign I needed. She's never been that far gone.

There is a bloom of orange light outside—a flame. Aunt Nora is in the backyard, smoking a cigarette. She looks a million years old. Tonight, she found out her sister was buried in a mass grave.

Aunt Nora's accelerated aging makes sense. I think maybe I am a million years old, too.

"Mom," I whisper. "Aunt Nora's smoking. You should come yell at her."

Somewhere, Mom sighs.

The soup pot sits in the sink, soaking. I turn on the faucet, wait until the water is so hot I can hardly stand it, then I scrub the pot.

Cleaning up my sister's mess.

Part 2

Across the Universe

25

Mae

ISS Location: Low-Earth Orbit
Earth Date: 24 November
Earth Time (EST): 15:21

t is November now. Almost Thanksgiving.

We are at an apple orchard because that is a thing people do here in Boston. They pick apples. Then they take them home and bake pies, because there isn't much else to do with a bushel of apples. When Ben insisted we celebrate my birthday, I told him he had to plan it because I am not interested in a birthday without my parents, and this is what he came up with. He said it's good to get some dirt underneath your fingernails. Typical geophysicist.

After, we are going to the Dresden Dolls concert. Maybe it will be fun, but I feel bad about dancing when they're dead.

This is not the first birthday party I've had without my parents.

I had three whole birthdays without Mom's cakes and Dad making thermodynamics jokes whenever I blew out the candles. I don't remember my first birthday with them, which was when I turned four, except for the ball pit. I remember being in the McDonald's ball pit with my mom, how she held me in all that color. How she kept pressing her lips against my cheek. I'd been a little frightened of that sea of plastic, but I already knew she wouldn't let me go, not ever. That there was someone who would finally hold on to me for dear life. I think that's the day when I knew I was home.

Sometimes, now, when I am alone, I just whisper, "Mama." I feel like she hears me. I will never tell anyone I do this.

I say *Mama* when I wake up in the middle of the night and I feel the pressing. When the sheets are heavy and I start thinking about the hundreds of pounds of dirt in that other pit, the one without color. The one Mom was in for so long before they took her out.

Mama.

I close my eyes and I picture Mom and me in the center of that galaxy of plastic spheres, the smell of French fries in the air, those little red and blue and yellow and green planets orbiting us. Mom, encircling my body like the rings of Saturn.

"The tree of knowledge," Nate says, resting his hand on a knobby trunk. "From Eve herself to Isaac Newton watching an apple fall, the *malum* really is the fruit of all knowledge."

There are rows and rows of trees all around us. Not too many people, since it's the end of the season. It's a beautiful day. Blue, with puffy white clouds. Bright sun.

"Which one is Isaac Newton?" Nah asks.

There is color in her cheeks. Maybe it's the wind, but maybe it's because we're out here and it's good, fresh air and friends and a thermos of apple cider. Maybe Ben was right about the benefits of getting dirt under your fingernails. The tightness in my chest loosens a bit and, for a second, I feel hope. This day is going to be good. And it's going to make her better. Nate and I agreed that before we tell my aunt and uncle about Nah's problems, I can play one last card. The ace up my sleeve. Maybe it's more of a wild card. I've never gambled, but I feel like I am today. If my plan doesn't work, we tell them everything. This is naive, but I can't bear to make things more miserable for Nah during the holidays. It's already going to be hard enough.

I asked Ben if I could invite anyone I wanted to my birthday party, and he said yes, of course. So I invited someone that I hope will make things better. You can only stand hearing your sister cry herself to sleep for so long. In fact, you can't stand it at all.

But now, in this orchard, I realize that I am the dumbest smart person I know. Because Hannah already brought someone to my party.

She goes for a dangling Red Delicious, but it's just out of reach. Drew helps, his fingers grazing hers. Her eyes flick to his, hold. Then away.

"Ben," I whisper.

This panic, it's what you feel when the rocket has launched, but you missed something very important on the preflight checklist.

"Yes?" he whispers back. Then he leans closer. "Why are we whispering?"

I had no idea she was going to bring him. I haven't seen him since the day the Red Cross called, other than at school. Forgot all about him. Stupid, *stupid*. Why have my observational capacities failed me? Why did I not connect those dots?

I think this day is not going to be good.

Drew hands her the apple. Squeezes her hand once before letting go. Her skin, oh god, she's a rose when he touches her. Karalis skin doesn't hide a thing.

Now I know where she goes at lunch. When she gets on the train without me. When she climbs through her window late at night.

"I made a tactical error," I whisper. "A huge one."

"Birthday girls don't make tactical errors." He kisses my forehead. "That is a mathematical certainty."

I grab his arm, pull him from the tree and Nate's impromptu lecture on the history of gravity.

"Ben. You said I could invite anyone I wanted."

He nods. "Drew's nice."

"Ben—"

"Happy birthday, little sister."

I look over Ben's shoulder. "Micah. You made it."

they tell you if the airplane is going down

to put your oxygen mask on before you help anyone else

Apple Crate
Blossom Hill Orchard
Natick, MA

26

Hannah

should be over the moon that he's here.

I should be running, sprinting, vaulting into his arms.

Micah is here. He is standing a few feet from me, this improbable, beautiful blond surfer in the middle of a New England apple orchard.

But I can't move.

Micah looks at me, hazel eyes in sunny skin that I have bathed in and kissed and loved and missed. His lips turn up in that smile, the one he gave me when he walked out of the ocean, his board under his arm, stood over my towel, and said, "I'm Micah. And you're my future wife. So you better give me your phone number."

My body, it never does what is socially acceptable, the right thing. I know this because my body leans, it leans *back*. Against Drew.

"Are you sure?" Drew murmurs, so soft only I can hear it.

He's never met Micah, but it's so obvious, that claiming gaze. There is only one person who would think they had the right to look like they owned me.

I press against Drew and he lets out a soft breath. "Okay," he says.

Mae—brilliant, calm, cool, collected Mae—flails her hands. Actually *flails*.

"It's . . . so good to see you, Micah! Thank . . . thank you for coming. I, um . . . This is my boyfriend, Ben. He, uh, he goes to MIT and—"

Micah is ignoring Mae. Staring at me. The smile disappears from his face, and now he just looks confused. Because I was supposed to run to him. To be happy. To give him a big kiss.

But I just stand here.

"Hi," I say.

All those missed calls swim between us. The ones he missed. The ones I missed. On accident. On purpose. The awkward texts. The ignored texts. The photos that were promised and never sent. All the things we can't say, won't say. The entire month of March, and everything after. The wave.

He walks past my sister, toward me. Looks at Drew. Looks *harder* at Drew. At the lack of space between us.

Drew slides his hand into mine. Holds tight.

And now Micah stops. Goes completely still.

"Fuck," Nate whispers.

"So were you waiting to tell me about this when I came for Christmas?" Micah's voice is so quiet, that calm sea inside him getting ready to swell. "Or was I never supposed to find out?"

"I'm so sorry," I whisper.

"You're sorry."

"Nothing's happened," I say. "I promise."

He gives our hands a pointed look.

"Yeah, that's a lie." Micah turns to Drew. "So, what, my girlfriend fucks you, and you give her pills?"

I wish he'd hit me instead. I really think I do. Who is this boy?

Mae makes a startled, choked sound. *"Micah—"*

Drew starts to say something, too, but I beat them both to it. "If that's the kind of person you think I am, then there's nothing more we need to say here. So you can turn your ass around and go back to Logan Airport."

"I . . ." Micah shakes his head. "Fuck." He digs the heels of his hands into his eyes. When he looks back up at me I see what I feel every morning, when I first wake up, flash across Micah's face—all that shame and regret, all those what-ifs. "I'm sorry. I'm just—baby, what the fuck is *happening* right now? We . . . you're my . . . I don't understand."

"Is it true?" Mae says from behind Micah. She's staring at Drew. I have never seen violence on my sister's face before. I think she might hit him. "Are you the one giving her the pills?"

Her eyes, they are so big. Ringed with shadows. I hadn't noticed the shadows before.

"I . . . was," Drew says. "I'm not anymore. That was a mistake. A huge mistake."

He doesn't know what's in my pocket. Just because he's stopped dealing doesn't mean I've stopped buying.

"You asshole," Nate growls, stalking toward Drew.

Micah pushes in front of Nate, shoves Drew, his palms splayed across Drew's chest. Drew's hand falls out of mine and he backs up, his hands raised, as Micah stalks after him.

"Fucking right it was a mistake," Micah snarls. He has become one of the mountain lions that live in Malibu Canyon. "So you saw Hannah and thought, what, that you could take advantage of her grief? Get her high and then do whatever you want with her?"

He launches himself at Drew, but Drew's faster, dodges those tan fists.

"Stop it!" I scream. "Micah!"

"You're scaring her," Drew says, his hands at his sides. "I'm not doing this with you."

"Oh, we're doing this," Micah growls. "You drugged up my girlfriend—"

I grab Micah, turn him to face me.

"I sat in that room with my mom," I say, "and I kept hoping you'd walk through that door, Micah, and you didn't. You *didn't*." I close my eyes. "It's not about pills. It's not even about Drew. Or the wave. It's about you and me and her."

I open my eyes, look at him. At this boy who broke my heart. I have finally, *finally* told him the truth. About the acorn. About me. The three of us.

"Her," he says, his voice suddenly dull, all the fight gone out of him.

I nod.

Micah turns to Mae.

"I thought you said you didn't tell her." He steps closer to her. "That you'd give me a chance to make it right. Why the hell did you bring me out here?"

"Hey." Ben is there, next to Mae, pulling her away from Micah. He's so tall, his arms wrapping around her like the wings of a protective bird. "This entire thing is a shit sandwich, but you don't get to talk to Mae like that. Ever."

I look from my sister's stricken face to Micah. "Tell me what?"

Mae is so pale I can see the veins that snake down her neck. She turns to me.

"I didn't know what to do." Her voice is small and trembling, kicked to the curb. "I was so scared. The pills and . . . I didn't want to lose you, so I didn't tell you . . . I should have, but . . . I didn't know what you'd . . . I thought it would be another wave, Nah, another wave if you knew, and he said he loved you and it was a mistake and the wave made everything wrong and we all react in different ways to grief, which is true, you know, and I thought if he came, if you two . . . You said he was the Temperance card. Balance. I was trying—I'm so sorry. I'm *so, so sorry*." Her chin wobbles. I have never seen my sister cry. Ever. "I was trying to work the problem. I . . . failed. I should have told you."

"About *what*?" I am yelling. I am yelling because I know. And all I can do is yell.

"About Cathy," Micah says. "You said *her*. You said it's not about the pills, why you're with this dude. That it's because of you and me and *her*."

"I was talking about the baby," I say. "So who's Cathy?"

Micah's tan disappears.

I walk past Micah. When I reach my sister, I stop.

She looks up at me, so small.

"How long have you known?" I ask.

"A month," she whispers. "Thirty-seven days, actually, but—"

Nate steps forward. "Cuz. We didn't know what to do. She thought you might kill yourself, okay? Seriously."

I stare at him. "*You* knew?"

"We were trying to help you," he says. "That's why she flushed your pills. Why she invited Micah here. To help. To make you happy. She didn't know things had . . . changed for you." He gestures toward Drew. "You've been in a bad way, cuz. *Bad.*"

"So you *both* knew that my boyfriend was cheating on me and you let me think he . . . You let me keep planning to move back to LA and . . . What? Marry a cheating bastard because I'm too weak or—what? *What?*" I grab at my hair. "Why the fuck is everyone in this family a liar?"

"We're not. We . . . we love you, Nah," Mae says.

"No." I shake my head. "When you love someone, you have their fucking *back*, Mae. You don't let them stay with some asshole who is screwing some other girl." My eyes fill. I think about Mom. Did she know? She knew. I think she did. She died knowing. Oh God, she did.

"I've had your back," I sob. "You don't know it, but I have. You think I'm weak, that I'm upset about Mom and Dad dying—well, yeah, I am, but that's not all of it, okay? That's not all of it, and I've been protecting you so that *you* can fucking get out of bed in the morning. I've been watching out for you, and you . . . you were going to let me stay with someone who *betrayed* me, someone who told me to *get rid of my baby*. Why am I protecting you, Mae? Why? WHY?"

I shake my head. *Don't. Don't. It will kill her.*

"What are you protecting me from?" Mae steps forward. "Nah . . . tell me."

I turn away from her, wrap my arms around myself. Drew steps closer. I stare at the toes of his worn sneakers, the cuffs of his faded black jeans. I wish I could tell him that I broke my promise to him about the pills the day I found out my mother was in a pit. Because I'm in that pit, too.

Micah is behind me. I know it's him, so familiar. The endless churning energy of the sea. He kissed someone else. Someone named Cathy. He slept with her. Maybe more than once. Because he didn't love me enough. Or at all. I wasn't enough for Mom and Dad. Not enough for Micah. Just Hannah. If the wave had taken me, would anyone have felt this empty about me being gone? Mom maybe. But she'd have Mae.

I think the world would be okay without me.

It doesn't need me.

Just Hannah.

Just.

I wish the wave had taken me, too. I wish I'd been swept away.

Micah touches my shoulder. He's wearing the watch my dad bought him when he turned eighteen, a twin to his own—we'd called them Indiana Jones watches because it made them look like gentleman adventurers. My gift had been a photographic flip book I'd made out of all the years I'd been watching him surf, my camera pointed at the sea. Hundreds of pictures that showed him devouring wave after wave over the past three years. We liked waves then. Thought they were fun.

"Nah," he whispers, "I love you so much. The grief, it . . . I'd been drinking and I missed you and I've been losing my mind. I know you have, too. Like way more than me. But I swear, this is not . . . it's not *me*. I know that sounds like an excuse. It's not. But, please. *Please.* Don't be mad at Mae. I begged her not to tell you and she only agreed because she knows us, knows what we are. I ended it. Got my head on straight. I promise I will never fuck up like this again." He pulls me toward him, and he is so shattered that I forget to push him away. "You're my family. From day one, I told you that. I know if your dad were here he'd kick my ass, and I wish he could because I deserve it—"

And that. That does it.

"If my dad were here?" I look at him. Mae. Nate. Coconspirators. Liars. Betrayers. Can't fucking trust anyone. "If my dad were here, he'd be telling you he understood, Micah. You want to know why?"

"Hannah . . ." Drew says, soft. Giving me an out, a chance to do right by the miracle.

I don't take it.

This wound: It's for me. And for my mom.

"Because. He was just. Like. You."

I turn to Mae. I hate her right now. Knowing, all this time what Micah was doing to me, keeping it from me on the train, at the dinner table, in the bathroom brushing our teeth. Knowing about it and letting me stay with him. Letting me *trust* someone who was hurting me so bad. How could she? How could she let me stay with him?

"Dad was cheating on Mom. For over a year. With his research assistant. Rebecca Chen. Who is pregnant *right now* with his baby. Dad was going to leave Mom, Mae. As soon as we graduated. He was going to leave her. All of us."

And then I say the thing that took me, the day after we got the call from the Red Cross, to where the weirdos at Harvard Square hang out. The strung-out ones. With pills. I say the thing that hollows me out every morning. Every night.

"And maybe that's why she was alone. In the grave. Maybe he didn't try to save her."

Mae has been holding an apple. All this time. It falls out of her hand. *Thunks* to the ground. Rolls. She stares. Through me. Through . . . everything. She is not here.

I didn't know there was a flame blazing in my sister until it burned out.

"Mae." I say her name, a choke. A sob.

She just stares and stares. Ben wraps his arms around her, but her body doesn't move. Her eyes don't move.

She is not here.

I don't know where she went.

But she's gone.

What have I done?

The tears come, and I can hardly see, hardly breathe.

The orchard is silent. The sun goes behind a cloud. My sister turns away from me.

"Mae."

She keeps walking. Stumbles. Ben starts for her, but Nate holds him back.

"Mae!"

I scream my sister's name. But for the first time in our lives, she doesn't come when I call.

27

Mae

ISS Location: *Low-Earth Orbit*
Earth Date: *24 November*
Earth Time (EST): *20:09*

We make soup.

Aunt Nora and I. Baked potato.

The kitchen, the whole house, is silent. Just the sound of knives scraping against the wood chopping boards. Blades cutting into onion, potato. Water boiling. The gas flame hissing.

It is the last hours of my eighteenth birthday. We didn't eat the cake. Or the ice cream. I did not open any presents. Or go to the Dresden Dolls concert.

I don't know where my sister is. Not with Micah. He's already at the airport. He wanted to stay, to try again, but Nate said no.

When I'm done making soup, I will go up to my room and I will lie down on my bed and stare into the dark until the sun comes up.

And I will wonder, for the first time in my life, if the social worker made a mistake.

Every time I picture my dad, his face is blurry now. What Nah said, what I know about him—the truth turned every memory of my dad into a watercolor that got left out in the rain.

I will never leave you, he'd said.

We searched for truth together. But he was lying all along.

"Did she know?"

My words peel at the silence, to the hurt underneath.

Aunt Nora's knife goes still.

Then: She nods.

Is this what drowning feels like? Knowing your life is ending just before the dying begins?

"None of us knew . . . about the baby," Aunt Nora says. "And from what Nate told me when you all got home today, it sounds like your father didn't know, either. At least not before he left for the trip." Her fingers tighten around the knife. "But your mom knew about . . . her." My aunt's voice breaks. "She thought this trip . . . she was hoping she could . . ." She shakes her head. "I told her not to go."

I stare at the mounds of potato beneath my hands. The skin is still on because Mom says the soup tastes better that way.

Just how you like it, Mom.

"Nah said . . ." I grip a raw potato, squeeze. "She said maybe he didn't try and save her. That's why their bodies aren't together. Because he didn't . . . because . . ."

There's a clatter as my aunt lets go of her knife and crosses to me. She grabs my shoulders.

"Listen," she says, fierce. "Your dad was doing a bad thing. A horrible thing. But he loved her—not in the way he used to, but he did love her. I believe that. And he was a good man in every other part of his life. Good people make mistakes. Okay? He would *never* have let her die. You know that. Deep in your heart, Mae, you *know* he would have done everything to save her."

No. From now on, I only believe something, or someone, if the fucking math checks out.

And this math—it doesn't check out.

Add up all the days for that whole year that he was lying to us—about where he was, who he was with, what he was doing. Subtract all the plans we made for the future *as a family*. Divide that whole family. What do you get? A fraction. Not something whole.

"What do we do about the baby?" I say. Somewhere in LA, Rebecca Chen is carrying a little piece of my family.

Her hands drop. "Oh, sweetie. You don't have to worry about that."

I stare at her. "That's my sister. Or my brother. A *person*. It's not their fault. What he did." Just like it wasn't my fault that my bio mom didn't want me. "What do you mean I don't have to . . . Of *course* I have to worry."

If my bio mom had decided when she got pregnant that she didn't want me, okay, fine, have an abortion. I am all for choices. I wouldn't know if I didn't exist. But she had me. I'm *here*. And she turned her back on me. It'd be one thing if she'd given me up at birth, made the right choice, but she didn't. She just abandoned me to foster homes where anything could have—might have—happened to me. And she didn't even do *that* from the beginning. Social services came and found all the meth in her house, the baby with the dirty diaper, and they had to take me away. Because she'd literally *forgotten* about me. When I think about the things people might have done to me, bad things, things I might not remember until I'm forty and suddenly, suddenly I wake up in the middle of the night and—

Aunt Nora blanches. "I didn't mean—"

"But you *did*. We're not expendable," I say. "Me, that baby. Just because we're inconvenient. Just because things didn't work out the way they're 'supposed' to. We exist. Because people *chose* to bring us into the world. They didn't have to. But they did. And it's not our fault. It's not that baby's fault that Dad . . ."

I'm shaking. This anger rolling through me—I'll never pass my NASA psych evals like this.

"Mae, I'm so sorry. Sweetie—"

I pull away. "You know, I fucking hate birthdays. I always have."

It feels good to curse. To be a little like Hannah. To not be a good girl.

For goddamn once to just stop earning my place here.

"Mae . . . I didn't mean it, the way it came out. You aren't inconvenient. No! We *love* you."

"Love. What does that even mean? Dad said that to Mom, didn't he?"

She pushes back her hair, streaked with more gray than ever.

"Sweetie, that's different. Sometimes marriages, they don't . . . People change. But your kids—the love between a child and her father . . . That will never go away. Ever."

The look on Uncle Tony's face: *It occurs to me that I'm a dad without a daughter, and you're a daughter without a dad.*

"He was going to *leave* us."

"He was going to leave your mother. Not you." She grips my hand. "*Never* you, Mae. Your father loved you so much. More than anything. Frankly, more than any*one*. And I think you know that."

I think Hannah knows that, too.

"I hate him."

"You don't mean that."

"Yeah." I grab a towel and wipe off my hands, then head for the stairs. "I really think I do."

. ● .

I have been lying in the dark for three hours.

The only light comes from a moon lamp that Nate bought me when Nah and I moved in. A small little globe that glows white, with craters and everything.

I wish I were there. The moon. It'd be nice, for a change, to be the one who leaves. My bio mom, my parents, Riley—every single one of them is gone. Mom couldn't help it, but the end result is the same.

Everyone I love leaves me.

Maybe it's time to be the one who goes.

I've spent months thinking about not going to Annapolis, cancelling my interviews, not doing that final step because of Hannah. Because I don't want to leave her. Because I'm scared what will happen to her if no one is watching out for her.

But where is she now?

Not here, not with me, that's for sure. It's my birthday, which she ruined, and she couldn't even bother to come home. Because it's all about her. It's always about her. I shouldn't have kept Micah's cheating from her, but I'm sorry, okay, I didn't want to open my sister's bedroom door and find her dead from an overdose.

She should have come home. Made soup.

It's my birthday.

And she should have seen that I was trying to protect her like she was trying to protect me. She didn't want me to know about Dad. I didn't want her to know about Micah. Sometimes ignorance is bliss. Sometimes it's not best to know the answers.

I think I'd like to be the one who packs up the bags and walks out the door for good. Who gets on an airplane and never comes back. Maybe that's what I should do in June. I've been lying to my whole family, and to Ben. Told them I went to my Annapolis interview, even though I cancelled it after they found Mom. I'm not a liar, and that was a hard thing to do. But I knew that if I told anyone the truth, Hannah would know it was because of her, and she'd feel terrible. Shame spirals are not good for recovery. I'll have to tell the truth eventually, or maybe just say I didn't get in—which would be embarrassing. But maybe cancelling was a mistake. Because Hannah was right: Our family is done.

"Mama," I whisper into the blackness. Into the void.

It occurs to me that this is what I do all the time. I stare into the dark.

Dark matter. Dark energy. Darkest, deepest space.

There's so little light.

So little I know.

I keep replaying that conversation with Aunt Nora in my head. Thinking about my new baby sister or brother. And how quickly Nora was able to cut them out of our life. And now I'm in a whirlpool of thoughts I don't usually indulge in because they hurt and because there's nothing I can do about the past. But it's my birthday, and I can't help it.

I remember when Nah found out about her conception. Mom had gotten tipsy on too many margaritas one Cinco de Mayo and it came out: Dad had been telling her he wasn't ready, but it was Mom's birthday, and he said, *Okay, fine, we won't use a condom tonight, and if it's meant to be, then this is the only damn birthday present you're getting this year*. And then she laughed about how when she showed him the stick, he burst into tears and hugged her so hard she couldn't breathe. "Your father," she'd say, "truly contains multitudes."

I don't have a story like that.

I don't know the circumstances of how I came to be, but I doubt they involved a mom desperate to get pregnant, where I'm seen as a gift, and a dad so happy he cries. Maybe the circumstances were horrible. Maybe my bio dad is a rapist or a drunk or a total deadbeat. Or my bio mom doesn't know who he is. Maybe my conception is a sad one-night-stand story of barely remembered bad sex and Jell-O shots. Maybe my bio mom was broke or too young or scared or not ready. And when she found out, when she saw the stick that said I was coming, she hated me a little.

But the other thing I don't know is why she had me. Was she thinking about keeping me, or did she always know she'd give me up? Maybe I was a bad baby. Sickly or crying too much. Annoying. Not cute. I don't know what kind of baby I was, because I have no baby pictures. No home videos of me crawling. I do not know what I looked like until the first foster home, when I was one. And the only picture I have from that time, the state took so they could put it on their website. I've looked at those sites—it's like an animal shelter, kids being advertised for adoption, hoping for their "forever home." There are few things sadder on this planet than looking at the pictures of the older kids that no one wants. You can see it, in their eyes, you can see how much they want a family.

What exactly made my bio mom decide I wasn't worth the effort?

What made her sign me over to the State of California? A state that can't even balance its own checkbook half the time. She gave me to a system where statistics show upward of twenty-eight percent of kids are abused—and those are just the ones who fess up. I'm not the only drug orphan, I know. In fact, in all my research about Hannah, I've learned that the opiate crisis in America has created a swell of orphans, of kids whose parents do to them what my bio mom did to me—because they love the drugs more.

My bio mom didn't know I'd get to be a Winters, with smart parents who loved me and took care of me. This wasn't a case where some girl got pregnant and then got to choose the perfect family for her baby girl and it was all Hallmark beautiful. That wasn't my story. My story was seven houses in three years. Maybe some people just took me in for the money—you get real money for fostering kids. Or maybe they were just nice and good, but couldn't keep me. Or maybe they weren't. I DON'T KNOW. It keeps me up nights, all the things I don't know.

A short list:

- Why the universe is expanding
- What dark energy and dark matter actually are
- If life is possible on Mars
- If Dad's quintessence theory is correct
- How the first particle came to be
- My parents' last words
- How I will die
- If Nah will ever forgive me
- If Dad was really going to leave us
- What it's like to be in zero gravity, on a space walk, looking down at Earth
- Why Ben Tamura feels like home
- If it's me, something about me, that makes people go

There are no answers in the darkness. Just more questions.

I think about what River said, at Dharma Bums. About feeling everything no matter how bad it is. About waking up from the trance.

I sit up, lean my pillow against the wall. Cross my legs and close my eyes.

"Okay," I whisper. "Let's ride."

I ride the breath like a wave, not *the* wave, just one that brings me to the shore of myself, again and again.

In.

And out.

In.

And out.

I sit and sit, the thoughts sometimes racing, other waves that crash against my mind, never ending, but I let them go, let them crash.

H_2O and NaCl—water and sodium chloride. That's all a wave is. Elemental. Shifting. Changing.

Not permanent.

Not me.

The more I fall into the breath, the more I realize that the thoughts are just on the surface of me. I dive deeper. Sink. Beneath the waves—beneath *the* wave.

Stillness.

Quiet and deep.

Like all of space is inside me.

They say that the ocean is the closest environment to space we have on Earth, and more than half the human body is made up of water, so maybe our bodies know the language of the dark, of the deep, already. We just need to listen.

I listen.

And then: I feel.

Without the distraction of the thoughts, I can feel ... everything.

What Dad did—to Mom, to us, to that little baby in Rebecca Chen's belly far away in Los Angeles, and what Micah did to Nah, and what Nah and I did to each other, the lying.

I feel the weight of the ocean in my chest.

I don't push it away.
I don't work the problem.
I ride the wave.

In order for an object to float, it must contain some trapped air. That is the only way it can rise above the surface.

Eventually, the breath pushes me

up

up

up.

The wave recedes. For now.

I open my eyes.

Somehow, the darkness is a little lighter.

There's a tap on my window. Then another one.

I turn.

Ben is framed by yellow curtains, flakes of snow swirling all around him, as though just by meditating I've summoned him.

He spreads a gloved hand on the frosted pane and rests his forehead against the window and I can feel him through the glass.

The cold in me turns warm. Like soup.

I crawl out of bed and pull the window open. He is covered in snow. There is a storm behind him that must have started after Nate brought me home from the orchard. That long, silent car ride.

The wind is a knife, and it cuts through my thin T-shirt.

My moon lamp catches in Ben's eyes so that the night sky is now inches from my face. I don't feel the cold anymore.

"I wanted to kiss you good night," he says. "It's your birthday. And no birthday girl should go to sleep without a good-night kiss."

Did Dad knock on Mom's window late at night? Did he send her into zero gravity? And when she found out about him and Rebecca—was it like falling, or another kind of floating?

The wind is a knife. Serrated. Death by a thousand cuts, that's what this is. Caring about someone and knowing it will end.

"This is very romantic," I say, carefully. "And you came all this way in the cold, and I wish I could be the girlfriend you want, Ben, but—"

"You *are* the girlfriend I want," he says, leaning in a little, his hair dusted with snow. "And the one I have. How convenient."

"It's ANYTHING but convenient! I don't have *time* for this! For girlfriend things. I don't have space inside me for it."

"I love you."

Sometimes . . . sometimes you can actually *hear* Earth rotate.

I look at this boy who climbed to my window in a snowstorm. Who clings to the flimsy wood, patient. My quantum boy that I found in the chaos. And I want to grab him and never let him go.

But I can already feel what it will be like when he leaves.

I shake my head. I wish he hadn't said it. Everyone who has ever said that to me goes away for good.

"Yes. I do. I love you," he murmurs. "Right here, right now. The wave and your dad and your sister and Micah—no one, *nothing*, can take this moment from us. It's ours and I love you and if you don't have time, that's okay, because I'm not asking you for anything more than this minute. I'm not even asking you for it—I want to give it to you. A minute can be a gift."

His breath comes out in a puff, and I breathe him in, his heat melting me, melting that ice that built up so quickly inside. The physicist Carlo Rovelli says that time and heat are linked, that the only way you can see a detectable difference between the past and the future is when there is a flow of heat.

This heat I feel—does it mean that Ben and I have a future? Can thermodynamics keep two people from leaving each other? Maybe things got cold between Mom and Dad, and so there could be no future. No more time. No more minutes.

A *minute can be a gift.*

"I didn't open any birthday gifts."

Ben's eyes are sad. And hopeful. "I know."

Time is a gift.

I am learning this the hard way.

Sixty seconds. This minute, one minute with Ben. A gift.

His lips are a little blue, but he doesn't complain.

I kiss them.

Then I drag him inside.

As soon as Ben is here, in my room, I don't want him to be anywhere else. I want more gifts. More minutes.

"The universe is expanding," I say. "Maybe I am, too. Maybe there's more space in me than I thought."

He kisses me like we're in the final scene of a movie and the music is swelling and there's a sunrise behind us. It's a pretty good kiss.

Ben pulls away, looks around. "You failed to mention that this room is a wormhole."

"What?"

"Yeah. You tricked me, you minx." Ben is grinning, and it takes me a second, but then I see where he is going with this. Never fall for an MIT boy. "A minute in *here* is actually a whole *night* out there. Spacetime, man. Total mindfuck." He shuts the window, pulls off his scarf. "Well played, you. You've got me for the whole night."

I bite my lip, thinking. Micah would do something like this for Nah.

Ben leans close, his lips brushing my ear. "For science, Mae."

My eyes fly to his, and he's grinning, my person, and I almost say it, those three words, but I can't, I can't, so I just kiss them to him. He tastes like coffee and cinnamon.

"I feel like I'm living my entire life in the quantum realm now," I say.

Nothing makes sense. Reality isn't playing by the rules anymore. I have no idea what is going to happen next, no way to prepare. My parents are dead, my sister's on drugs, and I'm in the arms of a boy I'm already afraid of losing.

"We found each other there," he murmurs. "Remember?"

I nod. Colliding by the Charles. An experiment for science. His heart in the palm of my hand.

"No matter how much we discover," he says, "how many laws of physics we hold to be tried and true—none of this will ever make actual sense. Even if you discovered the origin of the universe, would it explain you? Or your parents, and what happened to them? Or this?"

He leans close, brushing the tip of his nose against mine.

"I . . . I don't know."

"Good answer."

Ben is melting, snow everywhere, and I help him pull off hat and gloves and coat, and as he kicks off his boots, my hands won't stop: sweatshirt and shirt and pants.

"Hey." He stops me. "I know I just made this grand gesture and found a nifty loophole to stay, but I heard you—when you said you don't have space. I can go. You can think about it."

I rest my hands on his bare chest, which is warm and soft. "I wouldn't have let you in if I didn't want to. And I think I've had enough space for one day." I shrug. "Besides, it's technically only a minute."

His answer to *that* is a slow, roguish smile that gives me no choice but to pull him to the bed and under the covers. I climb on top of him and whisper, "Say it again."

He pulls my face close to his, eyes on mine. "I love you, Mae."

As the words fall from Ben's lips, again and again, as he says them against my skin and into my mouth and as he fills me with them and with himself, I am safe, this moment and this boy a capsule speeding through space.

But.

The thing about wormholes—you reach the other side of the tunnel eventually.

After so many minutes, so many gifts, Ben's eyelids begin to drop: a sunset. I watch him sleep. Watch our night fade into day, our minute in the wormhole burning up as it hits the atmosphere, as the sun peeks into the room, spreads across the bedroom floor toward the bed. A wave of light. But still: a wave.

And I think: *I am going to lose you.*

i didn't want to walk away from him.

Train Seat
C Line
Boston

28

Hannah

S now isn't so bad when you have diamonds in your pockets and whiskey in your blood.

I turn to Drew. "I've never been kissed in the snow."

He leans toward me, and I turn my head up, waiting. I thought it would have come so much sooner. The orchard was hours and hours ago. The night is long gone—the sun is already starting to peek into the sky.

But it doesn't matter because here it comes, our first kiss, finally, *finally*—

Drew fixes my scarf, then rests his hands on my shoulders. I slide my arms around his neck, but he removes them, his fingers tangling with mine before he lets go.

"Not like this," Drew says, quiet.

I blink. "What?"

"Let's get some food. Coffee. Get warm." He's already walking toward the diner. "It's been a long night. Aren't you cold?"

He's walking away from me, toward the steamed-up windows, the neon OPEN sign, the turkey and Pilgrim decorations.

"What the *fuck*, Drew?"

He stops. Sighs. That tired sigh of everyone around me. That *I-wish-she-weren't-her* sigh.

"Hannah."

Snow swirls around him, and he is a poem. Does he know? Does he know how beautiful he is?

I wish I deserved him.

"I thought we . . ." I shake my head. "I broke up with him. I chose *you*. I stood there in front of him, holding your hand. Did I, like, read this all wrong or—"

"Hannah, you're high. And drunk." He throws up his hands. "I'm sorry if I'd like you to remember the first kiss I give you."

I stare at him. "Are you *seriously* fucking judging me right now? Because fuck you for that, Drew. You're the goddamn drug dealer, not me."

The party had been an accident, since of course we were supposed to be with Mae, eating cake and opening presents. But Mae and Nate and Ben had gone off, and Micah, too—with them or on his own, I don't know. They left me in the orchard because Nate said there was no way in fucking hell he'd play chauffeur to my dealer. Drew and I got a bus back to the city. Then we ran into someone. I needed the distraction. A few drinks, a joint. I haven't even had a pill. I've been so good. After today? *So good.*

"I don't deal anymore," he says, quiet.

"So you want some straight-edge girl now. Fine. Go back to your soccer-playing Christian girlfriend. I'm sure she'll be thrilled. Wish you had told me I wasn't your type before I broke up with my boyfriend of three years."

I can't even think about that now. What he did to me. And how breaking his heart still hurt so much. I turned off my phone. He'd been calling and texting and I just turned it off.

"What the hell, Hannah? I don't want—"

"Me."

He pulls off his hat, runs a hand through his hair. "That's not what I'm saying. Don't do that."

"Don't do what? Say the truth?"

Stupid. I was so stupid to think that he would want me. Why would he? Micah certainly doesn't. Cathy. Her name is Cathy.

Maybe it's because she's going to college. Not a C student like me. D student, actually. All those jokes with my dad I didn't get. All the references. The books he'd read to impress Dad, letting Mom smudge him even though sage makes him sneeze. I'm Just Hannah. A going-nowhere, average girl who just wants to have kids and make soup and read tarot cards. Just a basic bitch. I asked Micah what he saw in me, not too long before we left for Boston, and he said, "The future." And, at the time, I'd thought that was romantic—like we'd be together forever and he sees his whole future with me. But now I realize he didn't see me. He saw a *life* with me. But those are not the same thing.

My sister's birthday, and what did I do? Spent it getting fucked up with a guy who doesn't even want to kiss me. What an idiot I was, to think he'd kiss the hurt and the guilt away.

Drew must have been watching me all night, trying to figure out how to get rid of me. Now that I think about it, he didn't have a drink. Or take a hit of that joint. So it's been me, looking like a drunk junkie whore loser all night.

Drew steps closer. His lips part. A puff of breath floats through them, toward me.

"The *truth* is that I want you, Hannah. More than anything I've wanted in my entire life."

Some words are like diamonds. You can drape them all over you. Sparkle like an August night.

I step toward him, and my foot lands in an icy puddle. The cold reminds me: At the end of the day, diamonds are just rocks. And we're the suckers who empty our pockets for them.

Micah wanted me, too, at first. I could feel it, the way he couldn't keep his hands off me. Drew can't even touch me—look at him, look at him not even wanting to *touch* me, like I'm contagious or dirty. Because maybe I am. Dirty.

I pull my coat tighter around me. Back away. "I know what it's like to be with someone who wants me. This . . . doesn't feel like that."

"Because it *isn't* like that," Drew says, louder. "I'm not just trying to get down your pants, okay?"

"Well, *obviously* you're not trying to do that." Maybe I'm ugly now. The sadness, the pills. Maybe that's why he doesn't want to kiss me.

"Hannah, I . . ."

He stops. Looks at his feet. Canvas tennis shoes soaked through with snow. The storm caught us by surprise. Doesn't everything?

I am so cold. Every part of me is frozen. Snow whips between us, and I back away a little more.

Drew's thinking. Deciding. If I'm worth it. But we both know the answer. I'm not.

"This was a mistake, Drew."

He doesn't look at me. "What?"

"Being here."

"With me."

As soon as this is over, I'm taking a pill. Fuck it. Fuck everyone. Fuck me most of all.

"Yeah," I say. "With you."

When I walk away, part of me hopes—thinks—he'll run after me. Or call my name. But he doesn't.

He lets me go.

Like a shell you pick up from the beach, admire for a moment, but then throw back into the water. You don't see where it lands.

The ocean doesn't whisper, *Hannah. Hannah.*

It doesn't say anything at all.

• • •

The pill is in my mouth before I reach the end of the street.

If I pulled a card right now, I'd get the Devil: the card of addicts everywhere. *The devil made me do it.* My favorite Devil is in the Shadowscapes tarot, because it shows exactly what it feels like to be in prison. The Devil in that one is this beautiful but terrifying winged monster standing on top of a cave, juggling a heart in its hands. In the cave is a naked girl in chains, curled in on herself. I don't see how she'll ever get out.

I jump on the next train and ride the T all morning long. I like the C Line, even though it's more of a trolley than a subway, because it goes aboveground part of the time. So I just ride it up and down Boston, and I keep drawing a D, over and over, in the steam on the window—*Drew, Drew, Drew*. I go past Fenway, the "Cathedral" where the Sox play, and when the train slides underground I look up and imagine my angel as we zoom under Boston Garden, then we rumble beneath the dystopian buildings of Government Center. I have to get out at the end of the line, North Station, and change directions, then I ride the train back to Cleveland Circle, to the reservoir in front of Boston College, where I walked with Mom last Thanksgiving. We drank pumpkin spice lattes, and she told me it was okay I didn't want to go to college.

Then she fucking died, and now I ride trains by myself and think thoughts like: *Anna Karenina was brave.*

It takes brass ovaries to throw yourself in front of a train.

I only saw the movie, because I'm not smart enough to read the book. Mae read the book.

And then I have to try hard not to cry in public. Because it's wrong to want to die so badly when someone spent twenty-one hours in labor to bring you into the world.

It's warm in these old, cranky cars and I'm clean and young and don't look homeless, so no one bothers me. That's what you call privilege, I guess. It's a Sunday morning, and the other passengers are carrying shopping bags and children and are too busy planning next week's Thanksgiving dinner to notice the girl at the end of the car wrapped in an olive-green wool coat, her tangled hair covered with a thick knitted hat a drug dealer—*former* drug dealer—bought her on a whim because it has a pouf on the top that he thought might make her smile.

Just when I'm about to start feeling sad about Drew, my diamonds start to shine inside me. Pretty, pretty Oxy (Percocet's for babies) wraps itself around me and we are woven in each other, in love.

I smile.

I forget.

I float.

Pro Tip: Wear sunglasses. Put in earbuds. No one bothers you.

People come and go. I am here and not here. Not awake, not asleep.

In between.

In limbo.

No

one

sees

me.

I am invisible.

As usual.

I have to wait in the cold for the next train to take me back across Boston, knee-deep in snow, but I barely notice because I didn't just take one pill, I took two.

Maybe I should have taken them all.

Just.

Hannah.

I ride and ride and ride.

And then, around Coolidge Corner, the nausea hits, like it sometimes does, and I have to throw myself out of the doors when I get to my stop and luckily no one else is there to see me hurl up last night's whiskey into a snowbank.

Whatever.

I stumble across the tracks, and there's a blare, like the end of the world in surround sound, and I turn and a train, a train is coming.

Whatever.

There are sparks and a screech and the train is slowing down and so I keep moving because I don't want someone to have to clean up my mess on the tracks.

Whatever.

The snow is coming down hard now, and I can barely see, even though it's only—I actually have no idea what time it is, but the sun is still out, that pale Boston hangover sun.

Some people have been shoveling since last night, putting out salt. I stick to those parts of the sidewalk, carry myself up the twisty turns into the little hilly neighborhood behind Washington Square, to Aunt Nora and Uncle Tony's.

I'm nearly there, the cold so deep in me now I can barely move. I take a step forward and suddenly the world slides out from under me, staring up at the leafless tree in our front yard.

"Ouch," I whisper.

I am so thirsty.

The front door opens. "Jesus Christ."

My cousin is suddenly standing over me. It's hard to see him with my sunglasses on, but I think he's pissed. "Are you okay."

He doesn't reach out to help.

"Sure," I say.

Words are hard when you haven't used them in a long, long time.

He pulls off my sunglasses, stares at my pupils. My guess is that they are very small.

"How much did you take, Hannah?"

I shrug, and the movement shoves snow into my coat.

"Enough."

I sound like our drunk neighbor in Venice, the one we nicknamed Cuervo.

"Well, Hannah, it's clear you handle bad news with aplomb. It occurs to me Mae and I made a *huge* mistake not telling you your boyfriend was cheating on you while you were dealing with your parents' death. I think, judging by today's performance, you would have handled that with admirable maturity, with the calm of a ship's captain in a storm. Thanks for showing me the error of my ways." He turns around and heads up the walkway.

I lie in the snow a little longer.

They would never understand: What they did hurt *more* than what Micah did. So much more.

"Hannah." He is kind of yelling from the front door. "Get the *fuck* inside."

It's hard to stand. All the snow. Like sand, but shittier. My bones frozen.

I wish Drew had kissed me.

I wish my parents hadn't died.

I wish I were holding my baby.

I wish I were dead.

I need another pill.

When I step in the house, Nate shuts the door and then fixes me with a look of pure disgust.

"There is vomit all over your coat. Did you know that?"

I look down. So there is.

"Huh."

"Is that her?" Aunt Nora calls. She rushes into the room, stares at me. "Where have you *been*? It's nearly two in the afternoon!"

"The train."

"What?"

"I was riding the train," I say.

She looks at Nate. "Is that a euphemism? Does *riding the train* mean—"

"No," he says. "I don't think so."

The one she's thinking of is *riding the dragon*. But it doesn't feel like a dragon, Oxy. It feels like a phoenix, maybe. Because, after, you're just ash.

I pull off the coat, my boots, hat. All in a pile. Water all over the rug. Nice rug.

God, it's hot in here. Why the hell is it so *hot* in here? I pull off my sweater.

"I need some water—"

"Tony, get the car," Aunt Nora's saying over her shoulder, her voice sharp. She crosses to me, stares at my arms. They are covered in a red rash. "I'm taking you to the ER."

"What?" I try to pull away, but she has an iron grip. "I'm fine—"

Aunt Nora's shaking her head. "I can't believe I didn't see—"

Mae appears on the stairs, a shadow. "I should have told you sooner."

At first, I think she's talking to me, about Micah, about lying to me, but then I see she's talking to my aunt. Because she told her. About the pills. I stare at my sister.

"You fucking bitch."

Mae flinches as the words come out of my mouth.

I need a pill. Now. I need a pill, fuck, fuck, *fuck*.

"I trusted you," I say. The tears come, fast and hard.

She shakes her head. "No, you didn't. You don't. You never told me about getting pills from Drew, or that you wanted to be with him and not Micah. You hid the last postcard Mom and Dad sent us—I found it in your room. You didn't tell me about *anything*."

"Well, now you know why I didn't trust you, you *fucking narc*," I snarl.

"Enough," Nate says.

"Oh, of course. Defend Mae. She's your favorite and Dad's and everyone's. Of course, of course, because I'm Just Hannah—"

"Just the ONLY SISTER I HAVE." Mae is shouting. I have never heard this sound from her. It freaks me the fuck out.

"I know you're on a Class B narcotic right now and it might be challenging to fully comprehend what I am about to tell you," she says, "but do your best, Hannah: I DON'T WANT YOU TO DIE."

"Well, that makes one of us," I say.

She stares at me. "You are so unbelievably selfish."

My sister stands above me—in every way—looking down, her arms crossed, and I am so sick of her up there, always up there, being perfect. The heir and the spare.

"I don't *want* your help. I don't *need* your help. That doesn't sound selfish to me. I'm fine on my own. I'm sorry I'm not some scientific problem you can solve, Mae. You don't get a goddamn gold star for this one."

"Hannah, honey, *please* stop—" Aunt Nora starts toward me, but Nate shakes his head.

"She's fucking high, Mom. You can't reason with her."

"You want to go to space, Mae? I've already been there," I shout. "Zero gravity, Lucy in the sky with diamonds. Your fucking Starman is up there, too. Everything you study for, all the answers you're looking for: *I already know them.* I don't need advanced physics and Annapolis to feel weightless. To know the universe doesn't give a shit about me or you or anyone on this fucking rock. The universe does not have our back." I head toward the kitchen, toward water and the car in the garage Aunt Nora's about to force me inside. "As far as I'm concerned, the sooner you're in outer space, the better. Maybe you can do the Mars mission. Doesn't it take, like, four years just to get there?"

Her eyes fill—Dad called them tropical eyes. Blue, like the bluest ocean—and I hate her, I hate her.

This entire family, drowning in salt water.

29

Mae

ISS Location: Low-Earth Orbit
Earth Date: 25 November
Earth Time (EST): 19:08

Not all the soup in the world can fix this.

While they're at the hospital having Hannah drug tested and talking to doctors about how to make her better, Nate and I try to make minestrone, but once everything's cut up we realize we're out of stewed tomatoes. We give up on the soup.

"Ever heard of the comic Lenny Bruce?" Nate says.

"Comedy is not of great interest to me."

"Okay, well, anyway, he was super famous. And a heroin addict. I was reading up on opiates after you told me about Hannah and I keep thinking about this thing Lenny said, how he was certain heroin was going to kill him—but shooting up was like kissing God." Nate shakes his head. "How can we compete with that?"

What could I give my sister that could possibly be as good as kissing *God*?

"Hannah would love to kiss God. I think maybe that's all she's ever wanted."

I picture her, that night we put on Mom's lotion, pressing a hand to her heart and talking about the Something Else in her. God doesn't exist, obviously, but no one can deny the power of that idea. It's held most *Homo sapiens* in thrall since almost the beginning of human civilization.

"What happened to him?" I ask. "To Lenny Bruce."

"He died on his bathroom floor in Hollywood when he was forty. Overdose."

I hate the *Papaver somniferum*.

Like Hannah, the poppy that her pills come from grows tall and thrives in temperate climates. It comes in many colors, but we usually associate it with fields of red. Blood red.

They're pretty tough, for flowers, but the *Papaver somniferum* only blooms for a few days. Short life span.

The pod is where the trouble is. After the petals float off, you cut into the pod with a knife, catch the milky sap. Let it harden. And there you have it: opium. Smoke it, swallow it, shoot it into your veins. Crushed dreams and ruined lives.

The molecules in the poppy plant can chemically replicate the oxytocin we get from love or friendship or sex, and even that warm, gooey feeling when you're holding a sweet baby. It's why it feels so good. It's an excess dopamine release in the reward center of the brain.

Hannah doesn't have that sweet baby she wants to hold, but what is a baby, exactly? It's someone to care for. Someone who looks up to you. Who depends on you. Someone who you want to be your best self for. Ideally, anyway. Maybe that's her connection to Drew—maybe he provides oxytocin to her the way Ben provides it for me. But she needs a Ben, not a Drew. Not a drug dealer who is making her sicker. But she can get it from me, a little. It's human connection that gives you oxytocin. Which is a very good argument for me staying in Boston.

I don't want my sister to end up like Lenny Bruce. I want her to find other ways to kiss God.

"Nate?"

"Yeah?"

"I think that's more data than I can handle right now."

He nods. "Right. Sorry. Let's do a puzzle."

We do most of a puzzle. One of those color gradation ones that are really hard.

It doesn't help.

· • • ·

It's dark when they get back.

"Sit on the couch, Hannah," Uncle Tony says.

His tone—I've never heard him angry. But he is now.

She storms past me and throws herself onto the love seat, arms crossed. A hospital bracelet circles her wrist, and there are dark smudges under her eyes.

Aunt Nora follows Uncle Tony into the living room, looking equally exhausted. Nate starts to stand.

"Do you want me to head out?"

"No," she says. "This is a family discussion."

"I don't see how it's any of their business," Nah says, glaring at me, then at Nate.

Uncle Tony spreads his hands. "Kid, when you put everyone around you through hell, it's their business."

"I didn't *ask* to move here, to live with you. If I'm too much of a burden—"

"That's *not* what I'm saying," Uncle Tony growls. "You're not a burden, you're my niece, and I want you to have a good, *long* life."

For just a second, a look of remorse covers her face.

We are so lucky. What if we hadn't had relatives like them to take us in? Parents who could leave us money? What if we'd been poor, with horrible, abusive kin? What if they'd released us to the state, like my bio mom did?

So strange, to know we are the lucky ones.

"Everyone in this room loves you," Aunt Nora says. "And we've been worried sick about you." She fidgets with the little buttons on her blouse, and I catch her fingers shaking. "I should have seen what was happening. I thought it was depression."

"It's my fault," I say.

"No," Aunt Nora says, firm. "It's a disease. Annie's cancer was a disease, and it wasn't our fault or hers. Your sister's addiction isn't her fault—that's genes and bad luck and evil pharmaceutical companies the government isn't regulating. This is one equation you are not a part of, Mae."

I shake my head. "I should have told. It didn't have to get to this point. I tried to fix things on my own—"

"Any other betrayals you want to add to the list, Mae?" Nah says. Sneers. She actually sneers. I hate her drugs, and I hate how she is when she's on them, but I hate even more how she is when she's *not* on them but wants to be.

"Just to myself," I say.

I am tired of being seen as her enemy. And failing. Every day I fail with her, and I don't know how to deal with failure.

"What's that supposed to mean?" she says.

I look at her, Nate, my aunt and uncle. "I cancelled my Annapolis interview. I lied to all of you and said I did it, but it never happened. I'm staying here."

"What. The. Fuck." Nate's staring at me. "Are you kidding me right now? That's your *future*. You've worked your whole life for this!"

I keep my eyes on my sister. "You think I see you as some math problem I can fix. But I don't. You're my sister. And I love you." I am leaning so far forward on my chair that I'm almost on my knees. Begging. "And I'm scared. So I decided to stay so that we could beat this thing. Together."

Her skin goes blotchy. "I don't want that. Call them back, Mae. I didn't ask for that!"

"If you had cancer, like Annie did, I'd stay. This is the same thing. Like Aunt Nora said, you have a disease. You're sick. And if we don't treat it, you could die. Or at least have a really awful life."

"You are making too big a deal of this!" Hannah says. "Seriously. Like, I'm sorry I didn't come home *one night*—ground me or whatever. I don't need this, like, this fucking intervention, and I don't need you to give up your dreams, and this is so *stupid*, it's just so—"

Aunt Nora stands. "This isn't about last night. It's about all the weeks before that."

"But we'll start with last night," Uncle Tony says. He shoves his hands in his pockets. "You didn't even call, Hannah. Your sister's birthday, the first without your parents. We couldn't believe it. Thought something terrible had to have happened for you to pull something like that. Didn't want to worry Mae because she was already so upset about your dad, so we tried to handle it on our own. Your phone was off. I was getting ready to call the cops this morning, but then Mae told us about the pills. We were terrified. You were out in a snowstorm, on drugs. And then, considering who you were *with*—"

Nah throws a look of pure hatred toward the chairs Nate and I sit in by the fireplace. "You don't know Drew at all. You're just judging him because he's not like you, all brilliant and—"

"We're judging him because he sold you *drugs*, Hannah," Nate says.

"Not in forever!"

Nate rolls his eyes. "Forever? Considering you've known him for about a month, that means he sold you some, what, last week?"

"Fuck you."

"Hey." Aunt Nora glares at Nah. "There's no excuse for that. Your cousin loves you. That's why he's here. I'm sure there are a lot more things Nate would rather be doing."

"Then he should go do them," she snaps.

Who is this girl? Where is my sister, who rubbed Mom's lotion into my hands when I was sad?

Aunt Nora seems to read my mind.

"She's in withdrawal. They said she'd be . . . irritable. Among other things."

Nah gives an inarticulate growl. "I don't appreciate being talked about like I'm not here."

"And none of us appreciate being talked to like we're the enemy," Aunt Nora says. "We have to make some decisions about next steps. All of us."

She looks around, and I swear we're suddenly in a courtroom and she's about to give one of her opening statements. She's decided Hannah is guilty, and now there will be consequences.

"What are her options?" Nate asks.

"They want me to go to fucking rehab," Nah says. "Just because I came home one time on something—"

"It wasn't just one time," Uncle Tony says. "You already admitted that at the hospital. You've relapsed, and we have to—"

"Let's see both of your parents die in a tsunami and see how you cope, Tony," she says.

He gives her a hard stare. "Let's see you watch your daughter die of leukemia and see how *you* cope."

All of us flinch—Nah included.

"I'm sorry," she whispers.

"Do you see what this shit turns you into?" Uncle Tony says. "Do you know how lucky you are to be alive?"

"Tony." Aunt Nora gives a slight shake of her head, and he stands and crosses to the far side of the room, stares out the window. His hands are shaking. He's not mad, I realize: He's scared.

He doesn't want to go to another funeral.

Nah's hand floats to her stomach. I can see my sister retreating to wherever she goes when she thinks about the clinic.

"It helped last time, when you did the outpatient program," I tell her. "People often have to go more than once. When I was doing research—"

"I don't want to hear about your goddamn research, Mae!"

"Hannah, you have a serious addiction," Aunt Nora says. "You've already been in detox and outpatient group therapy this year alone. On top of that, you've suffered enormous trauma losing your parents, and the move, not to mention—"

She stops, uncertain, and Hannah stares at me.

"You told them about the clinic?"

"I had to, Nah. The secrets aren't helping."

"That wasn't your story to tell. Mom and Dad said that all of this was *my* story to tell!"

"When they were HERE," I yell. Then I remember that I have to be calm under pressure. I take a breath. "They said that because they knew and they could help. But now they're gone, and Aunt Nora and Uncle Tony have their job."

Aunt Nora's face softens. "Honey, your parents were right not to gossip about you. But they also had to hold a lot on their own, and I'm not sure that was such a good thing. Your mom especially, what with everything we all know now about your father. If she'd told me about this earlier, about everything you were dealing with, I could have helped."

I burst into tears. All of it coming up, like the wave: the truth about Dad and how hurt Mom must have been, her holding so much inside her, and Nah being so sick and me loving Ben but being too scared to tell him, and not going to Annapolis.

"I'm sorry," I say. "I'm sorry."

I don't know what I'm apologizing for. I don't think it matters.

Nate wraps his arms around me, then pulls me onto his lap like I'm a little girl and it's embarrassing but nice to cry into a T-shirt that says STRING THEORY with an illustration of a cat tangled up in a ball of yarn.

I can hear Hannah crying, too, but I don't look.

"Good, Buzz. Let all that shit out," he murmurs.

It does feel good. Like someone released a pressure valve I didn't know I had. I wish I could cry more. I see why people do it now.

"Mae," Hannah says. "I . . . I'm sorry. I am. I really am."

I look up at her. She's a little blurry.

"Then let us help you," I say.

"The doctors at the ER recommended Hannah do an intensive inpatient program," Aunt Nora says. "There's one out in Belmont. But we'll do the detox first and the outpatient program at Boston Children's. If that goes well, then the inpatient rehab won't be necessary—other than detox, Hannah will be home with us each night."

"It's Thanksgiving in three days," Nah says. "Can't I do all this after?"

She doesn't say: *our first without them.*

Aunt Nora's eyes well up. "Sweetie, we want you to have a lot more Thanksgivings. That's why we're doing this. You know we can't wait on the detox."

"What exactly . . . How does this detox thing work?" Nate asks.

Uncle Tony tries to explain, because Nah has gone silent, into herself. Every now and then, one of her legs kicks out, an involuntary spasm. I read about this—it's where the phrase *kicking the habit* comes from. Nah has done detox before, but she refused to ever talk about it with me. Just said it was worse than death.

But we know better now. Nothing can be worse than that.

Uncle Tony tells Nate the things I read about online. Detox is basically three or four days of Nah battling her own body. Like a knock-down, drag-out under her skin. Either she kicks the habit, or the habit kicks her.

"I don't need that," Nah insists. "The pills just help me feel normal. I don't even get high anymore when I take them, not really. If I can just get some Suboxone to taper off—"

"The fact they make you feel normal means you're addicted," Aunt Nora says.

It's true. The more opiates you have in your system, the more dependent the brain gets on those chemicals, and the opiates begin to have a normalizing effect.

"You heard what the doctor said: This can cause brain damage, Hannah," Uncle Tony says. "A stroke. Heart and cognitive defects. You don't get that Suboxa stuff, whatever it's called, until you've detoxed. It won't work otherwise, the doctor said that. We have to get you back to normal before you—"

My sister explodes.

"There IS NO GETTING BACK TO NORMAL. My parents are *dead*. There is no normal, not ever again. So don't fucking sit there and tell me that I'm gonna go to detox or rehab or whatever and then everything will be great, because it *won't*."

Uncle Tony goes red in the face, but Aunt Nora puts a hand on his arm and I think he literally bites his tongue. I bet he's drawn blood.

I stand and cross the room. Sit down next to her. "The pills won't bring them back," I say. "I know sometimes they help you forget how bad it is—but isn't everything worse, when the pill wears off? Worse than before you took them?"

Her eyes fill. "You don't understand."

I stare at her. "How can you say that, Nah? I lost them, too."

"But you don't know what it's like to be *me*," she says. Great, big fat tears roll down her face. "You have a future, a life. I have *nothing*. I'm probably not even going to graduate. I have lost everything. *Everything* in less than a year."

"You have me," I say. "You will *always* have me."

"I won't. You'll be gone by July first."

She remembered. The exact date that Plebe Summer begins. I didn't think she was ever really listening when I talked about school stuff, but she was.

"I told you, I'm not going," I say. "There are tons of schools here. You have me. Always."

For just a second, her eyes soften a bit, but then she sets her chin. Stubborn. "Mae, you knew my boyfriend was cheating on me, and you didn't tell me. I get you thought you were helping me, but you weren't. And now I can't trust you. So what makes you think I'll want to spend another second under any roof with you once we graduate?"

This is her addiction talking. I know that. But what if it's not? What if I gave up Annapolis for nothing?

"Enough. Enough of this." Aunt Nora's voice is trembling. "Do you know what I would give to have my sister back? To be sitting on that couch with her?"

She kneels on the rug in front of us, her hair a mess of black tangles. Nah looks like a carbon copy of Mom, almost, but Aunt Nora looks like her, too.

"My sister is dead."

This woman in front of me: This is how I would be, if I lost Nah.

"I have to remind myself of this every morning when I wake up," she says, "because I forget. I wake up and I think, *I have to tell Lila I had the most awful dream about her. This horrible wave, and I was searching in the rubble, looking and looking . . . and then I remember.*"

She clasps her hands together, tight, like she's praying, but there's no one to pray to.

"And I tell myself, I *have* to tell myself: *Lila is dead. My sister is dead.*

"Sometimes I'm angry at her. *I told you, Li. I told you not to go.* Because I did, and she went anyway. Stubborn as hell. Hannah, you're just like her."

Aunt Nora starts to cry, and Uncle Tony sits on the couch near her, his own face crumpling. Nate comes over, too, kneels beside her, his hand on her arm, the bangles from India he's wearing jangling quietly.

"It does something to you, being furious with your dead sister first thing in the morning." Aunt Nora shakes her head, wipes her runny nose with the back of her hand. "It's hardest around nine at night, though. That was our time. I would call her and she'd be making dinner. I'd be cleaning up. Sometimes the old grandfather clock downstairs chimes and I reach for the phone. Isn't that strange? I still reach for her."

She takes in a shuddering breath. Looks from Nah to me.

"When the sky is dark and the moon is out, I'm not angry at her anymore," she whispers. "I just want her help. I don't think I believe in anything—an After. But I still tell her, every night: *Help your girls, Li. Help them find their way back to each other.*"

She grabs our hands. "It's not good when sisters don't stay up together late at night. When they stop giggling and having secrets together. It's not good when they don't knowingly catch each other's eyes or borrow each other's clothes or do each other's makeup. I would give anything to be able to walk down a hallway, open a door, and see my sister's face. You both lost so much. But you have each other. Don't let the wave take that, too."

Hannah lets out a shuddering sob, her shoulders caving in. I wrap an arm around her and she falls into me, her head in my lap, like she did with Mom. I rub slow circles over her back, my palm against her thin shirt.

Aunt Nora stands, kisses us both on the head, then motions for Nate and Uncle Tony to follow her out of the room.

I run my hand through Nah's hair, just like Mom used to. The fire Nate built crackles, the sound a soothing background against Nah's broken heart.

"I tried," she sobs. "I tried to quit, but then they found Mom's . . . Mom's body, and I . . . I just *couldn't*, Mae. I can't . . ."

"That's part of why I didn't tell you," I say. "About Micah. I should have. I just didn't want to make it worse."

"I give up, Mae." Nah looks up at me with tearstained eyes. "I give *up*."

I don't know what this means. Giving up.

"It's not even December yet," I say. "We can get you tutors, get your grades up. You know, Scott Kelly was like you—not really into school. And now he's the American record holder for most days in space. I'm sure—"

She sits up. Wipes at her eyes. "I wasn't . . . Never mind."

I don't know what she wants. How to talk to her. To this person who craves nothing but pills and silence.

"What do you want, Nah? Right now. In your life. What do you want? Because I know that if we can figure that out, we can fix this. We can."

She pulls the backs of her hands across her eyes, smearing eye liner and mascara. "I think that's the problem. Part of it. I don't *want* anything. I don't *feel* anything. Everything I planned for—working with Mom at the studio, just being in LA and with Micah . . . it's all gone."

"Well, you could work at a studio here. Or go to yoga school. Are there yoga schools? You could—"

"It's not . . . Without her . . . I can't. I don't even care, Mae. You don't get it. I don't *care* about anything."

I remember that Mom told me something they would say at Al-Anon meetings she and Dad went to, the meetings for people who love someone with an addiction. They would say *Just for today*. And this sounds like what River was talking about at Dharma Bums, about being in the present, riding the ride.

"Then don't think about the future," I say. "Just think about now. This . . . moment. We can go moment by moment. I took a meditation class with Ben, and the teacher, River, she said all you need to worry about is the breath you're taking right now. So just . . . take a breath. Then another. And once you're off the pills for good, then maybe you'll want things again. Other things."

"You sound like Mom," she says.

"I do?" This makes me warm, fills me up. I smile. "Then things are much worse than I thought."

She laughs a little. "Yeah, who would have thought you'd turn into some guru?"

That laugh is a good sound.

"Mom and Dad are gone, but we're still here, Nah." I rest my hand on her knee. "We're still here. And no matter what happens, no matter how bad it gets, we can't give up. We have to do right by the miracle."

She stares at me, a little spark of light finally coming into her eyes. "Do right by the miracle."

As much as I hate my dad right now, I owe him one for that bit of light.

I nod. "Something Dad said in one of his talks."

"*Dad* said that?"

"Yeah. Last year. That Big Questions conference in Dallas."

Her eyes fill, face crumbling a little. "I didn't know."

"That's okay. Dad said a lot of things." I swallow. "He didn't take his own advice, though."

She shakes her head. "No."

"Aunt Nora says Mom knew. About . . . Rebecca."

Nah closes her eyes. "So she died knowing he didn't love her anymore."

I dig my fingernails into my jeans. "She died knowing *we* loved her. Fuck him."

She stares at me. Smiles. "Yeah. Fuck him."

It doesn't make me feel better. To hate him. How do you unlove someone?

She stands. "Still. Maybe he was right. About the miracle."

"You'll go—to detox?"

Three days of hell that will feel like three years.

My sister nods, then looks up past the ceiling, like she can see all the way through the atmosphere. "I'm still really mad at you."

And even though he's not there, even though he's just matter at the bottom of the ocean now, or in the belly of a shark, I know exactly who she's talking to. And I feel the same way.

30

Mae

A supermassive black hole is big enough to hold the mass of four million suns. There's a black hole at the center of our galaxy, but Earth is a safe distance from it, so we don't get pulled in. But I can't maintain a "safe distance" from my sister. She is the black hole that we orbit.

Neil deGrasse Tyson says that black holes could possibly be tunnels through the universe. I'm hoping we can get to the other side of this black hole. Back to the Hannah I knew without pills.

Today is Thanksgiving, the first without Mom and Dad, and the first without Nah, too.

Because my sister is in detox.

In a place with bright fluorescent lights and no sharp objects and strangers who don't know that after the big dinner we're supposed to all eat Mom's homemade cinnamon ice cream sundaes and watch at least one *Harry Potter* movie (this year we're on the third one, which is all of our favorites, and I bet Dad would have insisted we watch the fourth, too). Nate and Dad are supposed to argue about the aeronautical challenges of Quidditch, and Mom will decry the stereotype of Professor

Trelawney and how it gives everyone the wrong idea about people like Mom and her coven, as Dad calls Cyn and Mom's tarot friends. And Nah is supposed to be curled up on the couch with Micah, not some horrible Drug Boy who only wears black and probably secretly roots for the Yankees. And me? I'm just taking it all in.

But not this year.

This year, it just hurts too much to sit around the table. All those empty places. And knowing that, this year, maybe Dad's place would have been empty, anyway. Even if there hadn't been a wave.

I can't think about him. I can't. When I do, everything inside me goes completely dark. I become a black hole, too.

I wonder what Rebecca Chen is doing. And the wondering grows, because I think about my baby sister or brother and how it'd be really unfair if they were punished for what Dad did.

So I do something that surprises me, something spontaneous. Rash, even. I go to my room and send the email I've been writing and rewriting since my birthday, since I found out the truth about Dad and Rebecca, since Aunt Nora said, *You don't have to worry about that.*

My Brother or Sister 3:17 PM (November 28th)
Mae Winters <spacecadet@mail.com>
Rebecca Chen <rchen@mail.com>

I know what happened. My sister found all your emails with my dad. I'm writing you because I don't want this brother or sister I'm going to have to be punished for the poor choices of adults who forgot about the Butterfly Effect. This child deserves to know they have two sisters and that he or she or they are not alone in the universe. I want to be very clear: I think you're a bad person for what you did. I think my dad is, too. My family is hurting right now even more because of this. You should know that. Also, my mom knew about the two of you when she died. She was found in a mass grave earlier this month, alone.

I would like to be notified when my brother or sister is born. And I'd like to have updates and be part of their life in some way, because they deserve that, and Hannah and I do, too.

Mae Winters

I don't think I'm being disloyal to Mom by sending this email. I think she'd understand. She'd never want a kid to be hurt over something they can't control.

In the late afternoon, we make our plates and sit in front of the TV. Just me and Aunt Nora, Uncle Tony, Nate. We don't watch Harry. We watch *White Christmas*. A little early in the Winters holiday calendar, but I'm glad we do. Bing and Danny and "the girls"—I like the little cobbled-together family they decide to make at that Vermont inn. Strange, how a building falling down in a war zone can bring lonely people together. The *Sisters* bit makes me sad, though.

Ben went home for the holiday—he wasn't going to. Wanted to stay with me. But I can feel those three words between us. The ones he had the guts to say, and I didn't. I can feel him wanting more from me than I can give. Right now, everything is for Hannah. So I kissed him and told him to go to Brooklyn. Told him I'd see him when he got back. It wasn't what he wanted.

When it gets dark outside, I grab my coat and head down the stairs, ignoring the closed door to my sister's room. I say a quick goodbye, then head toward the T.

I'm on the Dharma Bums email list now, and they're having a special meeting tonight, so I'm going. I want to look for the secret in the silence. My dad was always saying that you learn more when you get quiet. I need to learn more. I think maybe I have too much specialized knowledge. I know a lot about astrophysics and theoretical physics, but I don't understand people. They are so different from theorems. So much harder to figure out. It's possible that the hardest person to understand is myself.

I need the silence to tell me what to do. To tell me if it really was the right thing to cancel that interview. To tell me how to help my sister in the best way I can.

It's cold tonight. No snow. Just banks of it left over from the storm. The D train rumbles behind me, a few blocks away, toward Boston Children's, and I look over the houses and trees to where Nah is waiting for us to pick her up tomorrow.

My eyes flick up to the sky, but the sight of the moon tonight doesn't make me feel better. It just reminds me how fast everything goes. The moon's one light-second away, so every time you look at it, you're actually seeing into the past. You're time traveling. And I just want to keep going back. Not forward. Back. And back. And back. But I can't.

I hurry down the sidewalk toward Beacon, to the T stop at Washington Square. The doors open and it's pretty empty inside. Everyone with their families.

I don't see him until I've transferred to the Red Line. He's sitting across from me, staring at nothing. Maybe he's seeing her. Trying to look past the stations that fly by, all the way back to Boston Children's.

Drew Nolan couldn't be more different from Micah if he tried. Micah was a sun god, bursting with light (even though he did turn out to be a horrible boyfriend who Nah refuses to ever speak to again), but Drew, he's all night. Late night. When you should be safe in bed night. His face is cut like stone. Sharp. Black, wavy hair. Paler than me. A perfect manga villain.

He feels my eyes on him and finally looks up. Goes paler, if that's possible.

From the look of him, he hasn't gotten any more sleep than the rest of us. But I don't care. The moment the seat next to him empties, I take it.

I keep my voice low, and he has to lean in to hear me above the roar of the train. "If you ever talk to my sister again, I'm calling the police.

And informing the school administration that you've been selling drugs to students. I know you're on scholarship, so I really hope you make the right choice."

Drew turns to me, broken and desperate, and I do not care. I do not.

His voice is a rasp, a fraying rope. "I love her."

"Fuck you."

I cannot believe I just said that. Or how good it felt.

I lean close to his face.

"You *sold her drugs*. Do you have any idea what she's been going through these past few days in detox?"

"She's in detox?" Relief and hurt wash over his face.

I'm surprised she didn't tell him. Maybe that was supposed to be a secret. But I'm done with secrets.

"Yeah, after a whole night out with *you*."

"She wasn't using with me that night. She drank, and I was watching out for her. Mae—"

"She could have died—she still *might* die."

I say this louder than I mean to, and an old lady a few seats down glances at us over her copy of the *Boston Globe*. I never realized how lucky you are, if you get to be a senior citizen. I used to feel sorry for old people; I don't anymore.

"These three days in the hospital—it's only the beginning." I am trying very hard to use my inside voice. "When she comes home, the doctors said she'll likely be depressed. Craving. Sensitive to pain. There's a higher risk of suicide. And if she relapses again and takes the same dose as she did before, her chances of overdosing are greater. You die from respiratory suppression. You stop breathing. You drown."

His voice is low, urgent. "I've been trying to help her. She just—"

"How? How have you helped her? By getting her high? By helping her forget who she is? You never talked to me. Or my aunt and uncle. My cousin. You could have told us. How bad it was. You didn't. And I know why. You didn't want her to be mad at you. To push you away like she pushes away anyone who tries to help her. So you'd rather have her *like* you than have her healthy. You're a fucking *coward*."

He flinches. "I know you don't believe I've been watching out for her, but I have. It's all I do these days. I'm not dealing anymore. I'm not giving her pills. She promised she was going to stop. If I try to bring it up, she pushes me away. You're right, she does that. But I can't help her if she doesn't let me in. She can't break up with you. But she can with me. If I'd lectured her, or if I'd told you—she'd have shut me out. For good. I thought if I could just show her she didn't need the pills—"

"So, what, you thought you could kiss it better?" I shake my head. "God, you're one of them."

"One of who?"

The train lurches, and I have to work very hard not to be pushed up against this creep.

"Guys never paid attention to me until my parents died. I never knew that was a factor in male attraction, but apparently it is. Suddenly, boys at school who are not my lab partners are talking to me. It's not because I'm the new girl. I think they like the idea of saving me, of being some knight in shining armor. They want to swoop in and get a little rush of oxytocin. I think they like the drama of it. We're these tragic figures to them. Being with us is like starring in an indie movie." I stare him down. "In your case, though, I bet you thought she could validate you somehow. Right? Like maybe you could be good again if you got her clean. Either way, it has nothing to do with Hannah and everything to do with you."

I've never said this out loud, and I'm suddenly wondering: Is *Ben* one of those guys, too? Because Riley was the only boy who ever showed interest in me all throughout high school, and yet suddenly a brilliant, MIT version of Ichigo Kurosaki meets me and wants to be with me after *one night* of astronautical engineering. Carl Jung would call this synchronicity, but Jung was a mystic more than a psychologist, and his reasoning is therefore suspect.

Drew shakes his head. "So you're suggesting that the *only* reason I'd be with Hannah is that I want to use her to feel better about my own piece-of-shit self? Because there would be no other reason to want to be with her, is that it?"

"You are misinterpreting my analysis—"

"I don't think I am. Not in this case. I think you got an A in AP Psych and you think you know everything. You're the smartest person on this train, and I'm a lowly dealer. I get it, I do: I don't deserve her. Maybe if I were like Ben, we wouldn't be having this conversation. But you're not accounting for the fact that someone might want Hannah for other reasons. Because she's beautiful and she sees the world in a way no one else does. She walks her own path, even when it's confusing and hard. She actually takes the time to get to know the kind of people the rest of the world writes off. No. All those things are irrelevant in your calculus."

"Don't tell me about my sister. You've known her for two seconds. You're not the expert on her."

Drew's eyes flash. "And you are? You live with her. You supposedly know her better than anyone, right? But here's what I don't get, Mae: If you're the expert, then how the hell did she get on the pill train to start? Because when I met her, she'd been on that ride for a while."

The T jolts to a stop. I can hardly breathe. My coat, sealing me in, a straitjacket. I feel like Mom, this enclosed space taking out all the air. All those elevators she hated getting into. I understand now, why she wanted to take the stairs.

I hate him. I hate him so much. I hate him more than climate change deniers.

"Except for when she was sober this summer, your sister's been swallowing pills for a year and a half," he says. "I've only known her since October. So how is this all *my* fault? Where have *you* been? Where have any of you *fucking been*? I'm the only person in this whole city who sees her. Who can't stop looking."

His words hit me with the force of the wave. He's right. I didn't do anything until it was too late, and even then it was Mom and Dad who figured out what her problem was. This is my fault. My parents drowned, and there was nothing I could do about it. My sister has been drowning for months, and I've been standing on the shore so close—but instead of looking out for her in that water, jumping in and pulling her out, I've had my eyes on the stars.

Selfish. I've been so selfish.

Maybe I didn't try to save her because a part of me knew that I'd have to give up Annapolis to do that. I'd hoped flushing her pills or calling Micah would do the trick. I was trying to pass her off to him, wasn't I?

I was willfully ignorant. The biggest crime you can commit.

Drew stands. "Call the cops. Call the damn mayor, if you want. I don't deserve her—that's true. But she's the one good thing in my life. And I know I can be a good thing in hers. And you're not keeping me from her."

I reach up and grab his arm, squeeze so hard he winces as I pull myself up. He's tall, taller than Hannah, even, so I have to stand on my toes to say what I have to say properly.

"You're right: You don't deserve her." I swallow. "But . . . you're also right about me. I have to . . . to recalculate my course."

He nods.

"Here's the thing, though," I say. "You almost took her from me. In a way, you already have. Her addiction isn't your fault. It's no one's fault. But easy access to pills—that *is* your fault. Not talking to my family so we can all keep her safe—*also* your fault. If you really love her, you'll stay away." I drop my hand. "Our family can't handle one more disaster, and that's all you'll be. You'll hurt her. You already have. And she'll hurt you. That's what she does. And then she'll feel bad about it. And it will make everything worse. We'll take it from here. Okay?"

Drew grips the bar above us as the train takes a sharp turn. "The difference between you and me, Mae, is that when I look at your sister, I don't see a problem. I see a solution." The smile he gives me is sad, and old. It's seen a lot of things maybe I haven't. "She's so much more than any of you have ever given her credit for." He leans forward. "And I'll tell you a little something I've picked up as a dealer. The pills, they have nothing to do with the stuff everyone thinks users take them for. Hannah doesn't take them because of the wave or the abortion or because she fell in with the wrong crowd."

"But . . . *why*, then?"

"I think you need to spend some time getting to know your sister better, Mae."

The train stops, and Drew turns, folding himself into the trickle of bodies exiting at Harvard Square. I stare after him long after the doors shut and the train starts again.

I sit on that train and ride it all the way to the end of the line, ride it like my sister did that morning when she was alone and cold and desperate and scared.

He's right: I don't know her. Not really. I thought I did. But I had to ask her what she wanted because I had no idea. And when I think about her now, the only adjective that comes to mind is *broken*. I don't know when she stopped being the person who sang along to *Hocus Pocus* or the fun girl who worked at the coffee shop by our house. The one who went to bonfires with surfers and loved jumping into waves and making goofy playlists.

I guess I wasn't looking.

Jean Cocteau—artist, writer, filmmaker—said of opium: *I owe it my perfect hours*. It makes me so sad, to imagine Nah's perfect hours being ones that are all alone, hiding, filled with pills to help her forget the wave and whatever made her start taking the pills in the first place. Covered in vomit, her lips blue from cold. Skin breaking out in a rash. I want to help her see what Ben showed me about time, how it can be a gift. How a minute, if you really let yourself live it, can be everything.

The past few days, I've been kicking my research into high gear. Thinking I was working the problem. I thought maybe if I could figure out *why* the pills were so attractive, I could provide an alternative. As though it would be a simple bait and switch. What, exactly, are the pills giving her that life isn't? And then how can I give her that thing in a healthier form?

But I don't think it's that simple. I've been trying to give Nah answers instead of asking her questions. It took a drug dealer, of all people, to point out my error. A drug dealer who is probably a lot smarter than I've been giving him credit for. Another error on my part.

I need to find a safe way to help my sister face whatever it is that got her started on pills in the first place. All that sadness she had even before the clinic and the wave. I think the answers might be at Dharma Bums, but I have to conduct more tests until I'm certain.

When the train stops at Kendall, I step off and walk toward the cushion that's waiting for me. The silence. The *something*—or Something Else—that hides in there, waiting for all of us.

this is what dying looks like.

Mirror

Room 365

Boston Children's Hospital

see what you are made of.

Toilet Seat

Room 365

Boston Children's Hospital

sit in a circle
stay there until
the beginning has no end

Door
Group Therapy Room
Boston Children's Hospital

the miracle can go fuck itself.

Suboxone Package
Medication Dispensary
Boston Children's Hospital

diamonds are a girl's best friend.

Opioid Addiction Hotline Sign
Copley Station
Boston

31

Hannah

Somehow I knew he'd be here. Waiting for me.

Drew sits beneath my angel like an offering. It's snowing again, and the flakes swirl around him, around her. It is so quiet here. Day fading to night. The garden empty, too cold for strolling.

He stands. Slow. He's afraid I'll run away again.

"They won't let me see you." His eyes are dark, a night sea. "I came. To your house."

"I know."

I heard his voice last night after I got back, even through my closed bedroom door upstairs. The one that no longer has a lock.

His voice, like the last lifesaver on a sinking ship, floating just beyond reach. For just one second, I wanted something more than a pill.

"Did you . . . I called." He laughs softly. "I even emailed you."

"I couldn't have anything in . . . there."

There.

Sweating through the clothes Aunt Nora brought. Shivering under starchy hospital sheets. My bones grinding against one another, muscles spasming, my body a traitor, punishing me. The nightmares, the wave and Mom in that grave and Dad running away from her, toward Rebecca Chen. Me, alone on an island in the middle of a sea and nobody will ever find me because I am invisible, I am invisible. Waking up alone, cold, cold, make it stop.

Finally saying, out loud, *I want to die*.

"You didn't tell me," I say, "that it was my dad who said we should do right by the miracle."

His face wobbles a little. "I didn't know if . . . it was weird? Me looking him up."

I shake my head. "Not weird."

Beautiful. Perfect. But not weird.

Drew is in front of me now, and his cheeks are so red from the cold, he must have been out here forever, waiting. He whispers, "Hannah, can . . . can I hold you?"

There is pure agony on his face, and so much hope. And fear. I don't know what to do with that.

I'm just trying to keep the lights on.

"Please," he says.

"Why?"

I'm the shell you throw back into the ocean, not the one you put into your pocket. I'm just a *shell*, I want to tell him. There is nothing here. Nothing left inside.

"Because I love you."

My eyes fill with the ocean.

He steps so close I can feel his breath on my cheek. "I love you so much, Hannah, so fucking much, and it's killing me right now, not touching you."

Through the blur of tears, I see this rope he's throwing me, trying to pull me in to safety.

Take it, someone whispers. *Take it, Hannah*.

Despite everything, Mom is still a hopeless romantic. She always has been.

I fall forward, against his chest, and Drew's arms come around me and he holds me close and tight as he lets loose a shuddering breath.

I look up at him and I try to find the words, but he says softly, "Wait."

Then he pulls off his gloves and runs his hands up my neck, his fingers trailing along my jaw.

"You should have a scarf on," he murmurs.

I smile. "At least I'm not wearing sandals."

A spark of light flies across Drew's eyes, like a bit of the meteor shower I once watched with Dad. It had been just us two—for once, without Mae. One of the best nights of my life is tucked away in this boy's eyes.

"I've wanted to kiss you from the moment you came up to me at school," he says. "I didn't want to sell you pills, Hannah, I wanted to *kiss* you. But I thought the pills were the only way to get you, to get anyone, to see me."

Maybe we see each other because we're both invisible.

"Drew . . ." I reach up. Grasp his hand where it rests near my cheek. "You don't have to—"

"But I do. I have to say this." He grips my shoulders. "I'm so sorry, *so* goddamn sorry, for what I did to you. To everyone I sold to. But especially you. If anything had happened to you . . . I don't think I could have . . . When Mae told me you were in the hospital, and I knew you were hurting so bad and I helped put you in there, it fucking tore me apart." His eyes fill. Spill over. "I don't deserve you. I know that. And your family's probably right, that I should stay away, but I just . . . I feel like that wave brought you to me. It washed you up on *my* shore. I wish it hadn't, for your sake. I wish your parents were still here, but they're not and I am, and, Hannah, I think we can help each other do right by the miracle. You already do— you're my miracle. Fuck, that's so cheesy, but you are. And I'm not him, Hannah. I'm not Micah. I would have come that day." His voice breaks. "I would have walked into the clinic and told you that you didn't have to do it if you didn't want to. And if you did, I would have gone in that room with you—I would *never* have let you do that alone, unless you wanted to. Because I see you, Hannah. I *see you*. Your kindness, your creativity, the way you give the whole world the middle finger, and—"

I kiss him.

Quick and soft, and then I pull away and murmur against his lips, so cold from waiting for me in the snow, "I love you, Drew Nolan."

Out of the corner of my eye, I swear my angel's wings flutter.

• • •

We thaw out from the cold on the frayed couch in Drew's living room, in front of a hissing radiator. I wish I could steal him away from here, from this place with dirty walls. There is a faint scent of stale beer, no decorations, no family photos. No loving touches. It's a place to crash when you're too tired or wasted to move.

"The radiator in my room broke, so it's better if we're out here," he says, tucking another blanket around me. "My dad's at the pub. Won't be back for hours."

"This time yesterday I was in a hospital bed. Your couch is perfect." I lean my forehead against his. "I'm glad to be with you. I don't care where."

"Me, too." He smiles. "How'd you get out of the house? Seemed like they had you under lockdown."

"I think they assumed because I'm not really athletic that I would never figure out how to climb out my window. It wasn't that high up, though. And all the yoga helped. I practically had to sun salutation my way out of there."

"You'll get in trouble, though. When they see you're gone."

I shrug. "Worth it."

I settle my legs over his lap and he reaches over and intertwines our fingers. "Was it as bad as I imagined—the hospital?"

"It sucked. Really hard."

"What happens next?"

"They're 'monitoring' me. If I stay clean, they won't send me to inpatient rehab. If I don't, then there's that. Either way, there's weekly group therapy in this lame-ass outpatient program." I roll my eyes. The return of Circle of Sad. "Random drug testing at home. Suboxone—this medicine that helps with getting me off this shit. They took the lock off my bed-room door. My aunt and uncle have never done this before, so once my aunt finishes reading all the books she bought I'm sure they'll figure out more ways to make my life suck. Right now they just stare at me a lot."

"What kind of books? Like, psychology books?"

"Let me see. There's *Don't Let Your Kid Kill You, Expecting Better, Addict in the Family* . . . I don't even want to know what the hell Mae's reading."

He pulls me a little closer. "I wish I could have been there with you."

My aunt and uncle have made it clear: I'm not allowed to date a drug dealer. Even a *former* drug dealer. Not that I care what they allow or don't allow.

"I wouldn't have wanted you to . . . see me like that." I frown. "I feel like you always see me at my worst. I wish you could have known me. Before."

Drew reaches beneath the blanket, pulls me onto his lap. "If your worst is a girl who hangs out with angels and convinces a hardened criminal to give up his drug-dealing ways just by being herself, by always keeping it real no matter how fucking messy things get, I'd say this Hannah's pretty great."

She's a shell, I think. But if I said that, it would break his heart. So I don't.

"Are you ever gonna kiss me?" I say instead.

I was the one who kissed him. He kissed me back, but still.

"You sure you want me to, after the other night? I kinda fucked that up."

"Don't be an idiot."

"See? Keeping it real." Drew smiles, and his eyes are playful and full of light.

He ducks his head toward mine, and his lips brush against my skin, soft and light, snowflake kisses that melt against me. So gentle. Careful.

"You won't break me, Drew." The hands resting against my cheeks tremble a little. "I'm stronger than you think."

He swallows. "I . . . I know you are."

I shift so that my legs straddle his hips, and that one movement un-locks something in Drew, whatever was holding him back. He lets out a low growl, pulls me close, crushes his lips against mine. This kiss is a homecoming, reminding me I'm not that girl shivering on the hospital bed, that my body isn't always a traitor. This kiss does right by the miracle.

A new height. A new high.

I open, open, open to him, to his breath and lips and hands, to his tongue and his teeth and his skin. Drew kisses me like he wants to pull me inside him, his whole body fusing with mine, sending sparks of light all through me until I'm dizzy, like we're on carnival swings that spin, faster and faster, higher and higher, and oh God, this new high feels so, so good. I ride this wave, let it take me all the way to the shore.

When he pulls away, my lips are swollen, and I'm covered with his scent, tea tree and cedar, like the inside of my mom's hope chest, which we had to put in storage.

"You smell like hope," I whisper against his lips. I can feel the blood fly under my face. "Sorry. That was weird. I just—"

He kisses me again. "So do you."

I want to believe him. So badly.

The high of the kiss melts away, and then I feel it, just like the doctor said I would: the craving. More, I want more.

That kiss, so good, so perfect—but it wasn't *quite* enough.

I need to feel . . . calibrated. Normal. Me. Just a little kick in my bloodstream to be *me*.

Drew reaches into his pocket. "I have one more diamond for you. Just one."

I stare at him.

On the one hand: *Oh, thank God, he knows me so well, he loves me, he has my back.* On the other: *I just got out of detox. He said he was sorry about the pills. What is he* thinking?

"I don't know if—" I start, but then the words, they don't matter anymore. Whatever I was going to say doesn't matter.

He holds up a velvet box. Not a pill bottle.

A bit of Yoko comes to me, slices right into my heart:

Each time we don't say
what we want to say
we're dying.

I want to say to Drew: *You can't save me.*

I want to say: *I wish it were a pill. I hate myself for that.*

But I don't. Because he keeps his eyes on mine as he opens the box. "It's small." His lips turn down a little, uncertain. "I hope that's okay."

Nestled inside the black velvet is a tiny teardrop diamond, just a sliver of sparkle, hanging from a thin gold chain. I know he spent everything he had on this. For me.

I die. For the fiftieth time this week. I die.

You can't save me.

I'm not worth saving.

"It's beautiful," I say instead.

Drew leans his forehead against mine. "From now on, these are the only kinds of diamonds I will give you. I promise."

I wish this was enough. That he was enough.

I wish I didn't still want a pill.

"Hannah." His voice is rough. "When . . . when I said I had a diamond for you. For a second, you seemed like . . ." His eyes fly to mine. "Would you have taken it? If it weren't a necklace?"

My eyes fill. I nod. "Yes. I'm sorry. Yes."

"Don't cry," he murmurs. "It's okay. It takes time. I'm here. Always. I'll carry you. I told you that before. I meant it."

I shake my head. "And I told *you* before—you can't carry me."

"Hannah, I would carry you across the damn universe if you needed it."

It is the perfect thing to say. I know that. I feel how perfect it is.

But if there is anything they made clear in detox, it was this: I'm on my own. As per fucking usual. No one can kick this for me. I have to do it myself. I have to not wish a pill were in a velvet box.

"But you can't, Drew. You can't get sober for me. I don't deserve you. This." I put my hand over his, over the box, and push it away.

"Yes, you do," he insists.

"You want me to tell you I'll never use again," I say.

"Yes."

"I can't, Drew. I can't promise you that." The ocean streams down my face and Drew holds me close and I hate myself for hurting him, for ruining this moment. "In the hospital, I . . . I realized something. The pills, they, they make me feel *normal*. Without them, my brain—it just doesn't work anymore. I need them. To get through senior year."

"You don't. I promise. You just have to get used to not having them again."

"You don't understand! Okay? You can't possibly. So don't talk to me like you do, because you *don't*."

"Okay. You're right. I'm sorry." He runs his hands across my back, long, soothing strokes. I never told him how I need that, but he knows, somehow he knows. "You said you were stronger than I think—than any of us think. I believe you. You are, Hannah. So strong. Look what you've come through already. You can fight this. I know you can. *We* can."

I cover my face, say the words through the bars of my fingers. Can't he see I'm in a cell I can't get out of?

"I can't. Not on empty. I'm telling you, my brain just doesn't—if I just had *one*—can't you give me—"

"No." He's firm. Gently slides my fingers back so he can see me. "I'm not holding, and I won't ever be again, and I will fucking kill anyone who sells to you, and that's a promise."

Drew takes the necklace out of the box, and I shake my head, but he slips it around my neck anyway, secures the clasp.

I start to cry for real. Horrible, ugly, pathetic tears. "Drew, please . . . Your cousin. Eddie. He likes me, right? When he was over that one time, he said anything I need, he'd get it for me."

"He shouldn't have fucking said that, and I told him so."

"But, Drew, he'll have something. Even just some Vicodin. Just, I need help to get through . . . please. I know you love me. I need you. I need your help."

"I do love you. I do, Hannah. All of me loves all of you."

"Not this part."

"Yes, *yes: this* part, too."

I cry harder. Because the way he says it—he's not on my side. He won't help. I thought he saw me, but he doesn't. If he did, he'd help me.

"Your mom loved Yoko, right?"

I blink, surprised he remembered from whatever rambling monologue that was from. "Yeah."

"Okay, well. Yoko—what would she say to you, huh? Or your mom? What would they say? To help you right now?"

I'm so tired. Days and days of detox takes it out of you. Everything hurts. Especially him. The desperate fear in his face. I think of the Fox telling the Little Prince: *You become responsible, forever, for what you have tamed.* The Little Prince knows that forever and ever he will be responsible for his thorny rose. And the Fox, too, if he tames him.

I don't want to be Drew's burden. His responsibility.

I'm such a fucking loser.

So fucking weak.

I don't deserve this diamond, this boy, this breath in my body.

"My mom can't say anything to help me now, Drew. She's dead." I slide off his lap. "And I think a part of me is, too."

An empty shell.

Nameless.

Nothing.

I lean down. Kiss him once. This is goodbye, but I don't say that.

I have died so many times this week.

32

Mae

ISS Location: Low-Earth Orbit
Earth Date: 5 December
Earth Time (EST): 14:25

There are so many silences—good ones, like when Ben hugs me tight or I sit on a meditation cushion—but this one scares me. The silence behind her closed door.

I keep thinking about how quiet my sister's death would be, if she overdosed: with respiratory suppression, you stop being able to inhale or exhale.

You forget how to breathe.

And now, when I open Nah's bedroom door, I forget how to breathe, too.

I don't know this person. This ghost sitting in the window seat.

An afghan Gram knitted a long time ago must have been wrapped around her at some point, but it's fallen to the ground. Nah sits, looking out the window, onto the street, where wind whips hard and vicious through the bare branches, staring at nothing.

It's been one week since she's been back. She hasn't left this room except for her therapy and drug testing at an outpatient clinic through Boston Children's. That's not entirely true—on her first night back after detox, Uncle Tony discovered Nah had snuck out of her window. There's an alarm on it now that will go off if she opens it. She's on home study because she refuses to go to school. She's failing all her classes. I'm not sure if she'll be able to graduate. I don't think she cares.

Aunt Nora hasn't signed her up for the rehab in Belmont yet, since her tests are coming back negative. But she said she still wants Hannah to go. They agreed that as long as her tests were drug-free, she could wait until the new year. I've been looking into research coming out of Europe and other places—maybe we're doing it all wrong. Maybe the Twelve Steps aren't getting Nah anywhere. There's no conclusive data on the method itself—shocking, really. And yet they seem to work for a lot of people.

I wish my parents were here.

The breakfast I brought up earlier sits on Nah's desk, untouched. Blueberry corn pancakes—her favorite.

"I'm going to Castaways," I say. "Come with. It'd be good—to get outside. And there's finally some sun! It's cold, but we'll bundle up. Ben will make you something with lots of chocolate. He does pretty good latte art—I bet he could do a tarot card for you."

Her hand goes to the necklace around her neck, a tiny diamond. It hangs just above Mom's Greek evil eye charm. She rubs it with her thumb.

"Did Drew give you that?" I ask.

She nods.

I saw him on our street once. Since Nah can't climb out the window anymore and she never comes downstairs, I think Drew might just be trying to be as close to her as possible. Gazing up at her window, like a twisted Romeo. But one look at Drew's face, and I didn't have it in me to interrogate him. I didn't know drug dealers wore their hearts on their sleeves, but this one does, and it's clear that heart belongs to Hannah, whether or not any of us like it.

At school, he's a ghost, like her. Staring through all of us. I think maybe he really does love her. I can't wrap my mind around a drug dealer not being a totally horrible person. It goes against everything I believe. He sold drugs to my sister. And I hate him for it. But I've asked around, and it's true: He's not dealing anymore. Maybe we're wrong to try to keep them apart. Maybe that's why she looks so empty.

"Nah."

She looks at me now, her eyes dull. That bright, vibrant green now a faded sage, like old paint in a doctor's office.

"I don't want to go," she says.

"What if I . . . snuck Drew in? So you guys can be together for a little bit. Would that help?"

I will break a rule. This is how desperate I am.

She looks at me. Through me. "I don't want to see him."

I cross the room and sit beside her. "You broke up?"

She leans her head against the wall, closes her eyes. "He can do better."

I snort. "You're kidding, right? He's a *drug dealer*. I know you're feeling bad, but—"

Her eyes snap open, and the first bit of light I've seen in them for a while flares. "He's *wonderful*."

I flinch under that stare. Drew called me out on my observational weaknesses, and maybe those don't only extend to my sister. Maybe I've spent so much time with books and telescopes that I don't see people anymore. Don't see them right.

"Okay. Then why don't you want to be with him?" I say.

I am trying to know her. To ask questions. But she makes it so hard.

Nah closes her eyes. Doesn't answer.

I squeeze her hand. "Listen. I've been thinking. After graduation, let's get an apartment. In Cambridge. Ben said he could get you a job at Castaways, and there's a really cool yoga studio nearby where I do meditation. They have a teacher training course. You'd love that. We can paint every wall a different color, like Mom always said she wanted to, but Dad said would be like putting the boardwalk in our house. What do you think?"

Her brow furrows. "You'll be at Plebe Summer. In Annapolis."

You know what always got me, at the end of *The Little Prince*? How he went back for her. For the rose. He spent all this time traveling the universe, discovering its secrets, but he wanted to go back to this rose who told him off, lied to him, was never willing to accept his help—so stubborn: *Let the tigers come with their claws!* Still, he was willing to be bitten by a poisonous snake, which was the only way he could return to Asteroid B-612, to their planet, so that he could be with the rose again.

I don't know if that's beautiful or demented. He chains himself to that little asteroid, with that rose who is going to be pricking him with her thorns for the rest of his life. But she's all he's got. And he's all she's got.

And so he goes back.

But he has to die to get to her. I think. Or at least be really, really hurt. He has to sacrifice himself.

Love is the hardest thing to understand. But also the simplest. It defies all logic.

I swallow. "I'm going to MIT. I mean, if I get in. It's obviously really hard. I have backups—Harvard. Well, Harvard's not a backup, but you know what I mean."

She stares at me. "What the hell are you talking about, Mae? I told you to reschedule the interview. I thought you—are you actually being serious right now?"

I'm not a great liar, but I try anyway. To make her think I am okay with this.

"Yes. Ben goes to MIT. So . . . you know. If I stay here, he and I can be—"

"You are *not* staying in Boston for me," she growls. "And you would never stay for some person you were dating. Not even Ben."

"Ben's a bonus. He's not the reason. Seeing Nate in the astronautical program has shown me how great their—"

She grabs my arm so hard I can feel the bruise form. "I am not your fucking responsibility."

But she is. We are taming her, and now we are responsible. Forever.

"You're my sister," I say, "and I love you and I think it would be really cool to have an apartment together and live near my boyfriend and Nate, too, and . . . MIT is amazing. I can still get into NASA this way and—"

"I don't want to live in your stupid apartment, okay?"

Mom, a little help. Please.

"But what will you do? School's done in six months. Are you going to stay here, live with Aunt Nora and Uncle Tony by yourself? You'd be so bored! And lonely." And maybe still on drugs. I rest a hand on her knee. "I know everything is so bad right now. But we need a plan. What do you want?"

She lets go of my arm. Stares into the street.

"Nothing," she says, soft.

She's like George Clooney's character in *Gravity*, floating off into space. Farther and farther into the darkness, with nothing but a country song to sing him to sleep.

Work the problem. I have to work the problem.

"Then I'll want for the both of us until you decide on something," I say. "And I want you to be happy. And healthy. And alive. You deserve good things, Nah. A good life."

She just looks at me.

"Starting with a brownie." You have to start somewhere. "I'm bringing you a brownie. And then you can teach me some yoga. The stuff you and Mom did. Will you? Downward cat? Or whatever it's called?"

I haven't seen her do yoga since the wave. Her mat is always out in her room, like she's waiting for the right moment.

"I'm tired." She closes her eyes and leans her head against the window seat wall.

"Then I'll bring coffee, too," I say. She's not the only Winters that gets to be stubborn.

She doesn't move. A statue.

"Okay. I'll be back soon. Coffee, brownie, yoga. Uncle Tony said he was gonna get a tree today, too. We could decorate later, if you want. We have some of the ornaments from LA. The egg from when we all went to Prague, remember? The one you love."

I pick up the afghan, settle it around her. She doesn't move.

I'm halfway out the door when she says, "Mae?"

"Yes?"

Nah opens her eyes long enough to look at me. "When you get to space, will you name a star after me?"

"Of course." I know she's trying to reassure me that I will still be an astronaut no matter what. I don't know how she can keep her eye on my prize and not have one of her own. "What made you think of that?"

"I was thinking. You know, in *The Little Prince*. That line: 'In one of those stars I shall be living . . .'"

When the Little Prince leaves Earth, he tells the pilot that when he looks up at the sky at night, the prince will be in one of those stars, laughing. "I shall not leave you," he assures the pilot.

And then a poisonous snake bites him. And he leaves Earth forever.

"Will you?" Her voice is insistent. "Name one for me?"

"Sure. We'll name it together. When I'm up there. I'll send you a Hubble image of it," I say. "After you see it, you can decide if you want it to be called *Nah* or *Hannah* or maybe—"

"You'll pick the right thing," she says, closing her eyes again. "You always do."

The sunlight moves across her, leaving my sister in shadows.

I stand in the doorway, watching her. "I'll be back soon, okay?"

She doesn't open her eyes. Already gone to the places I can't follow. A country song, playing in the dark.

33

Mae

ISS Location: Low-Earth Orbit
Earth Date: 5 December
Earth Time (EST): 15:37

Boston is a small world.

River is on my train, her eyes closed, palms on her thighs. Outright meditating on the subway. Her hair is covered by a turban so that she looks like a young Zadie Smith, and a thick scarf with a diamond pattern is tossed around her neck like a feather boa.

Mom, you would love her.

When she opens her eyes, I switch seats so I can sit down next to her. "You weren't kidding when you said you could meditate anywhere."

She laughs. "Gotta get your serenity on when you can, my friend. Especially during finals season. I would tell you never to go to grad school, but I doubt NASA would like that."

Who am I if I'm not the girl who's going to be an astronaut? I know I can't assume that taking Annapolis off the table means I won't be an astronaut, but it might make it harder, and it's already almost impossible.

I sink into the plastic groove of the chair. This tiredness, it must be what getting old feels like.

"What's on your mind, Mae?"

I've only been to Dharma Bums a few times, but River's a regular at

Castaways, too, so I've gotten to know her a bit these past few months. She hasn't heard the whole Winters saga, but she knows about the wave, and a little about Nah.

"My sister got out of detox last week."

"That's heavy."

"Yes." I pull at my gloves. "I'm trying to help her, but she . . . she's depressed. I don't know how to fix it. I'm not a neuroscientist. Nothing I do works. She broke up with her boyfriend. Both of them. If I could just figure out how to help her, how to *fix* this—"

"Then everything would be all right?" She raises an eyebrow.

"Well, not *everything*. But some things."

She cocks her head to the side. "How are you, Mae?"

"Me? I'm fine. But Hannah—"

"Mae." Her voice is soft. "How are *you*?"

I swallow. "I feel . . . like I'm on a spaceship with a hole in it."

River nods as she runs her fingers through the ends of her scarf. "I think everyone feels that way, at one point or another. The First Noble Truth, and all."

Life is suffering. These Buddhists don't go for the happily ever after. I think that is why I like so many of them. Normal people don't talk this way, but I have never been good around normal people. It's nice not to talk about TV or celebrities or diets.

"I keep trying to make sense of everything," I say. "But I can't. All the ways I know don't work. This guy in her life—he's a jerk, but he said something that was right. That I don't know my sister. And so I've been trying this past week—asking her questions. Just sitting with her. Trying to understand her. But it's not working. Nothing makes her happy."

"Ever heard of hungry ghosts?"

I shake my head. "Buddhist thing?"

"Buddhist thing." The train stops, and River glances at the door. "You on for a little longer?"

I nod. "I'm meeting Ben at Castaways."

"Okay, then."

River shifts so she's facing me better. The people around us have earbuds in or are reading books or tablets. Someone is talking loudly on their phone. Something about broken Christmas lights and a cat. All of us bundled in coats and scarves even though it's stuffy in here, holding bags from holiday shopping or backpacks heavy with books for finals studying. The floor is wet with melted snow. This is a good place for a dharma bomb to go off.

"In Tibetan Buddhism, hungry ghosts are these demons who keep trying to fill the holes inside them with people and things and experiences, but nothing ever satisfies," she says. "Never fills the hole. Never gives them lasting happiness. It's a fucked-up, never-ending cycle of misery. They live with the illusion that happiness comes from outside themselves, so they keep looking for the thing that will give it to them. Until they realize there is nothing in this world that will give them happiness, they will keep starving."

I stare at her. "Like in *Bleach*."

"What's that?"

"This manga series I love. There are these monsters that the main character has to fight—they're called Hollows. Ghosts who haven't passed over. They terrorize the living because they have unfinished business, and they roam around, trying to feed their souls, but it doesn't work, and then Reapers have to kill them for good or send them to a better place."

"Cool. When I'm done reading about gender constructs in the eighteenth century, I'll have to check it out." I laugh. Wow, am I glad I chose the sciences. "Yeah—hungry ghosts are definitely hollow. That's a good way of thinking about it. It's like when you're sad, and you think a new girlfriend or a new haircut or outfit will make you happier. But you get those things, and you still feel empty inside. Our suffering comes because we think people or things are for keeps. They're not. Or we think they'll solve our problems. They won't."

"My sister's a hungry ghost," I say. "I think she's been one for a long time." I frown. "But I don't understand *why*. I mean, it would almost make sense if I were the one with the problems—being a foster kid, all that. Hannah had this perfect life—my parents, good school, money. She's so pretty. When she's not on pills, she's really funny and weird, but good weird. I know she has depression—even before my parents died, I knew that. I just don't understand *why*. Or how to convert her sadness into something like happiness."

"You can't make her better, Mae. That's Hannah's job."

The train lurches to another stop—I glance at the sign on the platform. One more.

"But she can't *do* her job—of getting better. She needs help. She needs me. Or . . . someone. Something. I don't know."

I feel like I'm saying Ben's favorite words more and more these days. I hate that I can know so much about astrophysics and so little about human beings. Drew was right about me getting an A in AP Psych, but I don't know how that happened.

"Do you think you can control what's going on inside her?" River asks. "Or that you can fill the hollowness she's experiencing?"

"No. But I can show her *how* to do that—like meditation, right? Or figure out who can help her. I can't just accept my sister's depression, or addiction. Then I'd be accepting Hannah ruining her life. Wasting it. My parents—if they saw what was happening to her . . . I can't give up on her. That would be wrong. Selfish."

River's quiet for a moment. Twists a silver ring around her middle finger. When she looks up at me, her eyes have a slight mist over them.

"My brother died a few years ago," she says. "Heroin overdose."

People say things to me: *I'm sorry, Oh my god, I didn't know.* Silence, I have learned, is golden. I rest my hand over hers. River's fingers tighten around mine.

I am so afraid I will have to say those same words to someone someday: *My sister. Died. Overdose.*

"I spent years trying to help him. In and out of rehab," she says, her voice quiet beneath the roar of the train as it crosses the Charles, where, even in this cold, there are rowers pushing through the midnight-blue water. "My parents went completely broke. I'd get calls in the middle of the night to come pick him up in these shady-ass places. He'd cry, you know? Feel so bad. Wanted to get better. Couldn't. Manipulated us. God, he was so good at that. You never knew when he was lying or telling the truth. My parents actually *gave* him opiates once because he convinced them he'd kill himself if they didn't give him his stash back. He overdosed more times than I can count. I carried Naloxone in my purse—we all did—just in case he ODed when we were around. I had to use it twice."

"She's not at that point yet," I say.

But I have it in my purse, too. I did my research. It's the only drug that can counteract the effects of an opiate overdose.

"And I hope she never will be. But I hear myself in you, Mae. I hear myself living in constant fear. That I was going to lose him, that it was my fault. That I could fix him or find the answers he was looking for. And the fear of losing him—it made *me* a hungry ghost. Because I thought that without him, I'd die, too. In our practice, we call this *clinging*. We cling to the things and people we love because we think they are the source of happiness and light and life for us. But this isn't true. It can't be. Because nothing and no one lasts forever. You know this more than maybe anyone I've met. When we cling, we set ourselves up for so much unnecessary suffering. I was holding on so tight—but in the end, I lost him anyway."

River rests a hand on my arm. "You've got to let go of what you had as a family—before the pills, before the wave. Honor it, but let it go. You can't hold on to the past, Mae. It's gone. Something new will grow in its place, but you have to make space for it. At the same time, you can't live in the future. Because then you miss out on *now*. And now is the only thing you're guaranteed. You're a scientist, you know this stuff: It's the nature of existence. Everything winks out. Including, someday, you. We have to be okay in the face of that."

"I can't lose her," I say, my voice breaking.

The smile River gives me is kind, a smile from the other side of a journey I don't want to be on.

"My love, she was never yours to begin with." She reaches out, wipes my tears away.

Somehow, in the past few months, I've learned how to cry.

"You're telling me to give up on her," I say. "Give up responsibility. So I just let my sister be addicted so I can live my great life in the present moment and enjoy her for the short time we have?"

She shakes her head. "It sounds like apathy, like we choose inaction, but that's not what I'm saying. The chaos of life is still there, and we are still living and hoping and dreaming and loving and *helping*. But we aren't ruled by the chaos, by our fear of what might happen in the future. And we don't believe the lie that we can somehow control the chaos. That's impossible—it's *chaos*: by definition, not controllable. And once you realize that you, Mae Winters, can't control the outcome of your sister's addiction, there's freedom—in the chaos, you can be free. To show up for this day, this moment, this sister. Right here, right now. You can't control this ride—hers or yours. But how you *take* the ride, that's up to you."

"But what if . . . what if you're all alone on the ride?"

River's eyes stay on mine as she speaks, and it makes me feel like a captain on a boat, steering toward a distant horizon. "You're not alone, Mae. Not really. Your love for your sister, your parents—my love for my brother—and the love they have for us: That's for keeps, my friend. No matter what happens, through all the impermanence of things, that's for *keeps*. It's what makes the ride worth taking—even if there's sometimes an empty seat next to you."

The train slows and she raises her hands to adjust her scarf, and I see those words tattooed on the sides: ONLY LOVE.

"Hah-vahd," the announcer calls over the speaker.

"Your stop," she says.

I stand, unsteady.

"I'm trying to understand," I say. "But if I took your advice in space, I'd die. Control is very important to the mission. I really don't see the practical applications of this philosophy."

River leans back, gestures to the train car enclosing us. "Just ride the ride—you'll get it."

Zen people are infuriating. No answers, just more questions.

When I get to Castaways, Ben takes one look at me and turns toward the huge vat of coffee behind him. It's interesting to me that the name of this place is how I feel: like a castaway, a survivor of an ocean catastrophe, who has washed up on this strange shore—this new life that looks nothing like my old one. I don't know if I'm waiting to be rescued, or if I already have been, and I just don't know it. Sometimes it feels like I'm shooting up flares, and Ben is the one who sees them.

He fills a cup with steaming coffee, then slides the mug across the counter toward me. Our fingers touch, and it's the first time I've felt warm all day.

How do I keep Ben from turning me into a hungry ghost? I don't want to be like Hannah, shredded to pieces by these boys. And if something happens to Ben, or we break up, I don't want to feel hollow after. I don't want to kid myself into thinking he can make me feel whole.

I pull my skin away from his, from those fingers that are trying to intertwine with mine as he hands me my cup of coffee.

"Thanks," I say.

A look of confusion crosses his face, but he leans across the counter anyway and kisses my forehead. "I missed you."

It's been days since we've seen each other. I can't leave the house all the time and go off with my boyfriend while my sister's holed up in her room, hurting.

"I missed you, too. I can't stay long."

The coffee tastes bitter today. Too strong. Or maybe I'm just getting weak.

"I'm off in a couple hours. We could—"

I shake my head. "I have to get home."

"Okay." I can hear disappointment, frustration, worry. Fear. Love.

I think about what River said, how nothing is for keeps, but that we also have to ride the ride and be all in with life. But this is cognitive dissonance: She's telling me I have to both hold on and let go at the same time. Impossible.

"I'm sorry," I say. "I'm really out of my element here. I'm a better lab partner than girlfriend."

Ben runs a finger across the counter's scarred wood, watching me. Those three words I haven't said hover in the air between us. Ten days since my birthday, since that night he climbed through my window.

"I get that you're worried about Hannah," he finally says. "And you should be. It's really scary, what's going on with her. And you're a great sister. I don't want to stand in the way of that."

"Thank you." I rest my hand on his arm, and it feels so good to touch him. I think the social scientists are correct about the need for human contact. "I know I'm not being fair—trying to be with you and sort this out all at the same time."

I *did* warn him. But then he brought in Heisenberg and wormholes.

"I told you: I'm patient. And you did say you needed space. But." He tucks my hair behind my ear. "I don't think you're being fair to *yourself*. Mae, you need to have a life. It's not healthy—"

I think we are about to have our first fight.

"Ben, my sister is very sick. I'm all she has." I look around, but no one seems to be paying attention to us. It's finals week—everyone has better things to do than eavesdrop on the barista and his girlfriend. "You're an only child, and both your parents are alive. Nobody in your family has a serious disease. I don't think you understand what I'm dealing with! I can't just frolic around with you all the time."

I've hurt him, I can tell. I am SO BAD WITH WORDS.

"I wish I could explain with numbers," I say. "I don't mean to be rude about it—"

"I wasn't talking about me when I said you need to have a life. I know where I rank on your list of priorities. And I'm right where I should be, all things considered." Ben clears his throat. "I want you to go, Mae."

I freeze. Is he breaking up with me? I stare at him, and he must know what I'm thinking, because he reaches over and takes the mug out of my hands and then takes my hands, kisses the palm of the one that's shaking the most. Because I hold him. He'd said that before. I hold him in the palm of my hand.

"I meant Annapolis," he murmurs.

I close my eyes. Breathe. The feeling I had when I thought he was breaking up with me: hunger.

"I thought you'd be happy I was staying," I say. "Long-distance relationships don't usually work out."

His lips turn up. "I'm in love with a future astronaut who's going to be four hundred kilometers above Earth. I've had to make my peace with the whole long-distance thing."

There it is again: *love.*

"Well." I pull my hands away, gulp down the scalding coffee. "You don't need to worry about that for a while now."

"You told me that without fighter pilot experience, you were seriously hampering your chances of becoming an astronaut candidate."

I wanted to be as well-rounded as possible. Mission essential from both a military and scientific standpoint. I wanted to be a commander. Now I'll just be another rocket scientist. Much easier to ignore.

"I'll need to distinguish myself even more as an engineer, but not everyone chosen is military. I'll still . . . be in the running."

I don't care what River says about not being able to help Hannah. Her brother—that was different. *Heroin:* that's a very hard drug, the hardest. Yes, it's technically the same thing as Nah's pills, but my sister's not sticking needles into her arm. And once she's had time to process the grief and—

Ben hoists himself onto the counter, slides across it, and jumps down next to me, then pulls me close. For just a second, the roaring in my head stops. Hug meditation.

Goddamn you, Heisenberg. My person, in the chaos. But you lose people all the time, in chaos. It's the easiest way to lose someone. In crowded train stations, for instance. In amusement parks. In waves.

River's wrong. There's no freedom in the chaos. None. If you ask me, I don't think the Buddha knew how to work the problem.

Ben runs his fingers through my short strands of hair. "I want you here, always, but . . . it's your dream, Mae. You can't stay for your sister. It won't make her better. And you'll regret it, maybe lose your chance. You've worked so hard—"

"She's all I've got, Ben."

"No," he says, soft. "She's not."

"I know you mean that." I rest my palms on his chest. "But there are so many variables that can prove you wrong: women named Cathy or Rebecca, waves in Malaysia. Heroin and OxyContin and cancer and all the things, all the things that could take you. So many THINGS."

"Mae, it's too late."

"What?"

"It's too late to worry about the variables. You and me—this is already in motion." He rests the tips of his fingers against my cheeks. "Let me put it this way: We're on the rocket and it's already blasted off. Anything— everything—could go wrong. But we just have to sit back and—"

"Ride the ride?"

He smiles. "River strikes again."

I nod. "I saw her on the train today."

"Dharma insurgency?"

"I was ambushed." I sigh. "I don't know what to say, Ben. You and River want me to give up on my sister, and I can't. I won't. It's way too early to back off. I've got my whole life ahead of me—hopefully. But she might not." I rest my cheek against his for a moment, breathe in his coffee-and-wind scent, which is really the most wonderful thing, then step away.

"And, honestly, you saying these things—about how I'm not being fair to myself, not making healthy choices—it's not helping. I know you mean well. And please don't take this the wrong way, but I've only known you for two months. You don't know what's best for me. But I do."

He swallows, nods. "All very astute observations. I'm sorry for pushing. I just . . . It breaks my heart, not thinking of you in your uniform, or up in those fighter jets."

"It breaks mine, too."

Saying that out loud makes me feel more naked than that night he climbed through my window.

Ben pulls me close again, hugs me hard. I can feel all the things he wants to say but won't. I've never had someone be disappointed in me. I hate what it does to me on a cellular level.

My phone rings. Aunt Nora.

"Mae?" Her voice is a code red, high and shrill. "Hannah's not in her room. Is she with you?"

Sound waves, traveling. Grandma calling: *Honey? Something's happened.*

I stare at Ben, the phone falling from my hand. I see Hannah in my mind, asking me to name a star after her. Talking about the Little Prince.

Ben's picking up my phone, talking to me, his brown eyes—my mother's eyes—searching mine.

"Mae? What's wrong? Who was that?"

"I think my sister's going to hurt herself."

~~I want to die~~

34

Hannah

I decide to watch.

For once, just once, I want to see someone read my words.

I want to see what their face does.

If they care.

If they feel the same way, too.

I don't think I'm the only person who thinks these thoughts that I write down. These acorns, I think maybe they're inside all of us.

But maybe I *am* the only person.

I need to know.

If the words matter.

If any of it does.

If I do.

I'm at Copley Library, the beautiful one that Drew brought me to all those weeks ago, on what a part of me thinks of as our first date: the day we ditched school.

I ignore the tourists standing in front of the marble staircase flanked by lions, walk past the little cafe. I had tea there with Dad once. Earl Grey. Just the two of us, a father-daughter date. I hate missing him, missing this person who hurt us all.

I wonder if Mae and Drew and what's left of my family think of me that way. As the *person who hurt us all*.

I slide through the marble halls, past the dark wood doors, the sound of people's wet snow boots slapping on the stone echoing all around, then push through the double doors that lead to the library's inner courtyard.

Even though it's in the middle of Boston, this courtyard feels like a secret. It's instantly silent, like the whole world has been muzzled. It reminds me of an Italian villa, like some of the places my parents took us that summer we went to Rome. It reminds me a little of Greece, too—the columns. The last time we were there to visit Yia-yia's grave, I walked around the Acropolis thinking: *As soon as you die, it's as if you never existed at all.* All the artists are unknown. No names signed on statues, no plaques on buildings. Except for a few people—Plato, Socrates, all those old white guys—any ancient Greek who ever lived has been erased from Earth. Practically any *person* who's ever lived will be erased from Earth. That really bummed me out. But now I think maybe there's freedom in that. Nobody matters, in the end. Which means nothing matters.

A statue of a dancing woman holding a baby twirls in the fountain in the center of the courtyard, covered in verdigris. The water is turned off for winter, the base hidden by a pristine pile of snow. Like me, the statue is heedless of the cold, of the square patch of open December sky that dumps snow on her head. Unlike me, she is holding her baby. Happy. Playing. I watch her for a moment. Them.

I would have come, Drew said. Where would I be, who would I be, if it had been Drew and not Micah? Or if Micah had come? If I hadn't been on drugs and worried I had ruined the acorn inside me? You can't grow into a tree if your soil is soaked in opiates.

So many ifs.

It doesn't matter anymore.

I turn away from the statue and sit at one of the tiny wrought-iron cafe tables that are set up under the horseshoe-shaped portico that surrounds the space. I've chosen this table with care. Right under one of the bronze gothic lamps that hang from the ceiling, light pooling over it in the gathering dusk. The table sits in the path that connects the old and new wings of the library. People walk back and forth, back and forth. Not too many—it's getting late; the library will close soon. And it's cold and snowing. When it's warm, the courtyard is full, but now it belongs to me.

I take out my pen—a white paint pen I use for writing on metal, so it stands out. With it, I write my last acorn, carefully shaping each letter, pressing the pen down hard, but not too hard, or the paint will smear:

I want to die.

I stare at the words.

They are true.

I thought it might be hard to write them, but it's not.

I've been writing them in my head for so long now. It's a relief to put them out loud.

I wait a bit to make sure the paint dries. I pretend to check my phone because people look at you weird if you're just sitting doing nothing, but I have it on airplane mode. I've already told Mae what I needed to. I lean forward, look up to the sliver of sky that peeks into the courtyard. I wonder which one she'll choose. Which one will be named Hannah.

After a minute, I get up and cross to the other side of the courtyard and sit in the shadows.

For a while, people just hurry by. Trying to get out of the cold as quick as possible. Negative ten with windchill today. Can't blame them.

"Please," I whisper.

Just one.

Minutes go by—it's only me and the empty tables, the snow whipping past the stone arches, the statue and her baby.

Then.

A woman pushes through the door that leads out of the new library.

She stops by the table, looking at her phone. Curses. Sets her bag on the table. Stops. Stares at the table. At the white words on the wrought iron.

She stopped because of me.

Because of what I wrote.

She reads the words, and I can't breathe, watching her.

My reader runs a finger over my acorn, then looks around the courtyard. I shrink into my shadows, and she doesn't see me.

For just a second, she closes her eyes.

She gets it. I think.

She's been here, too. Maybe not now. But she's been here.

After a moment, the woman slips her phone into her pocket then walks away, into the light, the warmth, of the library.

I am suddenly so, so tired.

The chair scrapes against the stone as I get up. I cross the courtyard, walk through the snow, up to the bronze woman and her baby. I run my hand over the baby's head.

"Hello, you," I whisper.

The diamonds in my pocket slip past my lips. Enough of them to turn me into a star.

A little girl runs past the table, and I wait until she's gone, then take the cap off the pen and cross the words out. I wouldn't want a kid to read this. To feel this.

Turns out, it's not hard to erase yourself.

I start walking.

Out of the courtyard.

Out of the library.

Through the knife of the wind, through the snow, past the shops and their Christmas displays and the rushing people, and into the Boston Public Garden. Empty and quiet and dark.

And there she is, my bronze angel.

I lie at her feet. Make a snow angel.

when

the

wave

comes

i

let

it

take

me

35

Mae

ISS Location: Low-Earth Orbit
Earth Date: 5 December
Earth Time (EST): 18:00

HANNAH!"

Nate and I are running, tripping, sliding on black icy paths in the Boston Public Garden. A stone angel looms over my sister. She is going to take her. That angel is going to take my sister away.

Nate is faster than me—he reaches her first. I drop the phone in my hand, Drew's voice lost in the snow, and throw myself to the ground when I reach Nah.

"Is she breathing?" I'm screaming. "IS SHE BREATHING?"

He nods.

I fall on my knees beside him. "Tilt her head back."

I take the Naloxone out of my pocket, insert the nozzle into her nose. My hands are shaking.

"Just a sim," I tell myself, the words rushing out with my breath. "A death sim. That's all this is. Just a sim."

I push the plunger and pull the nozzle out of her nose.

"Two minutes," I say. I'm already pulling out a second dose, in case she doesn't wake up from this one.

Nate sits in the snow, pulls her halfway onto his lap. "Come on, cuz," he whispers into her ear.

I stare at my watch. One minute.

She's not waking up.

Oh god, she's not waking up.

"Nah," I whisper. Take off my coat, cover her, pat her body, shake her. "Brownies. Drew. Sunsets. Yoko. French fries. Soup. All the soup, Hannah. *Harry Potter* and Nate and Gram and Gramps and stars and blue nail polish and Mom's lotion and basil plants in the garden and tarot cards and—and—"

Nate picks up my litany. All the reasons she should stay alive. So many. Not enough.

Snow falls. In the distance, sirens. Closer. They are too late.

White foam begins to pool around her mouth.

Ten seconds.

"Tilt her head back," I say.

I push the nozzle in. Push the meds in.

Nothing.

Then.

She gasps. Her eyes fly open.

The wave recedes.

. • . •

Drew presses on the glass that separates us from where Nah lies in a hospital bed, his palms flat against the window, as though he could will himself into that room. He keeps saying her name, over and over. I don't think he realizes he's doing it.

"Thank you," I say.

I will be saying those words to him for the rest of my life.

Nah is alive.

She is alive because of him.

Drew knew where to find her. It is the only reason she is breathing right now.

My sister is lying in that bed, and I see her in the snow, her hair spread out over the clean cold of it.

Drew is silent.

"Drew." I rest my hand over his. "I'm so glad she has you."

He looks at me, eyes hollow. "I'm not. You were right about me. Everything you said, Mae. I..."

His eyes fill, and I think maybe there is nothing more lonely than seeing a boy cry. Nobody ever lets them. I like that this one can. That he does. That he cries for my sister.

"I could have stopped her. So many times. And I didn't. Not until it was too late. I was too scared to push her away, to lose her. But I almost did anyway. I can't believe how stupid, how selfish I've been. Your family's been through so much, and ... *fuck*. I'm so ... Sorry isn't enough. I'm so ..."

I look away. Look at Nah.

I rest my forehead against the glass. All that adrenaline from the past two hours has evaporated, and now I am filled with stones and sand and gallons of seawater. You can't reach the surface when you're this weighed down.

"Nobody can stop her, Drew. All the books say that. You and I made the same mistake. I didn't tell my aunt and uncle until my plan with Micah failed. I didn't want to lose her, either." When I sigh, the glass fogs up. "She told me to name a star after her. She was trying to tell me. And I didn't get it."

I didn't work the problem. I didn't think about the next thing that could kill me.

I would make a terrible astronaut.

"She meant it, Mae." A tear slips down his cheek. "The amount she took. She wanted it to work. She doesn't want to be here anymore."

With me. She doesn't want to be with me. I'm not enough to keep her here.

Aunt Nora and Uncle Tony trudge down the hall, looking ancient. I'm sure the hospital brings back too many memories of Annie, of the constant treatments. Of the medicine not working.

Uncle Tony's eyes fall on Drew, and he opens his mouth, closes it. Nods at him once. "Thank you."

"We appreciate what you did, Drew," Aunt Nora says. "So very much. But I think it's best for Hannah if you leave now."

He looks at Nah through the window, then nods. "Yeah. I understand."

Drew turns. Starts down the hall.

"I don't understand," I say.

He stops. Stares at me.

"Mae—" Aunt Nora starts, but I shake my head.

"If it weren't for Drew, we wouldn't be here right now. We'd be at the morgue, identifying her body."

I look at Drew. His hair is wild, dark and sticking up from running his hands through it, over and over, worrying about my sister. I grab Drew's hand, pull him back toward the window. "He stays."

I feel the shift then. The moment when I truly step over into adulthood, when everything I say doesn't get to be up for debate. They feel it, too.

This night, it has burned away whatever remained of my childhood. That's done now. I am the commander of my own life.

"Okay, then," Uncle Tony says.

They move Nah into the room she'll be in for the next day or so. She's not in here because of the overdose—the medicine worked, and she could go home right now, though she does have some hypothermia. This is a suicide watch.

I make sure Drew gets to see her before visiting hours end, since I can be here whenever I want, but he has to be out by eight p.m. I don't know what happens in that room, but when he comes out, he's a mess.

I surprise myself when I reach up and hug him. "I'll see you tomorrow."

"I . . . don't think you will," he says softly. "You're a good sister, Mae. She's lucky to have you."

He walks away, shoulders slumped forward, head down, and I don't have the heart to ask.

I walk into the room, and it is quiet except for the machines: beeps and whirs. Most of the lights are off except for a row above the bed, where Nah is sitting up. Her eyes are red, skin like tissue paper, an IV stuck in her hand. Mostly fluids, some medicine. I'm sure she's nauseous. The withdrawal is already starting.

For a minute, we just look at each other. Then I hold up my phone.

"I found a website. Where you can name a star after someone for seventy-five bucks." I try to smile. "Can we do it that way instead?"

My sister bursts into tears, and I surprise both of us by doing the same. When I get to the side of the bed, she scooches over and I lie next to her. I can't smell her rose smell, Mom's perfume she's been wearing since the wave. She smells like starch and a little bit sour, and a lot like winter. Deep cold.

"I'm so sad," she says. Her voice is scorched from all the vomiting that happened after she woke up.

"I know. I am, too."

We lie there, snow howling past the window, the quiet sounds of the hospital all around us. When the Russians are on a space walk, they just hang outside the ISS during each ninety-minute period of night, waiting for the next sunrise. It's too dark, too cold, to get any work done. Getting in and out of your suit is such a hassle that it's easier just to hang on to something and bob around in zero gravity. The Americans work through the night, but I think the cosmonauts have it right. Sometimes you just need to hang out and wait for the light. There's always another sunrise. You can't force things in the dark.

"You must think I'm a coward," Nah says after a while.

I shake my head. "I wish I could be like you."

She closes her eyes. "What a dumb thing to say."

"It's true." I squeeze her shoulder. "You're not afraid, Nah. Of anything. It seems like. I'm terrified. All the time."

"I'm so afraid of living that I'd rather die." She opens her eyes. "*You* literally want to fly to outer space on a *bomb*. You want to test fighter jets *in the air* to see if they work. What the hell are you talking about?"

I wave a hand. "I'm not afraid of heights. I'm afraid of . . . falling."

I'd started to believe that if I worked hard enough, I could control the outcome of any problem put before me. Eliminate all possibility of human error. Be two steps ahead of the universe itself. Maybe River's right. I'm clinging so tightly to everything in my life, thinking it will keep me from falling. From *failing*. But if you look at every space disaster in history, you know there is often nothing you can do. The *Apollo 1* team died in a training because when their cabin caught on fire, they couldn't get out—one of the hatches opened the wrong way. No one realized that was a problem until it happened. That was the engineers' fault, not theirs. They never went to the moon. They never went anywhere.

"You always land on your feet," Nah says. "Always."

I reach out and comb my fingers through her long, black hair. "Not anymore, I don't think. I'm beginning to realize I don't know very much."

She snorts. "Welcome to the club."

"But you're *okay* with not knowing. I wish I could be like that. Could like mystery. Ben's favorite words are *I don't know*. I HATE those words. I think the not-knowing is starting to drive me crazy."

She sighs. "There's something I don't know that's driving me crazy. Something I haven't told you."

Oh god.

Nah smiles a little. "Not a bad thing. I saw Mom. Twice."

"In a dream?"

Nah has very vivid dreams. We used to draw pictures of them when we were little.

"No. After the wave, I saw her doing yoga in her room—fish pose. And then I knew she was dead. She didn't say anything, but I knew. And then she came to my room after I found Dad's emails. And she was doing a headstand."

I open my mouth, but she shakes her head before I can say it. "I *wasn't* high. This was real."

Today I will suspend my disbelief. I will let there be a mystery. And I will not think about why Mom didn't visit *me*.

"It was just those two times?" I ask.

She nods. "But when I woke up here, I realized something. The headstand—her legs were in the same pose as the Hanged Man."

"That sounds scary."

"It's not. In tarot, the Hanged Man is dangling from a tree the way we used to on the jungle gym when we were kids—from his knees, not his neck. He's just hanging out. And he seems, like, enlightened. The card is all about looking at the world from a different perspective." She takes my hand. "Astronauts are the most badass Hanged Men, I think."

"Hanged *Women*," I correct. She smiles a little, but it doesn't reach her eyes. It never reaches her eyes anymore.

"I think Mom was telling me I need to look at the world in a new way. She couldn't give me a reading, so she became the reading." Her eyes slide to the window, the snow. "I just don't know how."

And I realize: I don't know, either.

"All the things I don't understand—about people and feelings and how to *be* human . . . You seem to know already, in your bones," I say. "I bet if you just meditated a few times upside down or closed your eyes and listened to the wind, you'd have your answers. For me to find anything out, I need to be in a space suit in zero gravity. And to get there, I have to acquire several advanced degrees and have the most dangerous jobs known to humankind. After beating out thousands of people to get those jobs, I have to live four hundred kilometers above Earth—just to figure out what you can in your bedroom." I squeeze her hand. "So who's really the genius here?"

"I'm not a genius," she says.

"But you are. In your way, Hannah, you're brilliant. I might know how to be an astronaut someday, but you know how to be a human today."

Nah's hand goes to the little diamond around her neck and she takes in a shuddering breath. I can see the missing in every Karalis splotch on her face.

"You told Drew you love him. I know you did."

She doesn't say anything.

"That's brave, Nah. Telling him. After Micah, and Mom and Dad. You could say it. Even though you knew you could lose each other in a second. You almost *did* lose each other. But you still said it."

"I broke up with him," she says. "Just now."

I run my hand over her hair. "Why?"

"My heart's tired."

"That's very unscientific," I say, after a little while in the silence. "But I get it. That's how it feels. These days."

She nods. We lie, watching the snow whip past the window. It was sixty-eight degrees in LA today. I checked.

"Did Ben tell you he loves you?"

I nod. And there must be something on my face that her genius self reads because those lines we both get when we're confused appear between her eyebrows. "You . . . you haven't said it back to him?"

It's a relief to confess.

"My heart's tired," I whisper.

I'll never forget the agony on Drew's face when he arrived at the hospital, certain she was dead. The way a part of my insides started to tear into pieces when I felt my sister's pulse, like it was in a distant galaxy and would disappear at any moment. No. *No.* I can't do that again, not with anyone else.

"But you love him. I know you do. It's so obvious." She stares at me, hard. "You *do.*"

"Every time I look at him, all I can think about is how it will feel when he dies."

Nah slips her hand into mine. She understands.

I look into her green eyes, and I see Dad. "I don't want to be a hungry ghost."

"What's that?"

"Buddhist thing. How we try to fill the empty places inside us with people or things, but it doesn't work."

"Things like pills," she says.

I nod. "And boys."

The snow falls. The hospital gets quieter. The nurse comes in to check her IV. Nate drops off flowers. Says good night. The room is dark and quiet.

The snow falls. My sister is alive. I will be her bronze angel tonight. Watching.

I think Nah is asleep, but then she says, "I'm such a loser."

"You're actually in very good company," I say. I pull the blanket up higher, tuck it around us. "Ben Franklin was an addict in later life. That shouldn't have surprised me, because he misbehaved quite a bit in his day. And the DEA raided Monticello back in the eighties because Jefferson had poppies planted there."

"The Founding Fathers got high?"

I nod. "It might account for them forgetting the rights of over half the population during the Continental Congress. Maybe all these years, we've just been cleaning up the messes of the most famous users in American history."

Nah snorts. "Leave it to you to give me a history lesson after an overdose."

"You can learn anywhere."

"Yeah," she says, her voice soft. "I guess you can."

I search her eyes, that bit of Dad in her forever. "Are you mad, Nah?"

"At what?"

"That we saved you?"

"Do you want the honest answer?" she asks, her voice faint as her pulse had been a few hours before.

"Yes."

Her eyes fill. "I don't know."

There are many stories from people who survived the wave, how they fought to hold on to the people they loved. Daughters and husbands and moms. They tried so hard not to let go. But it took them anyway. They didn't stand a chance against all that force and acceleration. Against nature. But Dad said the long shot is the best shot. So.

I wrap my whole self around my sister as she falls asleep. Hold on tight.

36

Mae

ISS Location: Low-Earth Orbit
Earth Date: 6 December
Earth Time (EST): 00:48

B en is waiting for me by the aquarium in the lobby.
For a second, I turn into Nah. Wish I could do a crazy thing: take his hand and run. Not look back, just grab his hand, outrun every wave that tries to follow.

He's sitting at a small table, next to a huge wall of glass that cages bright pink coral, a little stone castle, and darting sunshine-yellow fish. When he sees me, he bolts to his feet.

"Hey."

That smile. For a second, the clanging thoughts in me go silent. It is a Tibetan bell, ringing, deep and clear and ancient.

Good morning, Earth.

I try to smile. "Hi."

"How is she?"

"Alive."

He reaches out, wraps his arms around me. Coffee and wind.

"God, Mae, I seriously almost left with you. Just walked right out of Castaways."

He'd had to stay, since he was the only person working.

"Nate was with me. And I had Drew on the phone. He was amazing. He knew right where she would be."

My eyes fall on the aquarium. Will I ever see the bottom of the ocean and not think of Dad? I pull away from Ben, sit down at one of the tables.

My heart's tired.

He stays standing for a moment, watching me. I notice the empty paper coffee cups stacked on the table. His backpack on the floor. He has three finals next Monday alone.

"Have you been here this whole time?"

Hours. It's nearly one in the morning.

He nods. Slides into the seat opposite mine.

"I forgot to check my phone until just now," I say. "I'm sorry."

I can feel myself detaching from him. Like a space capsule from its rocket. *Hold on and let go at the same time.* Maybe this is a Zen koan— those riddles the masters like to come up with. If it's not, it should be.

"It's okay," Ben says. "Nate told me what was happening. I saw him with your aunt and uncle on their way out. You want me to call a car? I can take you home."

"I'm going to stay the night."

I don't want her to be alone. Don't trust her. That *I don't know* pulsing inside me. Ben's favorite words, my nightmare.

He leans forward. "How can I help?"

I look away from those eyes—my mother's eyes. Warm and brown.

"When Hannah was little—really little—she would do this thing. Play this game," I say. "She'd pretend to be dead. I'd walk into a room and she'd be lying on the floor, eyes closed, in some twisted position. Or floating facedown in my grandparents' pool at the Cape." I shake my head. "I believed her every time. And I would get so upset, you know? And shake her and scream and—not cry, I couldn't cry, but I'd *really* believe it. At some point she'd open her eyes or give this awful waking gasp or just get bored or whatever and she'd laugh and laugh at the look on my face." I wrap my arms around myself, the snow from the angel's garden deep in my bones now. "Even later, when I was pretty sure she was fooling me . . . I still believed her, a little. Because what if she wasn't pretending? I was so scared that, one time, it wouldn't be a game. That she really would be dead. And I could have saved her."

Ben reaches across the table, but I stand, move deeper into the empty lobby with its bright colors and happy murals, meant to cheer up sick kids and their families. No amount of sunflowers or smiley faces will fix this.

Ben stands behind me, close but not touching. "I want to help, Mae. What can I do? How can I make it a little better?"

"You can't."

He reaches out and turns me around. "Try me."

"Ben." I swallow. "I can't do this."

"Yes, you can. You're so strong, Mae. You're—"

"No. I mean—*this*. Us." I slide out of his grip. "My sister almost died tonight. Because I was with you. Because I missed you and I went anyway, even though I should have stayed with her, and it's my—" I shake my head. "I know what she did isn't my fault. But she tried to tell me. And I left her. I didn't see. I'm too—there's too much in my head right now. Everything's . . . It's like particle acceleration in here. I can't right now. I'm sorry, I'm so, so sorry. But I can't be with you."

Every mission requires focus. Anything that is not mission critical needs to be set aside. Ben is not mission critical. Hannah is.

He stares at me. "If you need more space, okay. Take it, as much as you want. But breaking up with me isn't going to make her better."

"But it will make *me* better!" I'm shaking now, and this day has to end, it has to. I see Drew, his palm pressed flat against that glass window, watching my sister come back to life. "I think about you . . . about losing you, and then I make mistakes with my sister because I'm worrying about the what-ifs. And every time I'm with you, I can't help thinking about it. There are so many ways to die, Ben."

"Yes. But there are so many ways to *live*. Together. For as long as we have."

"You don't get it! *We don't have time*. And River, her telling me to live in the present, just *accept* whatever is going to happen. Screw that. All that got her was a dead brother. But she's right about one thing: I need to let go. To not be so attached. So that's what I'm doing, Ben. I'm too . . . I'm clinging to you, *clinging*, and I—"

"Mae. That's not what she's saying, not what that *means*. She's talking about unhealthy clinging, like with Hannah. Fixing her is becoming your own addiction. And you know how addiction plays out. *That's* what she's talking about."

I pull my jacket around me tighter. "I'm sorry."

"Mae." His voice, gravel and crashing rocks, tunneling to Earth's core. "I'm not him."

"What?"

"Your dad. Is that what this is really about?" He steps closer. "I know what he did freaks you the hell out. But I'm not him. I love you."

I wish this were just about being afraid to be cheated on.

I see Drew, his face ravaged as he leaves Nah's room. And I see my sister in that room. In that hospital bed.

I don't know what to say. So I don't say anything at all.

Ben grips the back of one of the chairs. "You've never said it back."

"If you perform an experiment," I say, "and every time you do it, no matter the variables, you get the same results, what can you conclude?"

He blinks. "That your hypothesis is either correct or incorrect."

"Every person I say those words to dies, Ben. That's the result of my experiment." And then I tell him what I was telling myself in the elevator on the way down to the lobby. "You told me I wasn't being healthy— with the way I'm handling things with my sister. And you're right. Just not in the way you think." I swallow. "Before I met you, I trusted myself. I knew how to work problems and solve them. I could maintain focus. And knowing you has put me in this uncontrolled spin, and I have to recover, Ben. I have to."

Because I'm not afraid of heights. I'm afraid of falling.

I move toward the door. Out of his orbit.

"Before you met me," he says, "you had two parents. Your sister was sober. You hadn't been forced to move across the country and take care of that sister all by yourself." He crosses to me. "If you're spinning, Mae, and I agree that you are—it's not because of me. If you really want to end this, that's your choice. I'll accept it. But don't make me the fall guy."

I memorize his face in the moonlight that streams in through the window. The faint trace of freckles beneath his eyes, the thick brows, those long, dark lashes, the bleached tangerine hair. I know I will forget these details, just like I can't remember if Mom's teeth were straight or if Dad's lips were thin.

Everything, everyone, becomes a watercolor left out in the rain.

"You *are* like him. In the good ways," I say.

I could drink a case of you. Mom's Joni Mitchell song about Dad. Italian wedding.

It was grief soup—that last pot of soup Mom made. Dad's favorite, and he didn't get a bite.

I stand on my tiptoes and kiss Ben's cheek. Then I turn toward the elevators to take me back up to my sister.

I'm saving him. He doesn't know it yet, but I'm saving Ben's life.

And my own.

But then a cool, Pacific Ocean voice says, *Do you really think that?*

I don't know, Mom. I don't know.

Mad Matter Magazine Vol. 4, No. 12

Mad Matter: So, here's the million-dollar question: If we can't see dark matter, how do we even know it exists?

Dr. Winters: Well, mostly due to the gravitational effect dark matter has on distant galaxies. There has to be *something* creating these gravitational effects. For example, in Chile they discovered that the outermost stars in the Cosmic Seagull galaxy—which is 11.3 billion light-years away—race far too fast to be propelled by just the gravity of the galaxy's gas and stars. Some invisible matter is interacting with gravitational force, giving them a push and keeping these galaxies from flying apart. Dark matter, bullying stars around. This is just one example.

We see that there's this energy moving things—we see the *effect* of the energy—but not the energy itself. We don't know what it's made of, what it looks like. Or what it does beyond affect matter around it gravitationally. And yet most of the universe is made up of it. It's as ineffable as, well, the idea of God. Except we don't have actual proof of God. We do, however, have proof that dark matter exists. We just don't know enough about it yet.

Mad Matter: The way many physicists and cosmologists talk about dark matter verges on the religious. Substitute *God* for dark matter, and you could be a priest.

Dr. Winters: I've always felt scientists and the faithful have more in common than we've ever given ourselves a chance to see. At the end of the day, we're asking many of the same questions. I once traveled to India for an astrophysics conference and encountered scores of people on spiritual quests—yogis, meditators, all sorts. I felt like we were cotravelers on the same journey. We just had different guidebooks. They had the *Bhagavad Gita*, and I had *A Brief History of Time*. Not all scientists would agree with me on this one. [Laughs] I suppose I'm a misfit of sorts. All my favorite thinkers are.

Mad Matter: So how *do* you intend to get to the bottom of this mystery?

Dr. Winters: What we're doing is searching for interactions of particles on the subatomic level. Tiny, tiny little buggers. This will help us understand the fundamental structure of the universe. For anything we theorize in modern physics to make a damn bit of sense—how gravity behaves, for example—we can't move forward until we understand how these subatomic particles—these tiny buggers—interact with each other.

Mad Matter: And you do this by . . .

Dr. Winters: Smashing them. Forcing them to interact. Putting them together and saying, "Okay, now what? Now what are you gonna do when you can't get away from each other?" Only when they're together can we see what's possible.

c'est la goddamn vie.

Deli Counter
Zaftigs
Brookline, MA

37

Hannah

M y sponsor looks like she just walked out of a dark alley after kicking some serious ass. Leather jacket, long red hair, thick black eyeliner.

"I'm Jo." She holds out her hand. "And no, I'm not related to Jessica Chastain, but thanks for the compliment."

She *does* look a lot like her.

"Hannah. Not related to . . . any famous person."

Jo laughs, a bark more than a laugh. I like it. "Glad we've established that. Let's get the fuck out of here. I hate hospitals. What do you say?"

I smile, despite my earlier decision to hate whoever my sponsor is. "Yeah, okay."

Getting a sponsor was my choice. It's not as common for people my age to have one, but the group therapy thing just isn't cutting it. And when I want to use or when I just need to talk this shit out, I need someone I can call who understands what I'm going through. Mae tries. Nate tries. But they don't get it. I need someone who gets it. Not a therapist or a doctor, someone I pay to listen to me bitch who looks at the clock when we have five minutes left. I need to see someone in front of me who is surviving this. I need proof that I can, too—actual evidence. I'm starting to sound like Mae.

I have been at McLean Hospital for the past ten days. It went like this: an extra day in the hospital on suicide watch (even though they didn't say that's what it was), three days of detox *again*, then straight to McLean for ten days. This is where girls who like pills and tried to kill themselves go. The brochure said McLean is for people with acute psychiatric problems. Is trying to kill yourself an acute psychiatric problem, or just a rational response to the chaos of the universe? I channeled Mae when I asked the psychiatrist that. She smiled and wrote a prescription for Zoloft. I now take many pills each day so that I don't take pills. Zoloft for Sad. Suboxone to get off opiates. Sleeping pills I don't remember the name for. Something else for anxiety. Drew really should consider becoming a pharmaceutical suit. He'd make buckets of cash, way more than dealing. But I don't want to think about Drew because I crave him almost as much as the pills.

"You hungry?" Jo asks as we step into the elevator.

I shrug.

"Yeah, I get it. Depression's a bitch," she says. "The key is to find a few things worth living for. I found one, and it's near your place. You a Zaftigs fan?"

The Jewish deli near Aunt Nora and Uncle Tony's was one of Dad's obsessions.

"Good bagel chips," I say.

"Worth living for," she says. "Let's do it."

We go to the parking lot and she gestures to a red VW Golf that's seen better days. There's one of those COEXIST bumper stickers on it, with all the different religious symbols of the world forming the letters, and an illustrated sticker of the Golden Girls with the words STAY GOLDEN underneath.

"Life goals," she says when she sees me notice the girls.

I can't imagine being old. Or happy. They're always smiling, those Golden Girls. About what?

We get in the car, and she starts it up. The Seu Jorge rendition of

"Starman" floats out of the speakers—Bowie in Portuguese. I think my dead father is stalking me.

We are still not on speaking terms, I say to him.

Jo's car smells like cigarettes, but she doesn't light up.

"So, Hannah, your life totally sucks right now. I've got news for you: Your life is always going to suck a little." She backs out of the parking spot and whips out of the garage. "So if anyone feeds you some bullshit story about sobriety in which the sun is always shining, don't listen to them, because they don't know what they're talking about."

"My parents died in that tsunami," I say. "And I had an abortion. And my boyfriend cheated on me. And I had to move here from LA, and I fucking hate Boston, no offense. And I don't think I'm going to graduate. And I just broke up with a boy I think I really love. Oh, and I tried to kill myself. This all happened in the past nine months. I've accepted my life is always going to suck."

"A *little*," she says. "It doesn't have to suck a *lot*. When it's a lot, that's when we've got trouble." She stops at a red, glances at me. "But: *Damn*, girl."

My mouth twitches. "It's been a bad year."

When we get to Zaftigs, we slide into one of the leather booths, next to a zany painting of a corpulent woman. I love the art here. It's colorful and weird, like getting to walk around in the brain of a Venice boardwalk artist as they dream. Since it's the holidays, there are Hanukkah decorations and generic American holiday fare: pretty ornaments dangling from the ceiling, bits of holly.

I run my hand over a snazzy dreidel propped up against the salt-shaker. "They tried to bring holiday cheer to rehab, but it was sad. Like, mini Christmas trees next to the Suboxone dispensary doesn't help."

Jo snorts. "Aw, man. At least you got out before the big day." Four more days until Christmas. "I once spent New Year's in rehab. Fucking sucked. They gave us Martinelli's, and one of the alcoholics cried."

"Lame."

"How'd it feel, being in there? Being sober?"

I spin the dreidel, thinking. "I knew my mom wanted me there. That she wants me to see things from a different perspective. I tried to do that for her."

"And what did you see?"

"That I almost erased one of the last traces of her on Earth."

"So you want to get sober for her?"

I can see where this is going.

"I know I have to get sober for *me*. But she's my talisman, you know?" I run a finger over her evil eye, which might have saved my life. I mean, Mae and Drew and Nate saved my life, but still. I like to think Mom had a part in it.

"Okay. We can work with that."

Once we've got coffee and bagel chips and bowls of matzo ball soup, Jo takes a couple bites, then leans forward. "Ask me anything."

"What is this, exactly? Me and you."

Jo was matched with me through NA, some Narcotics Anonymous version of Tinder, where they put the newly sober with the not-so-newly sober in the hopes that the newly sober don't fuck up again. The hospital figured it all out for me, gave me some options. I liked Jo's hair and the fact she said *fuck* in the email she wrote me, so I chose her.

"Well, as your sponsor, I'm basically just here for you, man. Any time you think you might use, you call me," she says. "Or text, whatever. Modern world! Any time you need someone to talk to, or have questions, or need help working the Steps—I'm your girl."

The Steps. Right.

Whenever I detox, they're all about the whole Twelve-Step Program thing. *Work the Steps*, they say.

Step one, I've got: I admitted I was powerless against the pills—it's why I did what I did at the angel statue. Obviously that's not how you're supposed to work the Steps.

"What step would you say you're on?" she asks me. She slurps her soup, then gives a satisfied smack of her lips.

"Two," I say.

"'We believe that a power greater than ourselves can restore us to sanity,'" Jo says, quoting the pamphlet. "You agree with that?"

My mouth is full of soup, so it gives me an excuse to think. The soup's good. Mom never tried making matzo ball.

"I believe in a power greater than myself," I say. "Whatever She is."

If Dad had a grave, he'd be rolling in it. I don't know what that power is, but it's real. It's whatever allowed Pappoús to visit Yia-yia after he was already dead, their song—an old Greek love ballad—playing from an unplugged radio while they danced. I was there when it happened one night. I heard the music, even if I couldn't see him. Heard my grandmother laugh like a teenage girl when he said something funny.

"But the whole thing about the power restoring your sanity?" I dip a bagel chip in my soup. "I don't know about that."

"This is how you win step two: You eliminate *anything* and anyone in your life that fucks with your serenity. You feel me?"

I frown. "Yeah, I tried that. *I* fuck with my serenity. But eliminating myself is, I guess, not an option."

"Not an option," she agrees. "You have any friends who used who've died?"

I shake my head.

"You live in this world long enough, you will. I've lost a lot of friends. Sometimes they die on purpose, sometimes not. Either way, we use because we're not dealing with our shit. And at the bottom of our pile of shit, the *foundation* of our pile of shit, is the shit lie we tell ourselves: that *we* are shit. Sound familiar?"

I nod.

"You and me, we're gonna figure out how to make you not feel like a pile of shit. Because I bet that's when you throw back those pills. It's certainly why I did." She pulls up the sleeves of her shirt. She's covered in old-school-looking sailor tats—anchors and ships and mermaids—but if you look closely . . .

"Track marks," Jo says. "That's what the pills will lead to. They almost always do. Heroin's cheaper, easier to get, and the high hits you quicker. Same drug as your pills."

I never thought about myself that way—as the kind of girl who would stick a needle in her arm. But if someone had come into my room during detox with a syringe, I wouldn't have said no. They made me detox again, after the angel, and it was just as bad as the other two times. Third time is not a fucking charm.

I'm so tired.

"I don't think . . ." I swallow. "I don't think I can do this."

Jo pulls down her sleeves. "How many days sober are you?"

"Ten."

She holds up her hand. Black nail polish. Chipped. (I like her.)

"Count your fingers, Blue."

"What?"

"You like Janis Joplin?"

I shrug.

Jo pulls out her phone. Scrolls through it. Then she hands me her earbuds.

"Put these on. Close your eyes."

"Here?"

The look she gives me reminds me of Mom's Kali statue.

"Girl, you rode the dragon in the middle of the Boston Public Garden. Are you really getting bashful on me now?"

I put the earbuds in. Close my eyes.

Soft electric guitar. Then, Janis's whiskey-smoke voice, singing to a sad girl she calls Blue who's at the end of her rope.

Sit there, count your fingers. What else, what else is there to do?

The words, the song, it's a lullaby. Like Mom came from wherever she is and somehow she's sitting in this booth in Zaftigs and she's holding me in her arms and she's saying: *I see you.*

When the song ends, I open my eyes. Jo is a blur, a teary mess of wavy auburn hair and leather jacket and thick eyeliner. She reaches across the table and takes out the earbuds. Hands me a napkin.

"Every time you want to use, Hannah, you count your fingers—give thanks for every single day you've stayed clean. All right?"

I nod. It means: Do anything but use. Literally count my fingers if I have to.

"Day ten. You're a fucking badass."

I smile. "I don't feel like such a badass."

Jo slathers a bagel chip in cream cheese. "Remember: It's progress, not perfection. You fuck up, you try better next time. Like you are now. On my last day ten—girl, I had a lot of day tens—but my last one was six years ago. I'm twenty-five now. Ancient, right? So I was nineteen on that day. And my sponsor was this old lady named Lulu and she smoked like a chimney and she was a heroin addict from the East Village. She died last year. Sober, just old. Anyway, she gave me this song. And now I give it to you."

"Do you still need it?"

She wipes bagel chip off her jacket. "Not like I used to. That's why I'm your sponsor. But I'll always be in recovery. So will you—even if you're sober for the rest of your life. And I hope you will be. But being 'in' recovery never goes away. It's not a label, being an addict: It's just reality. You've got an incurable disease that's in remission. Understand?"

I nod slowly. "I think so."

"You will *always* have to stay on your ass," she says. "People talk about *mindfulness*. Shit, you don't need to talk to monks about that—talk to addicts. We are *experts* on mindfulness." She takes a swig of coffee. "We work the Steps. Every day. We count our fingers. If we don't, we're making snow angels in the Boston Public Garden."

In other words: Staying clean means we do right by the miracle.

"Someone in rehab said there's new studies being done—that you don't have to be stone-cold sober to keep from going overboard," I say. "There's, like, medicine that makes you not want to drink, so you *can* drink, you just don't want to. Stuff like that. It's, like, European or something."

Jo nods. "It's true that there's actually not a lot of great data for the Steps—kind of a problem when everyone's anonymous, right? And I won't deny there could be all kinds of ways to stay clean that aren't being explored. But the Steps worked for me. I've seen people do stuff like drink because pills are their problem. But the drinking usually leads back to the pills. We have this saying—fuck, we have a *lot* of sayings: *One is too many and a thousand is never enough.* That was true for me." She sighs. "We're all on our own journey, but my recommendation is to start with the Steps. Get clean. Get right with yourself and the people you love. Be okay being you without additives, know what I'm saying? Organic, free-range Hannah Winters."

I smile. "Sounds delicious."

"It is, man. Tastes better than the inside of a coffin, anyway."

I stir my soup. "So anything I say to you is . . . confidential?"

Jo nods. "But I'll keep it real with you: If you tell me you're going to try to off yourself again, I'm gonna bring in whoever I need to, to keep you breathing." She leans her arms on the table. "Your file said someone told your sister where to find you—I'm guessing she and I aren't the only ones who want to keep you alive."

"My . . ." I can't stop seeing the look on his face when I said that whatever we had, it was done now. "Drew."

"Your Drew?"

"He was kind of my boyfriend."

"Was? Ah. The person you think you really love. But broke up with."

I shrug.

"Does he use?" She must see my hesitation, because she twirls her finger around our booth. "Cone of silence, okay? I'm just trying to get the lay of the land here. I'm not a narc."

I take a sip of coffee. "He sold to me. At first. But then he was the one who . . . He tried to get me to quit. He doesn't deal anymore. He doesn't use. We only took pills together once, and I've never seen him high outside of that one time."

She blows out a long breath. "I think you know what I'm going to say."

"You don't know him. He's . . . doing right by the miracle."

I tell her everything. The whole story. Of me. Starting with Just Hannah. Ending with Mae spending two nights in the hospital before they transferred me to McLean. I tell her about Micah and Drew and the clinic. All of it.

"So you didn't break up with him because you don't want to be with him, or because he was part of your drug life," Jo says. "You broke up with him because you feel like you're not good enough for him."

"I think I'm holding him back from getting on with his life after dealing. You know? Drew's kind of weirdly straight-edge when it comes to pills and stuff, but I think . . . he's addicted to me. A little. He wants to save me."

Jo crosses her arms. "I think he wants to save himself."

"Maybe." I push the bowl of soup away. "Honestly, I mostly broke up with him for selfish reasons. I just can't . . . I can't disappoint one more person. And I think if he—*when* he realizes that I'm not going to suddenly be not fucked-up, then he'll stop seeing me. Like I'd be invisible to him. That would—that would be so . . . It would shatter me, I think. And I'm scared of what I would do if I felt that way again."

The waitress comes by to refill our coffee, and Jo's quiet until we're alone again.

"Codependence is a bitch," she finally says. "I agree, he's got shit to work on. And I think you two need to work on your shit separately. And maybe someday the stars will align. But your problem right now, Blue, isn't whether or not to be with him. It's that the only time you seem to feel okay with yourself is when you talk about how he sees you and how good it feels to have someone see who you are and still want you. That's addiction talking. It's the same as the pills. Get your hit of Drew, feel okay. No Drew? Not okay." She leans forward. "You know you're really working the Steps when you understand that no one can be your inner lighthouse. No person can get you safely to shore." She points to her chest. "What you need—that light—it's in here. It always has been."

I can't help it: I roll my eyes.

"Yeah, yeah," she says, laughing softly. "Self-love shit. I know. But it's true. Other people, they come, they go. But watch me blow your mind right now: The only person you can *guarantee* will be there with you every step of the way until you die . . . is you." She rests her hand on mine. "So doesn't it make sense to be good to yourself?"

I stare at her, and she grins. "Dude." Jo spreads her arms. I notice a big lighthouse on her left forearm. "I think I just channeled my great-great-grandfather. He was a transcendentalist out in Concord, hung out with Thoreau and Emerson. That was deep, right?"

I laugh. "Yeah. Yeah, it was."

"Finish your soup while I tell you a story," she says, pushing the bowl back toward me. "My favorite ever."

The matzo is tender, soft. The broth reminds me of all the chicken soups Mom ever made me when I was sick. I can still feel her with me. With her Little Girl Blue.

"Okay, so I went to this weird but cool storytelling event in Brooklyn, and they were talking about these two old ladies. I guess their story was in the *Times* or something. They were best friends for a million years. Like, they were nurses or something in World War Two and, you know, gallivanted and shit. Lots of hot people in uniform—I don't blame them. They weren't even ladies, they were *broads*, you know? And they had the best names: Brownie and Mimi. I can't remember who was who, so we're just gonna say it was Mimi who did the interview with the *Times*. And she talked about how they maintained this friendship for decades. And then their husbands both died and these broads, who lived on opposite sides of the country and were, like, too old to travel or whatever, these gals would get on the horn and jabber every day. Talk about their health problems and the old days and curse and stuff. Super cool. Golden Girls. And then Mimi said one day she called, and Brownie didn't answer."

"She died?"

Jo nods. "Yeah. And they had video of Mimi, talking about that day—

that moment when Brownie didn't answer. And for a minute, you know, she looked a little lost. Her best friend dead, her husband. And you felt how fucking *lonely* and maybe terrifying it must be to be that old and have everyone dropping around you like flies and your whole life basically a memory, right? And everyone in the audience is about to start sobbing because, you know, it's *MimiandBrownie*, the fabulous duo, and Brownie's gone. But Mimi, she throws up her hands, legit cackles, and says—Hannah, she says: '*C'est la goddamn vie.*'"

Jo finishes her coffee, sets it down. "*That's life.* I'm here to tell you, my friend, *that* is how you find your serenity and don't let anything fuck with it. Whatever happens, count your fingers, and no matter how bad it gets—"

"*C'est la goddamn vie,*" I say.

"Hell yeah. One life. Use it or lose it, know what I'm saying?"

And for the first time since I lay down beneath the angel, I think: *Maybe I can do this.*

Mae

ISS Location: Low-Earth Orbit
Earth Date: 25 December
Earth Time (EST): 8:06

Christmas morning.

I wake up, rip it off like a Band-Aid.

The first one without them.

Gram and Papa's backyard in Cape Cod is a sea of white, the rose garden hidden under a fresh layer of snow. Little red blooms peek out here and there—hearty roses that refuse to give in to winter.

Some flowers find a way to survive no matter what.

Pines surround the property, towering over the yard, watchful, with a bit of forest between us and the neighbors.

I slide open the back door and step outside, careful to be extra quiet, since Nate is sprawled on the couch, sleeping. He's wearing the flannel pajamas with space kittens on them I got him last Christmas.

I can't see the ocean from here, but I can smell salt. That's about as close as I want to be to large bodies of water these days. Cold, damp air wraps around me, but I've bundled up. How many Christmas mornings did I spend out here with Mom, drinking her peppermint hot cocoa? No one else wanted to be in the cold, but I always did. With her.

The hole I told River about, the feeling like I'm in a spaceship with a hole in it—it's gotten bigger. Even though Nah is sober and might be okay, the hole keeps widening. I can feel it in my chest.

The more I think about what Dad did to Mom, to us, the more it feels like general relativity has been disproven. Nothing is certain. You can't count on anything. Not even physics.

I don't think the universe will ever make sense.

I close my eyes and imagine palm trees and the sound of the waves, the cafe up the street playing way too much Bob Marley and Sublime. The smell of Mom's garden—basil and oregano and the lemon tree, heavy with lemons for avgolemono.

When I open my eyes, I see a flicker of movement to my left and my heart stops beating. My sister is lying in a pool of sunlight, eyes squeezed tight, her ear pressed against the flagstones.

"Nah!"

Her eyes pop open, but she doesn't move.

No. Not today. Not any more days. NO.

I run, tripping over a stack of firewood as I rush past the covered patio furniture. "What is it? What's wrong?"

Those lines form between her eyebrows. "Nothing. I'm listening to the sound of the fire in the center of the globe."

Her pupils look normal. Color is good. No pills. Maybe she's drunk.

"I'm not using," she says, rising onto her elbows. "I'm being the Hanged Man. Seeing the world from a different perspective. Yoko says, *Listen to the sound of the fire burning in the center of the globe.* So I'm listening."

Humans are very surprising. Unpredictable. We are all quantum beings.

I really don't know anything.

Even though it's impossible to hear the molten core in the center of Earth—at least from a patio in Cape Cod—I find myself saying, "Can I listen, too?"

A smile I would classify as uncertain plays over her lips. "Really?"

I nod.

"Okay."

I lie down next to her, on my stomach. Even though it's cold outside, the sun has warmed the stones, and my many layers keep me warm. I rest my cheek against the stone and look at her.

"Now close your eyes," she whispers.

We listen.

We wait.

The sun lies over us like a blanket. Her breath is slow and even. The hole inside me gets a little smaller.

We are eight years old again, waiting for Santa. Listening for sleigh bells. Believing in magic. Together.

I press my ear against the stone. I hear Ben say, *We're living on a mystery.*

I crack open an eye just for a second. Nah's are squeezed shut, her brow furrowed in concentration. She is listening hard. I close mine again, try to catch the sound of Earth's center. I don't hear whatever sound its heat is making, but maybe that's not the point. Maybe it's the listening that counts.

"I can't hear anything," Nah says.

"That's probably because Earth's core is thousands of miles below us."

I don't know how far. I wish I could ask Ben. I wonder if he has ever pressed his ear to the ground and tried to hear the fire burning in the center of the globe.

I wish we were still together and I could kiss that ear. But it's also very distracting—that ear. Him, all of him. I think I made the right choice. I hope I did.

"I can hear the blood pumping in my veins," Nah says. "It sounds like lava. Like in this video they showed in chem." She laughs a little. "The one day I showed up this semester."

Nah is transferring to a special school in the new year, a sober high school full of people like her, all trying to get better.

I listen to the blood pumping in my veins. "The center of Earth is mostly iron," I say. "And seventy percent of the iron in the human body is found in our red blood cells—our muscles, too."

"You're getting all Bill Nye the Science Guy on me," she warns.

I smile. Thorny rose.

"Which *means*," I continue, opening my eyes, "that the fire in the center of the globe probably sounds like us, like our blood. Liquid iron."

I raise my head, and she raises hers.

"Yoko," she breathes.

"I don't speak 'weird.'"

Nah pushes up to her elbows. "She's trying to get us to see that it's in us. The earth. The center. *Dude.* The fire in the center of the globe *is burning inside us.*"

Oh, Ben would love that.

But . . .

"Or is it just a metal in the first transition series, atomic number twenty-six, symbol Fe for *ferrum*—"

"I don't speak 'weird.'" She leans closer, presses her forehead against mine. "I'm pushing my weird thought into you so you can understand it."

I laugh, a giggle. I don't think that sound has come out of me since August twenty-eighth.

"Okay." I lean into her. "I'm pushing *my* weird thought into you so *you* can understand it."

"Mae, you know I can't do advanced calculus."

"Dad says two heads are better than one."

Nah smiles. "He was wrong about the most important things, but he was right about that."

A bit of sunlight hits the little diamond around her neck, and I think about Isaac Newton, bending white light through a prism, discovering that all the colors are inside the light, even if we can't see them all the time. There's so much that's sitting right in front of us that we can't see.

I touch the tip of my finger to the diamond. "Do you miss him?"

"So much," she says.

"Then why, Nah?"

"He can't be what fills me up, you know? I have to be okay with just me. I can't think about boys right now. I need a break."

I nod. "Same. My meditation teacher talked about that. The hungry ghosts I told you about. How we try to fill ourselves with other people, but it doesn't help."

"Jo did, too. Ha! The sisterhood strikes again. She's on this whole self-love kick. Her ancestor, like, chilled with Thoreau."

"Really?"

"Yeah. Crazy."

I like Jo. I got to meet her when she dropped Nah off after their first meeting, and she reminds me of River. She gives it to you straight.

"Sit up," Nah says. "I want to give you your Christmas present."

We sit up.

"Should I go get yours? It's under the tree."

I went out on a limb this year: Despite all better judgment, I went to Salem with Nate and bought Hannah many witchy supplies. It was embarrassing shelling out cold, hard cash for crystals, but I love my sister.

"I can wait. This can't." She reaches into her coat pocket and hands me a piece of folded notebook paper. Her nails, like mine, are all different colors. We gave each other breakup nails, just like Mom did for me when Riley left.

I raise an eyebrow. "Hannah. You shouldn't have."

She laughs. "Shut up. Open it."

I unfold the paper. On it, in her messy handwriting, it says:

3468 Beacon Street
10:00 AM
January 5

I look up at her. "Um?"

"I called Annapolis. Your interview is on the fifth. Don't wear the pine-apple thing."

I grip the paper. "Nah. I told you, I'm not—"

"When I look up at the sky, I need to know *someone* I love is up there, looking down at me." She puts her hands on my shoulders. "We'll always be together, Buzz. Even if we're a million miles apart—*to infinity and beyond.*"

Her eyes are clear and shining. There is color in her cheeks. The fire in the center of the globe bursting through her. Through me.

Is this really happening?

Is it okay for me to go?

"I don't want you to be alone," I say.

"You giving up your dream for me fucks with my serenity."

The possibility of letting myself go to Annapolis unfurls inside me, a spiral galaxy of light and color.

"The ISS is only two hundred twenty miles above Earth," I say. "So, actually, you know, depending on where I am in its orbit and where you are . . . it might be closer than if we lived in different states. I mean, tech-nically."

She grins. "I love you, weirdo."

I wrap my arms around my sister, crush her against me. "I love you, too. To infinity and beyond."

Part 3

Little Universes

39

Mae

ISS Location: Low-Earth Orbit
Earth Date: 16 April
Earth Time (EST): 13:24

I AM GOING TO ANNAPOLIS.
   I have carried my acceptance letter with me for the past day, and I've pulled it out so many times to reread it that the paper has become fuzzy almost.
   I am going to Annapolis.
   I am going to Annapolis, and I can't tell my dad.
   I am going to become a fighter pilot, and then a test pilot, and then an astronaut. I am going to watch the sun rise and set over Earth sixteen times a day.
   And I can't tell my dad.
   The picnic was Nah's idea. She said one of Jo's rules is that you have to celebrate everything and that getting into my dream school constitutes as something *and* everything.
   It's a warm April day, perfect for lying around on Boston Common and eating Aunt Nora's red velvet cupcakes.
   I begged Nah not to play matchmaker and invite Ben. I made her swear on Yoko Ono's life. And then I made Nate swear on SpaceX's budget.
   So Ben won't be there.

Which is good. I think my experiment is working. It hurts now, yes. A lot, to be honest. Four months without Ben has been very extremely difficult. But I know that once I leave, once I go to Annapolis, this feeling will fade. I am an adolescent. As my hormones calibrate, these intense sensations will subside. It doesn't make sense to be together when I'm just going to get on a plane in June. Long-distance relationships are highly inefficient, and, more important, I am in training to be a self-sufficient astronaut. I can't be worrying about a boy when I'm trying not to crash a twenty-four-MILLION-dollar fighter jet or going through my preflight checklist in Star City, Russia. In being the one to leave, in severing ties, I am making the best decision for this mission. This mission being my life.

Still, I wish there were a heartbreak sim.

That hole in my chest is so big now, I'm surprised everyone can't see straight through me. I thought Annapolis would patch it up, somehow, but I feel almost worse. Which makes no sense. I even took my temperature yesterday, because I thought maybe I had mono or an undiagnosed respiratory condition. But I don't.

I've almost reached Nah and Nate when a weird Hannah-and-Mom kind of thing happens: A girl walks by me wearing a Pac-Man T-shirt, where Pac-Man is eating up all the ghosts, and I think, *hungry ghost*, and then I have a Newtonian moment. EUREKA! I realize that this feeling I'm having, the hole, and Annapolis not filling it: *I'm* just as much of a hungry ghost as Nah. I thought I was doing things to avoid ghostism, but I have had this condition ALL ALONG.

Getting Annapolis was all that was keeping me from falling right into this hole in my chest. Now I've been accepted, and there is nothing to distract me. Nah's sober, graduation's a couple months away, I'm on the path to becoming an astronaut.

And yet this hole, this hole is eating me alive.

I stand there in the middle of Boston Common, stunned. This is what those old sages were talking about, and Tite Kubo, the author of *Bleach*. If I died right now, I'd be a Hollow, and Ichigo Kurosaki would have to battle me, and that Soul Reaper would totally kick my ass. Hungry ghosts aren't just Hannah or the ghouls in *Bleach*—addicts or people with issues. Anyone can be a hungry ghost. EVERYONE is a hungry ghost.

I wrap my arms around myself and try really hard to feel my feet on the ground because I suddenly feel floaty, but not in a good, zero-gravity way.

I am an empty hole that nothing can fill.

Not even NASA.

I've lost everything.

Even the stars.

A thought that I have had many times since my parents died swirls round and round in my head, like space debris: *Who am I?*

If I'm not the girl who is going to be an astronaut, or the girl who *is* but isn't over the moon about it, then WHO AM I?

"Oh god."

I don't know who I am. I DON'T KNOW WHO I AM.

Am I a daughter? But if my parents are dead, then does that un-daughter me? As my quantitative value of being an orphan has increased, the qualitative value has decreased. Before the wave, I was a *lucky* orphan. Now I'm just a particularly unique one.

Am I a sister, even though Nah and I don't share blood? And if she starts using again and dies, then would I still have a sister, even if that sister doesn't exist anymore?

Am I a girl who likes manga and brownies and boys that smell like coffee and wind?

Am I a member of the armed forces?

An honors student?

A girl? But what is gender really?

An atheist? But I feel my dead parents and that is not very atheistic.

An American? Yes, but only as long as there is something called America, which might not be that much longer, let's be honest, or might be as long as ancient Greece, which would be a pretty good run, BUT THAT IS NOT THE POINT.

"Dad." He can't hear me, but I whisper his name again anyway, and my cognitive defects are becoming more and more apparent, and I think maybe the wave has filled me with something dead, because I am maybe dead inside.

I miss them so much.

I sit down right where I am, in the center of Boston Common, and I'm not sure I can get back up any time soon.

I am floating and sitting at the same time. I am living a Zen koan, an unsolvable riddle, like what is the sound of one hand clapping, which I never understood because ONE HAND CAN'T CLAP. And now I am holding up my hand and hitting the air—DAMN THESE ZEN BASTARDS. The sound of one hand clapping is nothing. So does that mean everything is nothing? No thing is a thing.

"Help," I whisper.

"Mae? What's wrong?"

I look up. Nah's standing over me, a worried frown on her face.

"Nothing." I keep clapping my one hand. "Nothing. It's NOTHING."

"Bullshit."

I stand up, a little off-balance, because I can feel Earth rotating now, and it's too fast.

My sister is so happy about the letter in my pocket. Annapolis was her Christmas gift to me. I can't tell her I'm empty. That the hole in my spaceship is so big, I might not make it back to Earth. So I just stare at her.

"Mae. Tell me what's up. You're freaking my shit out right now."

And if you're on a spaceship that might not make it back to Earth, and maybe you're all alone in a Soyuz you don't know how to fly, like Dr. Stone in *Gravity*, then are you REALLY alone? Because she saw a dead person and they helped her get home. And I can't help but feel like Mom and Dad wouldn't let me die up there. I don't believe in Hannah's Something Else. But if there's no Something Else, then why did Yuri—

"Mae, you are freaking me out. What is *wrong*?" She presses a hand to my forehead. "You're all sweaty. Should we go home, or—"

"When Yuri Gagarin came back from space, he said something weird," I say.

"Which one is Yuri Gaga—whatever?" Nah asks.

"Yuri Gagarin. The first human to enter space. 1961. Cosmonaut."

"So Russia beat us to space?"

"We got the moon. Hannah, that's not the POINT." I press the heels of my hands into my eye sockets. Earth is going too fast.

"Whoa. Okay. What did he say?"

My hands drop. "He said: 'I looked and looked but I didn't see God.'"

"About when he was in space, you mean?" she says.

"Yes. Can you believe it?!"

"Okay . . . so he was an atheist in the Soviet Union. What's so surprising about that? He's just saying he has proof that God doesn't exist. Or so he thinks." She rolls her eyes. "Typical rocket scientist."

I grip her shoulders. "But he *looked*, Nah. One of the foremost scientific minds in the world. He knew better. Why did he look? YURI GAGARIN IS FUCKING WITH MY SERENITY."

Yuri didn't just look: He looked—*and looked*. Like he was hoping to find something. Perhaps it was just dry Russian humor. But I'm not convinced. It's that second *looked* that's getting me. Looked *and looked*. Once: You're a cheeky atheist. Twice: You really looked for God-with-a-capital-G up there. Just in case.

She cocks her head to the side. "How could he not? You get up there, you have to wonder, right? Some of the smartest people in the world— Mom included—believe there's *something* out there. It's not just the weirdos and little people who believe." She leans in. "Also: He said he didn't *see* God. But everyone knows you *feel* God."

That gives me pause.

"What does God feel like?"

She loops her arm though mine, and we start toward where Nate is trying to get a tan.

"I think it's different for everyone," Nah says. "For me, it's that feeling

I get when I look at a kick-ass sunset over the ocean or when I realized Drew had been secretly using Dad's miracle life lesson on me all along. When I read one of Yoko's poems."

"But that's not God," I say, stubborn. "That's neurology. Psychology. Chemicals in your brain responding to outside stimuli."

"Every culture has its own name for God, its own way of talking about God. Dad said he was an atheist, but get him talking about the universe and he sounded downright *religious*. He just used big science words instead of woo-woo words, whatever. We're all talking about the same thing, I think. Remember what he said? *I don't need to pray. I just need to look into a telescope.*" She grins, sneaky. "He *looked and looked.*"

"I'll allow that it *feels* like an intelligence is at work," I say. "But Dad always said that the universe is like a complex symphony playing itself, and our job is to listen."

He also said he wanted to leave our mother. Maybe I should stop quoting him.

The hole widens because I am a hungry ghost and I want my dad to come back from the dead and make me a happy atheist again.

"Every symphony has a composer," Nah says. "And every orchestra a conductor. Remember *The Phantom Tollbooth*?"

I always loved that part, where the conductor conducts the rising of the sun. As though everything that happens in the universe is the result of a grand orchestra's symphonic dexterity, led by an all-knowing conductor.

"It's just a story, Nah," I say.

"I hate that word," she says with surprising vehemence.

"What?"

"*Just.*"

Before I can ask why, say more, we reach the blanket, where Nate is sunning himself, wearing a pair of tiny shorts and a little tank that says NEVER TRUST AN ATOM—THEY MAKE UP EVERYTHING.

"Good one," I say, nodding to the shirt.

He grins. "I bought you one, too."

Nah plops onto the blanket and holds up her phone. "I made you an Annapolis playlist."

The hole gets smaller. "You made a playlist?"

This is Hannah before the pills, back from the dead.

She smiles. "It was time, don't you think?"

I nod. "What's this one called?"

"*Rocket Girl*. But now it's clear I have to make a sequel called *Yuri Gagarin Is Fucking with My Serenity*."

Nate lets out a yelp. "Oh my god. We need to unpack that statement right the fuck now."

Nah glances at me. "Maybe later."

She hits PLAY, and Elton John's "Rocket Man" comes out of the little speaker, and I am very impressed because all of us know the words. We sing them together, and I'm also very sad because these two people I love have no idea that right at this precise moment I'm a rocket man, rocket man burning out his fuse up here all alone. When the song finishes, Nah hits PAUSE.

"That's it?" I ask.

"There are twelve more songs, but Nate and I have other programming for this afternoon." She looks at my cousin. Nods.

Nate sits up and hands me a small gift bag. "I was told to pass this along to you."

Ben.

I instinctively put my hands behind my back, but Nah reaches out and plucks it from him.

"If you don't open it, I will," she says.

I look at the bag. She sneaks a hand in, and I snatch it away. They stare at me, expectant.

"That gelato looks really good," I say, giving a cart a few feet away a pointed look.

Nate bounds to his feet. "Come on, cuz," he says to Nah. "You and I are going on a space walk."

I wait until they're well away before I pull out the tissue paper. *Ben touched this*, I think.

When I see what's inside, I stop breathing.

Ben has gotten me a piece of the universe.

Two hundred twenty-six grams of outer space are sitting in my hand. A meteorite. It is a polished piece of gnarled rock with a little gold stand to hold it.

There is a note.

To: Commander Winters
From: Mission Specialist Tamura

The specimen in this little bag fell to Earth around 2,200 BC (the geophysicist in me must inform you that this date was determined via carbon dating of the charred wood fragments taken from beneath the meteorite itself). This bit of the cosmos was discovered in a field called Campo Del Cielo — since you are taking Russian and not Spanish, I'll translate for you, Comrade: Field of the Sky. This bit of outer space you're holding in your hand (in your palm, where you also hold a certain someone across the Charles River), hit the atmosphere of our little blue dot after traveling 150,000 miles per hour.

Someday you will do the same.

You will go to space, solve mysteries, do somersaults in zero gravity, see sixteen sunsets and sunrises a day. And then, when you're ready, you will get in a little capsule and — just like this meteorite — hurtle through a blaze of fire before landing on Earth. From so far away, you will come back. I know it.

And I'll be waiting to welcome you home.

For Science —
Ben

Maybe Nah was right. God is a feeling. *This* feeling. Of empty and whole at the same time. Of holding on while letting go. Because that's what Ben did—he let go of me, but he never stopped holding on. If there were a wave and we were in it, I bet that water couldn't ever break us apart, not really.

Because it didn't break *any* of us apart. I can let go of my parents—of their selves, and my idea of who they were and who we were as a family—but I can still hold on, too.

Up to sixty percent of the adult human body is water. Water can't break itself. So the wave couldn't break my family because we are made of the same stuff as the wave. WE ARE THE WAVE.

I close my eyes and lie down, the meteorite clutched to my chest, pressing against the hole. Holding the universe in the palm of my hand.

I listen.

To the fire burning in the center of the globe.

To the laughter and talking and living noises of the people all around. Babies and children and adults. Life. Car horns honking and the faint sound of a guitar. The bell of a passing ice-cream vendor.

The sounds swirl around me, in me, through me, waves, *the* wave. All these atoms—this blanket I'm lying on, this air I breathe, this meteorite, this heart, this skin, these people, and these trees—none of it solid, all of it shifting and changing and moving, just atoms held together by dancing electrons.

Solidity is an illusion. We know this. We know that nothing is actually solid in the way we think of it, it's just simply the varying levels of resistance of the electrons in the atoms of objects that come into contact with one another.

Nothing is solid.

Everything changes—everything.

But . . .

I grip the meteorite.

River's hands: ONLY LOVE.

Dad didn't stop loving me. He's dead, but he didn't stop loving me. And Nah almost dying, hurting herself, that didn't mean she didn't love me—it meant she didn't love *herself*. And even though people have left me, I am still surrounded by people who haven't: Gram, Papa, Nah, Nate, Aunt Nora, Uncle Tony.

And now Ben.

I have lost so many people, but there has never been a time in my life when no one loved me. Even my birth mother might have loved me. She gave me up because she knew she couldn't care for me. Maybe she loved me enough to let me go.

Everything changes, but love is the constant.

Love is the constant.

In this crazy experiment of life, with all its variables, all its unknowns, that is the only thing that doesn't change.

And if love is the constant, then love is the only safe bet.

Everyone leaves; everyone dies.

But love doesn't.

Like atoms. It changes, morphs, but it never dies.

There are some things you don't need an equation for.

The hole in me gets wider, deeper, but it's not a hole. It's an air-lock, burst wide open because I don't need to stay locked in this capsule any-more, looking through a tiny window, on the outside of the universe looking in.

I'm not empty.

I am filled with the universe. I come from that same atom the entire cosmos was born from. I'm not just filled with it, I am it. I am the universe.

I am zero gravity and stars being born and dying and black holes and *quintessence*—I am filled with dark matter, with an energy field that's expanding with the universe. So if the universe is expanding, then ALL OF US ARE EXPANDING WITH IT.

We're all part of this vast Etch-A-Sketch that is constantly reshap-ing itself. When we die, we get shaped into something else, we *return* to that creative energetic essence we came from. We're not just this one *thing*—we are ALL THE THINGS. This is quintessence, the Philosopher's Stone. This is what Dad was on the brink of. This is what he was listening for. The point of it all.

There is a little universe inside each of us. We are filled with planets and stars, light and gravity, dark matter and a million other mysteries we may never understand. And the greatest mystery of all is that *we are immortal*. We will be reshaped, again and again, by the universe itself. And we will never die.

My parents aren't dead.

The wave didn't take them.

They never left.

Their atoms are just dancing to a different tune.

They're not ghosts.

I'm not a ghost.

I am alive. Here and now and ALIVE.

And I'm not hungry. Not anymore. Not even a little.

I'm full.

are you a mother if you lose a daughter?
are you a daughter if you lose a mother?

Ice Cream Cone Wrapper

Boston Common

Boston

40

Hannah

My sister is walking through Boston Common in a daze, a rock clutched in her hand.

I glance at Nate. "Should we be worried?"

"I don't think so. When's the last time Mae suggested crossing the Charles?"

Ever since she and Ben broke up, Mae has refused to get on any train that goes over the Charles River, into the north of the city, where Castaways and MIT are. Now she says she's getting on the Red Line—the train that would take her closest to a certain rock nerd. Just as soon as she makes a pot of soup.

My fingers immediately go to the necklace I haven't taken off since Drew put it around my neck.

I miss him so much.

But I know Jo is right. If I'm going to figure out who I am outside of the pills, outside of Micah and Mom and Dad and all of it, then I need to be on my own. And the way I miss Drew, the way I *crave* him—that's my addiction looking for a hit. And he deserves to be more than that.

That's what I tell everyone, including Drew. It helps, us not being at the same school anymore. But only a little.

Every time I think about running to him, I think about how it would kill me, it would fucking *kill* me, if he ever looked at me the way Micah did and said, *I can't carry you.* And he would. Because I'm a burden. On everyone who cares about me. I can see the way I exhaust them, the worry and stress. My sister almost gave up *everything* for me. I ruin people's lives. It's the only thing I'm good at.

Jo would say that's the depression talking. "Stop drinking your haterade," she'd say.

But it's true.

I do what I'm supposed to. Call Jo when I'm two seconds away from giving my "jeweler," my dealer in Harvard Square, a call. I go to meetings. Sometimes I talk at them, but usually I just listen and drink too much coffee.

My day looks like this: school and group therapy—at school since we're all addicts—an extra meeting at NA on hard nights, coffee with Jo or my new sober friends or making soup with Aunt Nora or taking a walk with Mae. TV. Bed. Where I lie awake and count my fingers.

I hate my life.

But at least I have one. Use it or lose it, right?

C'est la goddamn vie.

"Must have been some gift," I say to my sister as we near Park Street station.

She turns to me, eyes bright. "It helped me figure some stuff out."

"Including Ben?"

Mae's phone buzzes before she can answer. She glances at it, frowning. Then her fingers fly across the screen and she stares at it, openmouthed. She blinks. Smiles.

"What?" I say.

Her expression turns uneasy. Guilty.

"Don't be mad," she says.

"And the day was going so well," Nate mutters.

I take off my sunglasses. Stare her down. "What did you do, Mae?"

Count your fingers. Count your fingers.

How bad can it be?

"When you were in detox over Thanksgiving, I emailed Rebecca Chen."

The sunshine and happy of the day falls away so suddenly it's like tumbling into a well.

"Why the *hell* would you do that?" I say.

"I wanted to know about the baby," she says softly. "Our brother or sister. It's not their fault."

"That kid's not our—"

I stop. Realize. They are. That baby my dad and Rebecca have—technically, they're related to me.

I shove my glasses back on. "Stay out of it, Mae. Just. Leave that whore alone."

My sister's tropical-sea eyes turn as dark as the Atlantic. "I'm sure there are people in my bio family who wanted to forget me just as easily."

"Mae. Jesus. I wasn't saying—"

She steps closer to me. "It's not her fault."

"What the hell do you mean? It totally *is* her fault."

Pot, kettle—I know. I fell in love with Drew while still with Micah. So maybe I understand Dad more than I want to. But I didn't break up a family.

I see the look on Micah's face, though, when he thought Mae had betrayed him in that orchard, brought him there just to hurt him. He'd been like her big brother. And how sorry he was, how sad. I believe him, a little, that the grief had made him do something so crazy. But I chose Drew. So maybe I broke up a family, too.

Mae holds up her phone. "No. It's not *her* fault."

And.

There.

Curled up in a little pile of blankets, is a baby girl. Rosy, puffy cheeks. A little pink bow around her tiny head. Bitty hands covered in mittens. Her eyes are open—bright green, just like Dad's. Just like mine. She has his nose. That same all-knowing expression.

"What . . . what's her name?" I hear myself whisper.

"Pearl," Mae says. "After the Three Sisters."

"Orion's Belt." Nate lays a hand on my arm. "A constellation. Also known as the Three Sisters. The Arabic name translates to 'string of pearls.'" He sighs. "That was . . . nice of her. Rebecca."

"Fuck Rebecca," Mae surprises me by saying. "If this little girl, if Pearl, stands a chance of doing right by the miracle, she's going to need us. Her sisters. Her mother obviously has no moral compass."

Nate whistles. "Remind me never to get on your bad side."

Mae crosses her arms. "I want to meet her. As soon as possible."

I stare at her. "What? You mean, get on a plane and . . . No. *No.* We'd have to see that woman."

Mae gives me a strange, fleeting smile, and I swear for a second it's Mom looking out at me through her eyes, or maybe even Yia-yia. Someone older and wiser. "Don't you want to hold her?"

I look at the picture again. My heart burns.

I nod.

I do. I want to hold my baby sister.

"Then we have a trip to plan," Mae says.

. • • .

I wonder if it's disloyal to Mom to want to hold Pearl.

I think about this as Mae and Nate plot about how and when we'll go to LA, what we should do about Rebecca. Aunt Nora won't like it. Because of Mom.

But I'm already wondering what she smells like. What she'll feel like in my arms. I don't know if that makes me a bad daughter, a good sister, or both.

We go home, and I help Mae make Italian wedding soup. Ben's favorite, she says. It has been so long since we made soup just the two of us, but here we are, side by side, chopping and sautéing and stirring.

This isn't crisis soup. This is happy soup. But I can't help thinking about the last time someone in our family made it. That was *my-husband-is-cheating-on-me* soup. Now it's *I-love-you* soup. At least, I think it is.

"You have to tell him," I say, ladling Dad's favorite food into the large glass mason jar Mae is taking on the train with her.

"I know." She looks into the pot, wistful. "I wish I'd worked the problem sooner. Four whole *months*."

I rest a hand on her arm. "All you have is now. Go get your boy, Mae."

"You really are the genius of the family. I have to work so hard to know the things that are so obvious to you." She brightens. "Have you considered theological studies? Or psychology? I think you'd be a great—"

"Okay, now you've lost it. Go! Grand romantic gesture, remember?"

She kisses me on the cheek, grabs her mason jar of soup, and skips—actually *skips*—out of the kitchen.

When Mae crosses the Charles with Nate, I go upstairs.

This house used to be the place we sometimes stopped by on our way to the Cape for Christmas or Thanksgiving or summer vacation. Now it's this other thing. Not my home. But also not just a place to crash for the night after a long flight across the country.

This idea of *home* has been getting to me a lot lately.

This past week, to be exact.

I'm so proud of my sister. So proud. And happy for her. It makes me smile to imagine her one step closer to space.

But I don't know where that leaves me.

For a minute there, I thought I was okay. That everything would be okay. Going to meetings, counting my fingers. Jo is cool. I missed Drew, but I was really okay. Now I'm beginning to feel what it will be like when she's gone and it's just me and Aunt Nora and Uncle Tony. Nate will be around, but only on weekends, and only until he graduates. And I can't bear it. I really can't.

I don't know what I'm going to do with my life. I have no plan. Nowhere to go. No dorm to move into. No apartment with Micah. No best friend that I'm getting a place with.

I have money. My parents made sure of that. I know I'm lucky in that regard. Drew has to make his own money to help chip in for rent, to buy tea tree soap and deodorant. But what good does the money do me when I have nothing to spend it on but pills?

Everyone keeps telling me they're proud of me. For what? Not getting high? Not killing myself?

Seeing what Mae's accomplished just underscores how much I have utterly failed at life. We had the same parents, the same schooling, the same chances. I even had a leg up, since she didn't even become a part of our family until she was three. But she never lets being adopted bring her down. Didn't let Mom and Dad's death ruin her life. And now she's going to Annapolis, and she's about to figure things out with Ben. And I am here in a big, empty house. Alone.

My head is starting to hurt, and I reach up to pull the rubber band out of my hair, but it gets tangled, and I can't get it out, I can't even get a fucking rubber band out of my hair, and suddenly it's too much, too fucking much.

I remember throwing up all over this hair in the snow after they woke me up under the angel, and Mae trying to hold it back, and I was so disgusting that night.

And I decide, right now: One of us has to go. Me or the hair.

A haircut is easier.

I go to the kitchen and grab the shears. For a while, they were hiding all the knives and such, but it's been four months since I overdosed, and everyone thinks I'm okay now.

I'm not.

But if you tell people that, they never stop watching you and asking you stupid questions and using that pity-grief voice, so I don't tell them. I mean, my aunt and uncle took off my bedroom door when I got back from rehab to make sure they could check on me all the time. And there are random drug tests each week, sometimes more than once, here and at school. I don't know what else the adults in my life could do to me, but I don't want to find out.

I sit in front of the mirror in my room, and I see my mother's face. This is the thing no one thinks about. When you look like your dead mother, you stop wanting to see yourself. It hurts to look at you. It hurts everyone to look at you.

Aunt Nora calls me Lila sometimes, by accident. She doesn't always realize it. One time she did, and her face got so sad. Because just looking at me reminded her of Mom.

I am tired of looking like my dead mother.

I am tired of seeing her when I brush my teeth, when I walk by clean windows.

I grab a chunk of my hair, but just as I'm about to cut, I remember Mom running her fingers through this hair. Braiding it. Helping me dye strips of it in funky Venice Beach colors: blue, pink, green. Putting those pink foam curlers in it when I was little. Bows, rubber bands, scarves. Twisting it idly around her finger when we had our long talks. I haven't cut it since before the wave. It goes all the way to the middle of my back.

The scissors fall from my hands. I scratch at my arms, the monster inside me that wants more diamonds clawing at me from the inside out.

"I hate you."

I don't know who I'm talking to: myself, the monster inside, or Mom, for leaving me.

I pick up the scissors and I start chopping. Chopping and chopping, waves and waves of my mother's black hair falling off my head and the tears pour out of me so fast and hard that I can't see what I'm doing but I still keep cutting until there is no more hair to grab, there is nothing left, just little stubs. As if the wave has come by and torn me up by the roots.

When I'm done, I feel lighter.

So light I could fly away.

41

Mae

ISS Location: Low-Earth Orbit
Earth Date: 16 April
Earth Time (EST): 22:23

Nate lets me into the dorm room he shares with Ben, grabs a duffel bag, and says he'll see me in the morning. He adds an exaggerated wink and hip shake because he can't resist.

Ben won't be back until late, it turns out. Lab, class, study group. Nate doesn't tell him I'm here. A little surprise, like a bit of outer space in a gift bag.

I put the soup on Ben's desk, then wander around his side of the room, which is much tidier than Nate's. I am not surprised by the rock collection on the windowsill, or the meditation cushion. There's a picture of us pinned to the corkboard above his desk, one Nate took when we were at Castaways. I stare at the girl in the picture, at her huge smile, at the way she looks at the boy. And I think, once again, that I am the dumbest smart person I know.

Ben has a copy of Dad's book—*Dark Diving*—on his shelf, and I pull it down. It's filled with underlining and highlighting, sticky notes. For me. He read this for me. I turn to the back, to Dad's picture. I remember when Mom took it, how she had him lean into the sunlight just so, how she'd brushed back a lock of his hair and he'd caught her hand and kissed it.

And now there's Pearl.

I turn to the dedication: *For my girls: May you always find light in the darkness.*

My eyes fall back to the picture of Ben and me. Maybe that's what we all are for each other. Little lamps, lighting the way home.

I hold the book against my chest and curl up on Ben's neatly made bed, with its plaid comforter and very fluffy pillows that smell like him. I open to a part Ben has highlighted and put exclamation signs beside:

My colleague, physicist Carlo Rovelli, says, we live in "a world of happenings, not of things," likening his observations to the happenings of the sixties, when people would gather on a whim to do something crazy and unexpected—for no particular reason other than that they could and they wanted to. Though quantum mechanics is a very specific set of rules that provides an excellent description of the behavior of subatomic particles, I like to think of particle theory and quantum mechanics as the hippies of physics. The work scientists are doing in these realms show us how dynamic and ever-shifting the universe is, how it's constantly engaged in such happenings. This is high-vibe science, where everything is in relationship, jumping from one interaction to the next, connecting, over and over. We could say that the very essence of the universe is connection: this particle with that particle, this atom with that atom. Particles move in swarms, like birds or bees, together, unpredictable, but together. In relationship. Continually. It is restless and searching and expanding and curious. The universe is so damn curious! The particles go here, there, then here again. Like my daughters, searching for shells on the beach.

My dad is saying that the universe doesn't want us to be alone. It won't *let* us be alone. Any of us.

I wish I could ask him *why*. Why did he fall out of love with Mom? Why did he do what he did? Maybe it's just particle theory. Love jumping from one person to the next. He loved Mom, then he loved Rebecca. Without malice or intent. Love exists in the quantum realm. Predictably unpredictable.

I read and the darkness gathers, the sun goes down. My eyes grow heavy.

I wake to the sound of a key in the lock, the soft *thud* of a heavy backpack hitting the floor. A sharp intake of breath.

The door shuts, and then there is the *click* of the desk lamp, the mattress sagging, a warm hand on my shoulder.

I open my eyes. Ben's wearing the thick, black-rimmed glasses he only puts on late at night, and his hair is a mess, and all I want to do is run my hands through it. He has the most awestruck expression on his face, looking at me. Like me being here is a scientific discovery.

"You're going to die," I blurt out.

He blinks. "Yes . . ."

I sit up. "I think . . . I think I'm okay with that."

River's right: Nothing—no one—is for keeps. Not Mom or Dad or Nah. Not Ben. Not even me.

"Someday you will leave me," I say. "Or I will leave you. In this current collection of atoms or sooner. And it will hurt. But it will hurt more to not have this—to have *you*—while I can. I want to be here. I want to be *now*."

Ben doesn't say anything. He just holds out his arms and everything in me sags in relief, and then I'm in his lap and he's kissing my head, his arms tight around me.

I let myself fall into him, for him. Every single one of us is in free fall all the time—me, Ben, Earth itself, the stars. We fall and fall, without end, together.

That's just physics. The falling. The always falling. Nothing ever lands, not really.

I look up at him, and I fall a little faster, and harder. I touch the tip of my nose against his. I'm okay with having nowhere to land, as long as I get to keep falling with him.

I take one last leap on my own:

"I love you."

Did you know that the sun isn't actually 149.6 million kilometers from Earth? It's smack-dab inside Benjamin Tamura.

"I know," he says, grinning. This boy is too smart for his own good.

"I have to explain some things I realized, but it might sound very weird because I was having an existential psychotic break in Boston Common earlier today. Which, by the way, was Yuri Gagarin's fault. I haven't had time to fully process it because I wanted to make soup for you."

He laughs. "I am in so much trouble."

I wrap my arms around his neck. "Me, too."

"You made me soup?"

"It's on your desk. Hannah helped. Italian wedding."

"My favorite."

"I know."

Ben rests his forehead against mine. "Tell me what Yuri Gagarin did this time."

"I thought it was personal," I say, straightening up. "That the universe somehow had it in for me. Taking away everyone I love. I was trying to outsmart it. I thought if I could stay two steps ahead, I would have more control over the outcomes. But trying to have control was just my version of being a hungry ghost. Hannah wanted pills, I wanted control, but it's the same thing—we've both been trying to outsmart the universe. But you can't! Mostly because the universe doesn't have a hit list. It's just doing its thing, and it's not personal—or, it is because I'm a part of it. Creation, destruction. Over and over. Me, you, my parents, Nah. My dad was a human, and now he's the ocean. BUT HE'S THE SAME THING HE WAS BEFORE. He was always the ocean, and the ocean was always him. JUST IN DIFFERENT FORMS. I can't fight that process. I can't be mad at the wave for being a wave, because I realized *I* am the wave. We share the same cosmic encoding." I stare at him, one final thing clicking into place. "I WAS NEVER AN ORPHAN BECAUSE WE ARE ALL COSMICALLY RELATED."

Ben blinks. "Yuri Gagarin told you all of that."

"He looked and looked. But I don't think he looked hard enough."

"What was he looking for?"

"God."

Ben watches me for a long moment.

"Um." He tucks my hair behind my ear. "Are you—and I will love you no matter what your answer is—but are you saying you believe in God now? Because it sounds like that's what—"

"Keep up, geophysicist! I'm saying I found MYSELF."

He just looks at me. Honestly, sometimes I question the level of instruction at MIT.

"Because I AM GOD. YOU ARE GOD. EVERYTHING IS GOD! Quintessence!"

Ben's face clears, and my wonderful atheist boy looks very relieved.

I think I feel just like Chuck Yeager did in 1947 when he became the fastest man alive by being the first pilot to break the sound barrier, flying faster than the speed of sound at level flight. In *The Right Stuff*, the flying aces are always talking about chasing a demon in the sky, like the sound barrier itself was a demon—and I think I just did the same. I beat that hungry ghost by a mile.

"Just so you know," he says, "that quote of Yuri's has been disputed."

"Really?"

He nods, very serious, his lips twitching. "Apparently, he was a believer."

I stare at him. "Now he's fucking with my serenity EVEN MORE."

Ben is trying hard not to laugh, I can tell. "Does that change your conclusions?"

"Of course not. Gagarin is irrelevant to the logic of my argument, which is sound."

"You're still God."

"Yes. And so are you. At the end of the day, the universe is clearly a proponent of equality."

"So, basically, you lay down on Boston Common and achieved enlightenment," Ben says.

"Basically."

He throws up his hands. "A couple visits to Dharma Bums and you're already a Zen Master."

I grin. "I progress through things very quickly."

"Like father, like daughter."

Ben reaches for his copy of *Dark Diving*. Flips through it to a dog-eared page. Reads my dad's words to me.

"When his dear friend Michele Besso died, Einstein imparted his theory on death to Besso's sister, in a letter of condolence. He writes, 'Michele has left this strange world a little before me. This means nothing. People like us, who believe in physics, know that the distinction made between past, present and future is nothing more than a persistent, stubborn illusion.'

In my search for quintessence—the meaning of existence through understanding what dark matter (and therefore the universe) is made up of—I find myself returning to this scrap of knowledge that Einstein imparted to a grieving woman and, perhaps, to his own grieving self. Is it possible that Einstein discovered true quintessence— the secret to eternal life that philosophers and alchemists have been searching for across the centuries? Perhaps the Elixir of Life isn't a tonic at all, but the simple knowledge that time is elastic and, as such, what we would consider a life's end—consciousness forever relegated to the past—is its beginning elsewhere."

"Houston, we have SCIENTIFIC PROOF OF ETERNAL LIFE!"

Ben laughs. "Maybe. But I think he's ultimately saying what we have to be okay with is not that we're going to die, but that we don't know what, exactly, or where or *when* we'll be when these physical manifestations of ourselves time out. So we have to live the hell out of the atoms we are right now and be okay with letting the form they take go when the time comes. But . . ." He smiles. "Maybe my atoms will always find your atoms."

I think of our kiss: *I am lost without you.* Quantum love.

"No object has a definite position except when colliding with something else," I whisper.

He nods. "You're my definite position in the universe."

"We're a funny pair," I say. "You love gravity, and I'm always trying to escape it."

"I'm so proud of you. I can't wait to be standing outside, looking up, and knowing you're somewhere above me looking down." His lips turn up. "But every astronaut needs to have her feet on the ground sometime."

Ben Tamura is my favorite gravitational pull.

I take his hand and kiss the palm.

"You hold me, too, you know," I whisper against it, the universe of me in the palm of his hand.

His eyes turn glassy.

"I'm so sorry, Ben. All these months. I—"

He stops me with a salty, sweet kiss. "Save your apologies for all the heart attacks you're going to give me when you're a fighter pilot, hm?"

I squeeze him a little tighter. "Thank you for the meteorite."

"I promise I won't get you rocks for every occasion. Despite being a geophysicist, I do have some self-control. But I thought you might like that one."

I burrow closer to him. "You know what's strange? If the wave hadn't happened . . . maybe I would never have met you."

He runs a hand over my head. "I don't think anything happens for a reason. The wave being the price we pay in exchange for this. I think a part of me would have found a way to collide with you, Mae, no matter what. Even if I had to take a quantum leap to make it happen. I'd have found you."

Because I'm his definite position in the universe. And he's mine.

I kiss him. I kiss him with all the kisses I haven't given him for over four months.

Then I pull back, stare at him. "You bastard."

I can't keep a straight face, so he just raises his eyebrows.

"When were you going to tell me that this room is a wormhole?" I try to sound extremely angry.

A minute out there—a whole night in *here*.

Ben grins, jumps off the bed, and bolts the door, then crawls back across the mattress toward me.

"You're the astronaut," he says. "Shouldn't you have seen that one coming?"

I rest a hand on the buttons of his shirt. "You're right. Maybe I should correct my course."

"I think we're finally on the optimal flight path," Ben says softly, laying me down. "Don't you?"

Only love.

So many ways to die. But so many ways to live. Maybe even forever. *Quintessence.* Always being. Never ending.

I nod. "Second star to the right and straight on till morning."

Benediction

maybe the empty places inside us
are just homes waiting to be filled

Table
Basement
Holy Cross Church

42

Hannah

If addiction is genetic, I don't know where I got it from.

Everyone in my family seems fine. Okay, on Dad's side, maybe Gram likes her after-dinner port a little too much, but she's a grown-ass seventy-five-year-old woman who's earned it. Mom's side might be the link: I'm pretty sure Pappoús was an alcoholic—no one says it that way, but he always had a shit-ton of ouzo on hand. Still, no one ever became an outright junkie. Went to rehab. Overdosed.

If Nate would just smoke a little too much weed or Uncle Tony hit the red wine harder. But no.

It's just me who's a loser. Jo would want me to reframe that, but that affirmation shit is just not working today.

Tomorrow, I'll have been sober for five months. Today doesn't count yet. I don't count a day until I wake up the next morning without using. Some people count it once they hit midnight, but we all know the hardest time is after midnight. In NA they give you sobriety swag in the form of chips that signify how long you've been clean. You can put them on a keychain or whatever. I have white, orange, green, and red. Next month, I'll get the biggie: a six-month blue one. It's like that time when I was collecting the Strawberry Shortcake Happy Meal toys, but not nearly as fun. I still want that blue chip, though.

Before I lay down under the angel to die, I was waking up every night at 4:03, which is the time my parents died—8:06—divided by two.

For the past three days I've been waking up at exactly that time. I'm trying not to read into it.

Especially since today is my birthday.

And also Mother's Day.

All things considered, that is some twisted shit, my birthday being on Mother's Day.

I read in one of the million pamphlets they gave me in rehab that suicide is the second-leading cause of death in the United States for my age group, and tenth overall.

It's why I decide to go to a meeting before the family celebration tonight. Before I have to pretend to be a happy birthday girl.

I'm in a church basement near BU. This particular meeting for Young People, as they call us, could be worse. Everyone is college-aged and pretty cool. Mae came with me once and called it the Tattoo Show. There's coffee and doughnuts from Dunkies. The speaker is this chick from New York who's a conceptual artist, and she talks about how her art helped her stay sober. And it just reminds me that I don't have anything like that, you know? Just my acorns. That's it.

Mae and I graduate next month. Somehow I've managed with my alternative school (not so alternative because it's still *school*) to get back on track. With lots of help from Mae, of course.

But then what?

It's a victory for me just to get out of bed and stay sober all day. What kind of life is that?

Aunt Nora keeps giving me these quizzes. All kinds of quizzes from magazines and online stuff, about finding your passion. One was called *What's Your Bliss?*

None of it's helping.

The only thing I *want* is a pill. And Drew. And my parents.

All things I can't have.

At least once a day, I think about calling Drew. But I know that I need to lady up, be on my own. I'm glad Mae realized Ben was good for her. She needed to be less independent. She's on this interconnectedness kick right now, and it's kind of funny. She really does sound like Mom. But I need to know who I am on my own, without pills or boys. I just thought after five months I'd have *some* idea.

We get in our groups and everyone talks, but I don't. My birthday gift to myself is not trying too much. For one day, I want to coast a little. I don't feel like telling my sad stories, but I listen to everyone else's. To the girl who fucked up last night and needed a fix so bad she stole the pain pills for her family's dog, who has cancer, so she's here, back at day one. To the boy who picked up a needle on Monday, then called his sponsor before he could stick it in his arm. To the insanely beautiful girl who looks like she could be in a J.Crew ad who tells us she just got out of rehab and she's not sure if she can do this, stay clean.

When we're done, I head toward the coffee. Pour myself a cup. J.Crew is right behind me.

"I like your hair," she says.

After I chopped it all off, Aunt Nora cried, then took me to her hair place so they could fix it. I like it. I feel stronger, in a way. More exposed, but also like there's less weighing me down. I think about how Mom wrote in that postcard how she chopped off all her hair, too. In Malaysia. So I guess we'd look even more the same, if she were here. Mae agrees that it would have been a good look on her.

"Thanks," I say.

She holds out her hand. "Jaipriya."

Her name brings back a memory, of Kirtan at Mom's studio, all of us chanting the names of Hindu gods in candlelight, the musician playing the harmonium—Jaipriya—leading us through the night.

I take her hand. "Hannah."

We drink our coffee. I want to tell her she *can* do this, but I don't want to overstep. At meetings, it can get weird real quick when people decide to start, like, life-coaching you. So we just drink coffee and talk about everyone's clothes and tats and wonder why all churches have this same weird, slightly musty smell, no matter the denomination.

"I hate Mother's Day," Jaipriya says, out of the blue.

"Me, too." I glance at her. "Why do you hate it?"

"I have a daughter. But my sister's raising her because . . . well. She's only two. But she calls her Mom."

"I'm sorry," I say, soft.

This. This is why I made the choice I made. Imagine me right now, with a year-old baby. I can't even get out of bed before ten. I think about killing myself every day. What if my baby had to call Mae *Mom* and Mae had to give up Annapolis to raise her?

Jesus fuck, man.

Jaipriya shrugs. "You'd think it'd be motivation enough to stay clean." She takes a sip of coffee, adds more sugar. "Why do you hate it? Mother's Day."

"My mom died last year."

"Oh, wow. I'd hate it, too, if I were you."

"It's also my birthday." I set down my coffee because my hand has started to shake.

She smiles. "'What if this darkness is not the darkness of the tomb, but the darkness of the womb?'"

The words sink into me. I like them.

"Did you make that up?" I ask.

She shakes her head. "Another poet—Valarie Kaur."

"Another? You're a poet?"

I didn't know a poet could wear a sweater set and khakis.

"Yeah."

My heart speeds up a little, like it does when I open *Acorn*.

"You have books out and stuff? Or poems in a magazine?"

Jaipriya shakes her head. "You don't need to be published to be a poet."

"Then how do you know you're a poet?"

She sets her coffee down. "I guess I knew for sure, started calling myself one, when I realized that writing was like breathing. There was no choice for me. I had to. My poems are the best part of me, the part the drugs don't get to lay their hands on." She cocks her head to the side. "Are *you* a poet?"

Even though we're in the basement of the church, I swear the sun bursts through the stained glass windows above and streams down, right into me, a rainbow of light. This is an outright *benediction*, and also you can't lie in church—it's really fucking bad luck.

"Yes."

"Half the romantic poets were opium or heroin addicts, so I guess the apple doesn't fall far from the tree. You're in good company, Hannah. Welcome to the club." She grabs her purse and slides it onto her shoulder. "And Happy Birthday."

I reach out, rest a hand on her arm. "Happy Mother's Day."

Her eyes widen, then she nods and hurries away, toward the exit. When she gets to the door, Jaipriya turns around.

"You want to hang out sometime?" she says. "Write or ... something?"

My chest fills with sparkling sea foam. "Yeah. Yes. I'd love to."

We exchange numbers, and hers is now included in the small handful in my phone—Mae, Jo, Drew, and the few remaining family members I have left. When she leaves, I finish my own coffee then get on the train, walk home, all in a daze.

I'm a poet.

I miss my mom.

I'm a poet.

This is my first birthday without them.

I'm a poet.

And even though the truth of this shines a little light into the darkness—tomb/womb—I'm still left with the fact that my future is as uncertain as ever.

What am I going to do after graduation?

You can't write poetry all day, I don't think. How am I going to stay sober when I don't even have homework or the goal of graduating to keep me busy, focus me even a little bit? And poetry doesn't pay the bills.

I need a job.

But who would hire an addict who's graduating by the skin of her teeth? What would I say in an interview when they ask about my interests, my plans? How could I prove that I am responsible in any way, for anything?

When I get to our walkway, there's a woman standing in front of the house, writing in a notebook. As I get closer, she looks up.

"Oh, hello," she says. "Do you live here?"

When did it start to feel normal, having my own room in this house?

"I guess I do." She gives me a weird look. "Yes?"

She reaches out a hand. "Lisa Cole—Realtor. You must be one of the nieces."

"Realtor?"

She nods. "For the sale. It's a beautiful house. It'll go like this." She snaps her fingers. "I hear you're going to Annapolis. That's wonderful!"

"That's my sister," I say.

They're selling the house. Why are they selling the house? Why haven't they told us?

"Oh, you're the other one, then. Where are you going to—"

The other one.

"Excuse me," I say, moving past her, up the walkway, toward the front door.

I turn the knob. Walk inside. Mae is sitting on the couch with Ben and Nate. They're watching the National Geographic channel, and she smiles up at me, but then she stops smiling because she sees my face.

"What's wrong?"

She's on her feet, coming toward me.

Aunt Nora walks out of the kitchen, wiping her hands on a towel. I can smell Uncle Tony's lasagna.

There are balloons. A cake on the table. Presents.

"I just met your Realtor," I say.

Aunt Nora goes still.

"Realtor?" Mae's face scrunches up.

I glance at Nate. He's looking at his shoes. Avoiding my gaze.

Secrets. Lies. This whole family of betrayers.

Mae turns to Aunt Nora.

"I had no idea she was here," Aunt Nora says. "Nothing's certain. We were just getting an estimate—"

"Why would you sell the house?" Mae asks.

Mae's voice is sharp enough to bring Uncle Tony out.

"Well . . ." Aunt Nora crosses her arms. Uncrosses them. Twists the towel in her hands. "The firm has offered me a promotion. An amazing opportunity." She swallows. "In New York, actually."

I just stare at my aunt. Her words gather speed, swell. Another wave.

"I haven't given them a definite answer," Aunt Nora says. "I thought we could have a family discussion and consider our options together."

"But you must want to do it," Mae says. "The Realtor's outside."

Uncle Tony shakes his head. "We just want to know what our options are."

"When were you planning on telling us this?" I say.

And I know. They were going to wait for Mae to leave, so she couldn't make the mistake of thinking about staying for me again.

"We wanted to wait until we had all the information we needed," Aunt Nora says. *Lies.* "There was no reason to say anything yet. And it's your birthday. Of course we won't go—*if* we go—until you're done with school. Not until August, at the earliest." Aunt Nora comes toward me and I back up, against the door. Too close. She's always too damn *close.* "And, Hannah, of course we want you to come with us. There are so many good schools there, or you could get a fun job. We could go to museums on the weekend—all sorts of things. A fresh start, honey. It'll be good for all of us, I think."

Cheer laced with guilt. Boy, do I know that sound.

Let's try to be happy even though your parents are dead, okay?

"Best pizza in the country," Uncle Tony adds.

Fuck pizza.

"But what about Jo? Hannah can't have a sponsor so far away, can she?" Mae asks.

How To Build A House

Imagine a lot of sticks

Stack them

Set them on fire

Watch them burn

It was one thing to live with my aunt and uncle when Nate was sleeping here most weekends, when Mae was down the hall. But there's no way they could want me to take up space in whatever tiny place they can afford to buy in Manhattan. Of course not. I'm just their junkie niece. They're empty nesters who probably want to go have a fabulous New York life, not worry that I'm going to overdose in their guest bedroom.

For a second, I think about my grandparents—but no. They're in a retirement community. You have to be over sixty-five to live there.

I don't have any friends to crash with. And, yeah, I have money and could technically get an apartment on my own, but I don't have a job or credit—who would rent to me? And even if someone did let me have a place, I'd have to be by myself. Ripe pickings for home invasion. I don't even have a cat. Maybe I should get a cat.

I am about to be homeless. Not on the streets, but a person without a *home* home.

A homeless orphan.

A homeless junkie orphan.

"And in the summers, Gram and Papa will be at the Cape, so you two can go there if you don't want to be in New York," Aunt Nora continues. "And we'll all be together for Christmas there, too."

No one would let me live in the Cape house year-round. That's for people who are trustworthy. Also, that would be super lonely and creepy, being up there all by myself.

Ben reaches for Mae. "Hey. I'll be in Brooklyn with my family in the summers. It's kind of perfect."

Jenga.

That's what happens inside me.

This news, this other freaking secret that Nate and Nora and Tony have kept to themselves for however long, it pushes me over and there is no getting up from this, from any of it, and I was just kidding myself, just kidding myself that I was clean, that I don't need—

"Nah?" Mae slips her hand into mine. "We'll figure it out. It'll be okay."

I pull my hand from hers. "You think?"

My voice is a slap. She leans back, like she can feel the force of the words against her cheek. I throw open the front door, and it bangs against the wall, hard. I guess it's all very dramatic—maybe I should have tried out for the school play.

There are concerned thises and thats as I step out the door, still holding my purse: "Honey, come back—" (Nora), "Hannah!—" (Mae), "Leave her alone, you guys!" (Nate).

I'm out the door. I hear Mae behind me and I just . . . fly. I'm running down the street, fast, throat burning, the cold spring night cutting into me. I am so out of shape, but I go and go and go. She calls my name, but I don't stop. I won't ever stop running away.

"Hannah! *Stop!* STOP, JESUS CHRIST, STOP."

Mae's desperation almost makes me slow down, but it's not quite enough.

For once the train is there, waiting for me, and I slip in just as the doors are closing. I tap my card on the kiosk and nod at the driver, my breath coming out in great, heaving gulps. As I'm making my way through the car, holding on to the bars that hang from the ceiling for balance, I catch a glimpse of Mae, hands on her knees, panting. Do we lock eyes and have deep internal realizations as my train speeds away from her?

No.

I sit down on an empty bank of seats and hug my purse to me. I'm stuck in my hourglass, the sand falling over me, faster and faster. It's already to my knees, and I haven't even had a pill yet.

We pass Zaftigs, then Fenway, and soon we're underground, Boston Common above us. I can feel myself checking out.

How much easier things would be for everyone without Just Hannah. Go to New York, go be an astronaut, go kiss a girl who doesn't bite.

"Hannah?"

For one wild moment, I think it's Drew and this will be like in a movie, where chance has brought us together and he will take me in his arms and everything will be okay and all I will smell is tea tree soap.

But the boy who called my name isn't Drew. Tall, scraggly, unfortunate tattoo choices. Those insanely beautiful Nolan eyes.

"Eddie?"

Drew's cousin grins and plops down on the seat across from me. "Long time, no see. Drew keeping you busy?"

The sand falls and falls.

"Drew and I . . ."

"Oh. Shit." Eddie takes off his Bruins cap, runs a hand through his hair.

"Yeah. It's . . . whatever."

The train stops at Copley and people flood in, out. Laughter, lots of Emerson students—arty and cool—and people with BU sweatshirts. The business casual crowd is here, too, reading their tablets or their phones. Eddie stands and comes to sit next to me. He smells like cigarettes and bad decisions.

"I was gonna give you a hard time about taking away my best dealer," he says. "Surprised he's not back up with it. Thought he only stopped 'cause of you."

I nod. Hold my purse closer.

"He's getting his shit together," I say.

I haven't talked to Drew in weeks. Sometimes I give in when he calls because I need a hit of his voice, but I'm always the first to hang up.

"Where you off to?" Eddie asks. The train jolts forward, and a group of girls near the back break into surprised giggles as they hold on to each other.

"I don't know," I say. What would it be like to be one of them, to be part of a happy little coven? "It's my birthday."

"Eighteen?"

I nod.

"You don't look very happy," he says.

"I'm not."

"Why don't you come out to Cambridge with me? I have to make a stop at a party—Fancy Harvard types." *Hah-vahd.* He says it like Drew. "You in?"

I shake my head. "No. I mean, thanks, but I don't party. Anymore."

"It's your *eighteenth* birthday. The fuck you talking about you're not gonna party?"

I open my mouth to say no. Obviously *no.* But then I see the girls from BU huddled together, laughing. Probably a little drunk. And I think about how I'm getting kicked out of my aunt and uncle's, and where the hell am I gonna go? And this opens something inside me, something raw and starving and gaping. A hole bigger than the pit they threw my mom into.

"Okay," I hear myself say.

"Fuckin' right okay."

Things Without Memory
Mirrors
Stars
Waves
Diamonds
Me

Bathroom Mirror
678 Leeds Street
Cambridge, MA

43

Hannah

should text Jo. I will. I'll text her right now. I'm going to a party, but I won't do anything. I won't. I reach into my bag, but my phone is dead. I'm never motivated to keep it charged, since I have zero friends and no boyfriend. I guess I could borrow Eddie's phone, but I don't ask.

Eddie starts talking about his kid, his girlfriend, and I listen. Nod. *Bad idea, bad idea* is going through my head on repeat, but I tune myself out. Soon we're at Park Street and transferring to the Red Line, which is fast and sleek. I hesitate before stepping into the train, but the doors start closing, and on instinct I jump in. *Bad idea, bad idea.* We get off at Harvard and Eddie nods to the punks camped out just outside the station with their guitars and cardboard signs and dogs. These are my people. The Justs. Square pegs in round holes. Maybe I will be homeless like them and I will write acorns on my signs and hope people give me quarters, or dollars, not just scorn or pity or an excuse to remember how lucky they are. Or I could be like Priscilla in Venice and join the freak show on the boardwalk: *Come see the girl who lost both her parents in a tsunami!* I look away from them before I can see my jeweler, my hookup. Before I can give her money in exchange for diamonds.

We walk past Harvard, where people like Mae are—people who matter, who belong. People who know what they want to do with their lives.

I take in a ragged breath, and Eddie turns, eyeing me. He reaches into his pocket and takes out a pill.

"For the birthday girl," he says.

I don't reach for it. I can't. Can I? My fingers itch. All that hard work getting better, and suddenly here I am.

"Oxy. Good stuff." He dangles it. "Going once, going twice . . ."

I take it and swallow the pill before I can change my mind. The sand in my hourglass falls faster. It's at my waist. Faster.

Way faster than usual.

We pass cafes with twinkle lights in the windows and bookstores and at least three Dunkin' Donuts. My high kicks in as we walk along the main road, much sooner than I thought it would. *Hey, old friend.* I follow Eddie when he turns onto a quiet side street with pools of light that spread across the asphalt like melted butter. I hear the house before I see it: laughter and music, a wraparound porch where smokers lean against the railing or sit on the stairs. It's your typical Cambridge house, made of clapboard, a couple stories high. These places all look like a Pilgrim could just stroll on out the front door at any second. Someone on the roof calls down to someone on the porch. They laugh.

"Nolan!" A skinny guy with ripped jeans and a faded black T-shirt jumps up from his seat on the stairs when he sees us. "Just in time, man." He glances at me as he throws down his cigarette. "This your girl?"

I shake my head. "Hannah," I say. "Just . . . Hannah."

"Sean."

"It's Hannah's birthday," Eddie says.

"No shit? We should celebrate." Sean motions us inside. "After you."

Eddie sticks out like a sore thumb among the Harvard sweatshirts and Urban Outfitters. He's so obviously poor—he's got *wrong side of the tracks* written all over him. It's clear he's the drug guy, and the energy spikes a little as Sean carves a path through the living room.

It's not a big place, and there are more people outside than in. I don't know what I expected a Harvard person's house to look like, but when I take a look around, this makes sense. IKEA chic, a little messy. Stacks of books. Half-empty bottles of wine, hard stuff. A few people sit on a couch, passing a bong back and forth. They shoot curious glances our way, one of the guys nodding at Eddie.

"What up." Eddie says this to the room at large, and he doesn't linger—he knows anyone who wants to buy will follow.

Sean pushes open a door at the end of the hall and calls inside, "He's here."

Five people are sprawled on the furniture and one of the girls claps. "My hero."

The room is painted turquoise, the lighting dim so that it feels as though we're underwater. A bed in the corner is covered neatly with a blanket, and a few beanbag chairs sit scattered around the room. There's a desk with a MacBook, a lamp, a cup of takeaway coffee.

I could borrow someone's phone. Call Jo. Have her come pick me up. I could, but the sand is at my neck, and it's so warm and cozy here. I flop down on one of the beanbag chairs.

Eddie takes out his plastic bag and opens up shop.

"A little present for the birthday girl," Sean says, handing over cash and then putting a pill in my palm. I don't know what it is, and I don't care because for the first time in weeks and weeks I am so, so happy. I swallow it. I watch while people come in and out of the room.

"You go to school around here, Hannah?" Sean asks, plopping down next to me.

I don't want to be the high school kid, so I lie. "Yeah. BU."

"Nice. Major?"

Fuck.

"English." Safe, right?

Sean nods. "Right on. My comp class is kicking my ass. Paper on Milton due tomorrow, and that's . . . not fucking happening."

We talk. Well, he talks and I listen, or I try to. I'm already half-gone. Sean is cute. Not as cute as Drew, but cute. A guy in the corner picks up a guitar and begins softly strumming it. I close my eyes, and the sand reaches past my lips. I ride the soft Oxy wave. I forget. About the promises I've made to myself, my parents, all the crap at home—all of it is gone. Eddie asks if I want to leave with him, and I say no.

"Hannah." Someone's shaking me gently, and when I open up my eyes, a stranger is looking at me, smiling. Wait, not a stranger. Sean. Harvard Sean.

"Sorry," I mumble, disoriented. The room is quiet. We're alone.

"It's okay. Just thought you might not want to sleep through your birthday."

"This is the worst birthday ever," I say, and the feelings come, and the sand, and I don't want to feel, not at all, because they will bury me alive.

"Then let's change that, shall we?" Sean holds up a pill and puts it between his lips, then leans in, so close the tip of his nose touches mine.

It has never occurred to me to have sex with someone who isn't Micah or Drew. And I haven't even had sex with Drew yet. But I am Hannah from BU. English major. My parents aren't dead, and I don't care about waves or rehab or any of it. I press my lips against his and feel Sean smile as I open my mouth to receive the pill.

Warm floating and breath and lips, another pill and I am here and not here, not anywhere, not anymore. Not. I am *not*.

Mad Matter Magazine Vol. 4, No. 12

Mad Matter: Do you think you'll find out the secret of the universe's origins—and, by extension—dark matter, in your lifetime?

Dr. Winters: I hope so. But it's okay if I don't.

Mad Matter: Really?

Dr. Winters: *[laughs]* Really. See, the universe has a way of throwing us a bone every now and then, and this is the one we get when we kick the bucket: When I die—and you, all of us—*we become the secret*. We become part of the universe itself, our molecules, enfolded back into the machine of life. So a part of me—admittedly, not the conscious part—gets to know the answers. In a way, every single one of us will one day know the secret of the universe.

Mad Matter: What do you think it is? If you had to guess.

Dr. Winters: My answer will disappoint you. It's not remotely scientific.

Mad Matter: Tell us anyway.

Dr. Winters: Love. I think the secret is love. I've been thinking about this for a long time, but I really got it this past year. It's been a rough one for me personally. But one day this spring I was sitting with my girls—we were eating chili, just a normal family dinner. And I looked into my daughters' eyes . . . and I saw the Helix Nebula. Right there, in both their eyes—a star. Amazing, how the human eye and the Helix resemble each other. And I couldn't help but think: The universe loves itself. It puts these little love notes to itself in all of us, in nature. About how utterly astonishing we are. So loving ourselves, one another, this planet, the cosmos—it's all the universe's own expression of deep, creative self-love. The universe is doing right by the miracle, too.

Mad Matter: It sounds like you already know the secret, Dr. Winters.

Dr. Winters: When I look at my girls, I believe I do. Yes.

44

Mae

ISS Location: Low-Earth Orbit
Earth Date: 10 May
Earth Time (EST): 19:17

Her phone rings and rings.

I call Jo. Nah's not with her, hasn't texted her or anything. Which is a really bad sign. Really bad.

"What about a meeting—think she'd be at one?" Nate asks. He's been driving me around the city for the past hour.

"She just got back from one," I say.

Ben leans forward, as close to me as he can be from the backseat. "Is there anywhere else she used to get her pills?"

We went to Harvard Square. We checked the angel at the garden. Drove all around our neighborhood. Went to the coffeehouses near our place. She's gone.

"I don't know. Jo said it was just Harvard Square. She's looking, too."

I call Drew. My sister can be mad at me for calling him later. I know she'll be ashamed that he knows her business like this, but I'm beyond caring about things like that right now.

"Hello?" His voice is uncertain. Maybe he's hoping it's her. Sometimes Nah borrows my phone, since hers is never on her.

"I can't find Hannah. I've looked everywhere."

"What do you mean you can't find her? What happened?"

He's trying to sound calm, but he isn't, not by a long shot.

"I underestimated maybe how hard the first birthday without them would be, and then we found out—"

"Wait—it's her birthday? Today?"

"You didn't know?"

He swears quietly. "No. She's not on social. We never . . . I had no way of—Shit. Where are you?"

"We'll come get you. I'm putting you on speakerphone. Tell Nate how to get to your house."

Nate pulls back onto the road while Drew directs him. Ben rests a hand on my shoulder. I grab hold of it. I wish Hannah could stay clean and I wish our parents weren't dead and I wish my aunt and uncle weren't moving and that the waves would stop coming just when it seems like the sea is calm.

Drew's waiting outside a run-down house when we pull up, hands shoved deep in his pockets. He still looks like a drug dealer to me, with his hoodie and the way his shoulders hunch up, like he's trying to disappear. Nah has kept Drew in the loop enough that he knows she has a sponsor, knows she's clean. But I haven't seen him since that night at the hospital.

He jogs over to the car and dives into the back seat next to Ben.

"Hey." Drew leans forward. He's thin. Gaunt, even. Like not being with her is eating him away. "Do you have Jo's number? Hannah might have—"

I shake my head. "She's the first person I called."

"I checked in with everyone I know from school—she hasn't showed up at any parties. I don't know if she'd know about them anyway," he says.

Nate glances at me. "Should we go back to Harvard Square, where her hookup is? Maybe it took her a while to get across the city—she got on the T."

I look at Drew, and he nods. The car is silent for a few moments, except for the sound of the tires going over bumps.

"What happened?" Drew finally asks.

I tell him and he rests his head in his hands, like he's going to be sick. "Why the fuck does she keep shutting me out?"

"She's not shutting you out. Jo thinks Nah needs to go it alone for a while, and I agree," I tell him. "Nah just . . ." I glance back at Ben, who's looking at Drew with concern. "Maybe you and Ben can talk later. He can explain, I think."

Ben nods. "I speak Winters now."

"If she's using . . ." Drew looks up at me, his eyes too bright, wild with fear. "If she goes back to her old dose—"

"She'll call Jo," I say. "I know she will. She's almost made it to five months. There's no way she'd go back to day one so quick. She *hates* day one."

"Every addict does," Drew says. "But that doesn't stop them."

Hannah is not going to die tonight. This is just a sim. Another death sim.

It's easier to face things when you're ready for them. Not even death can blindside you then.

We get to Harvard Square, but there is no Hannah. We talk to messed-up kids outside the train station, where they all congregate, steps from the university. One of them thinks he may have seen someone like her, but he can't remember. He's too high. Too gone.

When we get back in the car, Drew's phone buzzes, and he goes pale as he reads whatever text came in. His fingers fly across the screen.

"What?" I say. "Is that her?"

He shakes his head, brings up GPS. "I know where she is."

Nate glances at the screen. "Good—we're already going in that direction."

"What'd she say?"

"It was my cousin, not her," Drew bites out. "They ran into each other on the T."

He swipes through his phone and holds it up to his ear, eyes scanning the passing cars. I can hear it ring. The ringing stops, and someone on the other end starts to say something, but Drew cuts him off, his voice full of fury.

"I am going to fucking *kill* you for taking her there," he says. His cousin—I'm guessing it's his cousin—starts to speak again, and Drew growls, "Shut up. How much?"

The guy on the phone says something, a number I guess, and Drew curses. *How much?* means: How many milligrams? How many pills? How many chances to die?

Nate and Ben and I sit, silent, as Drew loses his mind on his cousin, anger masking the sheer terror I can see in his eyes. This doesn't feel like a sim. Not even a little bit.

Mom. Mom, please. Fix this, please.

When Drew hangs up, he falls back against the seat and stares out the window, the phone clutched in his hand. His face is so pale.

"Is she . . . She's using? He gave her something?" I can't breathe.

She's been sober for so long. It'll be too easy to overdose if she takes the same amount she used to. It says that in the books, the websites. The pamphlets from all the rehabs and doctors and places that were supposed to make her better.

"Yes. My cousin left the party, so she could have taken more." Drew grips the back of the driver's seat. "Faster, Nate."

"On it," my cousin says.

I have been here before. A pocket of spacetime that keeps happening, over and over. And I can't change the outcome. It is not up to me at all. It never has been.

"Creation. Destruction. Creation. Destruction."

I don't realize I'm saying this out loud until Nate says, "Buzz, you're freaking me the fuck out."

As we race toward Hannah, I feel a quickening, like I'm in the lab and five things have come together all at once, suddenly making sense. Making one thing true.

I close my eyes. Breathe.

Maybe we will get a chance to save her life again tonight. But in the end, Hannah has to save herself. She's going to have to believe she can do right by the miracle.

Tonight, my sister will live or she will die.

I can't work this problem.

I am not in control.

A strange peace settles over me. The fear and anxiety and horror of it all is still there. The urgency, too. I'm not giving up, not ever. But it's like when I'm meditating: That's all on the surface. Underneath: quiet.

Nonattachment doesn't mean not loving Nah. But this peace, this stuff under the surface of all the waves—that's the place I can be, no matter what happens. Death to the waves. Or . . . not to the waves themselves. Death to letting them sweep me off my feet. I can just . . . ride them.

This is what River meant.

It's just a ride.

Nate presses on the gas.

45

Mae

ISS Location: Low-Earth Orbit
Earth Date: 10 May
Earth Time (EST): 20:06

Ten minutes later, we're pulling up in front of a house on the other end of Cambridge, and Drew is out of the car before it stops. I run to catch up with him. A few people are smoking on the porch, but he ignores them, just walks right through the front door like he owns the place. He grabs the first guy he sees in the hallway.

"A girl—black hair. Pretty. Where is she?"

The guy holds his hands up. "Whoa, the fuck you—"

"Where. Is. She."

A girl sitting cross-legged on the couch glances at us after taking a massive hit from a bong. "She's with Sean. Down the hall. I'd knock if I were you."

Drew's face drains of color, and he lets go of the guy. He looks at me.

I shake my head. If she's with some other guy, then things are so bad. Hannah doesn't want anyone but Drew.

"Come on," he growls as he turns and heads down the hall. He stops for just a second in front of a closed door, then pushes it open.

"What the fuck?" a guy yells as Drew storms in.

Terror and misery and a thousand unnameable things flash over

Drew's face, and then he lurches across the room. I run to follow him, barely seeing the shirtless guy who's fallen off a bed onto the floor.

"Hannah," Drew's saying, already on his knees, leaning over the mattress. My sister's lying on it, topless, and he's shaking her. "Baby, wake up."

I am screaming words and she's not moving. I can't, she's—"NO."

I reach into my bag for the Naloxone, but it's not there. It's not there.

"Drew, I don't have it. The Naloxone. It must have fallen, I don't know, I don't have it—"

"911," Drew says, not looking at me.

"I thought she was sleeping," the guy says, staring at the bed. "Fuck. She was just—we were—"

Drew starts doing CPR, and I'm trying to unlock my phone, but my hands are shaking too bad. One of Nah's arms is dangling toward the floor, and everything I ever thought I believed or knew goes out the window because I am praying to who or what I don't know, but somebody has to be in fucking charge and I am praying praying praying to a God I don't believe in.

"911, what's your emergency?"

"My sister, she's . . . I think she's overdosed and—"

"Is your sister unconscious?"

"Yes," I sob. "Yes."

"Is she breathing?"

"I don't know. Drew, is she breathing?"

He shakes his head, intent on his work. Ben's in the room now, and I'm crying too hard to speak or think or hear, so he grabs the phone and talks to the woman on the other end and I fall next to Drew and grab Hannah's hand, which is cold, the fingers tinged slightly blue, and I know what that means because I researched overdoses and my sister isn't breathing.

"Hannah," I whisper, my forehead falling to the pillow. "Hannah, please."

Drew is working so hard, his mouth against hers, giving her all he can. "Come on, baby, come on," he says, pumping her chest.

I turn to the guy. He's staring at her, at us, but totally out of it.

"When did she stop breathing?" I shout.

"I don't know, I . . . I thought she was sleeping, I don't know. Look, I didn't do anything, she just—"

Brain damage begins four minutes after loss of oxygen, death eight minutes after.

Nate pushes his way into the room, and he's on the guy in seconds. "What did you give her?"

"I don't know what you're—"

My cousin shoves the guy, hard, and I'm surprised, but that's stupid—just because he's wearing one of my blouses doesn't mean he's not strong.

"Listen, you Harvard fuck, you tell me what you gave my cousin or I'll—"

"Okay, fuck, stop. Oxy, with a little—just a *little*—fentanyl in it." The death drug. The one killing everyone. "But it wasn't—"

"How much?" I say.

"Come on, baby," Drew says just as the other guy says he can't remember, maybe eighty milligrams, but she'd had something before he gave them to her and Drew says, "Fuck," and I have never seen someone look at another person with so much love and terror as Drew looks at my sister and then I hear the sirens.

My sister is dying.

"Come back," Drew says. Because she left. Because she's gone. *"Come back."*

Nate runs out and then the paramedics rush in and Drew moves away, his eyes never leaving Hannah. We all talk at once.

"What's her name?" the paramedic says, all business. She checks Hannah's pulse, frowns.

"Hannah," I say.

"Nalaxone," she says, holding out her hand. Her partner places a syringe in it and she takes Nah's arm, finds a vein, and slides the needle in. Nothing.

We wait.

Nothing.

My sister is dead.

Then—

Hannah gasps, her back arching as the air rushes into her lungs. I call out to her, and she looks at me, eyes glazed and wide with fear.

"You're okay," I say. "It's me. You're okay."

She doesn't say anything. I push past the paramedics, grab her hand. It's so cold.

"Hannah. It's me. It's *me*."

I wait, and the longer I wait, the more my heart sinks. Brain damage. I've lost her after all.

A sudden, deep knowing fills me: *I will survive this.* I love her, and I will survive loving her. Loving anyone.

"Mae?" she rasps.

"Yes." I'm sobbing hard, and I can barely get the words out. "It's me. You're okay? You're okay. You're okay now."

There's movement out of the corner of my eye, and Drew is turning around, his back to us, shoulders shaking, his forehead against the wall.

Nah turns over and vomits all over the floor. Everyone but me jumps back. I keep my eyes on my sister, one hand in hers, and I wipe her mouth with the sheet while the paramedics do things.

"Don't be scared," I say. "There's help."

"I'm sorry," she whispers.

"It's okay. Everything's okay now," I say.

I have to move so the paramedics can do their work, but I keep my hand in hers. They shine light in her eyes, and she winces.

"I was drowning," she says as they load her onto a stretcher. "But it was nice. Warm. I don't think it hurt them. Not the whole time, at least. Not at the end. I think it wasn't so bad."

A weight lifts off me then, as though a heavy bird of prey had been sitting on top of my chest since the wave. That had been the worst part, maybe, about all of this: not knowing how much it hurt when they died.

Hannah closes her eyes and sighs. I think she's asleep, but then she says, "It's okay that they weren't together. You're never really alone. I know that now."

"Miss?" The male paramedic gently taps my arm. "We need to get her in the ambulance. You can come with, if you want."

I nod and let go of Hannah's hand, then turn to my cousin.

"Nate, can you—" I start, but he pulls me into his arms and my words get lost against his shirt.

"Go," he says. "We'll see you there. Text me which hospital."

"Okay."

Nah opens her eyes for a second. "Thank you," she whispers to the paramedic.

She looks at my sister, surprised. Hannah's eyes close, and the woman turns to me.

"You've got a fighter here." She wheels Hannah out, past the throng of partyers, who stare at us all, shocked.

Drew is still in the corner, looking in the direction Hannah went.

"Thank you," I say.

He blinks and looks around, as if he's just noticing we're here. "I didn't do anything."

"You kept her here," I say. "You saved her. Again." I wrap my arms around him. "My parents would have loved you."

It's the highest praise I could give anyone.

When I pull away, Drew looks down, overcome, and then I kiss Ben because you never know how many kisses you get and then I hurry out of the room, toward my sister. My sister, who is alive.

When I Died
some deaths give
life

Bed Railing
Emergency Room
Mass General Hospital

46

Hannah

I guess some people need to get as close to death as possible before they realize they don't want to die after all.

Under the wave, I found out what I was made of. Realized no one is going to save me but me, that there is sometimes a choice—to stay or go—and that you might not know what you'll choose until the breath has left your lungs and somewhere, past the blood pounding in your ears and the *goodbye, world* of a poppy high, you suddenly come face-to-face with the voice in your head, the hidden you, that spark of light that has been singing you out of the darkness for as long as you can remember. And she is wise and beautiful—maiden and mother and crone—and she says, she says, *You are enough.* And now you have a choice: to float or drown, and if you are enough, then drowning isn't an option.

And just when you're not sure how to keep your head above water, you see your mother doing boat pose on top of the ocean. Making herself a lifeboat. Looking at you like you can be your own lifeboat, too.

And then, far away on the shore, you hear a voice you love say, "Come back."

So I did. I pulled my face out of that dark water, arched my back, reached behind me for my feet, and rode that wave that was trying to drown me, rode it all the way to the shore. One boat against the ocean. *With* the ocean.

But I didn't come back for Drew. Or Mae. Or even for Mom and Dad. I came back for me.

Because this darkness is not the darkness of the tomb. That's what the poem Jaipriya gave me was about. Rebirth. That poet was right: This darkness is the womb. One more chance to do right by the miracle.

I press my palms against the rough hospital sheets and think, *We did it.* I birthed myself, and it was a long and hard and painful labor, but I am alive and I am here. For good. Somewhere deep down inside me I knew—I *know*—that I won't get another chance. Use it or lose it.

"Well, Blue, you look like shit."

I open my eyes, and there's Jo standing in the doorway of my hospital room, arms crossed, a phoenix tat hissing at me from its perch near her elbow. She looks like she's just come from a goth biker meeting, all leather and ass-kicking boots and dark purple lipstick.

"I'm counting my fingers," I say.

Mae stands from where she'd been sitting in the chair next to the bed and yawns. Her short hair is sticking up in all sorts of angles, her clothes rumpled, and there are dark rings under her eyes, but she smiles when she sees me, and I smile back.

"I'm going to get some coffee, even though caffeine intake at two in the morning is not advisable." Mae glances at Jo, her smile turning into a little smirk. Attitude looks good on her. "She's all yours."

She and Jo high-five each other as she leaves the room, then Jo crosses to my bed. She flicks her long straight bangs out of her eyes then waits there, still as the Charles on a windless day.

"You were right," I say. "The only thing I was hiding from was myself."

Jo slides her backpack off and sits on the edge of the bed. "Lay it on me, sister."

"When my aunt and uncle said they were leaving, that freaked me the hell out. I mean, I know they offered to let me go with them and I wouldn't be homeless, but I *felt* like I'd be homeless. You know?"

She nods. "Walk me through your thought process."

"Even before I saw the Realtor, I was upset. Because we graduate next month and I don't know what to do with my life. Having a sister like Mae just makes adulting hard. Because it's like, no matter what I do, I feel like a lame-ass failure. She's literally going to be a rocket scientist."

"What Mae is going to be is irrelevant. What do *you* want? Who will *you* be?"

I have thought this question so many times, but it's different hearing it now, after everything that happened tonight. When I faced down the wave and decided to ride it.

"I want to be happy."

"What does happy look like?"

I close my eyes. And there it is: the little house, the garden, yoga, making soup. Kids and chili night, *I put a spell on you*, Drew.

"Having a family," I whisper. "Being a mom and just loving. Being loved. Maybe fostering some kids, like Mae was. I basically just want to be my mom—the Hannah version of her. But . . ."

"But what?"

"It's so retrograde. I mean, who says their goal in life is to be a freaking housewife?"

"Dude, fuck what anyone thinks." She shakes her head. "You know, I love certain things about the time we live in. I love that even though my parents are mad conservative, they've had to accept I have a girlfriend. I love that I get to vote and that women can run for president. I love that Beyoncé is in the world. You know what I mean?"

I nod.

"But . . ." Jo reaches into her jacket and frowns. "Okay, this is a conversation to be had over cigarettes. Ugh."

I laugh. Addicts, man. We do our best.

"*But,*" she continues, "what I don't like is this intense pressure for everyone to be fucking exceptional all the time. Or, no. This idea that we aren't *already* exceptional. I mean, yeah, we have to not waste our goddamn lives watching TV and shopping. That shit has to stop. But the life you're talking about: It's beautiful. And fuck anyone who shames you for wanting it. This one life: It's all we get. It's not about the likes and the degrees and the bank account. It's about the love, man. It's only about the love."

My heart breaks wide open then because I get it, I get it *so hard*: My mom didn't mean that our family wouldn't have been complete because I wasn't enough—*just Hannah*. It wouldn't have been complete because our hearts had more room in them, and that space was for Mae and for Drew and Ben and even my new baby sister, Pearl. And the little ones in my own future. I'm enough as I am, but if it were *just* me, I wouldn't be truly happy. Because I want my family. I want the love.

"Fuck, Jo. *Fuck.*"

"And that, my friend, is what we call an existential mic drop," Jo says.

I've learned something the Little Prince's thorny rose never did: A rose is beautiful whether or not anyone is admiring her, *choosing* her. Shakespeare said, "That which we call a rose / By any other name would smell as sweet." And it's true. Her beauty does not increase or decrease under observation—a rose is going to bloom whether you see her or not, whether you put her in your vase or walk right on by. She is not *just*. She *is*. And that's enough.

Jo unzips her backpack and takes a plastic bag out. She hands it to me. Inside is an old dish towel wrapped around a bowl—the most beautiful bowl I've ever seen: grayish-blue pottery with gold-filled cracks all over it. Somehow delicate and strong at the same time.

"My sponsor gave this to me the day I quit the shit for good—a little over six years ago," Jo says. "It's from Japan." She reaches out and traces the tip of her finger along one of the cracks. "It's a style called *kintsukuroi*. When pottery breaks, the potter puts it back together with gold instead of throwing the pieces away and starting over. It makes the piece even more beautiful—and much more valuable."

It hits me then, a memory of my mom singing along to Leonard Cohen in the kitchen while she makes soup: *There's a crack in everything . . . that's how the light gets in.*

I hold the bowl between my palms, the gold blurring as my eyes fill.

You are enough.

I start to hand her the bowl, but she shakes her head. "It's yours now."

"But I fucked up."

Jo nods. "Yeah, you did. *C'est la goddamn vie.* Remember, it's progress, not perfection." She rests her hand over mine. "Relapsing is a bitch, but you're gonna be okay."

"How do you know?"

"I talked to your paramedics. They said you thanked them. Usually, addicts are pissed as hell when they get woken up. They don't care that you just saved their life—fuck you because you ruined their high." She shakes her head. "One time, my mom woke me up—she had Naloxone in the house—and that's exactly what I said to her: *Fuck you.* To my own *mom.* For saving my life! But the last time I overdosed, I said thank you. I was so goddamn grateful to be alive. I haven't used since."

She hands me one more thing—a pamphlet about the Pink House. Jo had told me a bit about it—a rambling Victorian sober house, absolutely pink, in Cambridge's weirdo community, with ten bedrooms, all occupied by female-identifying former addicts. Jo runs the place.

"One of my girls is moving out," she says. "In June. I think this could be a good place for you to land while you figure out next steps. You can get a job, get involved. We have daily meetings. Support. A great kitchen with a big-ass soup pot. Even a poetry night." She smiles. "Think about it."

I stare at her. This isn't just a lifeline, it's an entire rescue operation.

"Yes," I say. "*Yes.*"

"This isn't some Disney happy ending," she warns. "You're gonna be working your ass off to get your shit together."

"I'm ready." I hold the little pamphlet to my chest. "Thank you."

"Thank yourself." Jo grins, then stands and crosses to the doorway. She pulls open the door, then turns around and holds up a finger. "Day one."

I nod. "Day one."

I finally understand the ending of *The Little Prince*. All my life I thought he had to die so that he could leave his body, which he said was too heavy to take with him the distance he needed to go. He couldn't leave Earth and get back to his asteroid otherwise. I thought it was like going to Heaven. But now I realize what he was trying to tell the pilot: Sometimes to find your way back home, you need to surrender the person you no longer are so that you can step into the person you're supposed to become.

I shall look as if I were dead, he said, *and that will not be true.*

That will not be true.

· ● ·

Drew is curled up on a couch in the waiting room, sleeping.

The TV mounted to the wall across from him is playing a rerun of *Golden Girls* on mute. (Life goals.)

It's three in the morning, and the room is empty.

I cross to him, kneel down.

I have brushed my teeth and washed my face and changed into the clean clothes Aunt Nora brought for me. I am wearing Mom's rose perfume. I don't want him to remember me covered in vomit, topless because another guy took off my shirt, surrounded by paramedics.

I watch Drew sleep for a little bit. Those dark lashes against pale skin. His hair longer than usual, messy. Raven's wings.

He's kicked off his shoes and there's a little hole in his sock and I decide that if the stars are aligned for us, and even if they aren't, I am going to buy him socks. He deserves some taking care of. This boy who has been so abandoned, orphaned not by a wave, but by his parents' addiction and indifference. Mae's the numbers nerd, but I know this much: When love is one-sided, the math doesn't check out. I don't want to only take. I want to start giving, too. Micah said he couldn't carry me. Drew said he *could*. Whether it's Drew I spend my life with, or someone I haven't met yet, I know this: I want to be in the kind of relationship where we carry each other.

I reach out, but before I even touch him, he takes a deep breath, my wrist so close to his nose, drenched in my rose scent.

"Hannah," he murmurs, still asleep.

For a minute, just a minute, I see him as an old man, with thick gray hair and a sweater and glasses slipping down his nose. My heart gets ten sizes bigger. Then it breaks into dozens or maybe hundreds of pieces. Because I know what's going to happen when he wakes up, what I'm going to say, and I hate it. I wonder if you can do *kintsukuroi* with hearts, too. Fill all the cracks in with gold.

Drew opens his eyes. Blinks.

He sits up and we look at each other for the longest time, all these months apart somehow having made the current between us stronger, and I throw my arms around him, hug him so, so tight. Drew presses his hand against the back of my head, wraps his other arm around my waist, and lets out a long, slow breath. Being in his arms is like lying on the beach, soaking up all that warm sand after a cold swim.

Maybe I don't have to do what I came here to do. Maybe I can stay on this beach a little longer. Forever, even.

When I let go, he pulls me close to him on the hard, dirty hospital couch, and I tell him about what I learned under the wave, about Mom and her boat pose, about being enough. He listens, those gray-and-gold eyes of his never leaving mine. They are almost the same color as the Japanese pottery Jo gave me.

"I love you," I say, when I'm finished. "Not just because you helped save my life tonight, but because you help save my life every night—you make me want to do right by the miracle."

I pause.

"But?" The light in his eyes dims a little.

Why do I have to keep hurting the people who care about me the most?

"I can't be with you."

Drew looks away, and I'm not sure what kind of calculus he's doing, but the way he bites his lip reminds me of Mae, working her problems. After a minute, he turns back to me. Nods once.

"I get it," he says. "You've got a lot to figure out. Right now. But when you're ready, in the future, you and I—"

"I don't know, Drew. I can't promise you anything. I have so much work to do. Jo's not kidding. This was my last chance. I know it. I can't screw up again. I have to be like Mae—I have to be focused on the mission."

There will be other waves. Different waves. I have to be ready. To not reach for a bottle of pills when they come.

"I know you're scared," he says. "I am, too. You died tonight. For a minute. I could feel you go. And I . . ." His voice shakes. "I understood the wave a lot better." He rests his cheek against mine. "Please don't go away again."

I run my hand through his hair. "I heard you tell me to come back. That's part of why I'm here right now."

"Then I don't understand why you think I'm not good for you." He leans back, his face a misery of confusion. "I can help. On this . . . this mission. I want to be here for you, to be with you, through whatever shit comes our way."

I want to give in, so bad, but somewhere Dad says: *We can do impossible things.*

I'm still mad at you, I remind him. But he's right.

"I want to be with you so much, God, *so much,*" I say, "but I don't think I can become the person I need to be—or get back to who I maybe always was—if I'm all tangled up in you. I've been basing my future around other people—working with Mom at the yoga studio, moving in with Micah.

I need to see what it feels like to base my future around *me*. And I don't know who I'll be at the end of that."

"You'll be *you*. And I'll be me."

I knew this would be hard. But it's so much worse than hard.

"This feeling—of us. Of this being *it*. I had that with Micah, too." I grip Drew's hand. "It was different—not like this, not so . . . certain feeling. But I really thought he and I would be together for good, you know? And now he's gone." The tears come, and I just let them run down my face. "Anything can happen. We might change—get older and not fit anymore. Or you might meet someone not all fucked-up—"

"I want *you*, Hannah," Drew says.

I look down at our hands, and I can almost see what they will look like with paper-thin old-person skin, age spots, gnarled knuckles.

"You get to be happy," he says. "You don't have to punish yourself."

I trace the lines of this face that is so special to me. "I'm not—I promise. I want the love. Big, *big* love. Family. All of it. When the time is right. I don't want to be alone forever—but I need to be right now."

I can't tell him how much I want that big love with him. Or that I want to do right by the miracle together. It wouldn't be fair to make him wait. Or to make a promise I don't know if I can keep.

We are quiet. For a long time. There is only the soft, strange sounds a hospital makes late at night, and the air conditioner, and Drew's breath, and mine.

"Okay," he finally says. He lets go of my hands. So quiet: "Okay."

I brush my lips against his, quick, then stand. "I have to go now."

Before I take back everything I said. Before I throw myself into his arms and never, ever leave. I have to go. Now.

He doesn't get up, just nods. I stand. Cross the room, sail away from the only port I've had in this storm. I am pushing out into unknown waters. I pull open the door and, just as it's about to close behind me, I hear him.

"Hannah."

I turn. Drew holds up the Chariot card I gave him all those months ago. He's been keeping it in his pocket, all this time. I never knew.

"You said the cards don't lie."

I see us in his kitchen, me pointing to that card.

So, the Chariot is about perseverance. To not give up on this thing you want, even if it seems impossible. It's all about creating a big change in your life. So whatever this thing you want is, you're going to have to be all in . . .

That slow smile of his spreads across his face. The hurt is still there, the longing. The terror of the past night, and all the nights before and to come.

But those are just cracks that let the light in.

It is so bright.

47

Mae

ISS Location: Low-Earth Orbit
Earth Date: 10 June
Earth Time (PST): 11:15

The Three Sisters in Orion's Belt was one of the first constellations I ever learned. They're super bright, very easy to locate. The sisters help you orient yourself.

Dad holds my hand up to the sky and traces my finger across its surface.

"Orion's the Hunter," he says. "There's his bow and arrow. See? And there's his head. His chest. And those three bright stars—that's his belt."

"To keep his pants up?"

Dad laughs. "Maybe. But, in ancient times, a belt could be very valuable—made of gold and jewels, even. So that belt is probably very precious to Orion. In fact, the Arabic word for the stars in the belt means 'string of pearls.'"

"That's a pretty fancy belt."

"It is, indeed. Many people call Orion's Belt the Three Sisters. I think I like that better."

"Me, too," I decide.

He presses my finger against each one, and I swear I feel the white-hot heat of those blazing pearls all the way down here on the beach.

"Alnitak. Alnilam. Mintaka. Whenever you're lost in the sky, just look for them. They'll help you find your way."

Hannah and I have asked Rebecca Chen to bring Pearl to the children's room in the central library in downtown LA, just off the atrium where we had Mom and Dad's memorial service. We arrived early and chose a table in a little corner, where hopefully no one will bother us. I have no idea what to expect—not a confrontation, I don't think. We're here to see Pearl, not get into it with our dad's . . . with Rebecca. But still.

Aunt Nora is at a nearby cafe, waiting for us.

We're sitting at a small wooden table by the picture books. I have been slowly spinning the globe that is on the table for the past fifteen minutes, my fingers running over the bump of Malaysia, traveling across the sea to Boston, across America to Los Angeles.

I am nervous.

"We should have played poker," I say.

"What?"

"American astronauts always play poker just before they board the spacecraft. It's good luck, which no one believes in, but maybe they do a little because everyone plays the game. They can't stop until the commander plays the worst hand."

"Why does he have to play the worst hand?" she asks.

"So he or *she* uses up all their bad luck for the day."

"I don't know how to play poker."

"Neither do I. But it can't be that hard." I frown. "They probably don't have cards here, though."

"Well, shit," Nah says.

I hold up the stuffed Buzz Lightyear I got Pearl. "But I think we're okay, because they *also* always bring a stuffed toy on board."

"Are you admitting to me that the smartest people in the world—and I'm including you in this, sister—are superstitious?"

I shake Buzz. "He serves a purpose. When you're launching, everything is strapped down. But not the toy. You know you've reached zero gravity when it starts floating around. Cool, huh?"

"Then I guess we'll have to get you one of these, too." She reaches down and pulls a bag from her purse. "Speaking of toys . . ."

"Something else for Pearl?"

Nah smiles. "For you."

I open the bag. Inside is a LEGO kit called Women of NASA. I stare at the two mini lady astronauts beside a shuttle.

"It's Mae!" she says.

It has always been a delight to me that I share a name with Mae Jemison, who became the first black woman to go in space when she launched on the *Endeavor* in 1992. Dad swears he didn't think about that when they named me, but I don't know. I think he was planting a seed.

"I love it," I say. "It will be awesome in my dorm room."

"Right? It's like the universe always knew you belonged up there," Nah says. "Someday there's gonna be a LEGO of you, I know it." She reaches across the table. "Mae. I'm so sorry, *so, so sorry*, for breaking the ISS you made with Dad. And for all the horrible things I said and did these past few months. Thank you for never giving up on me."

"I'll always love you to the moon and back." I grin. "Maybe even as far as Mars and back, if you're lucky."

I have forgiven Nah for that mean thing she said when she was on drugs. About wanting me to do the Mars mission. I think I forgave her the moment she said it. We both know she never meant it. That's a really long time to be without your sister.

She groans. "Please don't do the Mars mission. I don't think I could handle eight years without you."

"I suspect we'd both start failing our psych evals," I agree. I run my hand over this box filled with women doing impossible things. "And there are good things about Earth, too."

Ben. Brownies. Hannah's playlists. Nate's ridiculous T-shirts. My new baby sister.

I don't want to see Rebecca. I don't know how holding Pearl will affect Nah. And I don't have a lot of time to help with the fallout, if there is any. We graduated three days ago, and I only have a few weeks before I head to Annapolis for Plebe Summer. She seems to be doing okay, but you never know. You just never know.

"I'm fine," Nah says.

"Are you reading my MIND?"

"Yes. I always read your mind." She spins the globe and we watch it go round and round. "Obviously I don't want to see Rebecca. And yesterday was . . . intense. But I really am okay."

Nah took a walk on the beach with Micah last night. I don't know what they said, but when she came back to our hotel room, she seemed lighter.

"Are you and Micah friends now?"

"No, but we're good. I was so mad at him for not coming to the clinic with me that day. But when we actually talked about it, I realized he'd been just as confused and sad and scared as me. He just didn't know how to say any of that at the time." Nah sighs. "And it sucks, I guess, that I couldn't see that. I assumed it was because he didn't give a shit. It's so hard for guys. They're not allowed to cry, always told to man up."

"It fucks with their serenity."

I am enjoying the occasional curse these days. It's good to expand your vocabulary.

"Yeah. Drew and Ben and Nate—they're lucky. They're in touch with that yin side of them. They're not afraid to own their feminine energy."

I rest my hand on my chin, thinking. "I never thought about it that way. It's an evolutionary advantage, that's for sure."

"How so?"

I smile. "Well, Drew got the girl, didn't he? For a little while, anyway."

They broke up, and that was a good decision. But she still wears that necklace Drew gave her.

Nah reaches toward the globe and traces her finger over Boston. "For a little while, yes, he did."

I spread my palm across the Atlantic. We are holding the world in our hands.

"You know, if the fighter pilot thing doesn't work out, there's always submarines."

Nah stares at me. "After what happened . . . you would literally live *under the ocean*?"

"Not under it. *In* it." I lean forward. "This one astronaut candidate, she went to Annapolis, and part of why NASA dug her is because she'd proven she could thrive in an environment hostile to life—the ocean—by being one of the first female officers on a submarine. Plus, astronauts train in the ocean all the time because it mimics the microgravity climate of space. NASA has an undersea habitat on the bottom of the Atlantic called Aquarius—it's a whole sim for living on the ISS or doing space walks. Instead of wearing a space suit, you wear diving equipment."

"Mae, that is *fucking terrifying*."

I grin. "Or effing awesome."

"Poor Ben. Usually it's the dudes who become sailors and go to sea for months at a time."

"He knows who wears the oxygen tank in this relationship," I say.

Nah laughs, but then the sound dies on her lips. Her face goes pale.

"They're here," she whispers.

I follow her gaze. Rebecca Chen is standing a few feet away, hands gripping the bar of a stroller.

The three of us stare at each other.

There is hope in her eyes. I see the fantasy play out: connecting with the daughters of the man she loved. Being "there" for them.

I wonder, briefly, if there is a multiverse in which Rebecca and Dad are together, and she is making him very happy and he is getting to know his new daughter. And I wonder, briefly, if I could be okay with that. With them being together, a different family, one that is not ours. Would she make Italian wedding soup for him?

And I also wonder, briefly, if there is a multiverse in which Mom is happy, too.

Dad thought the multiverse theory was bunk.

This universe will have to do.

"I can't talk to her," Nah whispers. "Oh my God, I can't. I'm sorry."

"To Pearl?"

"Rebecca."

"It's okay. I'll take over command."

I cross to Rebecca. She tries to smile. I do not.

I still can't see Pearl. The stroller shade is up. Just as well. I don't want her to be traumatized by this conversation.

"My sister's boyfriend, Micah. They were together for over three years," I say.

She nods, confusion crossing her face. "Yes. I—"

"After our parents died, he cheated on her. That's part of why Hannah's staying by the table over there."

Rebecca turns very, very pale.

"I can't imagine we'll ever be friends," I say. "Not because you loved our dad. He was easy to love. But because neither of you factored my mom or my sister or me into your equation."

Her eyes shine and I know she is trying not to cry and it really bothers me that I feel bad for her. But I do. My dad was her Ben, maybe. And I know exactly how lonely Earth is for her without him.

"You're right that we did the math all wrong," Rebecca says. "But I want you to know that your father *did* take you into the equation— I think you know that a little, since you read the emails. You and Hannah were his whole life. I think part of why he didn't tell you was because he knew that if you said he had to choose, he would choose you girls. Instantly. Without a thought." Her lip begins to tremble, and she bites it. "I won't tell you you're too young to understand, because you're not. Love isn't rational. He and I—your whole family—learned that the hard way. And I will never stop being sorry for the hurt I've caused. I can promise you that."

I look at this woman, and I can't stop thinking that when my dad looked at her, he loved her. He died loving her.

Mom, help.

When Nah made that funny villain playlist about Dad's string theory nemesis from Harvard, Mom said something then that I only just now understand: "Our enemies are our best teachers—and sometimes, they become our closest friends." After Dad died, the nemesis wrote a beautiful article about him in the Harvard *Crimson*.

I didn't know how much I'd miss him, the nemesis wrote. *I didn't know he was my friend.*

Dad said we can do impossible things, but forgiving Rebecca Chen feels more impossible than being selected as an astronaut candidate.

"Was he happy?" I ask. "With you."

Her eyes widen a little. And the tears finally spill out. "Yes, Mae. I'm sorry, but yes."

"And did he know about Pearl?"

Rebecca looks into the stroller, where my little sister is hiding. Her face turns soft. She nods. "We didn't know we were having a girl, but he said he hoped we would. The last time we talked—the day before the wave—he said he liked the name Pearl. Because—"

"The Three Sisters."

She smiles. "Yes."

I think of my dad, floating on the ocean by himself. With all that love in his heart.

"I'm glad he knew," I say.

Tears fall down Rebecca's face. "Me, too."

I don't know if this is forgiveness, but it's a start.

There's a soft gurgling noise from inside the stroller, and Rebecca steps away.

"I think Pearl wants to meet her sisters." She looks over to where Nah is sitting at the table, not looking at us. "Take all the time you want," she says, then heads toward a shelf of picture books a few feet away.

I put my hand on the stroller, and I don't look down until I'm away from my new sister's mother. This moment is for sisters only.

I look down. There, nestled in a sea of pale green blankets, is Pearl. As if she knows I'm here, she opens her eyes and gives me a gummy grin.

Good morning, Earth.

"Do you want to hear something cool?" I whisper to her. "There is stardust raining down on us RIGHT NOW. And you're made of stars. And named after one. When you're a little bit older, I'll show it to you. Then you can always find your way in the sky."

She giggles and kicks her hands and feet.

I beam. "That is EXACTLY how I reacted when I learned that stuff, too. We're obviously related."

Nah stands as we reach her, and when my sister looks inside the stroller, she stares and stares, her face turning Karalis red, like it always does whenever she feels anything intensely.

"Do you think . . ." She swallows. "Do you think I can hold her?"

"Of course you can," I say. "She's our sister."

Nah takes a breath. Reaches inside. Lifts Pearl out of the stroller.

"Hello," Nah breathes.

Pearl reaches up with her little dimpled hand and rests it on Nah's cheek. They stare at each other for a long, long time.

Nah leans down and brushes her lips against Pearl's forehead. "Thank you," she whispers to her.

I reach out and brush my fingers across Pearl's dark hair. She has Dad's eyes. I am so sad that my father doesn't get to meet his daughter. That she doesn't get to meet him.

The anger I'd been holding inside me against my dad melts away. I guess babies do that. They melt things.

Pearl is giving us back our dad. Bringing him back to life. I can feel him, can almost hear his soft laughter.

I turn to Nah. "We have to let it go. For her sake. And his."

There is nothing more to say to Rebecca about what happened. And there is nothing we can do to change the past. My dad was a good dad. The best. And there is only now. *Only love.*

"Okay."

"And. When Pearl's old enough, we should eat it. The three of us. Don't you think?"

Hannah knows what I mean. The last of Dad's egg bake. Uncle Tony had had it specially frozen so we could take it across the country. We thought it was the last thing he made. But it wasn't. The last thing he made is lying in my sister's arms.

It's time. To let him go. Wherever he is.

Hannah's face turns splotchier. I don't think that is a word, but it's what happens on her skin.

"We'll take pictures," Nah says. "Get her a science nerd bib."

I squeeze Pearl's fingers. "Something to look forward to," I say to my baby sister. "Solids are awesome."

Hannah laughs.

I take our gift for Pearl out of my bag, and Nah settles her on her lap as I open it up to the part our little star in the constellation of us needs to hear the most, the part that is about our dad:

"I will live on one of those stars. I will laugh on one of them. And when you look up in the sky, it will seem to you that all the stars are laughing. Only you will have the stars that can laugh!"

Pearl grins.
We laugh.
And the stars keep shining.

An Ode To A Rose

Let the tigers come with their claws!
I am not afraid anymore
And neither should you be
You are loved
You ARE love
Don't you know that, silly girl?

Bedroom Wall
The Pink House
Cambridge, MA

48

Hannah

The Pink House is unapologetically pink, a gorgeous Victorian three-story rambling place that looks like it could be a bordello, if it wanted to.

The wide, wraparound porch is lined with wind chimes. Every different kind you could imagine. Mom would have loved it. There are huge honeysuckle bushes lining the porch, too, so that the air smells like a good day.

I've never seen a house like this, where the kids are in charge. There's graffiti on the actual walls, some of it very good, and crap everywhere: bicycle parts, abandoned craft projects, and the kind of random, busted-ass stuff you see in front of people's homes on trash day, but lovingly or cheekily repurposed, such as the dog bowl that now serves as an ashtray on the porch. There's an elaborate lamp with no lampshade near the stairs, and the scent of Nag Champa wafts from one of the rooms on the second floor, mingling with the scent of something spicy in the kitchen.

Over the fireplace mantel in the living room is a sign from the universe that I have made the right choice to move here: Someone has painted a quote by Yoko in beautiful calligraphy.

What is the most important thing? To love yourself and the world. In that order.

Jo comes out from the kitchen, wiping her hands on a towel. She gives me a wild biker-girl grin.

"Welcome home, Blue."

"Thanks. That sounds really nice."

Nate and Ben are coming by later with my boxes and some furniture, but I wanted to come here on my own first, to take this first step into the unknown by myself: Just Hannah.

"Come on," she says. "I'll give you the tour."

Despite the thrift-store furniture and scribbling on the walls, the place is immaculately clean. There's an order here, once you start looking. The books on the shelves are organized by color. Notes to housemates tacked neatly to a corkboard in the large dining room. Labeled bins: CLEANING SUPPLIES, THINGS FOR YOUR LADY PARTS, EMERGENCY CHOCOLATE.

"So, this is the common room," Jo says, waving a hand around the large, sunny living room. "This is where we hang for our daily meetings and other gatherings. You have to come to at least three meetings a week here. If you have Twelve-Step meetings somewhere else you also want to go to, that's fine."

This is part of what being in a sober home is. I want this structure, this support, even though the rules make me feel like a kid again. I need people around me to stay on my ass so that I keep the promises I've made to myself. It's too easy to stay at home and not go to a meeting.

"If you have guests," Jo continues, "they're welcome to be in here or the dining room or your bedroom and they can use the downstairs bathrooms, but we ask that you respect the privacy of the rest of the house. Especially since this is an all-female-identifying space. Lots of trauma here, you know?"

I nod.

I've heard too many sad stories in meetings—girls being hurt by their dealers, by guys taking advantage of them when they were out cold on drugs. Getting attacked. I still don't know what happened with Sean from Harvard. Mae said my pants were on. But I don't *know*. That alone might be enough to keep me sober for good.

"I have a friend coming to help decorate my room tomorrow," I say. "That girl I told you about from my meeting—the poet?"

Jaipriya and I have hung out once already. There was a poetry reading at Grolier Poetry Book Shop, which my mom used to go to a bunch back in the day. It's where she met Dad. The cashier asked if I was a writer, and I said *yes*.

"Right on. Obviously no drugs or alcohol are allowed in the house—that includes your guests. I will kick your ass out if you use here *or* anywhere else. No exceptions. Okay?"

"Okay. Yes."

"We drug test pretty regularly, and that's also mandatory. They're always done randomly, so you can't fool us. We depend on one another to support our sobriety, so we have to be on top of this." Jo leads me into a large dining room, with dark wood paneling and a pretty stained glass window. A rustic wooden table with mismatched chairs that seats at least twelve sits in the center. "We eat in here. We have group dinners a few times a week. I'll show you the schedule later. We make the meal together, eat together, clean up. It's really nice. The rest of the time, we all just do our own thing. But we often potluck it together. I've got a kick-ass curry on I'm gonna make you try. I call it Vicious Vegan Delight."

I grin. "Sounds awesome."

"We've got a cool garden out back. Gina will be thrilled to have you, if you like to do shit like that, which I don't. She's our resident green goddess."

"I'd love it. My mom and I gardened together a lot. I miss it."

I run my finger along the table, thinking. A dream's been forming in my head for a while now, ever since I started working with Ben at Castaways. I don't know if it was Mae's idea, me working there, or his, but I'm grateful. A job—one step toward independence, toward real life. A life outside the pills.

After graduation, I started working the morning shifts with Ben, making the sandwiches and soups and stuff for the lunch crowd, along with regular barista duties. I write acorns on the sandwich board outside.

And I love it. All of it. I really do.

"I've been thinking . . ."

Jo glances at me, eyebrows up. "Uh-huh . . ."

"Cooking chills me out. It helps me think. My dad always said that my mom did soup meditation. Remember I told you that whenever we're stressed or something happens, we make soup? Like, the night of the wave, Mae and I made chili. We weren't hungry, we just . . . had to." She nods. "I was thinking . . . I'm writing a lot now, but I need a job, too. I don't want minimum-wage barista work forever. What if cooking's one of my things? Like, how I contribute to the world? Food is healing. Making it, eating it. Growing it. I could maybe take some classes?"

Jo throws an arm around my shoulder. "Hell yes! I fucking love that idea. Mostly because I will directly benefit from whatever delicious shit you make."

I laugh, and it sounds good, that music coming from my mouth.

We peek into the sizable kitchen and the backyard, thick with trees and flowers and a big garden—tomatoes crawling up vines, rows of herbs, bunches of greens.

Jo tells me a bit about the others as she leads me to the second of the three floors. There are ten of us in all, including Jo, who's the oldest at twenty-five. A few are students at one of the many universities and colleges in Boston; many are like me, just working and trying to figure things out.

"We've got a lot of artists here," she says. "As you can see."

The upstairs walls are covered in a collage-like mural: flowers and suns and moons. There are five bedrooms on this floor, and a communal bathroom.

"There's a cleaning schedule, and you can sign up for your shower time if you need to be in there before work or something," Jo says. "We're strict about sign-ups and our commitments."

"Is it insane, trying to get in there?"

"Each floor has two toilets and two showers. Usually something's open if you need it."

All of the bedroom doors are shut except for one. Jo knocks, then pokes her head in.

"Hey, V. Got our new sister here. Come say hi."

My heart tightens at that word—*sister*. It's only been six days since Mae got on a plane for Annapolis. But I miss her.

A girl maybe a year or two older than me comes out. Her whole head is covered in dreadlocks, and she has an elfin face that reminds me a little of Mae.

"I'm Hannah," I say. "Nice to meet you."

"Valerie. You, too. So what's your deal?"

"Um . . ." I have a choice. Do I define myself by my addiction—or by something else? "I'm a poet. And I cook."

She grins. "Right on. I'm a painter. I did some of the stuff on the walls here. You should contribute to my zine. Like, a poem. I can make the art for it."

My words, with my name next to them. Not anonymous. Not secret. I can almost *feel* the stardust Mae is always talking about, falling on me. It tingles a little. All over.

"Okay. Yeah."

"Cool. Well, knock on my door any time you need something."

"Thanks."

Jo leads me across the hall, opens the last door on the left.

"And . . . here we are."

Pale yellow walls.

Thick wood floors.

A wide window overlooking a side yard crawling with flowers and bicycles.

A polished teardrop crystal hangs from the window, catching sunbeams and turning them into rainbows all around the room.

"My little present to you," Jo says, nodding at the crystal. A new kind of diamond.

The room is warm and cozy, big enough to roll out my yoga mat. I'll put a desk by the window, my bed in that corner, by the large closet.

A gilded mirror on the wall, so I'll remember I'm not invisible.

"Thank you, Jo. For everything."

"You won't want to thank me when you hear we have a curfew." I groan, and she cackles as she heads toward the door. "I have to check on my curry. You want to come down or do you want to soak this in before the guys get here?"

"I want to soak a bit," I say.

When Jo leaves, I lie in a patch of sunlight on the hardwood floor and look at the little tattoo on my right ankle, sitting in the same spot where Mom's Om was. Mine is one of Yoko's drawings from *Acorn*, a beautiful dot-art fly for her poem "Life Piece VII."

A promise. To myself. To my dead.

To dream of flying, to trust that I won't fall. I whisper the last line of the fly's poem, out loud: "Try to remember the feeling when you are awake."

"I remember," I say. "I remember."

The scent of roses and seawater hits me, and I turn my head. Mom is lying next to me, in corpse pose. Her lips are turned up in a smile, eyes closed.

That Death card I've been getting all year? It just means the end of one journey and the beginning of another.

I'm not afraid to die. But I'm not afraid to live, either.

"This is the last time," I say to her, "isn't it?"

Her palms are turned up to the sky, and her fingers twitch the tiniest bit. I reach out and hold my mom's hand.

Just like when I was a little girl, we walk home together.

Epilogue

Mae

ISS Location: Low-Earth Orbit
Earth Date: 29 August
Earth Time (MYT): 18:06

I t is the one-year anniversary of the wave.

The beach my parents died on is littered not with bodies or debris, but with white roses. Hundreds and hundreds of white roses.

For so long, it felt like Nah and I were the only ones who'd lost people in the wave. But here, now, surrounded by women and men and children from all over the planet who are crying, but also smiling and laughing and remembering, I realize we are not alone. Not one little bit.

This grief, it is collective.

This loss, it is the world's.

It is so beautiful here. I can see why Mom wanted to lie on this beach, walk in this sand, put her toes in this warm water. This gentle water, a sleeping giant. Even though a part of me knew better, I thought I would hate it. This ocean that took them.

But you can't be angry at water.

And I don't believe in God.

So there is no one to be angry with.

That's nice.

Nah carves the words in the sand with a piece of driftwood. When she's done, I stand beside her and slip my hand into hers.

Last Words
1. *Say thank you*
2. *Say I love you*
3. *Say these words until you die*
—HANNAH WINTERS

"Who do we say thank you to?"

"To Mom and Dad," Nah says. "The universe. Ourselves."

"I thought you and the universe weren't on speaking terms."

Nah smiles. "We had a heart-to-heart when I was in the hospital."

I look up at the sky, where the moon is already starting to peek through the sunset clouds and the ISS is making its rounds of Earth.

"Thank you," I whisper. To me. To them. To everything.

I turn to my sister, watch her lips move as she whispers the same words, her eyes on the water.

I lean my head against her shoulder. "I love you."

"I love you back."

We stand with our toes curled in the sand, and we don't leave until the sea has washed Nah's words away and the sun has fallen out of the sky.

"Are you ready?" she asks.

To say goodbye.

Am I?

"No. But also yes."

Some problems take a long time to work.

We walk into the water. Hand in hand. Nah's fingers tighten around mine.

We raise our arms. Throw our roses into the waves.

The sea takes them, like it took our parents, and, for just a second, I think I hear two long sighs deep in the heart of the ocean.

But maybe it's just us.

We turn our backs on the water and walk toward the lights of Langkawi and the present of our aliveness, which feels like it's wrapped in shiny paper. The ocean says *goodbye, goodbye* in its melancholy, lonesome voice, and just when I'm about to cross from sadness to despair, I remember something super cool.

I look at my sister. "You wanna hear something amazing about stars?"

Nah laughs and throws an arm around my shoulder. "Tell me."

"Okay, so the light that we see beaming from stars is actually thousands of years old, and it's possible that the light we see has traveled so far and so long that the stars the light comes from are already dead. BUT WE STILL SEE THEIR LIGHT. Isn't that awesome?"

My sister's eyes are shining just like Dad's used to when we talked about stars and planets. And when she smiles, her eyes crinkle up just like Mom's.

Gone, but we can still see their light.

Mental Health Resources

I wish I could show you
When you are lonely or in darkness
The astonishing light of your own being.
—HAFIZ

National Suicide Prevention Hotline (24/7, free, confidential):
1-800-273-TALK (8255)

SAMHSA's (Substance Abuse and Mental Health Services Administration) National Helpline (24/7, free, confidential):
1-800-662-HELP (4357)

Narcotics Anonymous (NA):
NA may or may not be the right path for you if you're suffering from an addiction. If you want to learn more about getting sober, or if you think you might have a problem, you can go to www.na.org, or find out more here:
https://na.org/admin/include/spaw2/uploads/files/EN3113_2008.pdf

Naloxone:
If you or someone you love has an opiate addiction, please, *please* keep Naloxone with you at all times. Many cities offer this lifesaving medicine for free or without a prescription. You can find out more here:
http://www.getnaloxonenow.org/find.html

Acknowledgments

This book was a lifetime in the making, a journey spanning the globe and my own spiritual topography. Sometimes I was alone, although, as Hannah says, we're never really alone; I was often with others—be they real or simply in the pages of books. (For the record, Yuri Gagarin is also fucking with my serenity.)

I want to thank some of those people below, but first, I want to say something I hope my younger readers especially will hear:

I've never taken a physics class in my life and was always intimidated by science. (Hello, Patriarchy). Working on this book gave me the permission I needed to explore a whole world of study that had felt off-limits and impossible for me since I was a kid. For all you girls out there who think science isn't for you—give it a try. I hope you take up lots of space in all the places you inhabit. Shoot for the moon—or even further. I'm rooting for you.

I'm grateful to the following people who have been with me on this journey:

First, I have to thank my sister, Meghan. This book has her DNA all over it. She has kept me afloat in many a wave. If you have a sister, hug her today—if you can—or do what mine does and send her a playlist of songs when she's sad. Meghan, I love you to infinity and beyond.

Sarah Torna Roberts: my forever kindred spirit. We might not share blood, but you will always be family. It took me decades to write the book I wanted to dedicate to you. Your unwavering belief in my work helped me leave it all on the page. You are my favorite person to solve the problems of the universe with—and one of the best people in it.

Zach, my definite position in the universe: I am lost without you. (And you know I mean that very literally, since I can't read a map.) Thank you for helping me see that I can science, for explaining all the things, and for watching all my favorite space movies with me—including *Gravity* in 3-D at the most expensive movie theater in Manhattan. Thanks are also in order for all the times you read this extremely long book and all your excellent insights about it. I love you to the moon and back. (Better yet, MARS and back).

Frankie Bolt: Thank you for your generosity and the deep, powerful read you gave this heart book of mine. So much of what makes this book tick should be credited to you. I bow down to your brilliance, and I adore you for getting my girls so hard.

Kate Farrell, my editor: Thank you for holding space for my work. Your trust in my ability and vision allowed me to shoot straight past the atmosphere. Writing under such conditions is like getting to see sixteen sunsets, and sixteen sunrises Every. Single. Day. Special thanks to everyone at Holt, especially Christian Trimmer, Brittany Pearlman, and Rachel Murray.

Jessica Welman: I can't begin to thank you enough for all your incredible insights into Mae. And for keeping my inner romantic in check. Well, as much as anyone can. I'm so glad your bed was across from mine freshman year.

Lisa Papademetriou: Your comments on the early pages helped me bring acorns to the next level. Thank you, thank you.

Laura Sibson: Your last-minute reading for me was so clutch! Thank you for your insights and wisdom on this complicated family.

Linda Fehst, the mother-in-law of dreams, for her ongoing support and an early read with incredibly helpful suggestions.

Brenda Bowen and everyone at Sanford Greenburger who were alongside me at the beginning of this ride: I am ever so grateful for all that you've done.

Thank you to the astronauts whose lives and work helped me understand Mae, especially Peggy Whitson, Chris Hadfield, Scott Kelly, and the NASA 2017 Class of Astronaut Candidates. You are all the right stuff.

Neil de Grasse Tyson said, "The universe is under no obligation to make sense to you." That might be true, but there are several people who have helped it make more sense to me, and made it easier to science the shit out of this book. This is a good time for curious people and I've been the grateful beneficiary of countless books and online resources, including the entire catalog of the On Being podcast. However, I'd like to especially thank the following scientists who were kind enough to take time out of studying the universe to help a layperson out—please note that ALL MISTAKES IN THIS BOOK ARE MY OWN (that deserved some Mae caps, methinks):

Dr. Chanda Prescod-Weinstein, who was so kind as to spend an hour on the phone with me talking about dark matter, axions, and the challenges for female-identifying persons in the sciences. Bonus: she didn't make me feel like an idiot for even a nanosecond. I know Mae would have had a new shero if she'd met this kickass science maven. You can find her on Twitter at @IBJIYONGI.

Colin Bischoff, who took time out of his busy schedule doing observational cosmology to read several pages of the book and school me on all things physics. He kept me from making Mae look like a dumbass, and I am forever grateful. He ALSO gave me the opportunity to casually drop into conversation that I have to return a physicist's email. You can find Colin on Twitter at @colinflipper. (Special thanks to Robin Kirk and Jenn Barnes for getting us in touch.)

Allison Campbell, my cool astrophysicist friend: Thank you for understanding what I was trying to do with this book, and advising me on dark matter and how an astronaut might go about having her cake and eating it, too.

Matt Anderson, for our lively email back-and-forth about geophysics: Dude, geophysicists are COOL. Thank you for making that so clear. Ben says hi.

There are many people who've been a part of helping me authentically portray Hannah's struggle with addiction. Since their experience with addiction or loved ones' addiction is their story to tell, I won't be naming them here, but I am in awe of their vulnerability and generosity.

A huge thanks to someone I *can* name, Dr. Diana Deister at Boston Children's Hospital, who was incredibly generous, answering questions via email and phone. All mistakes in the book are, of course, my own. The work she and everyone at this fantastic institution does on behalf of young people suffering from addiction is so incredibly important. Extra thanks to Megan Gallagher for helping me navigate the Boston Children's system.

Andrew Sullivan's article in *New York Magazine*, "The Poison We Pick" (Feb 19–March 4 2018), was incredibly helpful in understanding the nature of opioids, why people use them, and what we're up against with this epidemic. A powerful must-read. Also, we need to take down these companies that are killing our loved ones, and those in power who let them. Who's with me?

This book was mostly written in Bournemouth, UK, Bäch, Switzerland, Sitges, Spain, and Scottsdale, AZ—thanks to the housesitting fam for opening up their homes to me and trusting me with their desks and pets, and for my in-laws, Linda and Walt Fehst, without whom a certain rocket woman wouldn't have had a safe place to land this ship.

Huge thanks to my writers—students, clients, and friends—who cheer me on and keep my boat afloat. Big hugs to all my readers, who do the same. I love and appreciate all of you. I'm glad we all get to be on Earth together at the same time. We can do impossible things.

For all my spiritual teachers—the ones I know personally and the ones I only know on the page—thank you for your wisdom and your lifetime of doing the hard work of figuring out what it means to be human. I could never name you all, but here are a few who have personally helped me work the problem of being this particular collection of atoms: David Chernikoff, the MNDFL family—especially Lodro Rinzler and Adreanna Limbach—and, last but not least, Father John Unni at St. Cecelia's in Boston.

I've thanked a lot of scientists here, but there are scores of poets and musicians and writers and painters and makers of things who were with me every step of the way on this journey—you've met many of them in these pages. I think they know the secret Dr. Winters was looking for. After all, you can't spell Earth without "art."

For everyone reading this, and especially to all the people I know and love struggling with addiction (and the ones I don't know): you are the miracle. Let's do right by it together.